Empower

Publishing

Watch for These Titles
from Louise Gore Sayre-David

John Steel: The Man and the Legend
Green Sea Plantation
The Land Darkens
Springs Gift of Light

and *Empower Publishing*

The Turbulence and the Struggle

She Heard a Whippoorwill Series:
Book Four

By

Louise Gore Sayre-David

Empower Publishing
Winston-Salem

Empower

Publishing

Empower Publishing
PO Box 26701
Winston-Salem, NC 27114

This book is a work of fiction. The events and opinions related in this work are entirely the creation and opinion of the author and do not represent the opinions or thoughts of the publisher. All individuals described are the author's interpretation of history and creative imagination.

First Empower Publishing Books edition published
December, 2019
Empower Publishing, Feather Pen, and all production design are trademarks.

For information regarding bulk purchases of this book, digital purchase and special discounts, please contact the publisher at
empowerpublishing2015@gmail.com

Cover design by Pan Morelli

Manufactured in the United States of America
ISBN 978-1-63066-494-7

To the loving memory of my parents Webb and Dora Gore for their steadfast loyalty and capability to the needs and welfare of family, tenants and farmworkers alike as well as their effort to hold onto the land itself and especially during the hardship of the Great Depression.

—Louise Gore Sayre-David

Chapter One

After years of seemingly futility and frustration, Matthew found his life pulsing once more in contented fulfillment. Amy's infinite love and devotion were a haven that sheltered him snugly in the wake of the troubling storm that he had been immersed in for such a long time. His happiness with her was measuring far above what his dreams had harbored. Their honeymoon was filled with perfect communion, while they lived quietly and contentedly to themselves in the small suite of hotel rooms that he had rented for the duration of the winter months, or the length of time that he anticipated Congress would be in session. Even though they both missed the close contact with family and friends that they were accustomed to, and this was particularly true in Amy's case, this still did not affect their happiness to the point of causing them to feel lonely. They were so happily adjusted and in accord with one another that the company of others was not necessary for the good of their well-being.

While Matthew was away tending to Senate duties, Amy did what she had mostly always done, except for undertaking a few small personal chores that she did not call on the hotel staff to perform for her, since neither she nor Matthew had brought along a personal servant. An avid reader of history and biographical works, she read quite a lot, in addition to writing family and friends almost each day and doing needlework also. When Matthew entered the door though, she did none of these things. Her time was totally his. They took long walks together; sometimes in the falling snow, taking delight in the novelty of it drifting against their faces. They attended the theater some nights and attended Church on Sundays. Most of their free time though was spent together alone as they preferred it that way. For all the happy quietude though that Matthew had now in his personal life, it was beginning to be just the opposite with his political activities. He received a shocking blow when a group of avenging seeking radicals in Congress steered into motion by the joint effect of the two Republican Congressman Summer and Stevens, both of whom he already had heard a great deal about, made it known out in clear that Congress was not ready to seat the newly elected legislatures from the disloyal South. When President Johnson made his address to Congress in his vain attempt to inform it that as far as he was concerned; in so many words, the South had open reconstructed, with its branches of government operating as usual under federal control and state legislative bodies and got down to business as usual, the Radicals retaliated to his message bitterly and refused to seat what they referred to as the treacherous South, where they argued nothing had changed. Thus, a long tug-of-war between the president and Congress begun over the reconstructing of the South that was to eventually lead to an impeachment trial for the President, and a lengthy period of reconstruction in the South controlled by former casehardened Union generals. However, before this change of events was to take place which would began to materialize that coming fall in 1866 election when the radicals were to become such a tower of strength that there was no impediment to prevent them in pushing their bills through Congress ever President Johnson's vetoes, bills that were drawn and executed in their aim to make the betraying South pay for its sin in defying the Union, Matthew and Amy continue to remain in Washington until Easter. Because, by then, he had almost become disenchanted with politics altogether and saw no need to stay in Washington any longer. The atmosphere there spoke for itself. It was ascertained that the Radical Republicans were set to crush the southern planter and a whole society that had fought to keep a way of life and class of people that the South personified, forever. Moreover, it was assured that they had no intention of seating South Carolina or any other former Confederate state in the United States Congress which, on the whole, was biased and unfair. However, just how hard they would strike had not come to light yet, and that would be when they finally succeeded in pressing their Reconstruction Act of March 2, 1867 through congress to become law. This rancorous stage by the Radicals would not only be devastating to the already war worn and beaten South, bringing not only greed and corruption upon it, but a race consciousness was to result from its making that had never been there before and has yet to disappear. At all events, this being the state of the situation at Easter, with Matthew feeling in a certain sense that he had failed, he and Amy returned to Green Sea to be warmly welcomed by Eliza and Luke. After six weeks' vacation that was alternated in visits between Green Sea and Drakston Hall, they located in Columbia where his work was to be conducted from the Statehouse.

Matthew had rented a small house there, since Amy had told him that she thought they both would enjoy living in the house more than a hotel. Besides, she would like to plan their own meals for change, and did he not think that it would be rather nice to have a place where he could invite his friends from time to time? She had brought along two personal servants from Drakston Hall to do the household chores. Thus, it was not long after their vacation before they were settled down comfortably enough once more. She had not given the first thought of staying behind and packing Matthew off to Columbia to live alone while he continued to labor at his senate duties. She was devoted to him in full and was ready to adapt herself to any circumstance in order to be with him. Their vacation at home had held much pleasure for them, although Frank still kept his distance when he was in his uncle's presence. He had received them at Drakston Hall cordially enough, though the handshake that he extended to Matthew had been of short devotion and rather cold. In her excitement, Amy had appeared not to notice. This was partly due to her anxiousness overseeing the family members again as well as the prospect of getting acquainted with the newest addition and the one that she had not seen yet, who was waiting at Oak Grove. They had spent a great deal of their time there also, as Amy was delighted with the new baby girl that Martha had given birth to in February and who she and Bruce had named Laura. Maggie, who was almost six years old, was awed with her new baby sister, causing her mother to remark that she was going to be thrilled even more than that when her brothers started coming along! Consequently, starting with Laura's birth, Martha was to always secretly yearn to give Bruce a son, and it was most fortunate that she was unaware then that she would never do this, because Laura, this pretty baby daughter who people would say favored her grandmother Amy, was to be their last child. Mollie had also given birth a week after Martha. The Cooper baby was a boy. He was named for his father and Mollie's brother, his name turning out to be Brent William. Bill was proud that his sister had honored him in giving his name to that of her firstborn. He and Charlotte both doted on their new nephew. Mollie was sensible to the fact that her brother and sister had not been so lucky in love as she had been. This no doubt accounted for her choosing William as part of her baby's name, the name that he was to answer to.

Eliza has been thrilled over the birth of the two babies; also, had become quite fond of both. Though she did not see the Cooper baby near as often as she did the Randolph baby. She and Luke had been frequent callers at Oak Grove throughout the winter months and early spring. Martha would think of all kinds of excuses to plot the baby in Eliza's arms, both knowing full well that she did this for the sake of giving Eliza a chance to hold Laura and would be spared from revealing her intense eagerness to do so at the same time. They both were elated that Laura favored their mothers. By the spring of 1866, Eliza had resigned herself to the cold fact that she would never have a baby. Nor did she discuss the subject with Luke anymore. After almost six years of marriage, she and Luke were still blissfully happy together; she told herself that if there were to be no children from the union to accept and forget it and she had almost succeeded. Besides, things could be much worse than not having a baby in her arms. She could've lost Luke in the war like she had her brothers. But, thank God, she had Luke, so that was really all that mattered, anyway, she would reason. Luke was sharecropping again this year with the former slaves and since spring had been working awfully hard. Following her father and aunt Amy's visit home, her and Luke's life had become fairly quiet and uninterrupted routine, except for occasional visit with friends and attending church on Sundays. Most people were still trying to bring some semblance of order to their lives and were too busy with this to have but very little time for anything else. Eliza and Luke seldom saw Bill or his sister, Charlotte aside from the Sundays they came to the Baptist Church. It appeared that they had started attending the Methodist church which was located near Camden Plantation, more and more since Bill's return from the war. This was the church that Charlotte had gone to several times with Ore before his death, as the Camden's were Methodists, and it seemed that for some reason known only to Charlotte that this was the church that she held in greater favor nowadays. Bill was having great success with his sawmill. He had foreseen it was going to take a great deal of lumber to build back and repair what Sherman and his army had burned and torn down and was finding a ready market for every foot of lumber his mill could turn out. In addition to his lumber business, he was beginning to put the plantation under cultivation once more. Like Green Sea, acres and acres had grown up with brush. If Bill were courting any one certain girl, Eliza never heard about it. In the few times that interest in Bill's personal life had crossed her mind, she told herself that with all his involvement in the mill and the plantation too, that little wonder he had much time for courting! She would not allow her mind to think that perhaps she could be the reason for this. Bill was still pleasantly congenial with she and Luke both; as far as making any more effort though to talk with her alone, he never did. Nor had he since that day long ago at church. All in all, that spring and early summer had not brought any irregular happening to their lives from what they had been compelled to follow and get accustomed to since the war had in a sense turned their standard of living completely around, til it was made known early one summer morning when Luke came to the house for breakfast after he had seen to the feeding of the stock. As a rule, while breakfast was being prepared, he did this chore along with advising the hands in the work that he desired to have done on the plantation that particular day, sitting down to their breakfast Eliza noticed that Luke appeared to be upset over something. She waited for him to mention whatever it was obviously troubling him, but he hardly said two words other than responding to her few remarks, politely. Seeing that he had set his coffee cup down and was starting to push his chair back from the table to leave she waited no longer, saying, "Luke, what's wrong? You haven't said two words, except yes or no, all through breakfast."

"I'm sorry, dear, I suppose my mind has been straying off the usual trail it follows. I've been sitting here trying to reason out why I found the meadow fence, the part that borders the road, torn down this morning."

"No! Luke! Who on earth would do that?"

"That's the same question I've been asking myself ever since I sat down to breakfast. I can't quite settle on any explanation for it. I certainly don't think you or your father have any enemies. As for myself, I did have that run-in with Walt Hawkins. You remember he lost his job as a tax collector in election last fall. He still hangs around that gang at the Freedman's bureau. I saw him only a few days ago. There's no telling who's responsible though, with the country overflowing in carpetbaggers, scalawags, and shiftless freed Negros, who still think that someone's going to hand them a free living," he said rather hotly, which was a little rare for him.

"What about the hands, do you think they knew anything about it?"

"No, I don't think so. They appeared to be a shocked as I am, to realize that anyone could stoop to such a low trick. They said they never heard anything or saw anybody and I'm positive they didn't. The cabins are too far from the road for that, unless the noise had been awfully loud which it couldn't have been, because I didn't hear anything, did you?"

"No, I'm sorry, Luke, I didn't. Did any of the stock get out?"

"Fortunately, they didn't, or we would still be chasing them to heaven knows where. I turned mules in the small lot last night and left their stalls open. The horses and Bullitt were closed in, also."

"I'm so glad, Luke, that the stock's safe. It would surely put a hardship on us if we lost them."

"I know, darling, but don't worry about that. It didn't happen and maybe it won't. I've put Charlie and Sam to repairing the fence. I wanted to get all the corn layed by today but now I won't. I saw so much so much destruction during the war and especially when I reached Sherman's path, that looking at that fence seemed to bring it all back too vividly for my peace of mind. I couldn't wait to get it up again. Well, I guess I'd better get onto the fields, or there won't be much of anything done today," he said as he pushed his chair further back from the table and rose, leaning forward to kiss her on the cheek. "See you at dinner, dear," he added. Then, with his long, hurried strides he was through the doorway before she could reply. She sat for some few minutes gazing through the empty doorway after him. Now that, on top of all the other burdens that fall upon his shoulders, she thought. But, then again, maybe it would not happen anymore. She rose and began to do all her chores for that day too.

It did happen though, again and again as the assailants effected their purpose, whatever that was, through the same stealthy deeds that so far had taken place only in the late hours of the night. And, in each visit that they sneaked to Green Sea to do their evildoing, they were becoming bolder and bolder. After they had torn down the fence that ran alongside the road several times, they began stealing to the stables and opening the gates to the lots and stalls. The first time this happened, Luke and Eliza both had awakened to the sound of horse's hooves beating down the driveway as the riders hurried away. By the light of the moonlight streaming through the windows, they both jumped out of bed and ran downstairs to the front porch, hoping to recognize the culprits by their mounts, but they were too late. Luke, in his nightshirt and barefooted, ran across the yard and just made it in time to close the lot gate against a stirred and excited number of mules.

They both were so baffled they just stood and look down the darkened driveway in silence with their arms around each other's waist. Finally, they turned and went back inside. Neither slept anymore that night. The next time the attackers came was on a night that was mantled in total darkness. The moonless and starless sky had everything covered in pitch-black night. They struck right at twelve o'clock, herding mules from the lots and on out the gate, while the sharp cracking of their firearms was banging through the night stillness. The ringing of the shots instantly brought Luke and Eliza out of their sound sleep, started almost beyond belief. Neither had given any thought in regard to the attackers using deadly weapons to carry out their harassment. Nevertheless, they were not so stunned that it kept their feet from hitting the floor at the same time, with Luke shouting "Stay down and away from the windows, dear, and don't light the lamp!" He dashed toward the door, searching hurriedly for the doorknob. Grasping hold the cold like knob he was already going through the door, groping his way for the staircase, as Eliza was anxiously calling after him, "Do be careful, Luke!"

Running his hand along the heavy handrail for support, he made it down the stairs rather swiftly. Once his feet landed on the hall floor, it was only a matter of a few reckless and hasty strides before he reached the gun case that set just inside the library door along the center wall. He grabbed the first weapon that his hand reached which was Matthews six-shooter and within seconds had loaded it with well-practiced proficiency, as he had done countless times during the war in jet black night, also. Even so, by the time he got to the front porch and pulled the trigger, riders, horses, mules; and the whole pack were thundering down the driveway in flight. Abruptly, like a thunderclap as the bullets from the six-shooter were falling among the live oaks, the blast of a shotgun sending whizzing shots sailing in the same direction, boomed close by his ears. He whirled around in astonishment as Eliza was saying, "I hope I've filled their backside full, the dirty cowards!" He could've kissed her then and there for her bravery and also for her skillfulness in the handling of a firearm. But, his concern for safety was his uppermost thought. "Good lord! Dear!" He shouted excitedly. "Please be careful and get back inside! You shouldn't be out here, it's too dangerous!"

"No, Luke! I'm staying right here," she said unrelentingly, the tone of her voice plainly revealing her risen temper.

"Well, I think they're gone for tonight anyway," he replied, "So, we might as well lay our weapons down."

He took the gun from her hands and laid it on the floor, putting his arm protectively around her shoulders. In less than no time while they were standing there on the porch in their dilemma of confusion and trying to come up with an answer as to why had it all started here came Willie, Alan, Charlie, and Sam all running wildly around the corner of the porch, some caring lighted lanterns, with their wives following on their heels. Every face was covered nonetheless in fright looking as if Sherman's army were back in operation, raging a battle upon Green Sea. Promptly, Albert, Hannah, and Doss were all coming in a half run, too. Luke quickly called out "we're alright, everybody! It's that lousy riding gang again. This time though, I think they've turned out every horse and mule on the place, but it's too dark now to try to round them up. Go back to your house and try to get some sleep, but be back at daybreak, we'll go look for the stock then."

They all turned and went scuffling back in the direction of the cabins. Doss though was saying "Dem, no good varmints. I'm going to de stables, mister Luke, and if'm com back on this night, dey's goin get a pitchfork stuck in dem.!"

"Do what you like, Doss." Luke said, he would anyway. "I'd like to get my hands on them myself. Come on, dear, let's go inside, they're not coming back."

After getting settled down in bed once more, but remaining wide awake, Eliza said "Luke, what do you suppose their motive is?"

"I don't have the faintest idea, darling. Everything is in such turmoil these days, it could be a dozen or one thing. There's one thing for sure, the ending of the war didn't bring much peace. I'm going to the local authorities and report it. I realize there's little they can do, til we can identify whoever they are. Still, after tonight, I don't think it would hurt to let it be known what's going on."

"You wanted to finish gathering tobacco tomorrow, now instead, you'll be chasing mules. Oh, I'd like to ring their necks, Luke, for troubling you like this!" She exclaimed angrily.

"Well," He replied, pulling her closer to him. "I'm not too bad off with you and the hands here at Green Sea on my side. Though I want you to promise me, if there's any more shooting, that you'll stay inside. I don't think I could take it, if any harm should come to you."

"I'll try, Luke, but that goes both ways, you know. So, I can't promise. I lived in fear for three years, worrying about your safety and couldn't do one thing about it. This is different, we're together again, and I'm afraid if there's any fighting or anything else that involved you, I'm not going to be too far from your side." She told him.

It took all thc ncxt day to round up the mules and horses, while the ripe tobacco hung on the stalk and continued to ripen more, when it should have been gathered. Luke went to see the sheriff and informed him about the shooting and all the other molestation that had taken place. Whether though the attackers learned of his visit to the law and decided to lie low for a spell or became somewhat skittish of his and Eliza's answering shots, things stayed on a steady uninterrupted routine for several weeks. Nevertheless, it was the usual calm that always seems to precede a tempest.

That Sunday was out of keeping with the normal of late September in so much as the hot, humid day was more like the middle of July than the first week of fall; Eliza and Luke went on off to church that morning, never once had a thought that the molesters would come back on that day and especially in broad daylight, since it had appeared from the beginning that they had made an effort to remain unrecognized. Though at any rate, while everybody at Green Sea was at church, including the hands, they made their move. And, from all appearances in view of what happened they went for the sole purpose of playing an inhumane prank on that visit and nothing else, because outside of their ill-affected deed that was to bring a severely lasting impairment to Bullitt, they did not disturb another thing.

Although the day was rather uncomfortable weather wise, the buggy ride on the way home from church was pleasant enough for Eliza and Luke. As the mare pulled the lightweight buggy along at a moderate speed, they were taking delight in the slight breeze that the moving vehicle brought against their faces. Still, they were anxious to get home, as it was getting to be way past one o'clock in the afternoon. But, at last they reached the clearing and saw the mansion sitting in the cool inviting shade that the giant trees kept it shrouded in. Looking ahead in the distance they both were anticipating the moment of stepping inside its walls, that would grant them relief from the sweltering heat and also where they looked forward to spending the rest of the day with each other, since the summer months and harvest season gave them so very few lazy hours to while away and that was usually on Sunday afternoons. Suddenly though Eliza's eyes were drawn across the distant tobacco field where the view was open now as the tobacco stalks had been chopped down upon the last tobacco cropping. She had sighted a strange looking animal running wildly. There was something uncanny about the looks of it. Fear began to creep upon her, racing her heart when she recognized it to be that of a horse that had some peculiar object billowing out in the wind from its tail. The color of the horse was also odd looking; yet, there was something familiar about its carriage. Bullitt! Dear Lord! It was Bullitt! She gripped Luke's arm, exclaiming, "Luke stop the buggy!"

"What dear?" He said turning to look at her anxiously, as his eyes caught her gaze upon the racing animal. He pulled on the reins instantly, knowing that something dreadful was amiss.

For a moment, they both sat on the buggy seat as if they were frozen to it as a sound that was nothing like anything they had ever heard before began to close in on them. It was a constant struggling snorting ground that came with every labored breath that the horse drew. They saw him turn and, in a few seconds, he had come near enough in their line of vision to determine what had taken place while they had attended church. Someone had tied a large bundle of dried corn shucks to his tail! The swishing sound of the crisp shucks had caused him to keep in a continuous hard run to get away from them from the moment the pranksters had turned him loose. Instantly, Eliza jumped down from the buggy and gathering up her long skirt she was crossing the hedgerow road in a fast run, with Luke following just a fracture behind her. She began calling the stallion's name over and over, but Bullitt appeared to pay her no attention. He kept running up and down the tobacco fields, seeming as though he were following a path, although his gait was becoming slower and slower. Swiftly gaining the distance between him and them, Eliza saw why she had thought the horse was so odd looking in color. His whole body was drenched in a crystalline white lather. It looked as if every ounce of water and every particle of salt that his system contained had seeped through to his otherwise beautiful black coat. Still calling is name, her throat began to tighten as it was obvious to her that the high-spirited stallion had been running for hours and was now nearing his last mile if he was not restrained. With his straining for breath beating upon her and looking at the state he had been brought to, she was becoming frantic. Her eyes bathed with tears by now, she cried, "Luke! We have to do something. He won't last much longer!"

Indeed, Luke had become frantic too, for a number of reasons. Likewise, he knew that if the stallion did not stop running and soon, that he was going to fall dead before their eyes. As a matter of fact, he was expecting it, anyway. Then too, he had become desperate in trying to think of a way to protect Eliza from the attackers in case they were at the house. Anxiously looking in its direction and wondering what he would encounter once he got there and desiring to keep her away from it until he had gone and checked the state of things, he quickly suggested as a solution popped in his mind. "Stay here, dear, and keep calling him! In his excitement and fright, if he heed anyone's voice, it'll be yours! I'll dash to the stables and get the long clipping shears. He'd never let anybody untie those shucks. I'll be back as soon as I can!" Upon his last words, he was already running back across the field to the buggy, while he heard a Eliza holler after him, "Oh, Luke, please hurry!"

Luke did hurry. It was not long before he was back with the shears and the treat of sugar lumps that had always brought the horse to his side. He also had brought back rope for a lasso but was hoping he would not be compelled to catch Bullitt with it. He had no wish to aggravate the prostrated stallion any further. When he had reached the house, he had been surprised and relieved after taking a quick survey through the rooms to find that no one was there, and everything seemed to be in order. Then, he had rushed over to the stables and found that the other horses and mules had been undisturbed, too. He had known at once that Bullitt had been the lone target for their molesting that day, something that he could not quite understand. However, he did not dawdle in pondering over it. As fast as he could possibly move, he unhitched his mare from the buggy and threw a saddle on her and grabbing the rope and with the sugar in his pocket and revolver under his coat, he had snatched the revolver and sugar while he had torn through the house, he jumped upon the mare and raced back to the tobacco fields.

Now galloping hard and nearing where he had left Eliza, a burning anger spread through his whole being as he saw the anguish on her face and the near-dead Bullitt still running past her, while she cried his name over and over. He did not believe in killing but he was certain had the attacker appeared at that minute, his fingers would have pulled the trigger on his gun without so much as an exchange of a word. Leaping from the saddle he was saying "Here, dear! I've brought some sugar lumps! Maybe if he senses that you have a treat for him, he'll come to you!"

"Oh, yes! Luke!" She cried, quickly cupping her hands together and holding them out to him, "I'm so glad you thought of it! I know if he'll look in my direction now, he'll come to me!" With her hands outstretched in the same familiar way that she had always practiced when she had a treat for Bullitt, she swiftly ran toward him again crying his name.

Upon making his turn and starting back down the path that he had worn in the field by this time, Bullitt suddenly slowed his gait. He appeared to see Eliza for the first time. He seemed to set his eyes on her outstretched hands as his run became slower and slower til he was walking instead of running. Elated that she finally gotten his attention at last, she was now standing, having come to a complete standstill. Holding the sugar up to his foaming mouth, she felt nothing now though but utter defeat when he drooped his head and turned it a side, refusing the treat the he had constantly craved since he was a colt. She put sugar on the ground at his feet and began stroking his head with one hand while she grabbed her hat from her head with the other and started fanning him rapidly in what looked like a useless attempt to bring any comfort to the horse whatever. The white foam was spilling from his mouth in a continuous stream, falling all over her dress.

Luke had been standing motionlessly, eagerly watching Bullitt's behavior. Now, taking his cue, he stole quietly in a circle and slipping up behind him as closely as he dared, he reached forward with the long shears and clipped the cord of shucks that was dangling out and partially lying on the ground from the now sagging tail that was lathered a dirty grey-white color and void of any spiritedness for the first time since the day he had been born. Observing the stallion, Luke knew enough about horses to know that he and Eliza had been too late to save him from lasting impairment even if he were to survive, which was doubtful, taking into account that he appeared to be laboring harder for wind than when he had been running. Apparently, he was so near dead that he had given no sign of realizing that he had been freed of the menacing device that had doomed his lively nature. The only thing that he seemed to be aware of, excluding his misery, was Eliza's presence. He had snuggled his head as near to her as possible, seeming as though he was looking to her to mend his suffering.

Desperation covering her face, she looked at Luke and said,

"Luke, what shall we do? Can you think of any way that we can help him?'

"I can't think of a thing, dear, except make him as comfortable as his condition will allow, that is, if we even get him into the stables. He's run himself to death in this heat. I imagine his lungs feel as if they're on fire and to the point of bursting besides. I deplore having such a thought but maybe I should put him out of his misery."

Swiftly, changing her expression to horridness that Luke would be thinking of such as doing away with him, she cried "You mean shoot him?"

Luke let his eyes fall a good ways off as he replied, "Well, you can see his condition, dear. Even if he recovers, he'll be broken winded for the rest of his life. He'll never again be able to run any distance at all."

Indignant, that to realize the stallion had been reduced by ruthless deviltry to live the remainder of his days in a ploddingly state, she lashed out, "Well he can walk then! I'll never consult to his being shot! I don't think I could bear that!"

"I know what he means to you, darling, because he means a great deal to me also. I think it's only fair to warn you though, that his heart could stop at any minute. However, if that's the way you feel, I'll try to get him to the stables for you."

"Thank you, Luke. Tell me how I can help you with him."

"You ride the mare back, dear. There's nothing you can do. I'll lead him slowly."

"I don't want to ride back, Luke. Let me lead him." She pleaded.

Luke ran his eyes over her anxious face where the lines of tear marks showed vividly in the sweat and dirt and on down to her soiled dress, that she appeared to have no regard for whatever, and said, "Well, all right since he seems to want to stick close to you. But it would be less tiring for you in this hot sun, if you'll ride the mare back."

"I don't care about the hot sun or much of anything else right now, except to do something for him. Besides if he can endure the torture of this heat in his condition, I should be able to take a little, too!"

In spite of his own anger and disgust at the whole episode and grave outcome for Bullitt, Luke let a trace of a smile cross his face as he told her, "In that case, we'll both walk back. You don't think I'd ride and let you plod along beside me, do you?" She rested her eyes upon his for a second or two, exchanging a look with him that each could read as plainly as a book, making it unnecessary for her to comment to his statement. "Then, let's start," She said.

Every inch of ground that they covered on the way to the house, Eliza strained each and all her nerves to close her ears to the struggling gasps of Bullitt's convulsive suffering. She was almost ready to question her decision. But, after what had felt like a day and night to her, she and Luke had gotten him inside the lot, under a big spreading live oak where its leaves were gently rustling in what seemed to be the only place that contained any breeze in the humid afternoon. They began immediately to try to make the horse more comfortable. Taking a great out of care they rubbed him down and offered him water. He took one sip from the bucket and turned his head away. They looked at one another helplessly knowing there was nothing else they could do but wait on time to deal with the situation, cost what it may they had done their best. Both were aware then that improvement would be inchmeal, if indeed it all. Granted, as the weary day begin to slip away, they could observe no marked difference in the matter of his breathing. Except his coat which was starting to take on some semblance of its normal appearance, he could have been some other horse rather than the exuberant stallion they had known. The hands had been appalled when they had returned from their own church and learned what had happened. All of them, felt deep sympathy on Eliza's part, since they knew her devotion for the stallion, and tried to help in what fashion they could. It was evident though that little could be done. At long last, the peaceful, lazy Sunday afternoon and evening that she and Luke had envisioned with one another, had instead turned into a nightmare for them, ending with them falling into their bed totally exhausted from anxiety. The following day and the day after that, Bullitt showed no great change in his condition from what it had been on Sunday night when Luke and Eliza had finally left him and gone to bed. But, on the third day he began to appear on the uprising, and after a few more days had passed, days in which someone at Green Sea had been with him near around the clock ministering to him in every way that one thought would help, he seemed to be back to his normal self in so far as his breathing and eating was concerned. Even his looks now revealed no dissimilarity. Nevertheless, all this was misleading. When it came to him being the same horse physically and spirit wise it was nothing of the kind. Being quite the contrary. It was manifest from his behavior that he was a broken-winded horse, permanently impaired proving out that Luke had been right in what he had predicted. Several times, he and Eliza had watched the horse start to run, his feet bounding same as ever over the meadow turf with his white tail sailing high over his back. Then suddenly, his feet would plow into the earth, the lofty tail would start sloping downward and with his head drooped in labored breathing he would turn and slowly walk back to the shade of the live oak tree in the lot. It pained both of them to witness his impairment, knowing the stallion for what he had been in the past. But it was Eliza who was always touched the deepest as she wondered if she had done him an injustice by insisting, he not be destroyed.

Word of the vicious act spread swiftly over the neighborhoods. Luke spent several hours of many days in an endeavor to track down the culprits. All his efforts though came to no avail. He was not so dense that he did not know it could not be strangers, because whoever it was had to be well acquainted with the coming and goings of the dwellers at Green Sea. Yet, to point his finger at any certain person and charge them with the crime, he could not. At any rate, he took no more chances for several weeks, bring well-prepared to deal with the next attack should it come. Nothing else happened though for the rest of that fall and winter.

Though Eliza and Luke surely did not forget the unfortunate happening; still, there were other matters in the following months that helped push it from their minds, two things in particular, the 1866 fall elections and Matthew and Amy's visit home at Christmas time. With Congress still refusing to seat Southern delegations, what Matthew had feared came to pass. In the congressional elections that fall, as Southern conservatism and continuing "disloyalty" fell from the mouth of every revengeful inciter who could wag his tongue, the Radical's victory brought their goal within closer sight. It would be just a matter of a few months, and their plan for making the South pay for its firing shots upon Fort Sumter over five years earlier would be put to action.

Surprising to Mathew, he was one of the four lone Democrats to retain his seat in the state legislature in the Radical's sweep to power, though he did not hold onto it but a few more years. He finally resigned because he had no wish to buck the Republican majority, which made up a contingent of negroes and carpetbaggers, any further. What helped him to come to this decision though was the fact that other interests were beginning to dominate his mind more than politics, which were in reverse once again, the business of political activates becoming merely a job to get done. Of course, his main interest was the life he shared with the ever loving and winsome Amy and the close relationship that he still kept with his loved daughter and Luke. This other concern though that had been reeling around in his mind lately, pertained to something that was as astonishing to him to think about as it was to his family and friends when he announced the possibility of it on his visit home for the holidays. He and Amy were alternating their visit this holiday between all three plantations. Green Sea, Drakston Hall, and Oak Grove. A few days before Christmas, all the family and their closest friends had gathered at Oak Grove for the dinner party that Martha was giving in honor of Eliza's birthday and her own that had already passed. Even Frank had relented to Elizabeth's pleas and had gone despite him knowing that once he was in Eliza's presence, he would have to endure much distress. To be sure, his torch for her was blazing as high as ever, though as long as he did not see her be managed to control its intensity fairly well. Actually, at times if the whim struck him to want his wife, he would become so attentive to Elizabeth that she would start thinking perhaps she had been too hasty after all in judging her husband on the part of his obvious attraction for his cousin. At any rate, the party had progressed along pleasantly enough for everyone. Though there had been a few heated remarks made concerning the fall election and the South's perilous position, which now appeared to be under the thumb of every carpetbagger, scalawag, and Negro in the country. Nevertheless, in relation to that opinion, everyone there had been in total agreement with one another. The state of things simply made their tempers flare and especially if one had chosen to do a little nipping on the side, other than the fruit punch that Martha was serving. Another something that most guests were agreeing on mentally as they observed Matthew and Amy's open devotion was the fact that it was hard for them to realize that these two people had not been married to one another their entire married life, so obviously suited they were for each other.

Their happiness seemed to vibrate constantly, as much so as on their wedding day a year earlier. Eliza and Martha still took great delight that their parents had married, but frank was as aloof as ever towards his uncle. He did however for his mother's sake keep it from the degree of appearing disrespectful. All the same, when Matthew suddenly looked across the table and caught Amy's eye where she was seated beside Doctor Davis and told everybody that politics was not the only thing that his and Amy's life revolved around, because as of late they had become very attached to a little boy and were seriously thinking of adopting him, frank's face showed no less amazement than the astonishment that flared across Eliza's and Martha's. these three people would never have had the faintest idea that such a thought would pass through their parent's heads. In truth, Eliza's first thought was that, if anyone adopted a child, it should be Luke and her instead of her father and Aunt Amy. Still, she came through graciously enough when her father added, in wishing that he had been a little less abrupt with his news as sudden concern for her feelings wiped the smile from his face, "Mary Eliza, I'm sorry, dear. I realize how I shouldn't have sprung news of that nature on you so unexpectedly."

"Oh no, Father! Please don't think I wouldn't be happy about it! I think… Well… It's just wonderful!" She exclaimed, turning to Martha, "Don't you think so, too, Martha?"

Martha though was not as considerate with her reply as Eliza had been. She was thinking, along with not being too keen on the idea besides, that why her mother would consider raising a child at her age and the fact that she had three grandchildren to shower her devotion on was beyond her. Finally, she snapped, "I'm not too surprised! Pa used to say had he allowed my mother her way where the stray cat, dogs, and people were concerned, that Drakston Hall would've been overflowing in a week!" for once though in her life, no sooner had the words fallen from her mouth, Martha could have bitten her tongue off as she saw her mother's face drop toward her plate and her uncle follow suit in the rapidly falling silence; and she thought she would thank Luke for the rest of her days when he quickly took it upon himself to mend her crass statement.

"Speaking of not being surprised Martha," he said, "That goes for me too, since I've been aware of Mr. Carson's generosity for years. Your mother and Eliza's father share a remarkable trait that a good many others could heed to. I think it's a wonderful gesture on their part, and that little boy, whoever he is, will be one lucky chap to have them for parents, because whatever his life's been in the past, there's one thing for certain, he'll have plenty of love and devotion with these two."

"Thank you, Luke. I'm not positive yet that we'll get the chance to adopt him. However, I won't forget your kind words though." Matthew said.

Then, Amy looked up from her plate and smiled, "Well it's just a thought that's been in our minds as Matthew first stated, let alone so many details that'll have to be worked out, if we're that lucky to have him in our care. Anyway, if that day ever comes forth, I hope we'll be deserving of him and live up to your opinion of us, Luke."

Frank, whose face had lost its amazed look to one of disgust that displayed a scowl and knitted brow, did not trust himself to comment on the subject t at all. He thought it was the most idiotic notion he had ever heard in his whole life, telling himself that it would be like a shallow-brained Carson to come up with such and that he should not be too surprised. His heart swelled in deep compassion for his mother, who he though was going along with his uncle's foolhardiness not because she desired to; but because she was married to him and felt it her duty. While frank was busy with his silent thoughts, everyone else around the table were expressing views similar to Luke's with Doctor Davis' ringing on the edge of practicing medicine by telling them he thought it was the most wonderful healthiest thing they could do. Reverend Johnson echoed the doctor, saying "It takes a special kind of person, one who possesses a great deal of courage along with a lot of other good virtues to undertake the brining up of another's child; and I'm here to say that Matthew and Amy both more than qualify to this task."

"Father," Eliza suddenly interrupted, anxious to hear something about the child, "Who is this little boy and how and where did you and Aunt Amy make contact with him?" She had never called her aunt "Mother." To have done so, she felt would have been a dishonor to her own mother. Besides, her father and Amy both wanted it no other way.

Matthew chose his words carefully, "it's a long and complicated story, dear, that would take too long to go into for now, that is, all the people handling his case think it would be harmful in regarded to the child and the family that adopts him. Of course, there's always a certain degree of confidential information held back and especially if the child is not old enough to remember its own parents. Anyway, this much has been disclosed to me. His father was killed during the war, and the sad circumstances of his mother has made it impossible for her to make a home for him. Unfortunately, the few other family members couldn't take him, either. He's in the care of a young woman now, sorta on the order of a foster parent, who has knowledge of all the details. There're so many aspects of the situation to consider and a lot of things that'll have to be worked out legally, that it could take a year or longer. It's so uncertain, maybe it would've been wiser had I not mentioned it. But Amy and I do see him quite often since he lives near us, and I might add he's beginning to tug at out heartstrings."

"He'd win you over too, Eliza dear," Volunteered Amy, "and I'm afraid everybody else that's here, once they saw him. His tow-headed curls and those deep-brown concentrating eyes can near melt one's heart. I've come to dearly love the child and will be very disappointed If Matthew and I lose out on adopting him."

"Oh, I'll have no trouble loving him, Aunt Amy!" Eliza cried excitedly, "and I want you and father both to know that I for one will feel honored to have him in the family as my stepbrother! From this minute on, I'll be so anxious to hear all about him and how things are progressing toward his adoption, that I'll be worrying you with question and plying you with letters constantly. I do hope everything works out!"

Proud and showering her with adoration, Matthew laughed, "I guess that's why I had no qualms over blurting it out like I did. I knew you'd love the idea. Thank you, dear, we'll be sure to keep you posted."

Martha, still wanting to kick herself for her madcap ways, braced up to her rash remark and plucky as ever said, "well, what Eliza just said goes for me, too! I can't think of a thing to add to it except I would like to know his name and how old he is!"

Matthew chortled again, while Amy sent her daughter an approving smile this time, and said, "a very appropriate desire, Martha, I should think, and something that's escaped the conversation thus far. His given name is Whitney, and Amy and I both like it so much, we won't change it to anything else if he ever becomes ours. He's just a few months over two years old."

"Whitney!" Shrieked Martha, "Why, that's a family name on the side of Bruce's mother!"

"That's right! Martha." Matthew said, his face showing surprise. "I hadn't thought about that! I suppose that's because over time I hear it, for a second my mind shifts to the man who gave the South the cotton gin. Come to think about it, should he happen to become a member of this family, I can't think of a more fitting name for him."

Pronouncing it slowly and distinct, Eliza said "Whitney Carson." Pausing a few seconds, she went on, "Whit Carson, oh I like the sound of that!"

"She's already following the Carson family trait to shorten it. But I'm way ahead of you, my dear, since I've called him that and nothing else from the day I met him," Matthew teased.

"You would, Father!" Eliza laughed, pleased that it proved out, she was truly her father's daughter.

"Uncle Matthew," said Bruce, "I don't mean to change the subject from that little boy because I think it's just marvelous, but it's just popped in my mind to ask you if you'd mind taking a package back to Lucy for us, when you all go back to Columbia. The mail service is so unpredictable, I hesitate to send it by post. When I was in Columbia just before thanksgiving, I tried to persuade Lucy to come home and stay till after the first of the year, but she wouldn't hear it. She hasn't been home for Christmas since she took that teaching job there."

"I'd be most happy to take the package to her, Bruce," Matthew, told him. "We see Lucy fairly often, I ran into her on the street one day, shortly after settling down there. We both were knocked for a loop with surprise and even more so to find out that we lived only a few blocks from the other. The time spent there before going to Washington was always so short and packed of business, I missed out on seeing her then. I did go to Miss Taylor's school on one or two occasions, she had already left for the day though. Then, a note that she sent to the State house wasn't delivered in time for me to look her up, not once but twice! Anyway, it seemed that fate stepped in and saw that we finally meet again. We both laughed about our chance meeting, and I'll grant you, it felt good to see her laugh… it…" Matthew suddenly stopped, but Amy quickly took up where he left off.

"Lucy does seem to be fairly adjusted and more happier than she's been for a long time." She said, "Matthew dear, tell them about this school business that you've been discussing with Lucy."

"Oh, yes!" Matthew continued, glad to talk about anything if it would take his mind from traveling backwards. "Thank you, dear, for reminding me."

"School?" Asked three or four guests all at once. And for the first time, Frank's face began to soften somewhat, as the subject had been on his mind lately, and appeared to be sidetracking that ridiculous idea of his uncle and mother adopting a baby. At last, he was giving

Matthew a sharp undivided look, holding his ears open and with interest.

"Well, yes," Matthew went on saying, "With the state of things being such as they are now, it appears that our schools are going to be in jeopardy, also. So, why not start our own private school for our young ones, funded by private resources. That way no Republican can touch it, as no state subsistence will be involved. I've suggested this to Lucy, to come back here and teach rather than remain in Columbia away from family and friends. Competent and established teachers are hard to come by these days, with a war disrupting so many schools and the lives of teachers. There's Maggie, Stewart, and I could name a half dozen more. Besides, there aren't too many young women who holds a college degree from William and Mary in Virginia as Lucy does. Of course, the big question and catch is money since the war drained a good many of us. However, I do think it's a splendid idea and I'm surely willing to contribute what funds I can spare."

Though Frank was quite reserved with his son; still, he was a devoted father to Stewart. Moreover, when it came to the matter of Stewart's education, money would present no problem whatever. He can afford to send Stewart to the finest and most expensive schools in the world, but there was one drawback, and most people who knew Frank would've been surprised to know that. He had no desire to be separated from his son for so much as the length of one day or a night. In fact, he had been thinking about bringing a tutor to Drakston Hall to start the long process of Stewart's education. However, a teacher with Lucy Randolph's qualifications was seldom met with these days, anyhow, in regard to teaching in a private home. In addition to her ability to teach other subjects, she excelled in foreign languages. Now, he was thinking that if Lucy could be persuaded to come back to the low country, that troublesome question is giving Stewart the best schooling for his first years, anyhow, would be solved with him remaining home to boot! It was strange to him that he had not given a thought to Lucy Randolph in that respect before his uncle suggested it. Well, before he went any further into the matter he would see if anything could be arranged with Lucy.

Suddenly, to the amazement of most everyone there because it was not unordinary for Frank to go through an entire meal without saying one word and it had appeared that this meal would be one of those times, he told Matthew, "that won't be necessary, I'll fund the whole project. You just see that Lucy comes back here to teach these youngsters and that'll be enough."

His abrupt and least expected statement startled Matthew so till he was hard put to get his swallow of wine down before it strangled him. Amy, seeming to appear happier over her son's verbal words and contents itself, beamed broadly. At any rate, ever being able to see into the depths of Frank's personality further than anyone else, she was the one exception in being surprised. In realizing that it was Frank's devotion for Stewart that had prompted his remark, Elizabeth's face began to take on the look of ethereal glow as she studied her husband. But it was Martha's voice again that rang out upon the startled hush, saying, "Frank, you mean to say you're going to build us a schoolhouse?" As Martha was now taking several hours out of each day and away for many other duties that fell upon her to teach first-year education to Maggie, she was more than interested in getting something else arranged.

"Not exactly tomorrow, Martha, but in time. I think the most prudent cause would be to wait until we're sure of Lucy returning or locate someone else whose as competent as she is. I can't see building a schoolhouse and no teachers lined up." And, as Martha and all the rest sat in dumb silence in disbelief leaving Frank's long answer, he went on to say, "as a matter of fact, a schoolhouse is the least problems we have. Drakston Hall is large enough to accommodate a teacher and several children there is that entire west wing beside the ballroom on the lower level that is wasted space. We could use that for the classroom, even on rainy days the space would be adequate for the kids to play in."

"Why, Frank!" Exclaimed his mother, "That's an excellent idea." Happily, Elizabeth joined her, "and, Stewart and his little friends will be right there close so as we can keep an eye on them!"

Before everybody got carried away those that had children of or near school-age anyhow, Matthew thought he should put up a little warning signal. "Using Drakston Hall's vacant space is sound thinking, Frank, and no doubt it'll work out pleasantly for all concerned. I must warn everyone though that Lucy has a commitment to fulfill at Miss Taylor's for several months yet. And too, what her final decision is on coming back here to teach, I can't say or promise. I'll do my best though."

"Tell her," Frank said, "if she'll come back and teach Stewart at

Drakston Hall along with Maggie and any other child among our family friends whose parents wishes it, that I'll double her present salary and buy all the supplies she desires."

"That's a most generous offer, Frank, I'll tell her," Matthew said.

And so, in the fullness of time, Lucy would come back to Oak Grove and sitting with the other children in her classroom at Drakston Hall would be a small tow-headed boy whose legal name had become Whitney Carson.

Chapter Two

Between Christmas and New Year's that same week, the foamy, suds like cloud caps looming in the northern distance one cold, windy morning had foamed and churned the entire sky into a solid mass of overhanging dark steel grey by the dinner hour. Hearing the drone of the big bell at the house giving the signal to stop work, Luke leaned his rake against a huge pine and huddling his shoulders closer inside his lightweight work coat, he started walking across the field toward the mansion. He and the hands had been engaged for several days in clearing ground for the many tobacco seedbeds that the planting of next year's tobacco crop would demand. First the beds had to be laid out and cleared of brush and tree stumps that were piled back upon it and set to fire in order to rid the soil of insects and seeds of weed. The raking and burning of the plant beds were a must for the tiny seed sprouts or they would have been eaten or crushed out by weeds long before the lengthy period that was required for them to mature to planting stage. Invariably, it was Luke's habit to clear and pile brush in the forenoon and burn in the afternoons, a task that called for a watchful eye against setting the woods and timberland on fire. Noticing that the wind was much colder and stronger than it had been an hour earlier when he had looked at his watch, he raised his face skyward and concluded that the approaching storm in the cloud-curtained sky was too close at hand to be burning any beds that afternoon. Indeed, when he and the others returned to work after their dinner break, the cold, sleety mist soon began to fall. They kept on piling and clearing brush, but it was not long till they had built up a small fire to warm their chilled, clumsy hands by. Not more than an hour later, Luke saw that he and all the rest were standing around the fire, idle as much or longer than they spent at work; and even though it was only three o'clock in the afternoon he decided to continue in the bad weather would not accomplish much. Thus, he told the hands to gather up the axes, hoes, and rakes, and be sure to put the fire out, too, that they might as well quit till next morning. Though the slight sleet was beginning to stick to the treetops and show in spots here and there on the ground, he was positive the cold front would be gone by the next day. Cutting across the field once more though on his way back to the house, snow flurries began to blow and was falling rather hard when he reached the back yard. He ran up the back steps crossing the porch he opened the door quickly and hollered for Eliza.

As he stood in the open doorway, she came rushing down the back inside staircase, obviously surprised and pleased, saying, "Luke, you're back early. Oh! It's cold! Hurry and close the door!"

He kept the door open though, "Look! Sweet! It's snowing! I wanted you to see it while it lasted!"

"Snowing!" She cried, as she dashed on past him onto the porch and down the steps. "It is! It is! Oh, Luke! I don't think I've ever seen a sight more beautiful than falling snow!" And, it was pretty as it now was falling so heavy the ground was already covered in a white fluffy blanket, a sight that Eliza had seldom seen in her lifetime.

Luke had seen plenty of snow in his life, but he had never seen Eliza standing in it before with the crystal white flakes falling upon, and sticking to her beautiful hair, her long eyelashes; and her happy face as she lifted it toward the heavens. To him it was one sight in a thousand and one that touched him.

"Hey! Come back inside, you'll take a chill!" he called. "I didn't mean for you to go running out in the yard and get plastered like a Christmas tree!"

"I'm not that cold," she laughed as she looked at him and ran back up the steps. "It's so pretty one doesn't feel the cold so much!"

Helping her brush the flakes from her clothing, he took his jacket off and draped it around her shoulders, telling her, "You stay in it very long especially without any wraps, I fear you'd soon forget how pretty it is and start thinking how cold it is."

Still standing on the porch looking at the whirling flakes while Luke shivered in his work shirt, she asked, "Luke, do you think it'll snow long?"

"I don't know, darling. You know more about South Carolina snows than I do. Remember this is the first one I've seen fall here."

"I hope it does," she said. "We have so few snows."

"Well, whether you get your wish or not, I'd suggest that we go inside and watch from the windows, I think that would be a little more cozier," he said.

"Luke! I'm sorry!" she exclaimed, aware now that he was chilling rapidly without his coat. "here I stand draped in your jacket while you freeze!" She grabbed his hand. "Come on, no doubt the inside will be more comfortable for you!"

They rushed inside and on to her father's sitting room where they stood at the window a long time watching the hurling snow as it blew and began to settle over everything. And, instead of the storm ceasing it grew steadily worse, snowing the remainder of that day and night and on through the next day, finally ending sometime the next night; yet the cold front lasted for several more days with the snow remaining for a long period before all of it melted away. Thus, the snowstorm brought the happiest time to Eliza that she thought she had ever spent with Luke. Her father and Aunt Amy were on their last round of visiting at Drakston Hall before coming back to Green Sea for a few days, but that aspect did not dash their spirit of the setting. It was lively enough! With the severe cold abound and the ground banked several inches deep in snow, all outside work on the plantation stopped for a great many days save the necessity of caring for the livestock. Hence, she and Luke were vouchsafed an uninterrupted interval that did not call for them to follow a schedule of any sort an existence that had been granted in scant order since their wedding day and one that they now made the most of. They romped and played in the snow as though they might have been children rather than married grown-ups, chasing and throwing one another with snowballs amid the heavy-laden trees and evergreens. Luke would catch her and tickle her rib cage through her clothing til she would almost become breathless with the giggles, sinking down in the snow while she pleaded for him to stop. They even scooped up snow and built a snowman. Then when day drifted to late evening and long after the supper hour, they would pop popcorn in the fireplace and while they took delight in its butter soaked natural goodness, stretched out on the rug by the mellow glow of firelight, they would talk of anything and everything for hours. And, if she stayed locked in Luke's arms more frequently and longer in this period of time it was because from the beginning of the snow, she had felt that the pure, white flakes that had closed her and Luke together inside this novel, white world had somehow brought a glorification to their love making that had never been there before. Though, they had been husband and wife for years, it seemed that Luke's words of endearment whispered in her ears touched her heart no less profoundly than had they been a prayer. There was a sense of relaxation, a peace and calm about her that had been missing for so long. At times, as she would stand at their bedroom window alongside Luke with their arms encircling each other's waist looking out upon the white shrouded grounds, she would feel that she were sharing a closer rapport with God, also. Her mind would fleet back to another time when she had looked out upon the snow, positive now that her maker had let Luke come to her and spared his life during the war, too because He and He alone knew the full measure of the flamework the idiosyncrasy part of her nature and the depth of her way of thinking and feelings for Luke. Moreover, at long last, she knew that if she never truly accepted the tragic happening in her family, that God had now given her the strength to live with it and be happy and contented with Luke. But, the time grew around when the last of the snow disappeared as the cold front moved out and the days became warmer again in the winter sunshine. Her father and Aunt Amy's last turn of visiting at Green Sea was over and they had gone. Work on the plantation had begun once more and she and Luke's winter's paradise had turned to normal routine. That is to say, everything was running in its natural course, leaving out the ghastly head cold she had taken along with a hoarse rasping cough. There surely was no happy medium about that! Luke bundled her snugly in the buggy though one mild day and took her, over her protesting that she was not ill, to Doctor Davis' office. Of course, she came home not only with one bottle of "brown medicine," but two! One for her head cold and one for her cough. Seeing the medicine that he knew she detested to take, Luke had laughingly told her that maybe it was good for her well-being why the Lord did not rain down more snow upon South Carolina! She had replied with not a very straight face, "What's so hard for me to understand is the fact you're not coughing, too, Mr. Heyward!"

Although her cough and cold did seem to persist in holding on, both did improve along; nevertheless, she did find that she was not feeling as well as she should. One Sunday morning, the queasiness that had been in her stomach lately suddenly brought her leaping up from the bed and making a dash for the toilet chair inside the dressing room. She was sure she was going to start vomiting. She did not become worse though and it soon passed. But she did feel weak. She heard Luke's anxious voice calling to her, "Eliza, dear, are you alright."

"It's this dreadful cough, Luke," she said, as she came back through the doorway to see him standing beside the window, that was near the dressing room, with a disturbed look on his face. "At times it makes me feel as though I might throw up, I'm all right now, though."

"Are you sure, dear," he added, seeing that her face was still chalk white. "We don't have to go to church this morning, hadn't you rather we stay home and let you rest today?"

"goodness, no, Luke, I'm not ill. It's just that it appears, if I have to cough only once in the morning, here lately, it's worse than if I were to cough all day!"

"well, we'll go if you think you're all right," he said, seeing that the color was returning to her cheeks. "But, I don't want you to think you have to sit and suffer through Reverend Johnson's long sermon on my account. Truthfully, I'd prefer you stay in bed and take care of that cough. In fact, if it doesn't leave pretty soon, I'm taking you back to Doctor Davis."

"Oh, hurry and get dressed, Luke, or we'll be late. I'll take some mint along with me, and if Reverend Johnson sees fit to warn us of our sins longer than usual and I should start coughing, I'll plop some in my mouth and it'll take care of the nausea. So, don't worry about me. Besides, my cough doesn't make me feel like that except in the early mornings."

Neither she or Luke had the first though that it could be something other than her cough. All the same, the day did finally get around when Eliza did give a brief thought to the possibility. It was one gloomy morning near the middle of February, while she was looking at the calendar counting the weeks til spring, that it suddenly dawned on her that her monthly period was long overdue, a bodily function that had always been regular or nearabout. Her heart leaped as she studied the weeks once again to make sure. She coughed though and just as sudden she sank into despair as she thought about Hannah's seemingly constant perching about taking colds, telling her that colds would make her late besides a dozen other things. No doubt Hannah was right she reasoned. As much as she wanted to give Luke a child, she had given up long ago of thinking that she may conceive. Actually, in essence with that aspect of her marriage, she thought that had she and Luke been capable of being successful that they surely would have years back. Had not she searched for every possible answer and followed every hunch of her own in addition to any suggestion that the few people she had mentioned it to had hinted to her the few that she had expressed her longing for a child to, Doctor Davis, Martha, and Hannah. Why, she even gave way to Hannah's pleading and slept with one of Hannah's love potions under her pillow for several weeks once and still nothing happened! Of course, Luke had jested her time and time again for being as superstitious as the blacks. Anyhow, when Hannah had discovered that her remedy for that sort of thing had not brought forth any results either, she had stated, quite emphatically and indignant at that, "Hmph! Hit, Mister Luke den! He like dem young'uns O'min. me an' Mister Mathew qwine have no granchilin!" She had not been able to suppress her laughter when Hannah had said that, though she could tell that to Hannah it was nothing to laugh about. As a matter of fact, Hannah had made it fairly plain that she thought there was something lacking in Mister Luke's performance as well as her twin son's. Well, she did not know about Hannah's sons, but she did know her husband, and she would still maintain that their failing to conceive a child probably lay with her and her alone and not with him. Thus, that being her way of thinking, she sighed and brushed the thought of her period aside. Even so, later on that same morning when she met Hannah in the hallway, she suddenly got the urge to hear what she would make of it and if her own view had not quit convinced her, Hannah's remark stopped any further question she may have asked. "What I ben telling you," mumbled Hannah, "No surprise, all us qwine half-naked, hit dat cold, shonuf!" in truth, at this late stage, Hannah likewise had given up all hope of Eliza and Mister Luke's marriage being productive in the way of offspring not to mention Willie and Allen's unfruitful unions. It never would have occurred to Hannah that her twin sons had been born sterile, which did happen to be fact in their case. As far as that went, she had not ever heard the word and in the event of that happening and had it been explained to her, she most likely would have stated that such could not be!

Nevertheless, as things go, notwithstanding Hannah and Eliza's own opinion, the manifestation of the overdue period being something other than having a cold was soon to be disclosed, at least to Eliza. The dismal days of February had tolled into the first week of March. With the smell of spring beginning to be in the air and thinking it was going to be a mild march day, Eliza and Hannah decided that it was time to start the spring cleaning. Promptly, after breakfast they gathered all the soiled clothes, dresser scarves, curtains, blankets, and quilts and took them out to the wash house. Then, Hannah set out to inform Bessie and Ruth, who had been doing most all the washing that winter, that it was going to be washday and a big one at that. However, it seemed to be only a few minutes later that the sound of the sudden March wind whipping around the house came to Eliza's attention. She ran down the back stairs and was just in time to tell Bessie and Ruth as they approached the back yard not to start the fire. The wind was too strong. By then it appeared to have the fierceness of a lion's roar. The clothes and other washings were stacked in the wash house and Bessie and Ruth returned to their cabins and she and Hannah returned to the mansion. Besides, that new minister, Marsh Reed, who was assisting Reverend Johnson in holding the spring revival that week and whose captivating personality and inspirational sermons were gathering converts to the alter like bees to a honeycomb, was going to be a supper guest that night at Green Sea. So, it really was no suitable day for a big wash or cleaning house. She should have thought about that in the first place, she told Hannah as they began a few other smaller chores. And so, with her mind centered on spring and house cleaning such as replacing the heavy drapes in the bedrooms with the sheer summer curtains, the arriving of the new pastor and the revival, in addition to wondering what was taking place in Columbia concerning the little boy Whitney and her own private thoughts about the possibility of she and Luke adopting a child someday though she had yet to mention it to Luke, she had not wasted too much time in pondering why she still had not seen any sign of the cure of Eve! Now, having decided to take a bath and change into her dinner clothes, she would be wearing the same dress to church service that night, earlier than she normally would have since they were expecting a guest, she stepped out of all her clothing that she had taken off and let fall to her feet. She picked up her underclothes that she had laid out upon the bed and was crossing the floor toward the dressing room when she caught a glimpse of her bosom in the wardrobe mirror. Stopping dead still and with her heart leaping she began to stare. Then, remembering what Martha had said once about bosoms revealing a baby on the way before any other symptom, she started inching closer to thin unmistakable telltale sign in the mirror true evidence that showed she was carrying a baby! She let her hand fall gently on the still slender stomach, and in the gladness and excitement of realizing that the baby she had prayed and longed for so many years to give to Luke was lying there, her knees became so weak that she thought she might topple to the floor any time. Awe struck in wonderment, she turned and with somewhat quivering legs she made it to the edge of the bed and sat down. Seeming as though she were embracing her own body in the wonder of what had happened, she sat there for a long while with her arms crossed over her bosom while both hands gripped hard upon either shoulder. She thought of her other symptoms, the skipped periods, the morning sickness that she had thought was due to her cough, finally, when she thought her legs could be trusted once more, she rose and headed straight for the calendar that she kept in the dressing room. She turned it back to where she had marked her last period, that had started near the middle of December. December? This was March! Good heavens! She was over two months pregnant! Looking at the calendar again and counting days she wondered when the miracle of the tiny life that she now carried was conceived. She began thinking back to the holidays when she and Luke had been together a lot… The snowstorm! She was positive now that it was during those lazy, wonderful days. Oh, she must run to the field where Luke was breaking ground for the spring planting and tell him about their baby! This very moment Eliza made a dash for her clothes that she had stepped out of long minutes before that. Suddenly though, she heard the clock telling the hour. She would not have the time, it was too near the quitting hour and supper, plus that new pastor could ring the doorbell any minute! On second thought even if she were to have time, Luke no doubt would not like her running wildly in that roaring wind exposing her lingering cough. Cough? Colds? Hannah and her philosophy! No cold had caused her to skip that time of month, it was her and Luke's baby that now lay within her and that had been there all this time! Would Hannah be surprised and pleased as well as a little put out when she told her? Luke though must be the first to know. But, when on earth could she tell him? It must be in private and someplace that presented a feeling of closeness to it. With a guest for supper and the revival service later, there would not be any chance for hours. She supposed she could tell him on the way home from church. No, she did not think much of that idea. They would be too much in a hurry coming home, since Luke was very concerned in getting her out of the night air as quickly as he could. As a matter of fact, Luke had been so concerned over her lingering cough that he had gone so far as to suggest they skip the revival night service altogether. Knowing that he was very impressed with Marsh Reed, though, she had insisted that they attend. Besides, her cough was almost gone now. She knew what she would do, it had just come to her. She would tell Luke about their baby tonight, once they were in bed and she was snuggled down closely in his arms. No other place or time would be so perfect. Yes, she would tell Luke tonight at bedtime. The thrill of it brought goose bumps creeping over her body. Even so, had she had any inkling of what lay ahead of her in just a few short hours, a dark despair would have overshadowed the gladness in her heart tenfold.

Chapter Three

On the same day, at almost the exact hour that Eliza had made the joyous discovery of her pregnancy, there was a conversation, or perhaps an exchange of words would come near in fitting it's description, since Job was not too gifted in making sentences, going on in the Early Cole shack between Early's idiot son Job and his two brothers, who lagged behind Job in not too great a distance when it came to having any sound-headed, reasonable intelligence. Their discussion concerned another few words that had been exchanged between Job and Frank Drakston earlier in the day, when Frank had unexpectedly stopped at Early's to have a word with Early and, unfortunately, had not found no one home but Job. What Job was telling his brothers was not very clear, and indeed would have been quite difficult for a bright person to make anything of, least of all joseph and Jonah. But, where the average person would have disregard what Job was having to say Jonah envisioned a daring adventure in the telling and immediately started making plans in carrying it out, with Job gleefully looking on and feeling proud.

This particular day had been another restless one for Frank beginning early in the morning his whole body had seem to be as unsettled again as the howling wind singing through the tree boughs. A sound that even put his nerves on edge. Now, cantering Blossom back toward home, he was telling himself that, of course, he had numerous days like that when the wind was not singing, it came upon him now on days without wind when Eliza dwelled in his mind despite all his effort to focus on other things, such as Stewart's schooling. It had taken the party at Martha's during the holidays to convince him that he was not any nearer putting Eliza out of his mind than the moment he had come to love her. Though he had tried, he knew he would never get over losing her and especially to a man whose station in life had never ranked higher than that of an overseer on someone else's plantation. Come to think of it thought Frank in a sense, Luke Heyward had as yet to rise above the position even though he was married to Eliza. Indeed, if one were to allow one's thoughts to reflect over that aspect, as he himself was doing now and had rather often from time to time, one would have to admit that instead of Eliza's husband's status elevating, it appeared to be declining further all along. On every occasion that he chanced to pass Green Sea, did he not see Luke Heyward engaged in some downgrading task? Take the present time, how much lower could a man's work become than following behind a dumb mule all day long? Been out there since sunup eating dust. What would it be like to hold a plow handle all day? Still, by the same token, he wondered if he were in Luke Heyward's shoes, following that mule up and down that field, that he would be any more discontented and restless than he was now. He would stake his millions that for all his plowing and eating dirt, Luke Heyward did not have an unquiet bone in his body. Why should he, married to a beauty like Eliza? He bet that "overseer" never sweated and stewed with restlessness as he had this morning, til he was forced to ride a horse all the way to Charleston and back in order to wear his body down. But, he would have to admit it had helped because he thought he would have no trouble falling asleep tonight. He was more than ready to reach Drakston Hall, have super with Elizabeth and Stewart and then hit the hay. He thought he would suggest to Elizabeth their skipping church tonight. He was not getting anything out of that revival, anyway. The only reason he had attended so far was that no gentleman, such as himself, allowed his wife to go out after dark unescorted to church or any other place, as far as that matter. Though it was true that Elizabeth had become rather mesmerized, charm-struck, or something over that Marsh Reed, actually becoming one of his converts, this was one night she would have to forego his spellbinding sermon. If Marsh Reed were to preach to him all day long and night, too, he doubted very much that his sermon would move him. In fact, he was glad that he had gone to Charleston today, the hours that he had spent with Brad and Brent Cooper talking shop, had produced a measure of enthusiasm in him that otherwise he thought he had lost for good. Well! Fancy that! He had just stopped at Early Cole's to give him a damn good raking over about that stallion standing over there in the meadow pasture. First time that he had seen that horse since these bastards had caused him to run himself almost to his grave, and from what he had heard that might as well have happened. The very idea of those damn Cole boys selecting Eliza's horse for their pranks! He did not have to be told that they were the guilty party. Hell, he knew they were! He should have never gotten mixed up with those scums in the first place, made no difference how much he wanted to hit back at Luke Heyward! That damn stupid Early Cole! He was going to tell Cole that if he knew what was good for his health, he had better refresh his memory as to what the orders had been, which were to bring no physical harm to any people or stock. He had only meant for them to agitate that "overseer," such as hampering his work! And that business concerning the firearms. He had made it implicit to Cole that if firearms were to be used in stampeding the stock, the shots had better be fired into the air and not at any object, because if they ever put one little blemish upon Eliza, directly or indirectly, he would blow their brains out! In the matter of that stallion, it appeared that Cole had neglected his duty, seeing that his sons had followed orders correctly. Well, it was too bad that he did not find Early Cole home a while ago. It was also unfortunate that he had not known that Job Cole was the imbecile he was and the only person at that shack. Had he known that was the case, he would have rode on by. He was sorry that he had exchanged one word with the lunkhead. Why that stupid Cole would leave that idiot home by himself was a mystery to him anyhow. If Cole came home tonight and found his son and his shack burned up, it should not come as any surprise at all to him. On a windy day like this, that crazy fool had a fire built around that wash pot big enough to burn the whole county down. He had tried to tell Job that what he was doing was dangerous. He doubted though that it had done any good. He wondered if he could recall just what he and that nitwit had told to one another!

Unable to get anyone's attention while he had remained sitting in the saddle and calling out at the broken-down front steps, he had ridden Blossom on around that creaking shack of Cole's to the back yard where he had seen black smoke billowing. First thing, rounding the corner of the shack, his eyes had recognized Job standing near a big wash pot stirring clothes with a long wooden paddle, causing him to wonder wat was keeping it and Job, too, from catching on fire, as the wind whipped flames against it and within inches of Job's ragged clothing.

"Hello Job." He said.

Without moving his gaze in any direction other than the wash pot or changing his vacant expression, Job said "Hey, Mister Drakston." Bringing him to ponder again how Job had known who he was because as far as he could recollect, he had never spoken a word in Job Cole's presence before, and Job surely had not looked in his direction.

"Where's your father?"

His gaze still concentrated upon his stirring, Job asked, "You mean Pappy, Mister Drakston?"

"Yes! Yes! Your pappy, then." He snapped rather impatiently, regretting that he had taken the time to stop by.

"Pappy gone up the road a piece, brothers all gone, not with Pappy though."

"Where did your brothers go?" He asked

"Swamp," Job replied.

Though fully aware then to the extent of Job's idiocy, curiosity had made him inquire, anyhow, "Job, when was the last time you boys visited Green Sea?"

Finally taking his eyes away from the wash pot of boiling cloths and letting them fall in a somewhat dull stare upon him, Job had told him, "Green Sea, going to Green Sea, Mister Drakston... a visit to Green Sea!"

Sensing then that he should have left without asking Job the first question, he had said, "Job, forget it," and he started to move Blossom toward the road when on a sudden impulse he had decided to warn Job about the fire. "Don't put any more wood around that wash pot, Job, your clothes could catch on fire and burn you, besides catching this house on fire and burning it to the ground, also. You be careful!"

Job's faint nonchalant words reached his ears as he rode away, "Burn the house… Yes…Mister Drakston."

He supposed he should have made that fool put the fire out before he left. Job Cole's safety or that shack though, was not his responsibility. That belonged to that lazy, windbag Early Cole. Come what may, however, tomorrow morning he was going to locate that worthless cad and give him hell over afflicting Eliza's stallion. In the meantime, though, he was going to put Job Cole, Early Cole, and all the rest of that stinking bunch out of his mind and get a good night's sleep. There was Drakston Hall just ahead and it never had looked more inviting to him. He was bushed.

With the buggy robe draped warmly around her as she snuggled in the curve of Luke's arm, Eliza was keeping silent while he talked quite impassionedly and in earnest about Reverend Marsh Reed's zestful and some forward sermon, that they had listened to a short while earlier. However, much she wanted to keep her mind on what Luke was saying though, she knew she was failing. She had hardly heard a word he had said, and she was also positive that a great deal of Marsh Reed's sermon, too, had also bypassed her ears. Her thoughts had been and were still too absorbed with the conversation that she was going to have with Luke, once they had reached the house and gone to bed, to hear much of anything that anyone said. But, they should be home in a few minutes now, because they had almost come to the clearing. The hard wind that had blown all day had calmed considerably. It was still strong enough though to cause the heavily timbered forest to hum in its wake. Blowing wind that howled and especially at night had always depressed her and she was more than anxious to leave the woods and reach the open fields of Green Sea, leaving the humming tree tops behind her. On this night, Eliza told herself, she had no wish to allow anything to interfere with the singing in her heart. Maybe by the time they had reached the house and made ready for bed, the wind would be gone, and the unruly March day would end as peaceful as she knew she was going to be in the folds of Luke's arms, when she could at least tell him that she was going to have his baby. All of a sudden though as they were moving on at a brisk pace, Eliza thought the night's darkness had begun to grow lighter even though she knew there was no moon to shine these nights or one to be rising. It caused a strange fear to overtake her. She stirred somewhat from the cozy position where she was settled with Luke's strong protective arm tucked around her waist and felt the strength of drawing her back to his side as he said, "Doll, you better stay put a few more minutes, it'll be a little while yet before we reach the house. You'll become chilled moving around."

"I know, Luke," she said, "But—I—" while she continued to move to the outer edge of the seat, leaned her heard outside the buggy to look skyward.

He slowed the mare's gait.

"What is it, darling?" He asked, concerned over her behavior.

"No, Luke, don't slow down," She told him as a cold fear began to make her shiver.

"There seems to be a glow reflecting against the sky. I feel—," She paused then and held her breath, as a vision of grey ashes shifting gently in a mild morning's sunrise suddenly flashed before her eyes, blocking out the faint glow darken sky. She whirled back upon the seat and gripped Luke's hand in sudden shivering fright, telling him, "I'm afraid, Luke, please hurry!"

He rushed the mare, taking her at her word, “Don’t be frightened, sweet, what you saw is most likely the aurora borealis in the polar region, that’s not so unusual on a night such as this.”

As they were clearing the woods, “No, Luke,” she replied. “It wasn’t that. Oh, dear, God!” It’s green Sea! Green Sea’s on fire, Luke!” she suddenly screamed.

Luke jerked his head up and looked in the open space across the fields, which gave them a startling view of the spreading blaze, that was burning at the back wing of the mansion’s first floor. The wind was rapidly carrying the flame higher and higher as it turned the night’s darkness near to that of a red dawn. Holding firmly to the reins with one hand, he grabbed the rawhide whip with the other and gave the mare a hard whack on the rump, something he had never done before but time was so precious as he shouted to Eliza above her screams, “Stay in the buggy, dear , and hold on tight to me, don’t jump out! While they raced against time toward the growing flames, it seemed to Luke that all the horror he had seen and experienced during the war had been nothing compared to hearing Eliza’s terrifying screaming as well as his own anguish and distress on realizing that despite all his efforts to save Eliza’s home for her that in all likelihood nothing was going to save it, they both were going to be witness to the giant elegant mansion burning to the ground. And, the sudden peeling of the big plantation bell importing for miles only one message to its listeners this time of night brought the calamity of the fire pressing down upon Luke and all its shocking impact more than ever. Their thoughts were much the same aside from the vivid image of gray ashes piercing Eliza’s mind when plunging down the driveway with all the possible speed that Luke dared to drive the buggy at. Holding on fast to his arm, Eliza’s eyes caught and held upon the splendid white columns, the symbol that had always brought a wave from pride and devotion for Green Sea washing over her. They were still standing, amid rolling waves of smoke and sweeping flames, stately as ever. In realizing that she was looking upon them and the grand mansion itself for the last time, Eliza’s screams suddenly died, tightened into one big solid lumps of grief that lodged in her throat. Though she was astounded in terror-stricken disbelief that it could be happening, she still could move. She and Luke both had jumped from the buggy before its wheels had barely stopped spinning where he had brought it to a skid upon the lawn a good distance from the roaring blaze. The fire had now grown to the magnitude of releasing heat into the chilled night air; they felt its warmth upon their faces as their flying feet took them in the midst of the shout and cries of the hands, who were fighting frenziedly to bring the growing fire under control. They were dashing back—and—forth from the well with buckets of water and beating at the flames with wet sacks. The droning of the bell had begun to bring more people to the tragic sky scene; that is to say, those that had not already seen the light in the sky and had started, anyway. Everybody was doing as much as one could, but it was not enough to snuff out the fire that was rapidly eating everything in its path. It appeared that the fine furnishings and the exquisite decorations inside the mansion, such as the hand embroidered silk murals that adorned some of the walls, were added kerosene to the blazes. As Eliza had dashed forward into the heart sickening devastation with Luke and before he had joined the others in their futile attempt to extinguish the fire, she had heard his frantic shouts cautioning her to stay back from the blaze and not go inside the roasting, smoke filled mansion and even though she had no wish to heap further pain upon him, he just as well have held his breath. She took no heed to anything, his warning, her baby, nothing save the one compelling thing that her mind was willing her and her weekend, trembling legs were in pursuit of, the one thing that she knew she must and had to do… she had to save the family portraits! Some inborn drive in her Carson blood motivated her in reaching her aim and carrying it out despite the odds. She dashed inside the burning building and without flinching once or groping one inch against the suffocating house, her feet flew up the staircase to the last and highest portrait hanging on the wall. In a sense, it would never have become necessary for her to grope her way, anyhow. She had dwelled too many hours, days, months, and years in the mansion alone not to know and have every foot of its floors stamped forever in her memory, floors she had paced upon so much in her loneliness. Eliza had no idea how many times she had run in and out the burning mansion, snatching down portraits and carrying them outside. But, she was aware now that the flames were licking their way all around her as her hands grabbed another portrait from the wall. She thought, considering the distance she had covered to the door, running through it for what was to be her last time, that she had succeeded in saving the entire collection. In her confusion and torment though, both mental and physical because by this time the heat had scorched her face and hands, too, she was not completely sure. She whirled around and started to run back into the billowing smoke and crackling blaze, unaware of coughing with almost every short breath that the smoke had brought her to. However, she did feel the sudden grip of strong arms, holding her back. She did not know whose arms they were nor did she care. Suddenly, she heard shouts that the guest house had also caught on fire. She turned in seeing and hearing the beautiful chandelier in the hall fall and crash to the burning mahogany floor below, she were wishing that she were lying in the cemetery alongside Nat and her mother where she would not be forced to witness anymore. In spite of her striving to hold everything together during the war, now fire was destroying everything that had made or had been Green Sea, she thought. She did not think she could bear seeing the tall symbolic columns fall and crumble to dust and ashes and suddenly it seemed that she would be vouchsafed from going through the torture; because the fire, the shouts and cries, the roaring and crackling noise of the flames, her burning face and hands, the whole nightmare was fading into a blessed, darkness that was not lighted by fire eating madness. At last, she found herself sinking into the peaceful oblivion that she had wished for and she entered it with a will and quickly at that.

For the second time in her life, Eliza had fallen into a dead faint, but this time it was Luke's arms that she had fainted in. He gathered her limp body up and carried her a long way from the massive burning mansion, which had now become totally engulfed in flames. Having no wish to see it fall; either, Luke never once looked back. Laying Liza down gently upon the lawn, he hurriedly took his coat off, something he had not taken the time to do, yet; and gathering her up once again he laid her down upon it. Although numb himself from shock and wariness as well as being frightfully terrified with fear over her fainting he nevertheless waited not one second trying fiercely to revive her

During those trying minutes for Luke and Eliza both, Early Cole was having a hurried few minutes of conversing with his three sons. Early had been to Charleston that day; also, but had been later than customary in returning to his shack. Early's moonshine business had begun to capsize rapidly, even more so than what it had declined to during the war years. In fact, it was near diving to rock bottom and had been that way for some time now. Early would ponder for hours periodically, whether it was the quality that his moonshine had dropped to or had it dropped because of Walt Hawkins branding it in undeserving name. Anyhow, his time in Charleston that day had been taken up with buying supplies, mostly on credit, for his moonshining business and making an endeavor to solicit a few new customers. He was near worn out from sparing the energy that both dctails had demanded from him. Even so, seeing the light upon the surrounding dark sky and hearing the peeling of the big bell when he was still a good distance from home, Early set Maybelle on a flying course at once. Knowing now that the fire had to be at Green Sea as he grew nearer toward it, a cold suspicion began to form and take shape in Early's mind and became almost a certain fact and just as he reached his cluttered front yard that forever had been a landmark to the Cole's existence, he saw Joseph and Jonah speeding their mounts from the direction of the blaze. Simultaneously, all three men, reigned their mounts in among the trash and junk that made up the front yard. Job had also darted through the front door upon hearing their arrival and was standing on the rickety porch, looking as pleased as his vacant expression would allow.

Before their mount's feet had hardly gotten settled in the flying tin cans and other rubble, Early was inquiring anxiously, as he wanted to get a few facts straight before riding on, "Boys, ain't that Green Sea burning down and ain't you riding from there?"

"Shore is Pappy," answered Joseph, looking rather smug in the firelight that was shining through the open door from the roaring fire that Job had built in the fireplace.

"Since you're riding from there, I take it that you just may know something about what's going on up there, how did it start?" Asked Early, playing as if he did not have the slightest hunch.

"Now, Pappy," Laughed Jonah "don't play possum like that."

"Boys I'm afraid you've been mixed up in some dangerous business. That I don't quite understand, because kicking up a little dust and playing a few devilish pranks is one thing, but fire is another!"

Sending a somewhat oblique glance towards his brother Jonah, Joseph said, "Just following Mister Drakston's orders, Pappy."

Surprised and relieved that they had not acted on their own, Early asked, "What orders, when have you seen Frank Drakston?"

Suddenly, Job piped up with a few words, though his expression was dull as ever, "Mister Drakston said "Be careful, visit Green Sea, too!"

Early looked from Job to Joseph and waited for the answer to his question.

Finally, Joseph said, "Me and Jonah ain't, but he told Job."

Early sighed. He didn't know quite what to make of it, "So you boys have set fire to Green Sea on the orders of Frank Drakston. That shore was a grave mistake, son. It grieves me mightily that you did. I've always had a special feeling for Green Sea, you know that was where I got my education. Yes, that's mighty perplexing to me. I would've stopped you had I been home, Frank Drakston or no Frank Drakston!"

"Pappy, we waited for you a long time, them people was goin to be home from church in a little while and we couldn't wait no longer. You told us if you wus gone and Mister Drakston told us to do it, cause we wus binding to him."

"That is true, Joseph, I did tell you that for a fact. But, son, we ain't binding that much, for you and Jonah to go setting fire to Green Sea" Early pondered for a moment or two, then he went on, "Listen boys and listen careful. This is serious business, nothing like tearin down the fence! If it leaks out that there fire what's no accident, the law and that Luke Heyward is shore going to be asking question. You go in that house and stay there. If anybody should come by or ask when you come home, remember to say, "right then." And be shore… sure… To tell them that you're just come from the swamp!" `

"we'll do what you say, Pappy."

"Good!" said Early "Now I'm going on to Green Sea to see what that crowd up there has to say. I may pick up some useful information. I hate to ride up there though, knowing what I do. It sho—sure is a burden."

"We're sorry, Pappy, fer the burden" said Jonah

"Well, son, what's done is done, but I can tell you this, somethin' will sure be missing when I ride by Green Sea now when I'm on my way to O'Henry's" He looked at Job and shaking his head and putting a finger against his lips he continued, "Not a word , Job, to anybody, shh! Then, turned and headed Maybelle toward Green Sea and a hard gallop.

It has been a big house; thus it made a big fire. Urging Maybelle through the archway; for a second or two, Early was thinking were it possible that he could have been thrust back in ancient times and was seeing the burning of Rome with his own eyes! The falling of the many huge Gothic columns one after another, trailed by long burning tapers that sent trains of shooting stars into an overhang orange and inky curtain as they crashed into a roaring lake of fire below, were presenting a colorful pageantry of electrifying horror that generated an eerie feeling along every sudden guilt weighted nerve in Early's body. Early was not so stupid that he did not realize that he had loaned a helping hand in setting the stage for the spectacular and tragic occurrence, even if he had not applied the torch. In weighted guilt, he was on the verge of heading Maybelle back in the direction he had come. Nevertheless, observing that the fight to save the stables, the barn, and other buildings was still in progress, though the mansion and guesthouse had been abandoned to their fate, Early quickly concluded that the very least he could do would be to join in the struggle. He leaped off Maybelle and swiftly tieing to tie her to a limb under one of the live oaks that was near the road, he started hurrying up the lane. He had only gone a short distance; however, when his attention was drawn through the blinding rays of light and shadows to a small group of people on the lawn, who appeared to have something other than the fire on their minds for the present. Curious as always, Early trotted over and edged himself in among them, and instantly, he was wishing that he had given into his instinct moments earlier and left. The anguished face of Luke Heyward still bent over Eliza's unconscious body as he fanned her frantically with his hat, proved almost too much for Early's guilty conscience. The seriousness of the whole disastrous episode as well as fearing for the safety and welfare of his own sons caused Early to feel as though the cold blade of a dagger had been stabbed through him as he glanced at Eliza's Heyward's deathlike features. Early decided he should try to seek the information that he had mostly come for in the first place, quickly forging the opinion that maybe Luke Heyward would not think it odd if he voiced an inquiry or two, then and there since Luke had fronted him once or twice asking questions in connection with the Bullitt episode and all the other harassing incidents that had taken place at Green Sea. As a matter of fact, Early had come near telling Luke to ride to Drakston Hall and ask Frank Drakston who was responsible for the harassment at Green Sea. He had wanted to, but there had been the matter of involving his sons, and himself, not to mention his acreage. Accordingly, he had kept Luke waiting while he had looked seriously at all sides of the questions, finally ended up muttering a lie in spite of himself.

Now, clearing his throat making an effort to let his question sound as casual and offhand as he possibly could, considering the circumstances, Early ventured to say, "Mister Heyward, was the fire accidental or was it them vandals again?"

Albert and Doss, both of who were in the small group due to Luke's having called them away from the fire out of his concern over their age as both were getting well along in years looked at Early as if he were a fool. They both wore naked grief and terror, etched in every creased line on their faces, as they stood quietly and looked upon their mistress' stilled, scorched face. In fact, they had already told Luke, while tears had traced through the smoke and burns left on their cheeks, that they were certain they had heard riders speeding away just before they had discovered the fire. In any event, they did not approve of Early Cole asking Luke about it, then. Early though was not fazed one particle by their expressions or Luke's failing to reply, not yet. Usually nothing daunted him if he wanted to find out something. He repeated his question and when he did Luke lashed out it was doubtful more harshly, he had ever spoken to anyone. "Cole! For God sakes! Can't you see that my only concern right now is for my wife! Albert, she's staying out too long, see that someone goes for Doctor Davis and, Doss, if the kitchen isn't on fire, too, try to make your way around the blaze and bring me back the smelling salts!"

Hannah's cries fell upon Luke's last words as she came running through the shadows toward them. "Here dey is, Mister Luke, an' water, an' towels, an' quilt." She fell to her knees beside Eliza. "Lay her on de quilt, Mister Luke, I help yu'bring her to." She murmured through sobs as she started applying wet cloths to Eliza's face and hands.

For a passing second, Luke wondered about the quilt recognizing it as one from his and Eliza's bed he told her "Hannah you're not only a good woman, you're wise one, too" Hannah had remembered the wash that had been stacked in the washhouse that morning and had gotten the quilt and towels from there. The instant she had seen Eliza fainting in Luke's arms, she had recalled that other time when she had known the severity of Eliza's fainting, and, immediately, she had started making her way around the fire for the supplies.

Early Cole's head was not on his shoulders for nothing, he was also wise. Promptly, Early reasoned that Luke was absolutely correct for having ignored his question and in a manner, of calling him down to boot. Early saw that it had been most unbecoming of him to question Mister Heyward while he was so upset over his wife. Readily, he wanted to make up for his senseless thinking, exclaiming, "Mister Heyward! Maybell's the fastest mare in these parts anywhere! I'll have Doctor Davis to your wife in no time flat!" He whirled and had disappeared from sight before Luke had any chance to respond, whatever. As he and Maybelle sped through the darken and windy night, Early told himself many times over, 'that come morning. He was going to pluck a crow with Frank Drakston.'

They met one another, each on their way to see the other, when the sun had scarcely scanned the treetops. The near one-foot thick walls of Drakston Hall had cut out any sound that may have reached Frank's ears while the catastrophe had been in progress the night before. All through the ill-starred drama, he and Elizabeth had slept peacefully and soundly. A number of the house servants had observed the light in the sky and had concluded that it and the faint droning of a bell were near Green Sea, if not Green Sea itself. But, it would have taken the burning of Drakston Hall to have urged them in disturbing Frank once he had entered his bedroom and closed the door. However, when he and Elizabeth sat down to breakfast, the servants had come forth and announced that Green Sea had burned to the ground in the night. Assuredly, he and Elizabeth both had been shocked. Instantly, Elizabeth had started gathering up needful and essential items that are called for in such a situation. After frank's initial shock had worn off, his following reaction had been to think that it appeared that he was concerned for Eliza. In fact, he had made several suggestions to Elizabeth in the matter of what would be most suitable to take to Green Sea. Of course, he did not plan to go any near to Green Sea than passing on the road that ran by there, nor had he since that day that Eliza had so infuriated him at the flower bed. He still continued to sulk over her ordering him to leave and, sometimes, had been waiting for Eliza to apologize, because to his way of thinking he had not said anything that day, that was not fact and for her own welfare. At any rate, he was not quite set for the evil day that Early Cole's presence furnished, when they met that morning on a little way from Drakston Hall.

They drew their mounts to stop, facing one another in the middle of the road, both aware that if the glare that each was looking at was any signal flag, there chance meeting was not going to be pleasant.

Choosing to dispense with one word of greeting, Frank spoke first,

"Cole, I was on my way to see you, and my intention was to see you long before today. Anyway, I stopped by your place yesterday to tell you I don't want any more horses ruined. I've known all along that no one did that but those damn sons of yours! Some damn prank they come up with and choosing Eliza's stallion to pull it off with to boot! When I say one thing, I don't mean something else! Turning work horses and mules out is one thing but running one to death is another! That had better never happen again. I like horses!"

Preferring likewise to address Frank without affixing the usual "Mister" that he had always honored Frank with, Early said, "Drakston, I was sorry about that, but that was a mishap in a way. You see the boys told me that they just meant to tie them shucks to his tail only for a few minutes. They never dreamed the stallion was that high-spirited and was going to run like that. They done their level best to catch him, but finally had to give up and come on home, cause them people would be coming from church soon."

Early's excuses for everything had forever disgusted Frank. He was thinking that he might have known Early Cole would come up with some damn story that any intelligent person would never believe. He stared Early down and replied, "You heard what I said, Cole, and I damn well mean business!"

Calm as the spring morning, Early told him, "Well, Drakston, I've got some business to discuss with you, too, and was on my way to see you about it. What about the house? You know burning down houses ain't my cup of tea either!"

Had Early thrown a bucket of cold ice water in Frank's face, it would not have stunned him more rapidly or caused his heart to start pumping flaming blood of anger through his body more rapidly. With the fire in his eyes looking no less smoldering than a branding iron, he asked, coldly "What house? What in the hell are you talking about?"

Though he was aware of Frank's obvious anger, Early never backed off. "You know," he said, "I never would've thought that you'd told Job what you did, had I known you would, you could've had my plantation fer the tax money!"

"Told Job? What do you mean, Cole, and you'd better be fast in telling me!" Frank said as his face began to redden to a maddening crimson clear to his eyes.

"Telling Job to burn Green Sea last night! Job told Joseph and Jonah that you said to burn it!"

"Why, that son of a bitch! That son of a bitching idiot!"

"Wait just a minute, Drakston! Hold it right there! I don't like for my son to be called a name like that! I want you to understand that Methilda was a fine and decent woman, and I will not allow you to mud her like that.

Early's words had no more effect on Frank then had he not spoken them. The fire in his eyes seemed to be shooting sparks as he exploded in storming fury, "Oh, shut up! You good for nothing lazy bastard! I imagine if your wife were here today, she'd be the first to say that it would've done her a hellen's lot more good if you'd taken some the hard work off her while she lived, rather than making a play at protecting her name now! I should blow those god damn sons of yours to hell and back and you into the bargain as well! I only told that idiot of yours to be careful with that fire he'd built up, or he might burn that rotten shack of yours down!"

Washed over with guilt once again and more so now that he knew Frank did not approve of Green Sea becoming nothing but grey ashes, that his sons had brought about, Early said, "I didn't know, but didn't you mention Green Sea to Job, at all?"

"I merely ask him if they had been to Green Sea lately, I didn't know he's the idiot he is, or I wouldn't have said one word to him!"

"Well, Job does get things mixed up a little. If I'd been home, I would've stopped them."

"You goddamn right he does! To think I was concerned over that hell fired shack of yours, and your no-good bastard sons went and burned Green Sea, her very home right out from under her!"

Frank's referring to his sons as bastards again riled Early enough to brave Frank saying, "That's enough of that, Drakston, I can't see why you wanted to bring harm to that man in the first place." But, Early did see. He was almost positive that it was Frank's lust for Luke Heyward's shapely and beautiful wife. Still, he had not become so brave that he had the nerve to tell Frank so. He saw deep purple veins pulsing in Frank's temples and, on an impulse, thought that it was probably more wise to forget the "bastard" and not push Frank any further and, instantly, he was thanking his lucky stars that he had not revealed his thoughts. It appeared that Frank had gotten so wrathful and steamed up that he was suddenly coming out of his coat, disclosing as he did so not only one revolver on his person, but two!

It seemed that the reference to Luke had made Frank wilder than ever. As he throwed his coat across the pommel of his saddle, he lashed out at Early, furiously, "That's none of your damn business, Cole, and if you make one more remark in regard to that, I'll blow your head off here and now! You tell those damn firebug bastards, that if I hear another word about last night, their heads won't be on their shoulders very long afterwards; further, if you want to keep your own, you'd better make certain that there is never another mistake made and that they stay away from Green Sea until they have direct word from me to that contrary!" He turned and was racing out of Early's view back toward Drakston Hall before Early could have replied had he wished to. Frank might have told Early his sons were to stay away from Green Sea for all time, but his hatred for Luke kept him from doing so, and unfortunately, he sealed his own fate that day.

Early sat on Maybelle a good while looking down the empty road. Finally, he said out loud, "Methilda, I wish now that I'd let the Republicans had it. Yes, by golly it would've been better for everybody if I had."

He turned and headed for his run-down shack.

Chapter Four

Mockingbirds sat on blackened-charred tree limbs. The shrillness of their vociferous clamoring falling upon the deathlike stillness as Eliza stood at the site of the still smoldering ruins, the gaunt chimneys, and the powdery crumbling brick walls, staring at what had once been her home, while grey-white ashes sifted gently around her feet in the mild spring sunshine. After a spell, she lifter her bloodshot, tearful eyes above and looking at the excited birds through her blurred vision, she was thinking that not a chance but what their hearts were as troubled as her own over the fire wiping out their nest and, in all likelihood, their young, too.

For the present she was alone with her grief. Neighbors, close friends, and family had departed for their homes. Martha and Bruce, Elizabeth, the Wiltons, the Cooper's, the Clarendon's were away from home for a few days, Doctor Davis, and, of course, Reverend Johnson accompanied by the visiting minister, Marsh Reed all of who had come and loaned what comfort they could to her and Luke both had finally gone. Granted, she had heard Reverend Johnson quotes his usual saying, "everything has a way of working out for the best." She had looked at him and thought that she could not possibly disagree more with his self-persuasion. All she could see that the mansion's burning could ever bring would-be years of additional hardship for Luke and herself to endure. However, Marsh Reed had also had a few words to say too. He had quoted from the old familiar book in Ecclesiastes, "a time to weep, and a time to laugh, and a time to lose." At the end, he had looked at her and added, "If there's ever been a time to weep over waste, I shall think it's now." She had thanked him silently for understanding and had been certain that he was reading her thoughts as she returned his gaze. People had been kind though. The kitchen, which, ironically, was still standing due to last night's wind carrying flames and sparks away from it, was overflowing with home furnishings and baskets of prepared food. There was enough food to last a week or more for each and every person who live at Green Sea. She was positive that no one on the plantation would find the need to cook anything for days. Even Early Cole had come forth and done his part by riding through the pitch-dark night and fetching Doctor Davis for her. Luke had not left her side, since he had rushed to her and she had fainted in his arms, until a short while ago when she had insisted that he go onto the fields and start the hands back to breaking ground for the spring planting. Fortune's wheel had not turned against them all together. Besides the kitchen, the wash house, the barn, the stables; in fact, all the other buildings had survived the fire. Just the mansion and guest house had seemed to be doomed for destruction. All the animals have been safe too; she was so thankful for that.

She had not told Luke about their baby yet, nor had she told anyone else. Neither did she think that Doctor Davis knew, because he had not given any hint that he had noticed any body change about her person. All the same, she would have to admit that the doctor's examination last night had not been as thorough as it normally was or would have been had not Luke and Hannah already had her revived when he had arrived. It had been quite obvious though that the doctor was very upset over seeing the mansion going up in flames. He had walked through its door many times over the years, being hospitably and happily received not as a doctor but as a close family friend, enjoying numerous social occasions there. In any event, she would tell Luke shortly that she was truly going to have his baby. That unusual queasiness in her stomach was still there. She did not know for what reason she was holding off from telling him, unless it was for her wishing everything to be more in order; if that day even came, when she did tell him. She had no desire to share this wonderful news with Luke while they stood and stared at smoking ruins with tears in her eyes. Somehow, that just did not seem to be the thing to do. She would wait till they were settled down in the kitchen. Yes, the kitchen had become their home. As a matter of fact, she and Luke had slept there last night—well, cried in one another's arms would be nearer to the truth. Shelter had been generously offered to her and Luke at Oak Grove, Drakston Hall, and Elms' but she had thanked everybody and declined, remaining firm and steadfast in her decision not to leave Green Sea for as much as one night. Luke had readily agreed with her.

Save worrying about Luke and her father, what she had most feared during the last year of the war has now become a reality. Every time that she heard the huff of a mounted horse, she had trembled in fear that Union Calvary from Sherman's army was coming to set a torch to Green Sea. Now, the grand and unique mansion was gone—a heritage and landmark of three Carson generations—gone to powdered ruins and ashes. But, thank God, she had saved the portraits, yes, every last one. Though her throat still burned and felt irritated from smoke and vapor exposure, her face remained reddened from heat, and her hands scorched with blisters forming here and there; nonetheless, she had saved them. What was a little discomfort in relation with saving all those faces that could never be replaced? A legacy to be handed down to her and Luke's baby. What about all other things though that did go up in flames or was still smoldering in smoke; for example, her father's many volumes of books with their leather bindings, the beautiful solid brass and silver chandeliers that were nothing now but grotesque heaps of scarred twisted metal the huge brass besteads burned down to a charcoal black, only ashes though where the rosewood and mahogany beds had set, and the shattered and burned crystal, china, and silver? How could she and Luke ever possibly replace all that? Even with God's blessing, she seriously doubted if they would ever be able to replace half of it. Well, assuredly, fire encouraged by the March wind had devoured all of it last night and, in time the wind would finish carrying all ashes away and that would be the last of the many things that this seemingly small plot of ground had held. There was only one thing that the fire and wind had not taken and that was her memory of all the years that she had been sheltered inside these crumbling walls—that she would hug and hold to her forever. In fact; even now, she could almost hear the echo of voices and laughter that had vibrated in this very spot in time passed. She was determined that she would not give in. She still had Luke, did she not? Thus, things could be a lot worse than they were.

Eliza's eyes fell away from the smoldering wreckage and found their way straying over the grounds and fields and finally toward the live oaks that bordered the drive where she saw Luke coming back from the field after starting the hands back to breaking ground. He was walking, and from his carriage it was manifested that last night's tragedy had taken its toll upon him. Dear Luke, what would her life have been compromised of had he not come to Green Sea? Certainly, there would have remained a void within her that no one else could ever have satiated or possessed. She deplored to think what might have been without him. She had told Luke at Windsor years ago, she would forever be happy with him at any time, in anything, and anywhere. Still, on the other hand, what about Luke? She would never question his love for her. But, would his burdens have been lighter had he not come to Green Sea? Suddenly, her heart swelled in love for him, bringing tears smarting to the surface of her burning eyes as she thought about the load that Luke carried on his shoulders. She started walking toward him, her feet measuring steps faster and faster until she was running to reach his outstretched arms, though she had not been aware of it. He gathered her close to him—both clinging to the other in silence, til one or two sobs escaped from her throat in spite of her trying to hold them back.

"Try not to cry anymore, darling," he said. "I'm worried you'll become ill." Just as quickly though he added, "But how can you help it? It tears me to pieces; also, to look at it"

She let her arms fall from around his neck to rest at his waist, saying as they started walking up the lane with their arms encircled tight around the other's body, "I'll be alright, Luke. How could I be otherwise with you beside me?"

He tightened his arm about her.

They reached the kitchen and sat down on the one kitchen doorstep. Looking at the ruins, Luke brought both their thoughts out in the open when he finally said, "Eliza, dear, the hardest part about last night is yet to come, you know. How I dread to wire your father."

She drew her arms tight her about him. "I know, darling," she said, "and no doubt that father will be deeply grieved. But, I also think that he'll be more concerned about our safety and the others who lived in the mansion with us and what we're going to be up against in the future, rather than the loss of the mansion itself."

He did realize that the greater part of what she had said was true. Then again, he was aware that she was only making an endeavor to be brave herself—as well as trying to give him the courage to wire Matthew Carson the shocking news that the house he built mostly himself and had been so devoted to, was lying in ashes.

"Drive in with me to Charleston, then, and I'll wire him," Luke said soberly. He looked at her dress that was torn, soiled, and had burned holes near the hem at the bottom. "I'm sorry, dear, about your clothes, we'll have to buy you a dress or two while we're there."

They both were still wearing clothes that they had worn to church the night before. His attire was in a much worse condition than hers was. Knowing him for the meticulous man that he was when it came to his person and his dress and how conscious he had always been of what she wore, she almost burst forth with sobs again. However, she made a stab of steadying her nerves and faltering throat muscles plus swallowing a time or two and told him, "That won't be necessary, Luke, Martha and Carolina brought me a number of dresses and underclothes too, you know we're all about the same size. I don't think there's a pound of difference between Martha and myself. I just haven't gotten around to any personal grooming and dressing yet. I have Hannah this very minute altering some of Bruce's things for your own self." Despite all she almost let a faint smile show as she went on, "Remember, there aren't many men in this neighborhood that's as tall and handsome as you are, so you'll have to take potluck!"

He did smile at her, knowing that she was making a plunge once more to lift their spirit. It was true that he was taller than most their acquaintances with her father and Bill Clarendon being the exception. He, Bill, and her father were all on the same build, lean and tall.

"With such flattery as that, Mrs. Heyward, how can I miss," he said, hugging her closer to him.

Suddenly, it seemed the situation was not so bleak after all. She was on the verge of telling him about the baby, but he was saying, "speaking of tallness, I'll go see Bill about buying some lumber. Coming up the lane a while ago, I was observing this kitchen and I think I'll add two large rooms on to it. A bedroom and a sitting room we can't possibly live in it otherwise or I should say in any comfort. Furthermore, it looks like we'll be in it a few years, anyhow. So, I want to make it as likable as I can for you."

"Luke, you don't have to do that now. You're already too busy with starting the planting. I can make out somehow. What I told you that day at Windsor is true now more than ever."

He took her blistered hand and planted a kiss upon it. "I was thinking about that coming from the field," he said. "Sweetheart, God willing, I'm going to build you another mansion someday. No, I won't promise that it'll be the grand house that set out there where those ashes are, but I promise when I do build one, it'll be worthy of you. Meantime I plan to make this as comfortable as possible for you."

"But, Luke, you'll need most of our cash to plant and care for the crop and supplying the hands with what they'll need also."

"I know, I've thought about that, too. Bill has quite a supply of good seasoned lumber at the present though. That was his purpose to make this trip. He told me it was time he got rid of it. Seems the weather held up a lot of building through the winter months. Anyway, if he doesn't find an immediate buyer for the entire supply, I'll see what I can arrange with him. Bill has passed all prospects with his sawmill. It may be that he'll wait til I get this year's crop harvested and sold. If not, I suppose I'll see Brad Cooper and sign a bank note for money to carry us over again this year."

Her sudden lift of spirit vanished swiftly. It was apparent that another mortgage was in the making against Green Sea's lands. The road ahead looked long and hard to travel for Luke and herself too. After all the years of longing and praying for a baby, it seemed that she could not have gotten pregnant at any worse time, that is, in terms of giving Luke something else to worry over. She began to rise from the steps, saying, "Luke, I'm sorry. It's way passed the dinner hour. There's plenty of food. I'll put it on the table."

"No need to hurry, doll, I don't feel much like eating, anyhow." He rose, too, the smile appearing at the corners of his mouth again. "I guess though if I'm going to build you another mansion, now's the proper time to start toward that goal, and I most certainly won't be able to ever accomplish it on an empty stomach!"

She took hold of his hand. "We'll build it together, Luke. Come on and let's eat, then we'll go to Charleston and wire my father. He'll have to know. I'm thankful he was in Columbia instead of here and spared seeing it fall in flames."

Bringing a little order to their disrupted lives once more as they began living in the small crowded kitchen proved to be a greater task for Eliza to cope with than any expectation, she may have foreseen. Fairly often, numerous tears washed down her pale and drawn face—tears that she made every effort to keep hidden from Luke. It appeared that the sudden upheaval that had been spent upon them was affecting her emotional nature and heightening the queasy feeling in her stomach more than she had counted on. Several times she had been forced to leave the table and a few mornings later when she suddenly became deathly pale and fled out the kitchen door retching, Luke jumped up and followed her saying, as she leaned her head against the rough outside wall, "What is it, dear?" Thinking that the fire was the cause for it, he put his arm around her shivering shoulders. "I know, darling, it's hard for you to live and eat in this kitchen, but you're going to become very ill if this keeps up. I've noticed for days that you haven't eaten enough for a bird. Please, dear, won't you try a little harder to accept it for the sake of your health and well-being and for me, too, darling? You're probably worried about your father coming this weekend, aren't you?"

Her nausea had begun to leave her. "Well, I will own to the fact that I've though an awful lot about how it's going to be for him when he rides up that driveway, but that isn't it, Luke." She raised her head up and leaned it now against his chest while he gathered her closer in protection from the morning's chill. "Oh, Luke, I love you so and wanted it to be different, you know, in a special place, at the proper time and everything. But, it seems plans so often have a way in going astray, don't they?"

He had become slightly confused over part of what she had said and was becoming upset over it. It seemed that the fire had disturbed his wife more than he cared to give thought to.

"Well, yes, they do, sweetheart, but please try to put it out of your mind as much as possible. Come on, darling, let's go back inside it's chilly out here, I don't want you to take more cold" He told her.

"Neither do I, Luke, relieve me from any more colds and coughs." She said, as they walked back through the door. "Sit down, Luke, and eat your breakfast and stop worrying about me. In fact, I think I can eat a few bites with you. Some experience," she rattled on as Luke began to eat, though somewhat apprehensive, "A few minutes ago I couldn't bear the sight of food, now it sorta looks rather tempting. I guess though I'll have many experiences to cope with that'll be completely novel to me, but I can assure you every last one will be welcomed and beautiful to me, no matter how uncomfortable!"

Oh, God! He thought, No, as his last gulp of coffee almost strangled him. Anything, dear God, but Eliza's mind becoming deranged! He didn't think he could take that and, it must be, because she had voiced the terrible happening that they had experienced as being beautiful, more or less! While his heart pounded in his ears and seemed as though it were beating upon drums in his chest, he stared down at his empty coffee cup, trying to gain the courage to observe her. What would he see when he did let his eyes rest upon Eliza's face? She seemed to be so quiet, all of a sudden. Would he see a dull, disinterested face or perhaps eyes that had a frantic and raging stare about them? Still hesitant to look at her, he let his gaze move from his cup and trail across the table to her plate and stop. Finally, his eyelids slowly lifted, and he looked at her. Suddenly, while he thanked his

God silently, all his fear for her sanity began to run on a wild, plunging course downstream! There sit Eliza, with her lovely wide-awake face and beautiful alert eyes, returning his gaze! As profound relief washed over him in tender softness, they stared at one another for a long, wonderful minute. Then, noticing the cunning mischief filling her eyes, and the pixie smile that had begun to curve her warm, enticing lips, he suddenly felt as if someone had belted him smack in the stomach! It couldn't be! Yet, he was certain that Eliza had been trying to tell him that she was pregnant!

Rising from his chair, he made an attempt at asking, but his words were partly broken with emotion and wonderment altogether. "Eliza darling—it can't—not after all these years—not now—you aren't—?"

"Yes, Luke, my darling," she laughed, "I am. It is true, that I carry your baby at last!"

While he stood in stunned disbelief, she rose, too, and walked around the table to him. All he did though was stare at her, til she asked, anxiously, "Luke?"

He took her in his arms but still did not speak for what seemed like minutes, holding her next to him as though he were protecting her from a hurling storm from some apparent evil. Finally, he asked, "But—when—how long have you known, sweetheart?"

"Well, for a certainty, Luke, only a short while," she said as he sat back down in his chair and pulled her down with him. And, sitting on his lap with her arm around his shoulders, she told him everything.

"Lord's mercy! Lord's mercy! I wish I'd known. Think of all you've gone through these past few days. You may have and could—" He broke off from saying what he was thinking that it was a miracle she had not already miscarried.

Reading his thoughts, she laid a finger upon his lips. "No, Luke, I didn't, and I won't! I'll carry our baby full term and I'll have it!"

He hugged around her and asked again, "How long did you say—I wonder when—" his voice lagged and stopped once more.

"Well, it's sorta hard to be exact in something like that. But, my guess is that it happened sometime through those lazy, wonderful hours, when I lay in your arms so much during the snowstorm, remember?" She teased with that pixie smile of hers again.

He grinned, "How could I ever forget that, darling. Oh! Eliza dear!" He hugged her tighter than ever.

"Well, in case you do," she jested, "Come September, we're going to have evidence of those days around to remind you!"

Rumpling her hair and giving her ear lobe a tug, his grin rippled through the kitchen in laughter. Just as suddenly though it died away as it dawned on him where they were sitting. His face turned grim. "To think you'll be carrying our baby and giving birth to it in a place such as this. Darling, how I wish I could spare you."

"Everything will turn out all right, Luke, I don't want you being anxious over me. You have too much on you as it is, besides worrying about this place. I'll agree it isn't the mansion with its comfortable rooms. But, I'm healthy and I'm still young," she laughed, "so I'll be all right."

"Well, I'm certainly going to see what I can do toward making our living quarters more inviting," he paused a moment, then went on to say, "Eliza dear, under these circumstances, the summer months will be very trying for you. Have you given any thought as to accepting shelter at the other plantations for a while anyway? Of course, I'd miss you terribly, as I'm afraid some nights I wouldn't be able to get away from all the work that'll be required in gathering the tobacco. But darling you'd be more comfortable at Drakston Hall or Oak Grove. My feelings can be thrust aside. All that really matters to me is your welfare, something that's very essential for your health as well as our baby's."

She was thinking that Oak Grove was entirely too far from Green Sea and on no account would she even consider living in close accommodations with Frank Drakston, but she told him, "No, Luke, I can't say that I have because my home is Green Sea, and as long as I can stick my head under any type shelter that's here, this is where I shall stay! No question that either of these places would be more comfortable, come summer. But I think it's important that one's heart and mind be at ease, also. Come what may, I shall remain right here where we can be together as we've always been. You're still my main concern, darling, and it will always be so, if I should have dozens of babies. I'll never leave your side under any circumstances, unless I'm forced to do so."

Her boundless love near melted his heart. He drew her close to him, brushing his lips from one cheek to the other, showering them in kisses. "September," he muttered, "what a nitwit I've been, sweetheart, not to notice anything."

She pulled away, telling him, "No I've been the nitwit, Luke, listening to Hannah and drawing my own conclusions, which were groundless in the first place. Weeks ago, I should have known for certain and told you, then. After all, Eve's bothersome curse had never been late before!"

He laughed, "That's why I feel like such a featherbrain as many times as we've made reference to that troublesome and unhandy business! Poor Eve, at times, I've been inclined to feel that perhaps she and all the women who have followed her paid a little too heavy for that garden episode!"

"Well, she did temp Adam, you know, in their falling to the weakness of the flesh!"

"So it's said, but he was there, wasn't he? Come to think about it, I don't imagine that it took Eve too long in persuading him to bend to her will!"

She chortled, "I think you may have something there, Luke," as they threw their arms around one another's neck.

Luke's mirth though never lasted very long; his thoughts were back upon their grim situation again. His next remarks revealed what was worrying him as clearly as if he had expressed it verbally.

Quite soberly, he said, "I hope it's a cool summer."

She hushed his words with a tender kiss and told him, "Luke please, I'll be alright." He observed her for a fairly long minute. Then, a smile began to play at the corners of his lips.

"Eliza darling, I don't suppose I've been a complete lackbrain after all when it comes to my observation of some recent variations. I was just telling myself when I sat down to breakfast that one pleasing aspect emerged from all our calamity! At least, Caroline's dress had finally gotten filled out quite properly!"

"Luke!" She exclaimed, blushing, her hand flying to her bosom!

"Oh, sweetheart," he laughed, "I had to get back at you for scaring me half to death with all that beautiful experience talk of yours. For a few minutes there, I thought you'd gone wacky! Furthermore, in case my remark has caused one grain of skepticism to start whirling around in that lovely head of yours, I'll clear it up. Although Caroline is the type of girl that is quite appealing to the opposite sex, she could never do for that dress what you're doing for it, and believe me, darling, I wouldn't change a thing about you for all the world and what's in it!"

Making an endeavor to keep a straight face and at the same time affect a somewhat prudish manner, which was indeed rate for her, she studied his face for a moment and meekly replied, "I believe you, Luke." However, her sudden newly acquired prim composure lasted for only a short few seconds before she gave way to giggles, with him joining her as they held on to each other blissfully happy, and their joy went ringing through the kitchen as merrily a though they had been sitting in the elegant dining room of the mansion.

Notwithstanding her mirth with Luke though, once she felt her father's arms about her shoulder it was quite the contrary and in reverse to what her outlook had been a few days earlier. The laughter she had shared with Luke turned bitter sobs as her father held her warmly, pressed to his chest.

"Father, I didn't take care of it very well, did I?" she quieted her grief enough to ask. Shaken profoundly at the sight of the tragedy and seeing her living in the crude kitchen. It became necessary to steady his own voice before replying, "Mary Eliza dear, no daughter or anyone else could ever have stood by Green Sea in steadfast devotion any more than you have, it would upset me terribly dear, to learn if you've talked yourself into believing that you had failed your home in any way. I'm just thankful to God that you, Luke and all the others are safe all of you did all that was possible to save it. Now, let's do our best to accept it as we've had to do with so many other unfortunate happenings.

"It's hard, Father, to look at those ashes and remember all the things that made them up."

"I know, dear," he said, still holding on to her.

"It's so comforting to have you here though, I know now it's what I truly needed." She pulled back somewhat and looking beyond the doorway where they stood, she asked, "Where's Aunt Amy, isn't she with you?"

"Darling, she didn't come. She wanted to very much, but the doctor nor I as for that matter, thought she should make a long train trip at this time."

"Oh Father, I'm sorry, Aunt Amy isn't seriously ill, is she?"

"No, dear, not really, or the doctor assures me that's the case, thank God! It's—well—using the doctor's phrases, 'female disorders' a natural process for women her age, so he says. That wobbling and lurching train, tossing its passengers repeatedly and especially when it jerks itself to a stop every few miles, would've aggravated her condition too much. Anyway, she sent you her love along with a large box of personal things that she thought you might need, and there's several more things outside in the hack that we both want you and Luke to have."

"Thank you, Father, and I do hope that Aunt Amy will soon be feeling better. I understand, but I miss her already.

"I know what you mean, dear."

She turned and stepped over to a rather restful looking, cushioned chair that Elizabeth had brought from Drakston Hall and moving it a little way out from a pile of quilts, lamps, and other items that were stacked on a table nearby she said, "Come on in, Father, and sit here. Doss can bring the things inside later. I'm so anxious to visit with you. We have so much to talk about."

While Matthew took his seat, he glanced around the crude, cluttered kitchen. He could not remember when he had last stepped inside it. Though he could see she had improved its state considerably, it still looked worse than what he had visioned it would with them living there.

She had taken her seat near him and was saying, "It doesn't look like much, does it Father? But, Luke plans to add two rooms right away."

"Yes, that's what he was telling me." Matthew said.

"So, you've already seen Luke?" She asked quite excitedly.

"Yes, he and the hands were breaking ground near the road as I was passing. I stopped and visited for a few minutes."

She looked down at her hands, folded over the other in her lap. But, just as quickly she lifted the still wet long lashes that set off her beautiful eyes, and he saw a sudden glaze pop in as she smiled and said, "Luke's already told you!"

"Yes, darling, he did but I wanted you to tell me, too, that's why I haven't mentioned it." He bent forward and took her hand. "It's the most wonderful news that I've heard for a long time; I couldn't be happier over it. Luke is overjoyed also, but we both are very concerned about you living in this place through the summer months."

"I know, Father, and I realize it won't be easy to adjust to something like this," she indicated with a sweep of her other hand, while her eyes scanned around the room; "but, I couldn't be contented living one week any place, other than Green Sea. Though my surroundings at Oak Grove or Drakston Hall would give me the same body comfort that I've always been accustomed to, neither would be home to me. No, I have no plans to leave Green Sea, pregnant or otherwise!"

Matthew was suddenly becoming proud of her spirit and decision to stay. He smiled, "I don't believe you'll leave, either, dear. I see too much of the true Carson fighting spirit in you for all this to get you down." He patted her hand fondly and learning back in his chair again, he studied her face for a moment and went on, "A grandchild, I can hardly believe you're carrying a Carson heir. Will Amy be surprised and happy when I tell her?

"At times, Father, it's s almost beyond belief to me. I've longed to give Luke a child for so long, only to know nothing but disappointment, year after year. Yes, no doubt that Aunt Amy has given up thinking in terms of my ever becoming a mother and will be shocked to hear of it." Now, it was she that was studying him in the pause of conversation. She had seen an additional light shine in his eyes each time his wife's name was mentioned. "You're very happy with Aunt Amy, aren't you, Father? I can see it in your face."

"Yes, dear, I am. She's contentment, tenderness, and warmth, after years of bitter loneliness and troubling storms. I love her very much just as I did your own mother." His voice halted and his eyes fell upon the floor. Then, he broke his downward gaze and lifted it upon her again. "I've never forgotten Anne nor shall I ever forget her, we shared too much for that. But, for years, dear, it was a constant raw wound of reality. I would reach out and there was nothing there. I hope and pray that you and Luke will live out your lives with one another and you'll never feel the need to recall what I'm telling you now; but, Mary Eliza dear, if you should ever find yourself without Luke, God forbid, remember this, empty arms make for an empty life. What I'm trying to say is that Anne's presence is gone from my life, but thank God I can reach out and hold Amy's to me."

"It makes me happy, Father, to know that you're happy. I truly love Aunt Amy. It's not because I see so much of my own mother in her, which I do. It's for her true self and her own goodness that I love her."

"Thank you, darling. In all respects, I couldn't have expressed my own sentiments more faithfully than that." His eyes left her once more and moved around the kitchen walls somewhat. "Speaking of your mother, dear, reminded me. Luke said you saved the family portraits."

"Yes, Father, I did. Having no place to hang them though, I put them away for the time being. I could get them father, if you—" She broke off and started to get up from her chair.

"No, dear," he said quickly, "you sit still. I can look at them some other time. All those faces are very vivid in my mind, anyway, especially your mother's. it was wise not to hang them in here, the smoke from the cooking would in all probability have damaged them."

"That's why I put them away, Father, I didn't want any harm to come to them. Caroline came yesterday and helped me wrap each one and label them, so they would be easy to identify in case someone wished to look at some certain one. I'll hang them again when I have a place worthy of them." She said sadly.

Although Matthew was still shaken from the devastated ruins that had met his eyes, instead of the white columned mansion that he had been so proud of, he forced himself to be as cheerful as the situation would permit for her sake. In a sense, he regretted that he had mentioned the portraits. Then again, he wanted to let her know how he felt. "Well, I'm thankful, darling, that you saved them. But, I'm still shivering from hearing how you risked your life in those flames in order to do so. I've lost my two sons, dear, and it's been rough to take. I—well—I don't think I could bear losing you, too." Abruptly, overflowing with emotion in thinking of what could have happened to her, he fell silent for a moment or two before continuing on, "Please, dear, for my peace of mind, promise me that you'll never take a chance like that again."

"I promise, Father, and I'm sorry I've caused you this anxiety. Still, thinking about how Caroline stared at Phil's face yesterday, it seems to make all the danger I faced worthwhile." "How is Caroline? Hasn't she accepted Phil's death yet?"

Looking at her father rather questionably before replying, she said, "No, I really don't think that she has, not in her heart, anyway. Father, you haven't given up all hope, have you?"

"I fear, dear, that I have. It's been almost two years since the war ended. I've written letters to every branch of service and numerous personnel, put notices in newspapers, and exhausted every other source of information that I can think of in regard to his disappearance; not one lead have I uncovered. It grieves me to admit it, but I have no hope left."

She dropped her eyes again. "I don't feel that way," she said solemnly. "I've never expressed this to anyone before, but ever since Gettysburg, when I think about Phil it's as though he's somewhere other than his resting place. It's not that way with Nat, or Mother as far as that goes. I feel that they're gone, and I've tried to accept their deaths. With Phil though it's a different matter."

Matthew scrutinized her for some minutes. Finally, he told her, "I'm glad, dear, that you can think of him in that way. It's better than having no hope at all as I do. In fact, after I left Luke awhile ago, I've come to an important decision." He reached forward once more and took her hand. She looked up at him, her eyes set to his direct, listening anxiously while he went on to say, "Mary Eliza dear, since God has willed you to be my only living child and the fact that you're carrying a heir to Green Sea as well as your husband being a man that I respect and love as if he were of my own flesh, I'm deeding the lands of Green Sea to you and Luke to hold jointly. The operation of Green Sea has fallen upon Luke to carry through and manage. Therefore, it's no more than right for him to have the privilege of running it to his own choosing. With the holdings remaining in my name, Luke is stalled from securing a loan or transacting any business of any kind here without my approval and signed signature. I think that's a little too much for a man of Luke's integrity to be subjected to." He stopped once more, but for the first time she saw his handsome grin spreading wildly, "Besides, I don't think you and Luke would throw me out if I should chance to come back here to live!"

"Oh, Father, Green Sea will always be yours. It grieves me terribly that the house you and mother mostly built and furnished is gone, and you're prevented from enjoying your usual chair, your pipe, your slippers, I could go on and on—"

"Don't worry about me, dear, I'll be all right. The same prevails for you and Luke also and you're making do. Like I said, let's try to put it out of our minds and look to the future. Since Amy isn't with me, I plan to stay at John's while I'm here, that is, at night. We'll have a chance to visit some if he isn't called out to a patient, something we haven't done for a long time."

"Doctor Davis is going to have some help before too long, didn't Luke tell you?" "No!" Exclaimed Matthew. "Who?"

"You recall Doctor Davis telling us about that young doctor, Seth Roalf, who he worked with in Richmond? Well, he and his little boy, I understand Doctor Roalf's a widower, are probably on their way now. Doctor Davis has finally induced him to come to the low country and join his practice."

"That's great! John needs some help; he's not getting any younger."

"That's true, and I'm afraid we all have come to depend on Doctor Davis too much and in all likelihood too often. No sooner than I told Luke about the baby, he packed me off to the doctor for a thorough examination. Anyway, he was telling us about it while we were there. Doctor Davis also asked about you and Aunt Amy."

"Well, it most certainly seems as though there's a lot of good news, too. A grandchild on the way and a new doctor coming among us!"

"Father, I've wanted to ask before now, but we've had so many things to talk about. How's the little boy, Whit? Have you adopted him yet?"

"No, not yet, but I'm still working in trying to get all the legal matters cleared toward it."

"Supposing then, that you do adopt him, Father, are you certain you want to deed all of Green Sea to Luke and me?"

Her deep thinking always amazed him.

"Yes, dear, I am. As I've stated, you're the only child I have now, my last living heir. In the case of Whit, remember he's just passed two years old, which, of course, means that there are a lot of years left before he becomes of legal age. In the meantime, someone would have to act as his guardian, anyway. Furthermore, if Amy and I do adopt him and it should ever come to pass that we aren't here to see to his welfare, I have no qualms about you and Luke doing what's right in that aspect. Don't forget, too, that by law he'll be Amy's child as well as mine. She gets a substantial income from the earnings of Drakston Hall that I advise her to put in trust. So far, I've been able to provide for Amy since we were married, and it hasn't become necessary for us to spend her income. Anyway, when it comes to the matter of Whit's security, I surely don't see him lacking for anything, considering the vast wealth at Drakston Hall."

"No, I suppose not." She looked through the doorway into the distance. "Whit, Doctor Roalf, or his little boy will never know the beautiful mansion that set once out there under those trees, but Luke says if all goes well, he plans to start building another house in a year or two."

"See there!" Matthew said cheerfully. "Luke will do it, too!" Before too many years I expect to feast my eyes upon another house setting in that same spot where the first Carson Cabin set, and I'm certain if Luke has anything to do with it, that it'll be a house deserving to every foot of land that's called Green Sea."

In point of fact, Matthew was displaying much more optimism than he felt. He knew a lot of crops would have to be clawed from the soil of Green Sea before Luke would be able to build another house even half as grand as the massive one that had been reduced to ashes and rubble. Another something that he had no intention of revealing to his sad hearted daughter was the fact that his plans to bring Amy and Whit, he had no doubt that he would adopt Whit, home to Green Sea in the fall had now gone astray. He was well aware that when he and Amy did come home, that now they would be forced to live at Drakston Hall. He was not quite ready to do that yet, since one could hardly say that he and his nephew were shoulder slapping kinsmen as he and Franklin Drakston had been. Though, come what may, he was still resolute and by no means had no plans on letting the recent tragedy deter him from going ahead with the adoption of Whit, though it was almost manifested that Whit would be brought up at Drakston Hall rather than Green Sea, where, of course, he would have preferred Whit to have been raised. Now, he would struggle along with the Republicans awhile longer. But, the adopting of Whit was something he had to do and could not put off much longer, He wished it were so that he could tell Mary Eliza his main reason for becoming so attached to this little boy. However, a man had to stand by his word of honor, did he not? Now, while he observed the sadness on his daughter's face as she remained silent and seemed to have her thoughts miles away, he was saying, "Mary Eliza dear, I know it's only natural for you to have wondered why I would think of adopting a two year old child at my age, but believe me, dear, once you see Whit, you'll come to love him as much as Amy and I do. I—well—I'd prefer to reveal a few details to you that has been disclosed to me concerning the matter—though on my word of honor I'm prevented from doing so. Therefore, if you have any questions in your mind, dear, please—for me—lay them aside and try to understand. On my word of honor again, darling, I shall hope that you realize, although I've come to love Whit, he or a dozen like him could never take your place in my heart."

She turned her face back to him. "Oh, Father, doubting your devotion is something I wouldn't do. To me, your adopting this little boy is not at all surprising, knowing you and Aunt Amy both as I do."

She smiled, "in spite of it, I still feel secure in your love."

He smiled back, "That's my daughter. It's for certain, I can always count on her. On my next visit to Green Sea, dear, it may be so that I'll be allowed to bring Whit along with me. I'm anxious for you to meet him. Amy simply adores him. She told me that if Whit wasn't just around the corner from us, which makes it very handy for them to visit with one another, that she feared she'd forget doctor's orders and come along with me. She also has Lucy Randolph that she can visit with, so she shouldn't be too lonesome. In fact, since we moved to Columbia, Amy and Lucy has become rather close."

"That's wonderful, Father. How is Lucy? She looked so sad and alone when I saw her last."

"Her life is tragic, dear. That's about the most seemly way to put it, in my opinion. I would never have thought that she held such an unmeasurable love for my son. Though she realizes that he's gone; still, she seems to be as totally devoted to him as though he were living and they were man and wife."

"They were almost, had it not been for that awful war which prevented it."

"Yes—I know—a most grievous and unfortunate circumstance. I think though, that Amy and I have helped Lucy's burdened heart somewhat in regard to that matter, by prevailing upon her to lay aside what may have been and try to accept and not despair her life away. I believe in her knowing that I've had to do the same, more times than I care to think about, that she feels a certain rapport with me and realizes that I understand her sadness and have her welfare at heart. In fact, she plans to come home in the fall and take that teaching position at Drakston Hall. I'm to see Frank and work out all details for her while I'm here."

"Father! That's wonderful! I'm so glad she's coming back home!"

"It pleases me, too, dear, because I'm positive that in the long run she'll be happier here among family and friends, than had she chosen to live in Columbia permanently." He got up from his chair and pulled out his watch from a small waist pocket in his trouser top. "Dear, it's getting later than I thought. If you don't mind, I think I'll take a little walk and stretch my legs some before Luke comes in from the fields." He said.

She rose, handing him his hat. "Of course, Father," she said, knowing as sure as she breathed where he was headed to. "We'll wait and share some of our chit-chat with Luke you'll still have time for a long walk before he gets here and supper's ready."

He squeezed her hand and brushed her cheek with a kiss and was out the door.

Moved to tears, she stood for some time and watched the tall, still trim, nimble footed figure making his way across the unplowed field—where last year's corn crop had grown and where turtle doves were scampering here and there at the sound of his footsteps—as he stepped lively toward the plot of ground that held the ones who were now gone from his life but, in no respect had he ever banished his frequent pilgrim visit to their graves when he came home to Green Sea. Noticing the straight shoulders and high head that made no mistake in revealing his undaunted courage to stand up and face this additional hard knock that fate had dealt him, to her he looked as tall as the heavens that he was walking under. Instantly, a new will of strength began to bubble within her; she resolved harder to live by his example. Reaching for the hem of her apron, she dried her despairing tears and turned away from the door. Moving more briskly than she had for days, she started preparing supper. She even began to chant a little song.

At best, the following days were burdensome though. For the most part, although she made every effort to hold onto the heartened spirit that her father's visit had given her; nevertheless, it seemed put to trial and wallowed at a low ebb, often enough. So as to give Luke extra help with the spring planting and outside work; and too, because the one room kitchen would hardly require a maid, and the fact that she and Luke did prefer to have a little privacy she was preparing most all their meals again. Shortly, before noon one day as she was hurrying with the preparation of dinner, cooking at the same huge grate in the big fireplace where all the delicious meals had been served in the mansion over the years had been prepared, she heard someone rap upon the door frame. She had left the door open since the spring days were beginning to be rather warm. Swiftly, taking a look and concluding that dinner was done, she set the steaming pot of food aside, gave her damp, disheveled hair a sweep with her hand, and in an old faded and ragged dress that she had discovered in the wash house after the fire and which she had slipped on to do the cooking in, she went rushing to the door. Suddenly it was doubtful that she had felt any worse that day at the flower bed when Frank had caught her dressed in rags. If blond, handsome Bill Clarendon though—dressed every much as impeccable as Frank had been gave any thought to her attire he did not show it, as he turned his grave expression from the pile of burned wreckage and grey ashes to look at her warmly, grasping on to her hand as she stepped through the doorway. And, although that being the case; even so, she was unable to comprehend why his presence and the touch of his hand sent her weakened spirit crashing into nothing and brought tears swimming to her eyes as they stared at one another.

"Eliza dear," he was saying, "I'm so sorry, I came as quickly as I could. I was gone longer than I expected, I just arrived back in Charleston this morning. I truly regret that I wasn't here to lend what support and comfort, for what little it may have been to you and Luke both. I heard that it burned almost two weeks ago."

Her throat had tightened, but she did manage to mutter "Yes—It happened—several days ago." She dropped her eyes and stared at his hand still clasped to hers. "No one was able to do anything, Bill. It was windy that night and it burned as though kerosene had been poured on it. It's—I just wish—that—," her voice quivered and broke off.

Moving his hand from hers at last, he placed it under her chin and lifted her face to meet his and, as they looked at each other again he had the same feeling that he had when they had met after the war. He longed to take her in his arms and comfort her and felt that had he done so she would not have pulled away; yet, he made no move in putting his instinct to the proof or relenting to any desire he may have held, admitting to himself with some reluctance that whatever her feelings were at that moment—he knew beyond question that it was Luke Heyward who held her heart. Still, he reasoned that this aspect should not prevent him from asking her what she had started to say but found so painful to talk about. Besides, he sensed again that it was something she wanted him to know.

"Eliza dear, tell me what you started to say. I'd like to help if I could. We are old friends, and if nothing else I could listen." He said.

She looked toward the ruins. "Oh, Bill, it's so hard for me to express, you see, I've always held a dream that someday I'd have a child born in that same house as I was."

He thought her remark a little odd and one that he had not been expecting. Taking into account what she had been through though, he brushed it aside. As with all the rest of the Heyward's friends and acquaintances, he likewise had come to look upon their marriage as being a childless one. He didn't know quite what to say and was telling himself that his reply could not have sounded shallower to him, when he told her, "try not to think about it, dear. I realize that's easier said than done though."

"Yes, when I'm reminded of it every single minute it seems and especially when I'm inside that kitchen. My telling you this may not seem very proper, but right at this moment conventions mean very little to me," she said as she set her eyes to his once more. "Bill, I'm going to have a baby. After all these years what I've prayed for has finally come to pass and look at what it'll be born in!"

He was startled.

"A baby! Eliza! You're going to have a baby! When?"

"In September, if all goes well, and I pray that it will."

"Of course it will, dear! Why—that's wonderful news. I can understand your feelings concerning the mansion, but look at it this way, dear, what your baby's born in is not that important. The important part is yours and its welfare and comfort." He shifted his glance to the drab looking kitchen. "So, you do plan on living here?" He asked.

"Yes, it's home, Bill. I want my baby born here."

"I can see why you'd feel that way, but Eliza you can't live in one room," he was saying as his eyes began to move upon the kitchen's dimensions, as if he were measuring and already planning improvements.

"Well, Luke does plan to add two more rooms right away. In fact, he's been waiting to see you about some lumber."

He smiled at her. "It appears that Luke's mind and mine are running together. I was just figuring how this place could be altered to fit your needs and certainly make you and him both more comfortable."

At the sound of huff beats, they turned their heads.

"There's Luke now, Coming to dinner. He'll be glad to see you," she told him, and he saw how her face brightened as Luke reined his mount close to where they were standing jumped from the saddle—reaching one hand out to circle her waist while he brushed her cheek with a kiss and extended his other hand toward him all in one motion, saying, "it's good to see you, Bill, hope everything's well with you."

"Hello Luke, I'm terribly sorry and shocked over your misfortune here, and as I've told Eliza I regret I couldn't be here before now." Then, he smiled, quite cheerfully. "I don't imagine this has been done many times, if ever, offering sympathy and congratulations all in the same breath, but that's what I'm doing," he said, giving Luke a hearty handshake.

Beaming instantly, Luke looked down at Eliza, who suddenly seemed to be in much better spirits. "She's told you," he said, "Thank you, Bill. We're very happy about it and I might add astonished somewhat, also!"

"Well, it's sure wonderful news and I'm very happy for both of you."

"If you two will excuse me," interrupted Eliza, "I'll get dinner on the table. Bill, you will stay and eat with us, won't you? It'll give you and Luke a chance to visit longer."

Bill looked at her and laughed, "I was hoping you'd say that! This weary traveler is famished."

"Well, in that case," she laughed, finally. "I'll hurry. It'll be ready in a few minutes." She stepped back through the door.

He called blithely after her, "I'll be waiting!" Turning back to Luke though his air of levity that he had maintained in her presence changed considerably. "Luke, Eliza was telling me that your plans are to build onto this kitchen, right away."

"Yes, although it's a busy season to start a building project, I have no choice except to start and try to get it completed, anyway, by the time the baby's born. People has been kind and thoughtful, the Drakston's and Randolph's have generously offered us their hospitality for as long as we would accept, but Eliza wants to remain here; and to be honest I have to admit I go along with her, traveling back and forth between either of those places and Green Sea would put a double hardship on me this summer. Still," he looked toward the kitchen door, "I can tell you again, that I'm plenty worried over her living in this place, too."

"Well, we'll have to see what we can do about it. I have plenty of ready lumber just waiting for a hammer and saw."

"I thought about that and I've been waiting for you to get back, so perhaps I could work out some arrangements with you about buying what I'll need here."

"I'll be glad to work out any arrangement, but only on one condition." Bill said, his lightness of spirit returning again.

With some disquiet, Luke asked, "How's that?"

"That you allow me to make you and Eliza a present of every board that it takes!"

Luke was overwhelmed. "Bill, I don't know what to say. In a sense I feel that would be overdrawing on your generosity a little too much."

"Nonsense! Luke! It's not that much. I want to do this. Remember the Carson's have been our dearest friends over the years, and I feel that had this tragedy been spent upon Clarendon Plantation that you would've been among the first there, giving aid in whatever capacity was available to you and it most certainly wouldn't have been measured. Besides, your other expense is going to be heavy enough, such as windows, doors, nails, roofing, and a number of other things."

"I won't argue that point with you, Bill. I hope we won't be living here too many years, but one can never tell. So, I want to make it as comfortable and pleasant for Eliza as it can be made."

"I agree with you on that score and we'll do it, too! Listen if you'll work all your plans out and give me the list Sunday of what you'll be needing, Come Monday morning I'll have the wagons loaded and send them on over; that is, weather permitting."

"Thanks, Bill, I appreciate that. I have most everything worked out, just a few minor details left to consider. I've been drawing and planning every night after supper for the past week."

"Luke," Bill suddenly exclaimed, "A thought just popped in my head! With as many men as there are in this neighborhood that's capable of using a hammer and saw, thank God! The Yankees didn't do away with all of us! I can't see you struggling alone on this project and working a crop, also. It's too much for any one man to tackle. Why not let me see Bruce and tell him to spread the word in his neck of the woods and I'll do the same in mine, that there's going to be a 'working' at Green Sea, you just set the date. That way most all this work could be finished in one week!"

Luke had felt that his admiration for Bill Clarendon had reached its height years back in the dignity and reputability that Bill had comported as he bowed out his near winning Eliza and making her his wife, though his deep affection for her had been evident while he did so. Now, he was aware that he had been wrong. He thought he had not ever scratched the surface in coming to know the depth of Bill Clarendon's nobility and moral strength. He looked Bill full in the face and told him so.

"Bill, a few minutes ago, I spoke of overdrawing on your generosity. Well, as of now, I've changed my mind concerning that. I think your supply is so unlimited that no way could I or anyone else lower its fullness. That's about the best way that I can think to say thanks to a man, that I'm hard put to know how to thank."

"I appreciate your kind words, Luke, and allowing me to help. I was hoping that you would give me the privilege to do this, when I heard Eliza say that you planned to add the additional space." He extended his hand to Luke and laughed, "had you refused, I had planned on pleading with you in behalf of the baby!"

Shaking his hand heartily once more, Luke laughed, too, "In behalf of the baby, Bill, no further persuasion is necessary. Let's go to dinner!" However, as he and Bill stepped through the doorway, his mind was for removed from the kitchen. It had traveled back to a morning in 1860 when he had pressed the gold coins inside Betsy Green's palm and said, "Take it in behalf of the baby."

Long minutes before Luke and Bill had gone inside to dinner, Doss had stepped from out of nowhere and led their mounts away to the stables. In a way, the three older house servants; Doss, Hannah, and Albert had taken the burning of the mansion every much as hard as Eliza and Luke had, if not more so. Still, out of the three servants, it was Doss who appeared to be the most dejected in spirit. Hannah seemed to be adjusting quite well to living in one of the many abandoned slave cabins, and Albert was not around anymore to be compelled to look upon the ruins. Matthew had come to his rescue. Having observed the snow-white head, knowing that his age and training made him almost worthless as a field hand, Matthew out of his goodness of heart had taken Albert back to Columbia with him. He was certain that Amy would fit Albert into their household, restoring him to doing something that would merit the training that had been distilled in him since the day he had been born at Green Sea. Doss was going his own way as usual, barring his grief over the mansion. Luke had ceased in telling him to do anything. However, ignoring Doss was easy to do in view of fact it was not necessary to point out chores to him. He worked continuously, chopping wood, keeping the yard neat, and doing endless things for Eliza that he thought would make her life more easier. As a matter of fact, Luke was comforted in knowing that Doss was always close by Eliza, when he was away in the fields. He was certain that if Doss could in any manner prevent it, no harm would come to Eliza if it came to his giving his life to protect her. Therefore, Luke respected Doss' feelings and left him alone. All in all, the burning of the grand house though—not only brought grief to these former slaves, upsetting their living pattern in their old age; but it brought a period of lean years to Eliza and Luke—years that saw them rich exclusively in two things, love and land. The rest was very meager as Eliza had foreseen.

Chapter Five

On Monday of the next week, wagons of lumber from Bill's sawmill started rolling toward Green Sea. Luke made a trip to Charleston and bought the other materials that he needed; and beginning one week to the day of Bill's visit, the singing of saws, the clattering of boards, and the pounding of hammers began. There were no less than ten capable, well-qualified carpenters among the clan of men who had gathered for the "working". The late March day had also been well-timed, as it seemed the elements could not have been more propitious. It appeared as though the cloudless, gentle, warm day had come in all spring's splendor to live down the, sometimes, windy ravages of March, touching one as softly as the down of a new baby chick. What breeze did fan across the worker's faces every now and then brought nothing but mouth-watering delight, that made them fly their hammers that much more zestfully in anticipation of the dinner hour. The aroma of fresh baking bread, pies, and cakes in addition to roasting ham and chicken, and the sight of the long plank table set on sawhorses at either end out in the yard under a live oak tree had given everybody the feeling that a social gathering and picnic were in progress rather than a "working". As the men had gathered to lend their assistance to Luke with his building project, without anyone suggesting it, the women had come along, too, to assist Eliza in feeding them. There had been huge baskets of prepared food and numerous uncooked items brought by Martha, "Miss" Amelia and Caroline, Charlotte, and several others, including Mollie Cooper from Charleston.

In process of making ready for the noonday feast, rather often it became necessary for some of these comely women to parade to and fro between the big fireplace and the banquet table under the live oak and, so far as the men were concerned this was additional spice added to the fragrant atmosphere. Each time their glance chanced to catch one of these pretty figures in their scope of vision, it was no less affecting than had someone suddenly thrust the spirits jug under their nose, causing one's already high enthusiasm to increase something like several notches. And, when the big bell did finally sound over the clacking noise to signal that all was ready, there were many feet scurrying down rafters and beams; for by then, quite a number of these good helping patrons were every much as eager to enjoy the company of these fair ladies as they were to pray upon the rich flowered, appetizing dishes—containers of food that were spread so abundantly that one could scarcely see the red and white checkered cotton table cloths that were hiding the rough planks of the makeshift table. Moreover, by late afternoon or perhaps in some cases a little earlier, if a few more of these befrienders began to lag somewhat with their hammer or saw, due to overstuffing on feeling the need to quench their thirst more often than they should have with the highly patent beverage of the "spirits jug" rather than what the bouncy maidens had to offer—they in a sense had earned this respite; and the others could come close to forgiving because it was astonishing to see what the workers had accomplished since the first nail had been driven.

To be sure, the women had had a full day; also, since they had prepared supper for the men as well as dinner. But, by the same token, they had gossiped a lot, too. Those that had not already known about Eliza's pregnancy heard about it on this day; indeed the news could not have been more surprisingly and happily received. Martha had hilariously told Eliza that she would loan but not give Laura's infant baby clothes to her, because she expected to use them again herself, sometime. Besides babies, another topic of interest among the ladies was the new doctor, Seth Roalf and his little boy, Seth junior who had recently arrived at Doctor Davis' from Washington. It appeared that Doctor Roalf had already made the acquaintances of the Wiltons, having been a dinner guest at Elms the night before "Miss" Amelia thought the young doctor was very good-looking with a charming personality to boot. However, if Caroline held any views pro or con for the doctor, she kept them to herself. Anyway, long before the subject of Doctor Roalf had been exhausted there was hardly a woman present from the Wiltons that did not have a hankering to meet the doctor, not when they were off-color below par, naturally, but on social basis.

As the guider for the men, Bill had seen to it that work continued on til one could barely see how to drive a nail in the dusk of nightfall. His aim had been to leave Luke with nothing to do but build the steps, put in the windows, hang the doors, and paint. When he finally called an end to the "working", he had reached his objective. Strange as it was, though they did not see one another too often anymore, the unique relationship—ever holding the other in high esteem that had existed between these two men from the very beginning was as strong and steadfast as always. Even though there was no disputing the fact that both loved the same women, with one having lost her and the other winning her, for all that, they were never uneasy in the other's company as Luke and Frank Drakston were. Of course, there was no question what made this possible. It was Bill's honorable behavior toward Eliza. From the day that she had told him that she loved Luke and was going to marry him, Bill had made no other move in conquest of her, nor had he allowed his eyes to betray any feeling he may have held. True, he did not shun her as he still remained friends with her, her father, and Luke. Just the same, in this warmhearted amity though that he shared with them, he was careful not to let his emotions affect nothing but just that, when he was near Eliza or perhaps held her hands. On this day, for instance, he had given Eliza no more attention, even less than he had the other women present. As a matter of fact, all through the dinner break he had mostly kept close to Caroline, carrying on quite a friendly little chat with her. Thus, any disquietude that could have risen in a situation such as that, Bill quelled it before it surfaced to the open.

Assuredly, Frank had been nowhere around on this day. Most the workers who had gathered to give Luke a helping hand were not too surprised at his absence, and especially those who were more familiar with his nature. Nonetheless, his failing to be there was due to other factors known only to Frank not withstanding his peculiarity. In the first place it would have been doubtful if wild horses could have dragged Frank to Green Sea for any cause or occasion. He was not quite ready to view what he indirectly had brought Eliza to. Then again, he had become intensely furious when Elizabeth had given him the news that Eliza was going to have a baby. As Elizabeth stood in shocked disbelief, he manifested his love and his jealousness once more for his cousin, lashing out at his wife, ruthlessly, "Don't ever mention her having a baby for Luke Heyward to me again!" Elizabeth had turned and left him without saying another word. To a certain degree, as long as the Heyward marriage had not produced any offspring it had been easy for Frank to imagine that Eliza was not even married at times. Now, hearing that she was going to become a mother, sealed her marriage to Luke more firmly than ever, and to Frank had taken her that much further away. Another something that irked him tenfold was the fact that Eliza had chosen to live in a "hut" rather than accept his invitation to come live at Drakston Hall for a long as she wished to. He had sent Elizabeth to Green Sea bearing his personal written message, but Eliza had refused to accept his hospitality at the time that he was truly concerned for her. He could barely endure or abide with the situation any longer, he reasoned; whereupon, he whirled on his heels and proceeded to find Elizabeth and apologized to her for his rage, suggesting that it would be a wonderful and most convenient time of year for him to take her and Stuart on a trip to New Orleans! She would be able to meet his other relatives, a pleasure that so far had been denied her. He was sorry that he had not taken her before this. What did she think of the idea? Besides, he wanted to stop in Columbia and see his mother—he never breathed one word of desire to see his uncle—he was lonesome to enjoy a visit with her again, it had been rather a long time since he had; did not Elizabeth agree? If Elizabeth did not wholly approve of their being gone during the "working" at Green Sea, she was delighted that Frank for the first time since their marriage had asked her opinion instead of suddenly ordering her to make ready to leave! Thus wise, the day that all the other neighbors had flocked to Green Sea, despite their own work that needed attending, to help Luke and Eliza, Frank was far away from Green Sea on an extended visit to show off Elizabeth and Stuart to his relatives! Furthermore, it was little wonder that he kept Elizabeth slightly confused when it came to question of his devotion for her.

In any event, what Bill had proposed and set in motion had paid off beyond his or anyone else's expectation. The day had been a complete success without Frank's help. After supper had been served to everyone, the Heyward's had seen their friends off with a warm thanks and, when the last buggy and wagon had gone trailing one behind the other and were lost from sight in the darkness of the live oaks—they turned to one another and drawing each other close—they stood for some minutes in the first rays of moonlight and viewed the architecture that had resulted from Luke's design, the framework that he had sketched and worked on for a number of nights by candlelight til bedtime. Suddenly, a surge of optimism began to rise in them, something they had not felt for quite a while, as they envisioned the coming summer with a more rose-colored perspective. They went inside and walked from room to room on the newly laid white oak floor, mentally placing the furnishings that had been given to them, here and there. Indeed, the newly constructed parts had added a pleasing supplement of space to their living quarters, and once they were through with adding the finishing touch, the kitchen had almost disappeared from sight and their home was to give the appearance of a neat, rural house that might have set in some New England village rather than on a twenty-five thousand-acre southern plantation. The additional two rooms had been built onto the front of the kitchen, extending the entire length of the structure and way beyond several fleet and continued on to parallel with the back. A back porch had also been added along the complete back part, new and old. The only part of the kitchen that showed from outside view was the end where the big chimney stood, and in time those boards were covered with newer lumber. The high ceilings on the inside that Luke made sure his plan called for, also demanded a tall gabled roof that covered over the kitchen roof as well as the new part. It sloped sharply down in front with a wide overhanging cave. The front door was centered with tall, wide shuttered windows on either side. One stepped from the front steps direct into the living room. Luke had not designed a front porch in his remodeling. A porch required some sort of posts. To have displayed columns on a small structure such as that or fashioned any type of pillar of lesser size, to him would have been a parody, defaming the huge stately columns that had been so much a part of Green Sea in the past. Therefore, he cast off all thought of a front porch, altogether.

Immediately, he and Doss began building the front and back steps, using brick that Doss had scratched out of the mansion's burned wreckage. Each evening after Luke came in from the fields, they worked until dark and, when they started building another chimney, sometimes, they would work til bedtime. Luke placed the chimney at the opposite end of the big kitchen. The chimney in the new part that he had built which consisted of the living room and bedroom was placed in the living room but close enough to the bedroom to provide some warmth for it too in the winter months. The bedroom had two doors, one opened to the living room, the other had been placed between the end of the kitchen wall that the bedroom paralleled with. Once everything began to take shape, Doss perked up in spirit and was a great deal of help to Luke. With the exception of the shutters, which were painted white, he and Luke painted the entire house a soft grey. Actually, Doss did most of the painting while Luke was busy getting his crop planted. But, at long last, the job was finally completed outside and inside as well. There were white ruffled curtains hanging at the windows, rugs upon the polished floors, and the furniture placed. Eliza had placed the easy, oversized chair from Drakston Hall beside the fireplace for Luke. There was a comfortable rocker facing it which she would occupy. This rocker was a gift from Martha, after Martha had learned about the baby. She had told Eliza that a easier rocker for rocking babies to sleep had never been made. Martha's chair was to come in for a plenty of rocking, and Eliza was never to dispute her claim. At any rate, Eliza and Luke could at last look upon their home with a certain amount of satisfaction and pride. They did not refer to it as the "kitchen" anymore, because the kitchen had rapidly turned into a house—their home. Granted, they would not have thought of comparing it to the mansion in any degree; yet, there was something about it, some charm that pleased them. Most of all though, they were cozy and comfortable once more, and the house was surely adequate and plenty good enough to receive their baby. This was the most important part of all to them, because they both had wished for it to be born at Green Sea; still, in something other than a crude one room kitchen. Now, it appeared as though their wish would be granted to them.

Along with the new life and tender leafing of spring, Eliza felt her baby stir within her for the first time. She took as much delight from this seemingly miracle as she did seeing the dogwoods and redbuds unfolding in masses of color. Somehow, in this budding and blooming of a new season the resplendence of wild daisy's and blue cornflowers, the nakedness of the land being clothed with a rich cloak of summer green, the grievous loss of the mansion came to her thoughts less vividly as she waited for her baby. She had begun to increase in body, but she carried her baby gracefully. It was no fault of Luke's that she was not pampered as her mother had been when she had carried her and her brothers. Even though Luke was nothing but tenderness and concern for her wellbeing, this in no way could bring back the easy, carefree life pattern that she had once lived by. Her responsibilities were heavy. As the normal run of summer was, the work ever seemed endless. Besides the ordinary duties of her house to keep up, there was the garden work, the canning of fruits and vegetables for winter's use, plus she made an effort to help Luke with the crop in every way that was possible and most the time over his protest. At times, the tobacco crop demanded every hand on the plantation, even Doss despite his averseness for field work, to keep the suckers and blooms from destroying it before maturity; and those were the times she gave no heed to Luke's objection. She would put on her bonnet against the sun and swiftly top blooms and pull suckers as she trudged heavily up and down the long rows of tall, thick-set tobacco, where a breath of fresh air seldom sifted. Her general health was excellent. Though carrying a baby in the summer heat and under such conditions was a burden. Sometimes, notwithstanding her happiness over her pregnancy she would despair when her body ached from sheer tiredness and sweat steamed in such profusion that it would literally run down her legs. Yet, in spite of this discomfort and pain, her mind was more concerned with Luke than it was with herself. Whereas before in summers past, he had worked from sunup to sundown, now he stretched his day's work from the crack of dawn to way passed dark. It seemed as though he were held continuously in a high-pressured grip that was driving him beyond any man's endurance. He had grown extremely thin and gaunt once more in this summer of 1867. She sensed the reason for his pressing himself so was because of the mansion's burning and his promising to build her another. Thus, one day she took it upon herself to tell him how she felt. He had hardly taken the time to eat dinner that she had prepared before he was brushing her cheek with a kiss and making a grab for his straw hat, going back to the fields without taking a rest period.

"Luke, wait," she said, as he was going through the door, "If all the mansions in God's world were at my disposal, they would be of no use to me whatever without you. I know you said that you would build me another, but, darling, please don't do away with yourself and what we have together in your effort to make that promise come true. There would be no joy in it for me that way."

Each word that she had said had fallen hard upon his ears and reached his heart to the quick. He turned back and hung his straw hat upon a nail on the back—porch wall. He stepped back to the table and sat down in his chair. He looked at her deeply, where she still remained sitting at the table. He smiled, "Sweetheart, those apple dumplings are awfully good, I think I'll try another helping."

Her wise message had gotten through.

On top of everything else that had happened at Green Sea that spring and summer, there were other matters though that had ensued in and out the State of South Carolina that had also concerned Eliza and Luke. The radicals who had erected their "paying machine" with solid and well-greased wheels, now had it running quite smoothly over the battered and worn southland.

The Northern military commanders had moved in, besides the continuing migration of more carpetbaggers and numerous other northern citizens and private groups, all claiming to have come to the South for the purpose of supporting the newly freed negro, however much they helped the negro though is still to be questioned. At any rate, the fourteenth and fifteenth amendment had finally been ratified by Congress and added to the Constitution, giving every person born in the United States warranted citizenship and the right to vote regardless of race, past employment, or color. Walt Hawkins had come into good fortune once more, gaining the position of county sheriff through his yankee friends—an office he was to hold for several years. There were race riots and mass disorder. Hawkins had his hands full, with usually a full jailhouse. Colored troops drank and sometimes became aggressive toward southern whites. The whites fought back by burning negro schools that had recently been set up to educate the colored race, and many secret societies were organized by the whites in order to protect themselves, their homes, and their families, so they alleged, from the negros and the unjust northern aggression. There were hangings, floggings, et cetera. One of these not so secret societies was the famous hooded Ku Klux Klan, whose members rode upon the shadows and dark of night clothed in their white hoods; and the leader of one particular group in his neighborhood was no other than Frank Drakston! True, Frank had not marched one step or fired the first shot to preserve the South's cause in its long struggle for independence, letting family, friends, and others shoulder the responsibility while he made his millions. Even so, this fact did not hinder him from standing up and defending the Klan and everything it advocated. In fact, through the Klan he had gained a new interest in life, almost deriving as much pleasure from it as he had making his fortune, and he was never accused of shrinking in his duty to it. He gave generously in money, time, and energy to its function. He became known, and none too indiscreetly at that, for his capability and his bravery as a leader. His daring feats with the military and Walt Hawkins caused Elizabeth many anxious hours. But, be that as it may, what no one was aware of except Frank and the sheriff was that Walt Hawkins would usually lead his deputies, if he could possibly feign it in anyway, in another direction other than in pursuit of Frank and his riders. Besides Frank Drakston's immense wealth, there had been something about his eyes and cold, calculated manner that day at O'Henry's store that had put a fear in Walt Hawkins he was unable to forget. The sheriff was positive if Frank saw fit to do so he would not bat an eye much less count to three in pulling the trigger of those pearl-handled revolvers, which it was rumored that Frank wore always and everywhere, making no exception for any occasion! Therefore, the sheriff preferred to stay clear of Franks range, unless, of course, he could drum up some excuse to have a reason to call on Frank at Drakston Hall, something that gave him a feeling of being socially intimate with the Drakston's. Anyhow, when Luke refused to join Frank and his group and ride as one of these loaded vigilantes, he and Frank came near a bitter exchange of words and the wide breech that had existed between them from the first became more distant than ever. Luke gave Frank his reasons for not joining, not in defense of his stand, because he felt he did not have to vindicate his views to anyone; but he did have a desire to let Frank know his mind once and final. In the first place, he had given three years of his life away from his wife to preserve the South's cause and while doing so had seen enough killing, suffering, and destruction to last him a lifetime. Then again, less a killing at green Sea, Luke felt that about everything could happen had already taken place there! He shared a good rapport with the former slaves at Green Sea and had had no problems with any others that he was aware of. Moreover, last of all but not least, he did not have the time or energy to devote to this society because he was too busy trying to scratch out a living for Eliza and himself and preserve the lands of Green Sea in addition to seeing to the welfare of his several tenant families. In short, he was not a man of leisure and money as Frank Drakston was!

At first, Frank's reaction was untold fury toward Luke. He called Luke a coward and cussed him repeatedly, all in private, naturally. Later when the storm of his fury though had calmed somewhat, and he had gotten around to giving the situation more thought he began to see it all in a different light. His conscience, for the first time since the mansion had burned at Green Sea, began to ease up some. He told himself over and over that he was doing something for Eliza that her own husband refused to do. He was defending and protecting her and her home! To be sure, there had been no more night rides upon Green

Sea since that early night in March and, with Frank's mind working as it did, it was a sure bet that the Coles were to stay away from Green Sea for a long time, despite his constant loathing for Luke and the distaste he felt over Luke's refusal to join the Klan.

Summer was to pass through at Green Sea with another good crop season, and the harvest had fallen upon Luke. He and the hands were preparing the flue cured tobacco for market, picking out the trash leaves before the tobacco was packed in large casks to be shipped. The cotton was getting heavier each day, bursting out in big fluffy white balls, spreading a white cotton blanket over the fields. The hands were busy picking it, also, plodding along up and down the long rows with their cotton sack tied around their waist, while a hot September sun beat down upon their bent backs. And, the time for Eliza's labor was drawing nearer and nearer til the day came when it was upon, she and Luke. Nowadays, although she had no taste for it, Prudence as well as Daisy did field work and outside chores. Very seldom did Prudence cook at the big fireplace in the kitchen anymore. This area of chores had fallen almost entirely to Eliza since the mansion had burned, and on this night as she prepared Luke's supper the telltale signs of her pending labor began. It was September twenty-third, the eve of her seventh wedding anniversary; and a little earlier, too, than she had been expecting her baby to arrive. She finished cooking supper, at last, when Luke did finally come from the tobacco barn to eat, she sat down at the table with him as usual. Though she only toyed with the serving of food that she put on her plate. Seeing how tired he looked, she desired putting off telling him as long as she could. She went on to bed with him as usual; also, having an inkling there would be plenty of time for him to be upset over her. Luke fell asleep instantly. She didn't. As a matter of fact, she never fell asleep and, at three o'clock in the morning Luke awakened to find her out of bed. He jumped up and bounded through the living room to the kitchen where he found her sitting at the kitchen table, her arms crossed over the other with her hands gripped to either shoulder. Bearing to another hard pain that had seized her. Though the candlelight was faint that she sat by, he could still see the force of the cutting pain upon her face.

Thinking she had been up only a few minutes, he rushed to her, saying, "Good Lord! Darling, why didn't you call me?" as he swept her up in his arms and carried her back to their bed, pulling the light covers snugly around her.

She had seen something near suffering on his face, too, when he had found her. He had known without her saying so that her labor was in progress. Now, as he was making a grab for his pants by the light of the waving moon streaming through the window, she tried to reassure him, "Luke, please don't worry so, I'll be all right." She hoped that he would not become knowledgeable to the fact that she had been sitting, what time she had not been walking, in the kitchen for three hours!

He swiftly reached for her hand and squeeze it in a most intimate way that set it apart from the many other times that he had done so, "I'll run for Hannah, sweetheart, and be right back," he said.

She lay there in the quiescence of night, that time of night when it is hard not to vision the whole world as being wrapped in a blanket of slumber and thought about the numerous times during her pregnancy that she had heard Luke say he wished it were him bearing the burden of carrying their baby, instead of her. Presently, she heard the thud of his running feet upon the hard-packed path between the kitchen and slave cabins, where Hannah and Doss lived in the nearest one to the kitchen; and in less than no time, she heard the voices of Hannah and Doss as they padded behind him. Yes, no two ways about it Doss had come, too. She heard them enter the kitchen and promptly Luke was to her side asking anxiously, if she thought she would be alright with Hannah and Doss while he rushed to fetch Doctor Davis. She endeavored to ease his mind once more. He kissed her quickly and gripped her hand, clinging to it somewhat hesitant before he turned away and was gone again. She had been almost ready to tell him that he need not be in no great hurry to summon the doctor. It was true that she knew very little about the course and steps of one giving birth, only what Martha had enlightened her to; but something told her even though the stork had started on his way to deliver her baby at last, he still was not going to make a fast flight!

In the hush, she could take in most of Hannah and Doss' conversation and heard Hannah say to him, "Ol' m'n y'us knows what to do, nothin' likes plenty of hot water in a birthin'!

Then, Hannah was creeping softly into the bedroom with a lighted lamp, its wick turned down low. In the pale amber glow, she saw that Hannah's face; also, was drawn and anxious an entire bed of deep channeled furrows, as she laid her work hand as lightly as a breath upon Eliza's brow and gently stroked back her hair once or twice, after which she started making her as comfortable as was possible; and doing a number of other things that they would not be able to dispense with in the traveling of this unfamiliar road that she was embarking upon. There was something though about Hannah's weathered, soothing hands that gave Eliza confidence and promise, loaning to her a near feeling of her long-departed mother's hands and, as another hard pain cut through her she clung to them tightly. Hannah said, soft, "Take deep breath an' doan h'ld back, hit'll com' sooner." The pain left her tired and shaky. Hannah tucked another blanket around her feet and legs and sat quietly beside the bed til she seemed to feel some better. She lay alone once more in the still, grey-black dawn. Hannah had told her, "Better get dem min som' breakfast started," and she had gone back to the kitchen. Eliza heard her now rattling dishes and pans every now and then in making sure that Luke and Doctor Davis had steaming coffee at their disposal, as well as hot biscuits, grits, ham and eggs, cheese, butter, milk, honey and at least two different kinds of jam; once they entered the door. She heard the chain for drawing water jangling upon the small iron roller, as Doss lowered the bucket into the well again. It appeared that Doss was taking Hannah at her word and filling every available pot and kettle in the kitchen and, if the slashing of his ax at the wood pile had been any sign, Eliza was positive that he had chopped near a chord of wood! She heard the beat of a horse's gallop. Luke was back! How he must have hurried, probably rode as if he were back riding in Jeb Stuart's cavalry raids! Did she hear the faint squeaking of Doctor Davis' buggy? Yes, it was coming up the drive, too. Poor Doctor Davis, she was sure that Luke had routed him from his sleep unnecessarily. Luke was waiting for the doctor. There! She could hear them in the yard. Now, they were inside! Doctor Davis was saying, "I'll have a look at her, Luke, and report to you in a few minutes." The doctor sounded very professional. Poor Luke, there he was already pacing the floor and Doctor Davis had barely greeted her, much less started any examination of her. She surely hoped that the doctor would say that she was making more progress than what she had thought, so Luke would be spared all those steps!

Luke looked anxiously at the doctor, as he stepped through the bedroom door that opened into the kitchen and chose to shut behind him. "Let's sit here at the table, Luke," Doctor Davis said, striding toward the cup of coffee that Hannah had just poured and set down upon the table that was laid with breakfast.

Luke stared for a moment at the closed bedroom door. He wanted to go to Eliza, but did as the doctor had suggested and followed him to the kitchen table. He did not sit down though. He remained standing and still looking at Doctor Davis questionably, while the doctor got settled in his chair and lifted his coffee cup once or twice, gulping down the strong coffee somewhat eagerly.

After what had seemed to Luke was entirely too long, the doctor finally got around to stating his prognosis of Eliza's confinement. "Luke, I'd certainly been more pleased to have seen that Eliza had made more progress than she has, but this happens in a lot of cases and especially with the first baby." He said.

Luke turned his head toward the clock upon the mantel. Why, it was just passed six o'clock! He did not quite understand what the doctor meant. Though he wished to God that were the fact, surely Doctor Davis had not expected Eliza to be ready for delivering in a mere three hours! Somewhat puzzled, he replied, "I regret, too, Doctor Davis, that she isn't closer to delivery, because I've prayed that she won't have long hours of suffering in bringing our baby into the world. Maybe though, we're expecting more from her than we should, it's only been a few hours, now."

Doctor Davis looked up, studying him for a long moment.

"Apparently, Luke," he said, "Eliza didn't want you to know til it became necessary, so you wouldn't worry over her and get some rest last night. Your wife has already been in labor not just a few hours, but actually more than twelve hours!"

Luke was stunned cold. Hard fear seized him. So, even in her distress and pain, Eliza had put him first in her thoughts. He was positive he had never been so deeply moved and scared

altogether. "No Doctor Davis, I didn't know," he said, quite solemnly. "She will be all right? You're not trying to tell me—," he could not go any further with the question.

Seeing that Luke's face had gone an ash white, suddenly the doctor quickly said, "of course, she will, I didn't mean to alarm you. I only meant to warn you that it's going to be several more hours before that baby comes, you might as well go on about your business, for the present, anyway!"

"Can't you do something—I mean—well—speed—." He went no further with that question, either.

Doctor Davis ran his eyes over him again, slowly. "No, Luke, I can't" he said, rather emphatically. "In matters such as this, we have to let nature take its course. That baby will move when it gets ready to move!"

Luke waited no longer. "Will you excuse me, doctor," he said, as he turned and crossed the length of the floor between the table and the closed door with very few swings of his feet. He had the highest regard for Doctor Davis, but he did not go along with the doctor's seemingly notion that Eliza giving birth to a baby was any day's occurrence, and that he should see it as such.

"Certainly, Luke," the doctor replied, shaking his head. He was thinking that sometimes he had more trouble with the father than he did the mother, and from all appearances this was going to be one of those times.

Some of Luke's fear though had begun to rub off on the doctor by middle afternoon; because, by then, it was plain to be seen that Eliza was in agony and, from all the signs that he had been disclosed so far in the course of her labor, it was almost a definite fact that she would never have her baby without the use of instruments—a procedure he had no wish to revert to until the last step had been taken. There was too much danger involved—infection and hemorrhage with her—to say nothing about the, sometimes, inevitable sorrow of having to sacrifice the baby's life in the process. She had waited a long time for this baby. He knew the torture of her pain, but he was going to take every measure possible to save her baby for her; and also, do the very best for her that lay in his power. No, he would wait a few more hours, though added to his worries would be what to do about Luke! He was certain that among all the fathers he had seen, he had never seen one so wrought up with emotion. In fact, he had been forced to ask Luke to wait outside the bedroom on two or three instances today. Luke seemed to think that his presence would ease his wife's suffering to an extent. Well, he held a different opinion. He was sure that Eliza held back from giving way to her pain when Luke was in the room for fear of alarming him. Hannah was all the help he needed, anyway. He much preferred Luke going on about his business; for instance, seeing about his tobacco, instead of pacing the floor, looking as though he might collapse from fright and straining most any time. Here he was again asking the same question. He had asked it repeatedly, times without number, it seemed.

"No, Luke, I can't give her anything for the pain. If I could, I most certainly would. I do have chloroform that I plan to use at the time of delivery that should help her bear the pain, but I can't give it to her at this stage. She has to do most the work to bring that baby forth; and she surely would cease all effort if she were put into an oblivious state where she was unaware of what was happening to her besides the many other dangers. I deplore her suffering, too, but such is the trials of childbirth, sometimes. Unfortunately, your wife is one of those women that will ever find it difficult to give birth in any case. She has to have that baby, Luke, you or I can't have it for her. I'm going back now to check on her. If there's any need to call you, I'll do so."

"What about the baby, doctor?"

"I'm almost certain the baby's still all right. Its position is all right, thank God! However, I don't want to falsify the situation. I may not be able to save that baby, Luke. If I fail though, it's not going to be before I give it every possible chance, without, of course, putting Eliza in grave danger to do so."

"Thank you, Doctor Davis. I asked you that question in case circumstances should call for my viewpoint. Eliza's safety is to come first, if it should come to that. I wanted you to know.'

The doctor stepped back to the bedroom and closed the door.

Luke looked hard and long at the bedroom door that the doctor had just disappeared through, shutting it firmly behind him again. He was hard put to figure out why Doctor Davis preferred to keep the door closed anyway, because the late September day had become unusually hot in the afternoon—another factor to add to Eliza's misery. It appeared that the doctor was solidly set against performing any duty whatever, except behind a closed door and assuredly after he had made it plain that he had rather be left alone and preferred him to go on about his business! Good God! Everything had its place, situations varied. What was modesty, if that were the case, in a trying time such as this? Eliza was his wife and he was certain that she wanted him with her. He knew it by the way her hands had gripped and clung to his and the way her eyes had followed him each time he had left her, naturally, by the doctor's request! Doctor Davis should realize that things had changed and, where Eliza was concerned, to be sure, they had changed a great deal. This was 1867. The days of the plantation master sitting in his elegant library of leather-bound volumes and imported furniture, sipping brandy and most the time with the attending physician to keep him company to boot, both of whom in all probability being absent upstairs when the baby did arrive, leaving everything up to the midwives to take care of though the doctor would be praised for all the credit, those days were long gone! Granted, Eliza was far from the plantation mistress who lay abed all decked out in satins and lace with a dozen or so attendants fluttering and fussing over and around her, sponging, fanning, and preforming every little task or trying every remedy known in childbirth in an endeavor to make her comfortable. Besides the doctor, Eliza had no one but Hannah, and Hannah did not have a dozen hands! She could only do so much. He felt that if his wife had gone along with his desire to bring the other doctor along to attend to her as well as Doctor Davis. He held Seth Roalf in high regard and had from the moment he had met him. He was young, alert, and from all reports, highly capable. The neighborhood came into a streak of good luck by the arrival of Doctor Seth Roalf. It was not that he was saying Seth Roalf was more competent than Doctor Davis. It was the age factor. Doctor Davis had actually gotten to be almost feeble in appearance. In truth, he should be home resting. There was no question that Eliza's hard labor was taking its tool upon him, and it made no difference how much the doctor desired to keep the door closed and him away from Eliza, her screams and moans were reaching his ears, anyway. Her torture slashed at him like a knife on his own flesh. It seemed to him that her moans were becoming weaker and weaker. Though the times that she had screamed out had pierced his very soul, he; nevertheless, had felt a few seconds of relief in thinking that maybe the baby was finally coming, and she would be spared any further pain. But, no such luck.

Women died in childbirth; it happened all the time. No, God, he silently prayed, please let me be free of any such thought that I could lose her. He would never have desired a baby of their flesh had he known it would have come to this for her. They had been happy without children. Was this the cost of their passion for one another? There that business about Eve's curse was coming to his mind again. Well, what had actually happened in essence, between Eve and Adam, he did not know. The truth of essence though between Eliza and himself, he did know, and why he had been spared all pain of the flesh, while his wife had to suffer the consequences of their mating in anguish and torture, was a little hard for him to absorb. They had conceived that baby together in happiness and joy. Why could it not have been his lot; somehow or to her, to share her agony as well in giving birth to it?

Luke walked to the back porch and, from the top doorstep where he had planted himself at twelve o'clock, Doss' dusky, tired and concerned face lifted in question once more. It looked as though Doss had whittled away an entire block of wood, but Luke noticed he had taken care to pile the showings in a neat pile close by.

"She's still in labor, Doss." He told him.

"Too long," sighed Doss, as he sent his knife sailing back down the smooth piece of wood that he held in his hand.

"Yes, I know," Luke replied, turning away. Dejectedly, he walked back inside the kitchen and sat down at the kitchen table. The plate that Hannah had laid for him in early morning was still in its same spot. He had not eaten a bite all day. Hannah, Doctor Davis, and Eliza, too, before she had become so filled with pain that she had ceased to talk, had told him he should eat something. He had not been able to eat though. He was too upset to think of food much less eat nay. He had no idea how long it had been since the doctor had gone back to Eliza and closed the door in his face. It seemed he had lost track of all time. He lifted his slumped head and looked at the clock. Dare God! Five o'clock! He dropped his head back to his hands. Almost twenty-four hours, how could she stand much more of this excruciating labor that was no less in pitch than had she been some terror-crazed animal caught in the purgatory of a steel trap in some distant wild? He knew she had given over and above all the strength that she had to give, time and time again, today. In the severity of the hard pains, he had seen her often bite down on her lips to keep from giving in to the torment. Her pretty lips had even begun to swell and look bruised when he had left her. In fact, Eliza's whole body had become worn and totally spent hours ago. What should he do? Should he send Charlie for Doctor Seth Roalf, anyway? Suddenly though, as he sat there weighing the idea of sending for the other doctor, Doctor Seth Roalf and all other thoughts were swiftly put aside as the penetrating hush of the room—a quiet all of a sudden that seemed as if he were sitting in a tomb hit his ears and other sense with all the impact of a cannon shell exploding through the house. All sound had ceased in the bedroom! No screams, no moans, no baby's wail, no nothing! He sprung to his feet, and; in truth, actually leaped within inches to the fastened door, jerking hold of the doorknob and flinging the door wide open. The horrifying scene that met his eyes was one he was never to forget, nor was he ever able to forgive himself for leaving Eliza's bedside in spite of Doctor Davis' pronounced manifestation that he do so. In the few seconds that he halted in petrified disbelief as a suffocating wave of heat, blood, sweat, and chloroform washed over him, he caught the first glimpse of his baby making its endeavor to enter the world through a channel of flowing blood that was soaking the white bed clothing and everything else that it came in contact with so rapidly, there was only one word for it hemorrhage; and the doctor appeared to be in some sorta stupor with his hands completely motionless and Hannah stood beside him seeming as though she were frozen, holding a receiving blanket in her hands and crying silent washing tears!

Luke knew there was no time to ponder and ask questions. Seconds were ticking away, and everyone was precious if his wife who gave every appearance that she might be breathing her last breath, and his baby were to be saved! As he vaulted to the bed, he yelled for Hannah to open the other door, and then, disregarding the doctor he began to work frenziedly and mechanically to bring the baby forth from Eliza's body. His hands had suddenly become someone else's they were not his own, as he skillfully moved them into doing what they had done in likeness times before that moment when he had helped some prostrated animal in bearing their young. In the sweep of less than a minute but what had seemed like the space of a year to him—where he had struggled through a dark illimitable jungle, he at last was holding a blood coated baby in his hands and by some miracle which shocked him further he heard it give a faint wail as he thrust it into Hannah's waiting arms, telling her to take care of it. Wheeling back to Eliza and seeing the blood still gushing forth, he shouted, "Doctor Davis, please help me!"

Abruptly, Doctor Davis appeared to have come out of his trance and within and instant was making all the effort to stop the bleeding, while Luke made a dash to take the pillows from under Eliza's head in order to lower her body against the hemorrhage. Slipping an arm under her head he raised her up and, as he pulled the under pillow away, if the situation had not been so

critical he could have almost laughed. All day, Eliza had lain with the biggest butcher knife that the entire plantation laid claim to under her pillow! He felt like throwing it out the window and briefly wondered if Hannah would ever believe in this particular superstition any more after this day. He knew she had put it here, no doubt saying to Eliza, "To cut the pain." However, the knife had not surprised him too much. He had known all about Hannah's "love potion" under Eliza's pillow that time, but he had not had the heart to tease Eliza about it because he was well aware of her readiness to put more faith than she should have in Hannah's old wives' tale, or, as for that matter, any other folklore that the Negroes on the plantation believed in and practiced. Out of respect for Hannah's credenda though and his desire not to hurt her feelings, he did not throw the knife any place, he merely laid it aside. He was far too troubled to think about the knife, laughing, or doing much of anything right then. He was too shocked at Eliza's death white face and closed eyes that met deep blue black circles under them and too busy trying to pry her hands loose from the brass bar at the head of the bed that she was still gripping to. Her hands seemed as though someone had nailed them tight. When he got them unfastened and before he could get her positioned in the way that he thought was best, her eyes opened for barely a second and she faintly mumbled, "L—uke" and fainted dead away in his arms!

Sometimes later, when the long, exhausting day was finally pulling its own door shut, and the edge of nightfall had begun to spread its cool skirt of grey-black hues over the warm earth the storm of fear and disquiet that had been blowing far too long appeared to have turned into another direction, and the little house had taken on some peace and order about it once again. Leastwise, Eliza had been revived and the hemorrhage regulated, though her condition remained to be questioned. With Luke's help, Hannah had tidied up Eliza and the bed. Her hair, which had been soaking wet, had been rubbed dry and dressed somewhat. She had on a fresh clean gown and the bed had been changed and made up with clean linens, too. Moreover, the baby, a boy, had been bathed and dressed in its little white flannel gown that Eliza had stitched herself, and now was lying snuggled in his blanket upon the bed beside her. She did not realize he was there though, nor had she hardly known when he was born, or indeed if she had a baby at all.

Doss had received the news with a grin that had expanded clear across his face, revealing every tooth that was left in his head. Luke told him to go to the tobacco barn and tell the others that Green Sea had been blessed with a heir at last. He also sent word for Willie and Allen to pack the tobacco away and close up everything, because he could not leave Eliza to see to it himself.

Hannah, who was ready to drop from exhaustion, had also gotten her orders from Luke to go to her cabin and rest. He would see to Eliza and the baby for the reminder of the night. Knowing the trying time that he had been through and the fact that he still had not eaten anything, Hannah and the doctor both raised their eyebrows in concern at this news. Nonetheless, Luke quickly reduced their misgivings by pointing out to them that he had gone without sleep, sometimes no food, and very little rest for stretches of twenty-four hours or more on numerous occasions—while he had been riding with the mighty and one General J.E.B. Stuart. They gave no further hint of their objection.

Now, lamps had been lighted for the night and Luke and Doctor Davis were standing beside the bed observing Eliza. The doctor leaned forward and gently pulled back the lids of both eyes, looking closely. Rising up, he said, "She's sleeping, Luke, probably won't wake for hours."

"Thank God," Luke replied, sighing deep with relief.

"I think I've got the hemorrhage stopped, Luke. However, I don't want to mislead you. Sometimes, as it is in some cases where the flow of blood is heavy in childbirth, it's a little hard to tell how well it's checked itself."

"I'm praying, Doctor Davis. Judging from the color of her face, I'm certain she could not go through another, as severe as the first one, anyway."

"Well, maybe she won't let her sleep as long as she will, don't arouse her. One of the best signs of all that she's doing all right are the bedclothes."

"The bedclothes?"

"Yes, as long as you don't see that bed being rapidly soaked with blood, everything's going at a normal pace."

"I'll watch closely, Doctor Davis."

The doctor turned aside and started gathering up his medical and surgical supplies, packing them back in his old worn leather bag. Somewhat dispirited, he said, "Luke, I'm sorry that you had to do what you did. I guess I'm getting to be older than I realize, or something's wrong that I'm not aware of. For a moment or two there, I had a black out, became dazed, and right at the time that Eliza needed me most."

Though Luke did not know what had caused the doctor's black out he felt that the closed doors, causing the bedroom to become overly heated, had played a big part. Still, all his annoyance for some of the doctor's bedside manners suddenly disappeared. And too, he had never been one to dampen an already low spirit.

"Doctor Davis, you owe me no apology, though I'll confess something to you, I was scared to death! I'm sorry, too, that the day brought so many long agonizing hours to Eliza, forcing you to endure them along with her. I feel you've given beyond the average man's endurance today. Hours ago, you should've been home resting instead of still standing on your feet. I'm positive I couldn't have taken today what you have, and I want to thank you a hundred times over."

The doctor's face and manner brightened considerably.

"Thanks, Luke, for understanding. You know though, I wouldn't say you've had an easy day, either, in more ways than one. You need food, rest, and sleep yourself."

"I'll be fine, Doctor Davis, as long as Eliza is doing all right. Besides, every time I look at that bundle over there beside her, I get so keyed up, I feel as though I'll never want to sleep anymore!"

"Well, he's certainly something for you to become keyed up over. Although he sure was stubborn in presenting himself to the outside world, I don't think I've ever seen a finer looking infant," Doctor Davis said, closing his medical bag and reaching for his hat.

Luke, already elated to the heights over his son, needed no further encouragement to draw the doctor's attention to the baby again. He walked around to the other side of the bed where the baby lay and pulling back the blanket from its face, he said, "Doctor Davis you can see what his hair looks like now, since it's gotten dry."

The doctor, adding more steps to his wearisome day, walked to Luke's side and began viewing the baby once more.

"Doctor Davis, who would you say he looks like?" Asked Luke surprising the doctor a little and amusing him, too.

The doctor's grim face finally took on a smile. "Well—that's sorta difficult to say."

"You know who he looks like," interrupted Luke, laughing, "You're afraid you'll deflate my new father ego by saying he doesn't favor me, so I'll say it for you. He's a Carson through and through!"

The doctor clearing his throat, gave forth with a little chuckle.

"Luke, I fear I'm going to have to agree with you, wholly. I remember it well, he's the image of his mother when she was born, Phil too. The same full head of dark brown curls, the same chubby cheeks, the same lips and mouth, the bushy eyebrows; in fact, he could be her again over."

"I'm glad he looks like his mother," said Luke. "He'll be one handsome man."

"I wouldn't debate that point with you, Luke, even if he didn't look like his mother, considering the looks of both his parents."

Luke grinned, "You're a kind and thoughtful man, Doctor Davis, but we're going to have to let the Carson's take credit for this baby's looks."

"I know someone else who's going to be mighty happy and proud, and that's Matthew." Said Doctor Davis.

"Yes, I plan to wire him first thing in the morning if Eliza is so I can leave her. It'll give me great pleasure to wire Mr. Carson something other than bad news, for a change."

"Well, I think Doss has my buggy outside, I heard those wheels grinding. I'll get on home. Charger is no doubt anxious to be back in his own stall."

Luke tucked the blanket back around the baby and walked as far as the bedroom door with the doctor. "Thanks again, Doctor Davis" he said, "Forgive me for not going any farther in seeing you off."

"That's all right, Luke, I understand. I think Eliza is so exhausted, she'll not wake till morning, so I'll be back to check on her then," the doctor told him as he turned and walked wearily across the living room and out the front door, closing it softly after him.

Luke stepped back to the bed. He turned and picked up a chair and placing it beside the bed, he sat down. The cadence of night creatures was heavy in the air, coming to his ears vividly through the open window. He got up and walked to the window to close the nights' chill off Eliza and the baby. Noticing a dazzling full moon rising to start its journey across the night cloaked sky, for the first time in ages he thought of Windsor, rose blossoms, and Eliza in a white dress. A night just like this night, he thought. But that was June, this is September. September? Why, today was September the twenty-fourth, his and Eliza's seventh wedding anniversary! He had not even thought of it! Eliza had given him a son on their anniversary! He turned from the window and sat down again. Suddenly though, as he looked upon her face, his emotions finally gave way to all the overwhelming trials that the day had brought to him. He dropped his head and surrendered to the conquering sobs.

Chapter Six

Likewise, almost without distinction in common with Luke; that is, relative to what she was doing at that moment, Rachelle Fillmore—Lee was looking through a window, too. *A*s she was washing the supper dishes, she suddenly let her hands slip from the plate she was holding and both plate and hands submerged in sudsy foam and sank to the bottom of the dishpan in stillness. God's painting of saffron, cherry-colored spirals, forming coils of multicolored rosettes bursting in bloom upon a grey-blue meadow in evening's western sky had caught her attention and caused her face to glow with delight form its prettiness, the blending of colors, heaven's candlelight gleamed in gray-hued shadowy dusk. As she ever did with anything that brought any delight or joy to her, her first thought and desire was to share it with John. She turned her head from the pretty view that she was admiring through the kitchen window and looked over her shoulder toward the table where John sat working, as he did most every night after supper. She noticed that the rainbow-like streaks of light were reflecting upon John's papers that were spread out before him on the table, an area she always made available for him as quickly as she could each evening, hurrying in gathering the supper dishes up so he could begin his work. She started to draw his attention to the unusual and pretty sunset, but on afterthought she decided not to disturb him since he appeared to be rather deep in whatever he had his mind on. John worked hard. He tried to make every waking minute account for something; still, it seemed they were never able to expand their holdings or have any money left over from their living expenses to start building the nest egg for Beth Anne that they often talked about. Times were hard though. The country was still suffering from the chaos of the long war. Most people were trying to amass and gain back some portion of their former existence that war had destroyed for them, in some cases having no money to spare for the luxury of buying even a newspaper; and John's paper had a small circulation to begin with. Thus, when it came to ever putting aside a dowry for Beth Anne or anything against a rainy day, so to speak, their chances looked to be slim indeed. Never did she despair though, nor did she ever think in terms of what might have been had she married Doctor Seth Roalf, who she had completely lost touch with after he had left Washington for Richmond during the war. The love that she and John shared and what they had together made her life seem rich, anyway.

She started to turn back to her dish washing, but just at that instant, Beth Anne, their less than two-years-old daughter, scrambled to her feet and toddled across the floor to where her father sat, tugging at his arm. Though Rachelle had thought that her daughter would stay put with her playthings, a few clothespins, her rag doll, and a few more worthless items that she had gathered up that day during her play and assembled upon the kitchen floor, until she herself could finish the supper dishes, that aspect did not appear to hold any more. Rachelle took her hands from the dishpan and reached for the kitchen towel, hanging upon a nail driven into the kitchen wall near the window. While drying her hands, her smile glowed more radiantly as she observed her husband and baby. Though John had appeared to be lost in his work, his mind had not been so absorbed that he did not know his daughter was there, and, as for that matter, nor was it ever. He adored her. Rachelle saw his lame, crippled arm reach out awkwardly and slowly to gather Beth Anne closer to his knee. John had gotten part of his wish. Their baby had been a girl born on December first, in sixty-five. However, as far as their baby inheriting her features as John had said he hoped she would, in no way had his wish been granted, and Rachelle was most certainly please that it had not! Their baby could never have gotten those enchanting deep blue eyes with long curled up lashes under heavy brows, dark-brown flowing curls spilling over her

head, and the pretty full lips and perfect shaped nose from the Fillmore's! Yes, Beth Anne was an almost two-year-old miniature of her father. Rachelle secretly suspected that John was very proud and happy that his daughter looked so much like him in spite of what he had said. John had named their little girl. Of all the names they had discussed, he would always come back to Anne or Beth. Finally, he had decided to call her by both names, Beth Anne. Why did he like the names so much? He did not know.

Looking at father and daughter together, Rachelle for the first time in months wondered about their baby's lost heritage. What would their child miss out on in life—if anything? No, there was something, Rachelle was certain about that, probably many things that Beth Anne would be denied. Rachelle was as sure about that as she was her own name. She was positive that John was of noble heritage—a past of family friends, maybe even wealth because John's whole person spoke of the highest culture, all lying somewhere though lost to him forever, apparently. She did not think about John's past in terms concerning herself. It was for him and their baby, not herself, because she had no regrets or qualms over what might have been or could still be, once his past was revealed. She loved John. She had taken him—all of him—the John she knew and married him. Thus, it would ever be that way with her. She loved and was loved in return. That was all she had asked for from the first, anyway, and she had gotten her hope and desire vouchsafed.

John was saying to Beth Anne, "Come over on the other side, darling, and Daddy will lift you on his lap."

His lame arm could not support his baby's weight.

Rachelle hurried across the room. "I'm sorry, John, I'll take her," she said. "I thought she'd stay put with her toys till I finished the dishes and not be bothering you while you work. She should be in bed, anyway. Come to mother, Beth Anne, so Daddy can work."

"She's all right, dear, I'm not so busy that I can't give my daughter a few minutes," he said, planting a kiss atop Beth Anne's curls.

Beth Anne reached her chubby hand up to his beard and gave it a rather hard yank.

"O—h!" He groaned. "Now what if Daddy pulled your curls like that?" He playfully ruffled her hair.

The baby laughed, gleefully while her father disheveled her curls. When he stopped though, she turned her attention to his papers and slapped both hands down upon them, causing several to go sailing to the floor.

"No! Beth Anne," scolded Rachelle, as she bent over to pick the papers up and lay them back on the table. "Come on to mother and let her get you ready to meet the sandman before you really get in trouble." Rachelle held out her arms.

"You've already scattered Daddy's papers besides pulled his beard, young lady!"

Beth Anne was a happy, contented baby. Without any fuss, tears, or whatever, she willingly held up her arms to her mother.

"Say goodnight to Daddy," Rachelle said. Beth Anne piped out heartily, "Ni—Da—Da!"

John laughed and reached his hand up to the baby's cheek, caressing it as he said, "Goodnight to you, you pretty doll, I fear with your charm, there'll be one or two men left with a broken heart someday. But no man's going to capture you for a long time, if I can help it!"

"No, not for a long time, John, so don't start worrying about that just yet," laughed Rachelle, taking the baby and disappearing through the doorway.

Presently, Rachelle was back saying, "That phrase, 'sleep like a baby' is surely fact wit*h* Beth Anne. She's already sound asleep."

"Well, one thing that account for that, dear, is the fact you're a wonderful and conscientious mother."

"I want to be," replied Rachelle, "and wife, too."

John grinned. "Well, my position is such that I can state, there's no complaint with you in that role either."

"I wasn't fishing for that sort of compliment, dear," Rachelle smiled, "To show that it pleases me though, I'll sort your papers as soon as I finish the dishes. First though, I guess I'd better pick up these toys before we stumble over them."

Turning more serious, John told her, "No hurry, darling, there's all evening. I can't seem to get this editorial written anyway, so I suppose I could sort them. Maybe then, when I return to my writing, I'll be able to concentrate on it more."

"What's the write-up about, John?"

"That same old bickering that's been raging for over two years now between President Johnsons and Congress. I'm afraid they'll vote to impeach him yet."

"What's your own feeling about it, John? I mean your personal view, not something you'd write in a paper for everybody to read. Are your sentiments with the President or with Congress?"

"I really don't know, darling. Everything's in such a state of utter confusion and has been since the war ended, I find it hard to take sides. I believe Johnson tries though. Maybe it's the way he handles it. Anyway, remember with me, the world's happenings are very young. In fact, that aspect is what I have my mind on tonight, rather than this editorial."

Rachelle looked up from where she was squatted on the floor, putting Beth Anne's toys in a box. "Want to talk about it John?" she asked.

"There's not much to say, dear, I've been through the same ordeal more or less so many times, that I much prefer not to think about it or talk about it."

"Another family's contacted you," she said, "and wants to meet you. I'm sorry, John. But truly, I haven't written any more letters, after you asked me not to."

"I know you haven't, darling. It's not exactly that anyway, it's something else."

Rachelle rose from the floor. She pulled a chair out from the table and placing it close to him, she sat down and reached for his hand. "Tell me about it, John, I want to help if I can."

"Oh, it's too—well—farfetched, dear, to even think about, much less discuss. You'll probably think I've taken leave to my senses. I shouldn't have mentioned it."

"No, John, I won't think no such thing. I can see whatever it is, that it's very important to you. Please, let me share it."

"Well, I ran across a notice today that was taken from a South Carolina newspaper that I can't put out of my mind. A state senator, I really can't even remember his name now but the papers at the office, had run this notice in regard to his son who was listed among the missing at Gettysburg. HE's never had a trace of information concerning him since the battle. The part that almost made me have cold shivers, Rachelle, was the description of his son. I fitted it perfect!"

"A southerner, John?" Surprise covered Rachelle's face. "Yes, and form South Carolina at that! I warned you how dumb it would sound."

"It's no such thing, John. It's not foolish at all. You've just said that this man's descriptive features of his son conforms with yours in complete likeness."

"So, I have, dear. But, do you realize how many men there must've been at Gettysburg who had dark-blue eyes brown wavy hair, and a height near six feet, who were listed among the missing in the battle? Most of all, darling, is the question of location. This senator's from the South rather than the North." He sighed. Then, after a moment of pausing silence, he looked at Rachelle and smiled. "You didn't by any chance get your colors mixed up that day, did you? I couldn't have been wearing grey instead of blue?"

"Right this minute, John, I wish I could say that I did. Though southerner or not, dear, let's write to him, anyway!"

"No, I don't think we should, Rachelle. Suppose we did, just stop and ponder how preposterous that would seem to this man. A Yankee soldier writing to say he fits the description of a South Carolinian's missing son! And too, we must not rule out the fact that the majority of southerners took their defeat quite hard. In fact, the common belief is that most South Carolinians are regular hotheads when it comes to the subject of the war. You wouldn't want this man to come up here and shoot mine off! Would you?" He grinned.

"Oh, John, I see you're not going to take it seriously. In answer to your question about the possibility of his shooting you, no, I don't think I could bear that."

"Well, in that case," he laughed, "I think we'd better forget all about this South Carolina Senator. Who knows maybe I'll run across another one and it'll be from the right location." He paused again in soberness. "Better still, maybe one morning I'll wake in a sunrise of knowing who I am."

"I feel so helpless, John." Rachelle said.

"Don't, dear, because you're half of me and I fear, the stronger half. You're sunshine in rain, light in darkness, and comfort in pain." He leaned forward and kissed her on the cheek. "See what you do for me. After this little chat with you, I think now that I can write that article, so I'd better start while the thoughts are popping." He picked up his pen and paper.

She looked at him for a long moment. She rose. "I'll finish the dishes. Then, I'll sort your papers, John." "Thanks, dear." He replied.

Chapter Seven

Raw, snow-like wind whipped around the little house at Green Sea. Eliza, sitting in Martha's rocker beside the fireplace that Luke and Doss had built, let her eyes slowly lift from her baby's face to look through the window at the dismal December day. Her visage was grim and she was dressed mostly in mourning attire once more from her small black hat that was adorned with a few tiny black plumes and a wide long black ribbon that tied to the left side of her throat in a big bow—to her glossy black high button shoes. She was dressed to leave in a few minutes to attend the funeral of Doctor John Davis. Two days earlier in the late afternoon, the doctor had suddenly fell dead of a stroke. Doctor Davis had been in his own home and in the room that served as his office at the time of his death and Doctor Seth Roalf had been with him. Doctor Roalf had attended to the aged doctor at once, but all his efforts to revive him had been useless. Within a very short while, Doctor Davis was gone. Eliza's heart lifted somewhat in knowing that the good doctor, who she and the whole neighborhood had loved, had been in his home with Doctor Roalf and not alone when he had died. She also gave thanks that his death had been quick, sparing him a lot of suffering and pain that otherwise could have very well been in his case. She felt that Doctor Davis had done too many kind deeds for mankind for that, and that undoubtedly God had seen it likewise.

Her eyes came back to rest upon her baby who she held at her breast. She observed the zest in which he savored her abundant supply of milk. Yes, no wet-nurse for her. She was nursing her baby and both Doctor Davis and Luke had readily agreed with her decision, though Ruth or Bessie could have adequately supplied her baby, instead. Both couples, Charlie and Ruth and Sam and Bessie, had babies of their own now born within a few days of one another and within a period of less than one month of her own confinement. Doctor Davis had questioned her about nursing the baby a day or two after its birth, saying if she desired to have it done, he would dry up her milk, though he thought it would be better if she nursed him.

"Oh course, it's Eliza's decision," Luke volunteered, "But, in regard to the mother's health, my own opinion is that it's wiser not to go against what nature purposed."

Doctor Davis had sent Luke a keen glance, saying, "And, it's my opinion, Luke, that with your common sense, a whole lot of people would've been much better off had you chosen to been a doctor of medicine rather than serving the ills of the animal kingdom."

As she continued to stare at her robust and healthy baby still nursing at her breast, the day of its birth and the period that followed when her life had hung at a critical point for a near twenty-four hours, came to her mind. She was aware now that Luke, Doctor Davis, and everybody else who was close to her, had been held in a state of trial and suspense as they had feared for her life. All of it though had been foggy to her. She had hardly known when her baby had been paced at her overflowing breast and indeed could scarcely recall it even now. The only part of those hours that did seem to stick in her memory fairly vividly was the one time she had awakened to see the strain on Luke's face as he sat by her bedside. She had tried to reach Luke's hand and tell him she would be all right not to worry so, but in her extreme weakness she had failed. Vaguely, she could also remember the concerned face of Doctor Seth Roalf bending down over her. On that second day after her baby's birth, Doctor Davis taking caution and, in his desire, too, to consult with another doctor, had acted on his own and sent for Doctor Roalf to come to Green Sea. However, notwithstanding her fogginess of that difficult time, she felt that she knew all that had taken place, anyway. It was as though her mind had been clear as a bell, because Hannah had seen to that! She felt that Hannah might have spared her a few details, though this had not been the case. Hannah had told her everything! It was, "Mister Luke had don' dis an' Mister Luke had don' dat. Dat b'by an' y'u, too, would shonough di'd, ifn not ben fer Mister Luke!" Hannah had told her dozens of times. There was no question that Luke had become bigger than the whole world to Hannah after she viewed him delivering his own baby.

Luke had never discussed that trying ordeal with her, nor did she think he ever would. All he had said to her concerning it was to tell her he would not have wanted to live any longer had she not pulled through, and if he could help it she would not go through that torture ever again! Well, she would affirm that any aspect of that possibility surely did not seem likely, if one stop to consider the fact that Luke had not shared her bed since the baby had been born! And near Christmastide and Luke was still continuing to sleep on the couch away from her, it appeared that he had meant what he had said! Just the same, she had survived and even though her face was hung in grief and sorrow today, no one could say that she did not look the picture of health these days. Hence, the way she saw it, Luke was carrying his idea of protecting her from that sort of thing, a little too far! Yet, for all his making certain not to waver in his obvious stand that there would be no more babies conceived between them, she was certain that there had never been a man more happier or proud than Luke had been the day he took the baby in his arms and stood at the bedroom door, showing him off to the hands as they softly tread in and out the kitchen. To be sure they had given this fifth generation Carson baby a thorough look, saying, while they did so, that he, "Sho favored Miss Eliza." Though she would have preferred their baby looking like his father, she was going to have to agree that the hands had been correct in their observation. The baby had no Heyward feature about him. He appeared to be all Carson.

There had been much discussion and even a small amount of controversy concerning the baby's name and christening. Her wish had been to name the baby for Luke. His wish had been to name it for her family. And also, they both had thoughts of naming the baby for Doctor Davis as well. So, they had compromised, with them finally settling upon, Carson Luke Davis Heyward! A rather long name, but they were already tagging the baby Carr, a good portion of the time, with Carson being said less and less.

Apparently, although Luke had been a Baptist for a good many years now, he had not laid all his Episcopalian upbringing aside since he had insisted on their baby being christened in the church. He had taken the matter up with Reverend Johnson when the reverend had come to Green Sea shortly following the baby's birth.

"Well, as you realize, Luke, our faith does not sanction the baptizing of infants. On the other hand, neither does it say that a baby can't be dedicated to God and blessed in God's house. If this is your wish, I'll take it up with the other deacons of the church, and let you know."

Luke had become a deacon in his church, long back. "Thank you, Reverend Johnson. It is my wish and Eliza agrees with me," Luke said. "I shall feel; then, that I've done all that is required of me in that respect until he's old enough to form his own opinions toward his salvation."

The other deacons had approved and the entire congregation had seemed to nod their approval; also, the Sunday that Reverend Johnson had announced it, and even though it was not expected to be a long blessing and prayer at all; even so, the reverend—true to his style of doing things—had not stopped til he had made quite a ceremony out of it! Nevertheless, she would never forget the pride and joy that spread across Doctor Davis' face as Reverend Johnson had declared the baby's name, introducing him to the congregation.

Seeing that the baby had fallen fast asleep, Eliza eased her breast away from his mouth and while she placed it back inside her clothes and buttoned her dress; she glanced through the window again and saw Luke coming toward the house with the buggy. At the same time, she heard Hannah's step upon the back porch and noticed how softly Hannah opened and closed the door against the strong wind and by habit how she had already started to putter around in the kitchen. Hannah was to stay with the baby while she and Luke attended the funeral service for Doctor Davis. They both had agreed that the weather was too cold to take the baby out, therefore, making it necessary that she nurse him just before leaving the house.

Despite Eliza's sorrow over Doctor Davis, hearing Hannah moving about in the kitchen had brought her mind upon Hannah's reaction to the stork bringing so many babies to Green Sea that fall. Every time she thought about it she could not help becoming a little amused. The coming of the three babies so closely together had sent Hannah's eyes examining and moving rather frequently upon her two daughters-in-law. But, after a few weeks had passed, Hannah's face dropped in disappointment as she concluded that she had been looking in vain. She began to grumble fairly often over her dashed hopes. One day as she was puttering around the kitchen and grumbling as usual, Luke had finally told her that it could very well be some physical problem that was preventing her in becoming a grandmother—that she should stop accusing her sons and, as for that matter, Prudence and Daisy; also, of being weaklings in regard to the matter of begetting offspring! Hannah had slowly raised from the hearth where she was busy among the pots and pans helping prepare dinner with nose in air and lips puffed out like sails, had let Luke know she thought he was talking nonsense!

"No, Mister Luke," she said, "Y'u be wong dis one time. All dem y'unguns, my boys an' dem gals j'st pl'in sorry lot!"

Luke had laughed and shook his head, realizing he might as well have kept his mouth shut in defending the bareness of Hannah's family.

Eliza started to rise from the rocker, but at the same instant, Luke opened the front door and quickly stepping into the room closed the door and held out his arms toward her, saying, "Let me have him, dear, I'll put him to bed while you gather the rest of your things." As he bent down and gently took the baby from her arms, he added, "Darling, wrap yourself up well, it's bitter cold outside. I have self-doubt over your braving that weather, anyway."

"Doctor Davis was always so good to me, Luke, I feel I have to go despite the weather," she told him, turning to pick up her heavy long black cape and gloves.

"I know, dear," he replied, as he laid the baby down in the handsome cradle that Matthew and Amy had brought upon their first visit to their new grandchild. The cradle having been placed closer to the fireplace that morning due to the severe cold spell.

Now heavily downed in her woolens, Eliza stepped to Luke's side and saw that his big strong hands had snuggled the baby down in its blankets with the mastery of the most adept nursemaid. Instinctively, he reached his arm out and laid it around her waist, while he stood beside the cradle staring down at the baby.

"I'm glad he has part of Doctor Davis' name, aren't you sweetheart?" He asked.

"Yes, I am, Luke, I was thinking about it before you came in."

Without saying a word to anyone and without so much as a whish of her many skirts or a tread of her rough shoes, Hannah had moved into the room with a big basket of mending and placing it on the floor at her feet she had comfortably settled herself in Martha's rocker. Doss had come into the kitchen from the back porch, which was usually his forte, and settled himself quite snugly in the corner by the kitchen hearth.

Although Luke appeared to go against his will to do so, he turned away from the sleeping baby, saying, "We'd better get started, sweetheart."

Hannah noticed that they both turned back at the door and looked longingly at the cradle. She merely nodded her head and smiled at them before they slipped through the door. That was all that had been necessary on her part in letting them know that she would be immovable between their baby and any danger. Knowing Doss was stationary in the kitchen as well, they were doubly certain that the baby was in safe hands.

As quickly as Eliza's feet hit the first doorstep, Luke saw her drop her head against the stinging cold wind.

"Come on, dear, let's get to the buggy fast, before you chill," he said, hurrying her along beside him in his long strides. "I've put side curtains up and Doss has the foot warmer packed with hot brick, so maybe it won't be too uncomfortable for you."

"What would we do without Doss and Hannah, Luke?"

"That's a good question, dear," he replied, helping her into the buggy.

The buggy was cozy. Somehow, fitted so tightly in the curve of Luke's arm that he had dropped firmly around her as he held onto the reins with his other hand; the feel of his body next to hers as she nestled warmly against him with the buggy robe tucked securely about her, Eliza felt an intimacy with him again—something that she had not felt for such a long time and had missed—a duration of time that she would rather forget than think about. It suddenly occurred to her though that this was the first time that she had been entirely alone with Luke since the baby had been born. She thought perhaps Luke was sensing the same suchlike feeling, because he had already turned his head to her several times and smiled; and once, had even bent down and kissed her! Luke had always been very attentive and affectionate toward her though. Still, as much as she was unwilling to admit it, in recent months he had been more prone to affect this side of his nature while they were in the company of others such as when Hannah was around the little house or as they were now rather than when they were alone with one another in a more propitious setting. Even so, since she loved him so deeply, any irritation that his behavior aroused in her at those times, usually evaporated as quickly as it flamed over her. At any rate, besides the coziness of the buggy or any other sensation it may effect, the very purpose for their being there should bring a message to Luke telling him more than any words she may ever express to him concerning this first personal problem that had arose in her marriage—a subject by its nature that she found so difficult to discuss with Luke. Well, she would wait and see if the circumstances that had brought them together in having this cozy buggy ride would change anything. Surely it would.

The church was crowded notwithstanding the weather. Doctor Davis had had a wide circle of friends and it appeared that the majority had come to pay their last respects. Among the numerous faces there were few that did not show the mark of grief for the man who had brought some portion of comfort to one and all alike. Even Reverend Johnson seemed to be more shaken and subdued than usual, and to the surprise of the mourners, cut the service shorter than was his custom. The reverend had attempted to convey in his message that Doctor Davis was merely parting from his many friends and this was not the end. But, as Eliza observed Luke, Bruce, Bill Clarendon, Brent Cooper, Doctor Seth Roalf, and Frank, granted Doctor Davis had been one of the few people who Frank admired, step forward to bear the casket down the aisle taking it to the small cemetery plot on the church grounds where Doctor Davis would be laid to rest beside his long-departed wife, she felt nothing but a sense of finality with the loved doctor

Everything, the reposing hush, the wind singing and whispering around the church, the stone-cold day, final farewell seemed to be manifest in all of it.

The burial had been rather swift, nothing like the day that Anne Carson had been buried; and mourners were beginning to turn away. The varicolored crepe paper arrangements that Eliza and the other women of the community had made up the preceding day were being placed; and once they were settled upon the cold banked mound, the reds, the pinks, the yellows and greens, to Eliza the warmth of color did seem after all to lend something to the poignant somberness, a promise of something other than finality. As she looked upon the bank of vividness through her tears and her thoughts of past association with the departed doctor, she became aware that a low, soft voice at her elbow was calling her name.

"Lu—cy, I'm so sorry, I didn't hear you. I didn't know you were here. I hadn't even seen you."

"I took a back pew, Eliza. When I arrived, the Church was almost full. I've been unable to reach you, till now."

Although Lucy's cheeks had filled out some, Eliza saw that the sadness in her eyes had never disappeared. She stepped closer to Lucy's side and laying an arm about her waist, she said, "How have you been? I thought I'd be seeing a lot of you after you came home in September, but I haven't. I don't believe I've seen you but once or twice. I suppose that in your teaching at Drakston Hall and my being a new mother."

Lucy's face seemed to grow lighter as she asked, "And, how is that adorable baby of yours? I see you don't have him with you."

"He's fine, growing like jimson weed. No, Luke and I thought it best not to bring him out."

"I think that was wise. I'm sure I've never felt a colder day unless it was snowing. I found that out early this morning when I went to Drakston Hall to pick up some schoolwork that I forgot yesterday. It needed my attention. I've dismissed the children until next Monday due to the weather."

Eliza turned her eyes back to the grave.

"I think I miss him already, Lucy."

"We all will, Eliza."

"I know Father's sad and upset, too, that he couldn't be here." Eliza said.

"I've been looking for Mr. Carson, I wondered why he wasn't here."

"He's in Washington for a few days, Lucy. Luke sent a wire to Columbia as quickly as possible, but he and Aunt Amy were still unable to get here in time for the funeral. Aunt Amy wired Father, then she wired us back."

Somehow, Eliza sensed a tone of anxiousness in Lucy's voice when she asked, "But, Mr. Carson and Miss Amy will be home for Christmas, won't they?"

"Oh yes, as far as I know now, nothing has changed toward that, and I can hardly wait. You know, Lucy, this visit is going to be special because they're bringing that little Whit to Green Sea for the first time. Father planned to bring him long before this, but things didn't work

"Yes, I know."

"That's right! I keep forgetting that you're well acquainted with Whit. Tell me, Lucy, what's he like? I haven't seemed to be able to put that thought far from my mind, since I truly knew the adoption was final."

A trace of a smile played on Lucy's face.

"You remind me of Martha so much. The nearer to Christmas the more she talks about the same thing. I'm positive she's asked me that very questions a hundred times. I'll tell you what I tell her, once you see Whit, you'll see why your father and Martha's mother couldn't resist him. I've missed him so much since leaving Columbia. Anyway, you, Martha, and Frank will not be disappointed."

Luke and Bruce, after seeing that the wreaths and everything was in order with the graves, turned at that moment to join Eliza and Lucy, with Bruce saying,

"I'm ready to leave now, sis, if you're ready. I'd better get you out of this wind, anyway, or Martha's going to have company with her cold. That goes for you, too, Eliza. Luke and I are used to the outside, but you women aren't."

"How is Martha, Bruce? Tell her I've missed her being here." Eliza said.

"Well, her cold does seem to be rather severe. I think she'll be all right though."

"I hope so, tell her; also, I'll see her in a few days to plan for our parent's homecoming." "Sure thing, Eliza." Bruce said, turning away. "You two take care, come on, sis."

"See you, Bruce." Called Luke, gathering Eliza close. "Come on, dear, we'd better get started, too."

Eliza took a long look at the grave though before she finally turned away.

On their way to the buggy, Eliza's eyes found the back of Doctor Seth Roalf as he hurried ahead of them. She noticed though instead of the doctor going in the direction of his buggy which was parked near theirs, he cut across the church grounds toward the Wilton coach where Caroline was standing beside its door, ready to enter. No doubt the doctor had asked Caroline to wait a moment, because she looked toward him and took her hand from the door handle. Suddenly, as Eliza looked toward them and even though she had never had the first thought in relation to it, she did not see the couple as they were—dressed in heavy winter clothing—their heads huddled together against the cold winter day. She saw Caroline in a lovely dress, holding a bouquet of pretty spring flowers in one hand while she gave the other to a beaming Doctor Seth Roalf. The vision did not startle her or upset her. Nor did she say anything about it to anyone, even Luke. Still, she could not understand why one second she felt happy about it, then the next second she had misgivings about it.

Going back to Green Sea though, Eliza nestled close to Luke's side once more, did discuss a lot of things with him. They talked about Doctor Davis not to mention several other subjects. All the same, the one matter that she would have liked to discuss with him and the one thing that was beginning to bother her a great deal, that subject failed to be mentioned. Nonetheless, that night at bedtime, despite their failing to bring the matter up, she was certain that Luke would come back to their bed. Lying awake, she waited and waited to hear him step upon the floor.

After hours had passed though or what seemed like hours to her, she did not bother to look at the clock, and he still had not come to her, she got up and lifted her baby from its cradle which at bedtime had been placed back in its customary place beside her bed. She laid the baby in her bed and crawled under the covers beside it. Hugging the warm and sleeping baby closely to the curve of her body, she lay once more for a long, long time crying silent tears upon its blanket. It was the one single time in her marriage that she felt Luke had failed her. She had yearned for the comfort that his nearness always gave her, and she had received nothing but cold, anxious waiting.

Her yearning for him had not been any more alive than Luke's had been for her. Even so, in his endeavor to protect her—not being able to forget less than three months earlier he had literally held his breath at times for fear of losing her—he could not bring himself to yield to his will and go to her. No question though had he known the depth of her anguish had turned to tears, he would have relented and chanced his stand. Granted, his sleep had been long in coming, too. Lying awake for hours, he had struggled with his conscience, fully aware that his behavior was distressing her deeply. In a hundred years, the thought would never have entered that he would see the day dawn when he would hesitate to take Eliza in his arms for fear of it resulting in their conceiving a baby. But that was precisely the case. Still, seeing his alluring wife in her regained radiant health and knowing her for the vital and passionate woman that she was, he recognized that his long continency was growing more fragile by the day and was reaching its limit. He thought that any man who was in his right mind and found himself in the same situation would never acknowledge otherwise.

Dawn saw him still having reached no sensible solution to his problem.

The sun shone warmly in a sapphire-blue sky. Standing at the window, Eliza was thinking no white Christmas this year when suddenly she spied the Drakston's elegant coach approaching her front door. Frank made certain that it was ever stationed and waiting at the depot for his mother's arrival, though he was seldom at the train station himself. Why Frank preferred to greet his mother no place else except Drakston Hall was something that only Frank knew the answer to—no doubt just another trait of his odd personality.

Dashing out the door and down the steps, Eliza saw that Matthew; agile as ever, had already planted his feet upon the ground before the carriage had hardly stopped and had swung a little boy down from the seat and stood him near at hand. The child looking somewhat withdrawn, now had one small hand clutched to the leg of her father's trousers, while he had turned back to assist his wife in descending from the carriage. Racing on to meet them, it was a good feeling to see her father's beaming face. Though the mansion was gone, following that first time when he had come home after its burning, she or no one else was ever to see despair on his face again concerning its loss. She noticed now that his expression was as bright as the sunny sky that draped the world above them. And, it was such a delightful joy to have him gathering her closely once more as he said to her, "Happy birthday, dear. It's so wonderful to see you looking so well." Then, she was swept into Aunt Amy's arms with her repeating a similar phrase, while she herself said, "Merry Christmas, Father, Merry Christmas Aunt Amy, welcome home!"

Now though, her father was taking the little boy by the hand and saying, "Mary Eliza darling, this is Whitney, Whit Carson, that you've heard so much about in the past year."

Eliza's face began to grow as serious and thoughtful as the child's solemn one that was turned up toward her while he stared at her out of deep-set brown eyes. For a moment she stared back, taking in the olive complexion and golden curls. In his light-blue suit, she thought a more handsome child she had yet to see. There was something about him though, that she could not quite grasp. She also began to feel as if she might start weeping, as her heart swelled within her.

She squatted down.

"Whitney Carson," she said. "Whit, I like your name as much as I like you. Welcome to Green Sea, dear. I bet you'll like Green Sea, once you see all the animals we have here." She did not push him too hard, taking the casual approach. "We have ducks, chickens, horses, pigs, and lots of things here that I'm sure you don't have in the city,

I'll have to show them to you right away. Would you like that?"

Whit merely stared and said nothing.

She tried again to win him over.

"Well, what do you say we all go inside? I know we have something in there that you'd like to see and perhaps hold in your arms. We have a little baby boy in there just waiting for you to see him. Would you like that?"

A slow smile began to appear on Whit's face, spreading wider and wider and, as Eliza saw it grow, she was positive she had seen the same smile before that—a smile that rapidly set her mind to work-stirring her to her very toes. Scattered words of previous conversations between her and her father in regard to Whit's adoption began to be uppermost in her thoughts. In addition to the classified information that he had spoken mystery about that surrounded this little boy. Then, all of a sudden, as Whit continued to smile at her with his brown eyes still gazing into hers as she stared him back, a good part of the mystery began to clear out; she was certain once she had time to sort out all the things that were running through her head—the long transition of adoption—the transfer of this child from its mother to her father and her aunt, that everything where Whit was concerned would fall in place. She knew she was staring and waiting too long in taking her quest inside; yet, she seemed helpless to move, for the moment anyway, in finally realizing the true circumstances of the adoption.

While her father stood in motionless silence, she barely heard Aunt Amy saying, "Eliza dear, it's apparent that Whit liked you upon first sight. He's usually very slow in making up with strangers."

"Yes—he would be—I mean—I hope he likes me," she replied. Her heart felt as if it were weeping tears inside her. "Because—well—I love him already."

Suddenly, she did rise, throwing her arms around her father's shoulder.

"Oh Father!" she said, "You have borne so much!"

"Then, you do understand, dear, what I so much wanted to tell you, but on my word of honor I was prevented from doing so?" He asked, giving silent thanks for such a wise daughter, as profound relief flowed through him.

"Yes, Father, the most important part, anyway."

"Well, since you're my only living child, I've prayed that it will be so. You see, the closest person to this child excepting Amy and myself, has gone to great length and through a lot of suffering I may add, as well as personal sacrifice, in order to protect him; and I cannot break her trust."

"I understand, Father, and I love you for it." She kissed him on the cheek. Then, she turned and embraced her aunt likewise.

"You're a truly good person, too, Aunt Amy, and I'm so glad you and my father walked into Whit's life."

"Thank you, dear, so am I," smiled Aunt Amy. "Whit's enriched our already wonderful marriage since he came to live with us. We feel very lucky and fortunate to have him entrusted to us."

Eliza turned back to Whit, squatting down before him again.

"Whit, may I hold your hand," she asked, "While we all go inside, so we can have a look at that baby?"

Whit slowly drew forward a plump little hand. Eliza wrapped her own hand around it, closing it tightly inside her palm. And, as she rose and walked down the walkway beside him while her father and aunt followed closely behind, she looked down at Whit's gold curls and told herself that in time they would for sure turn to a rich shade of light brown.

Once everybody had stepped through the door, it seemed that the meeting outside had never taken place and Whit had been accustomed to coming to Green Sea for the entire period of his young life. The atmosphere was warm and pleasant, with the little house smelling and looking like Christmas in every nook and corner. Holly and candles were on the mantel, mistletoe hanging above the doorways and a brightly decorated Christmas tree standing in a corner of the living room. The apprehension that had gripped Matthew while Eliza had stared at Whit, had long vanished. His joy over seeing his grandchild and daughter and the pleasure he took in observing what she and Luke had achieved in their living quarters, was very much evident and he told her so again and again. He did notice though that she had not hung the portraits. Though he did not mention it, nor did he ask to see them. On second thought he reasoned they would have crowded the walls of the small house too much. After a lot of exclaiming and cooing had been done over the baby while it lay in its cradle kicking and gurgling happily, he and Amy both went to the kitchen to greet Hannah, Prudence, and Daisy all of whom were busy in helping Eliza prepare pies, cakes, roasting meats and fowl for the family dinner and gathering that would be held at Oak Grove the next day. If the mansion at Green Sea had still been standing the dinner would have been held there. But, besides Eliza being without adequate silver, china, and crystal to set a table, the house at Green Sea was too small to accommodate everyone.

Thus, she and Martha had chosen Oak Grove for the family gathering. Another decision they had made concerned their birthday celebrations. With the mansion at Green Sea gone, the overwhelming fact that Eliza was a new mother this year which curtailed her coming and going to a great extent and especially at night, and the sad death of Doctor Davis having occurred between their birthdays, they agreed to dispense with the birthday celebrating for a while, anyway.

As well as bringing gifts for Eliza, Luke, and the baby—the packages having already been laid under the Christmas tree—Matthew and Amy brought gifts to the former slaves and their families, also. Matthew sent Doss to fetch the big canvas sack from the carriage. Doss came plodding back in right away with the sack throwed over his shoulders. He set it down in the center of the kitchen floor, whereupon Matthew sorted out the gifts, presenting Doss, Hannah, Prudence, and Daisy with theirs on the spot. He gave Doss the honor of distributing the others around the plantation, explaining to Doss who was to receive what.

While all this had been going on in the kitchen, much to Whit's delight, Eliza had kept her word to him. She had lifted Whit up in Luke's big chair and placed the baby in his arms. Whit promptly clasped his small short arms around it, though she sat on the stool at his little feet that scarcely reached halfway in the chair's bottom, helping him support the baby by holding her hand against its body. Presently, Matthew and Amy returned to the living room, and Eliza seeing that Whit's arms were wearing of this unimaginable novelty of holding a real live baby, suggested their putting the baby back in its cradle. Whit smiled that slow smile again and let go his arm's burden. Without anyone gesturing or suggesting that he do so, he then crawled down from the chair and stood waiting till Matthew got settled in its comfortable cushions. Then, he crawled up again and settled himself upon Matthew's lap. It was obvious Whit adored Matthew. By the same token, it was unhidden that Matthew adored Whit.

Hannah brought in a big silver tray loaded with cookies and a variety of sliced cake along with the coffee service and a glass of milk for Whit, placing everything on a console table that set in the center of the room. While Eliza served it, they all enjoyed a short but pleasant visit. Her father had already explained that their visit this day would have to be rather short, because they still had to stop at Drakston Hall a brief while before proceeding on to Oak Grove, where they would be lodging for the greater part of their homecoming. Eliza understood all this. She had no place for them to lodge. Matthew did take time though to catch up on recent happenings, including the death of his old and close friend, Doctor Davis. Eliza saw the unmistakable sadness in his eyes as she told him the circumstances. Time passed all too quickly though for daughter and father. It was time to leave, Whit was beginning to nod.

"Father, if you'd like to, we could put him to bed here for the time being."

No, I guess not, dear," he replied, looking at his daughter deeply. "I suppose we should be getting him on to Oak Grove as soon as possible."

She held her eyes straight to his, saying, "I Understand, Father."

Gathering the half-asleep Whit closer in his arms, Matthew rose from his chair.

Eliza and Aunt Amy rose, too, and Eliza still observing her father, gave forth with a light chuckle. "It seems so strange, Father, to see you playing the role of a new father."

"I imagine so, but it could keep me from growing old, you know," he laughed.

"I don't think you need to be concerned about that too much, Matthew," said Aunt Amy. It seems that years tend to subtract instead of add, when it comes to my father's appearance." Eliza agreed.

Matthew's grin spread somewhat as he made a start toward the door.

"Would it were my arms were unoccupied, I'd show you two women how much I appreciate the flattery. I might add though, nothing keeps a man looking younger than when he is flanked by such beauty as you two can claim to."

"Never mind! Matthew," said his wife. "In spite of your chivalry, Eliza and I meant every word because it's true."

Eliza walked on outside with them and as they were nearing the coach Matthew changed the subject, when he said to her, "Mary Eliza dear, tell Luke we're sorry we missed him, but we'll be looking forward to seeing him tomorrow though."

"I will, Father, and I'm sorry, too, that he isn't here. You might still see him, since he told me it would probably be late in the day before he returns from Oak Grove. Bruce had several head of livestock that he wanted Luke to attend to today."

"Well, maybe so, if we get moving. Come on Amy dear. Happy birthday, again, dear," he called as the carriage pulled away.

By then, Whit's eyes had opened wider. He raised his little hand and began to wave. Eliza stood and waved back at him till the coach had passed from view, thinking as she did so that God did truly work in a mysterious way. It was true, what had been made evident to her on this day had unnerved her, distressing her deeply when she gave way to it—fleeting moments of thinking what might have been while she had looked upon Whit lying in her father's arms. Yet, on the other hand, she felt a deep thankfulness, too, that Whit after all would not be denied his rightful station in life. Three people had had enough love and courage in their heart and enough trust in one another to make an endeavor to do what was best for Whit. As she turned back and walked inside the house again, she was asking herself, why had she not been more startled? Was it because in the depth of her being, she had known all along from the first mentioning of the adoption? Yes, she thought that this was indeed the case even though she had dismissed it from her mind, telling herself that her wild imagination was running away again. Would Martha, Frank, Luke, and all the rest see the real truth concerning Whit? Perhaps they would; then again, it could be they would not suspicion a thing. Well, she could not discuss it with anyone. It was a situation that she was helpless to do anything about, except accept it and keep quiet as her father and aunt were doing! However, since there was nothing she could do about Whit but love him, in the meantime she thought it would be wise of her if she got busy at trying to figure out what to do about the problem between her and Luke—a situation that was growing more tense and worse by the day! With their beautiful and healthy baby, what should be their happiest Christmas, from all appearances would be their worst! She thought she had succeeded in hiding her unhappiness from her father and she was glad. Besides, the delicacy of the problem would have prevented her

From discussing it with him, anyway. She surely could not tell him or anybody else, as for that matter, that her husband had quit making love to her! Even so, she had come to reason that it was high time she affected some more in doing something about it other than waiting for him to come to her. But what? She simply could not bring herself to ask Luke to come back and share their bed as her husband. Call it self-respect, pride, or whatever—when it came to that sort of business, she supposed her inbred dignity prevailed over and above any biological urge she may have. Still, by the same sign, she had no desire to share only a platonic relationship with Luke, either.

Maybe Luke saw her no longer as an attractive woman. She had not thought of that! No, how could she have such a silly thought as that, when he told her as often as he did, how pretty she was? Well, she thought she should risk laying that matter aside for the time being and think about what she was going to wear to Oak Grove tomorrow.

She walked over to the wardrobe, a generous and handsome gift that the Wiltons had made to she and Luke when the mansion burned, and began shifting various items around. Unlike when they had lived in the mansion, she and Luke shared the same wardrobe now. Moreover, it held the majority of their clothing. Suddenly, her eyes fell upon the beautiful blue peignoir set that her father had given her when Luke was gone to war. It had been taken to the wash house to be hand washed the day the mansion had burned; therefore, it was one among the few pieces of her clothing that had not been destroyed in the fire. Even though Luke had always remarked how pretty she was the few times she had worn it, it had been hanging far back in the wardrobe for months and months. It was lovely as ever, rather revealing though, she thought, as she kept staring at it. While a thought began to play around in her head, she reached inside and drew the somewhat seductive garment from the wardrobe. Holding it up to her, she walked over to the dresser and studied herself in the mirror. Luke was right, the color did become her. She did look pretty. Yet, it seemed her prettiness alone had not been enough to urge Luke back to their bed, lately! Perhaps he needed a little novelty something from the familiar to move him. Yes, she was pretty certain that was what he needed, and she thought this lounging set would help a great deal if not do the trick! There was more than one way to catch a mouse! She wondered why she had not though of doing something like that before this. Tonight, she would see just how pretty Luke thought she looked! Meanwhile, she must forget about that though and do what she started to do in the first place—select something to wear to Oak Grove. She most certainly could not go dressed in a negligee!

She hurried back to the wardrobe.

Supper was over. Luke, an attentive father, amused the baby while she readied up the table and did the dishes. Then, she nursed the baby and bedded him down in his cradle for the remainder of the night, during the time that Luke was taking his bathe and changing into his nightshirt, robe and slippers. Lukc came back to the kitchen, and together they packed the bulk of food that was to be taken to Oak Grove the next day.

"Luke, I'll go change into something more comfortable now, since all this is over with," she said, tucking the red checked cloth over and around the huge wicker basket as Luke set it aside. "Then, we'll relax by the fire for a while. Listen," she went on, "since we'll be rather busy in the morning, making ready to go to Oak Grove, what do you think about opening our gifts tonight?"

"Sure, doll, I was going to suggest the same thing." He laughed, "We'll sprawl down by the hearth and see what Santa decided to leave us on his first trip down our new and fairly clean chimney."

"Well," she laughed too. "I can hardly wait to see if he decided whether we've been naughty or good. I won't be long, Luke, I'll hurry!"

"And, while you're doing that," he said, "I'm going to fix us something to drink. Besides Christmas and your birthday, too, we should pledge honor to a lot of other blessing as well."

She called back, "That's so true, Luke," as she hurried from the kitchen.

He was sitting in his easy chair with a full wine glass in each hand waiting, when she to his astonishment—seeming to be unmindful of the flowing chiffon hugging her curves—breezed by him and took her seat opposite his chair. Though he was far from being cool and dispassionate to her attire he; nevertheless, appeared to be as he fixed his eyes upon her and leaned forward, handing her wine glass to her.

Rather slowly, he settled back in his chair again and raised his glass to hers.

"Merry Christmas, darling, happy birthday and many happy returns, but above all, thanks for that little fellow in the next room," he said, somewhat soberly, though he was still giving her a steady eye.

Over the top of her glass of Medeiva, she sent him a lovely smile. Then, she leaned forward and clicked her glass against his—her full bosom swelling over the plunging neckline of her thin gown as she did so.

Putting the glass to her lips, she let a small sip trickle down her throat before she replied rather coyly, "Thank you, Luke. But, as far as that little fellow in the next room is concerned, I'd be the first to say that I didn't achieve that, all by myself!"

While he never once let his eyes leave her and without so much as a sign of a smile in addition to making no comment to her remark, he took a fairly big swig from his glass and reached down and set it upon the hearth beside his chair. As he continued to stare at her and what to her seemed like an infinite silence, he finally said, "Set your glass down, darling, and come over here!"

She did as he had commanded, settling her glass down upon the heart, too. She got up and slowly crossed the distance between them and stood before him in silence.

He reached up and pulled her down upon his lap.

Cradling her tightly in his arms and between brushing her face with light kisses, he told her, "You're very enticing tonight, Mrs. Heyward. I'd say instead of looking like the twenty-five-year-old mother that you are, you look more like the sixteen year old girl that I fell in love with on the trail at Windsor."

Upon his last word, his kisses began to get bolder and bolder, giving her no chance to reply and; as they grew bolder still, the words she might have said were forgotten as she locked both arms around his neck and clung to him in a rising wave of long starved passion. He gathered her closer to him and rose with her from his chair, his intention to take her to their bed. However, once he was on his feet, he never took another step. Gentle, but at the same time somewhat quickly, too, he laid her down upon the rug that lay in the front of the hearth. He drew the folds of sheer chiffon away, exposing her nakedness. And, finding himself not in the glow of firelight but in the luminous power of the treasured gem lying before him, he savored the hunger of his desire for her body some few minutes before he mounted her and took her rather swiftly, in a bursting surge of rampant rapture.

Leastwise, she did feel pleasured and desired once more; yet, by no means did she feel completely satiated. She lifted her eyes to look at him and suddenly, feeling as though her person were far removed from her savage like behavior, she fiercely drew him back to her in cries of passionate demands to him.

He most willingly obliged her.

A long while later, as they still lay in one another's arms, he heard her say lowly in his ear," Luke—"

"Yes, darling."

"Will you promise me something?"

"If I possibly can, love."

"Will you promise that we'll never share again the kind of relationship that has existed in our marriage for the past three months?"

He let a long silence fall between them.

"Well, Luke?" She urged.

Her question had made him aware of something he had completely forgotten in his fiery copulation with her again, what he had strived and hoped to protect her from, their conceiving another baby any time soon. But, for all that, he was aware now that his long continency had run its course; for the present anyhow, because their senses had been too keenly awakened to each other's flesh once more, to live under the same roof with one another, vital and healthy, and deny sexual assuagement. In truth, he did not know how to answer her. He felt that it was not necessary to explain his actions of late to her, nor did he have any desire to. To talk about his fears, his anxieties, and her near death; to him, it would have spoiled the unique intimacy of their coupling together. Then again, he thought she did deserve to hear a few words fall from his lips, if merely touching upon the subject. But he was already planning to add a measure of teasing to what he did tell her.

"That's hard to do, dear, as none of us know what situations may arise, though I do want you to know that these past months without our making love together, have been long, difficult ones for me. Anyway—"

"Well she interrupted, "can't we say under the same circumstances, then?"

He thought for a moment.

"All right," he said, "We'll say under the same circum—stances. As I was going to say though, in case you should conclude that I'm shirking my duty from time to time, all you have to do is don this seductive outfit and start prancing!"

"Luke Heyward!" she shrieked. Her scheme had been as clear to Luke as if she had set a red light in her bedroom window, luring him forward, she was thinking.

Luke saw the sudden blush upon her cheeks and; in his eye, this rare personality trait, a passionate uninhibited warmth combined with delicate modesty, was one of her most appealing charms.

"Oh, darling," he laughed, tousling her hair. "Let's finish our wine and open our gifts."

They released one another and sat up, reaching for their drinks. They found that in the warmth of the fireplace, the wine had become fairly hot. They laughed about it though as they clicked their glasses together again and drank the warm contents down rather swiftly. Then, Luke jumped up and carted the Christmas packages over to the hearth, where they still sat upon the rug and opened them. He derived a lot of joy from seeing the glow of surprise in Eliza's eyes, as she saw what he had given her.

"Oh Luke—How pretty!" She exclaimed, her breathe holding in astonishment as she drew the navy-blue dress and cape to match, both trimmed in white stitching, from the box. Moreover, there was also a pretty hat to complete the outfit. Finally, she gave a long sigh. "But—Luke, you shouldn't have spent so much on me, darling."

"It's not that much, dear, and besides, although I appreciate the coat that Caroline gave to you after the fire, I wanted you to have another color other than black."

I know, Luke," she replied, aware by this time that he did not care for the color black in no case. "I'll wear all this tomorrow, Luke, just for you. Thank you, darling."

She leaned over and kissed him.

"And, you'll be the prettiest woman there, Mrs. Heyward," he told her, turning aside to hold up the handsome blue sweater again, that she had knitted for him. "And, as for myself, I'll leave that for others to decide, but I'm positive this sweater is going to look top-notch with my dark-blue trousers. Thank you again, dear, and for the fine imported tobacco pipe, too."

Suddenly, the clock setting above their heads on the mantel peeled its chimes.

Gosh!" Luke said, jumping upon his feet. "We've cheered Christmas in! It's twelve O'clock! Come on, dear, we'd better get to bed."

He gave her his hand.

Still sitting on the floor, she looked up at him and putting her hand in his, she said, "This is truly a Merry Christmas, Luke."

He smiled down at her.

"Yes, darling, it truly is," he replied.

And so, Luke's seed lay deep within her once again—taking root that same night, to sprout and start growing through long winter nights when she lay wrapped in his arms and through short winter days that seemed to her as though they had been set to notes of music—time that passed all too quickly—falling into spring time and Luke was saying, as he hurriedly got up from the dinner table since he was ever busy these days, "Doll, I'll be gone to Oak Grove, most all afternoon. It appears the mating season has given our Bessy the urge to pay a visit to Bruce's Samson!"

While he bent down to brush her cheek with a kiss, she remarked, "That means she'll be having a calf in November."

"Well—yes—I suppose so, dear," What an odd remark, he though.

"Luke, I know you need what ready cash we have to get the crop planted and gathered, but you're going to have to buy another cow that'll give us fresh milk when Bessy can't. We're going to need milk daily."

"Well, if you say so, dear, but we won't be without milk too long."

"That's true, and you and I could certainly do without, but Carr can't. I'm going to have to wean him a lot sooner than I had counted on. My milk may not be sufficient for him now. I pray he gets through the summer months all right, because I surely won't be able to nurse him all summer long!"

He walked back to his chair and sat down, the same old fear gripping him. He looked across the table at her. What a fool he was, he was thinking, living in a fool's paradise again, let fall what may! Although she was still slim as a reed, he should have noticed her paleness and especially the food she had pushed aside on her plate! He wanted to shout "No" over and over, but heard himself asking as calmly as he could, "Eliza darling, you're not—you're not going to be having another baby this soon?"

She raised her eyes to meet his.

"Yes, Luke, I'm pregnant again! It appears, darling, that once I got started, I'm not going to stop!"

"When—from all signs, I'd say three months! Of course, I'm not sure."

"Three months! Good Lord, darling! Carr won't be six-months-old till next week! That means you'll be having another baby in a year or maybe less!"

She could see nothing on his face but terror.

"Luke dear, don't panic. I realize I put you through many anxious hours when Carr was born, but he was the first. They say first babies are never easy. This time I'm sure it'll be different."

He rested his elbows on the table and let his face drop in his hands. Several minutes passed before he raised his head to say, "It's all my fault! You shouldn't be having another baby for years, if ever! No woman should have a baby every year, least of all you!"

His head fell into his hands again. His voice the ring of near vehemence. She had no way of knowing what thoughts Luke had held for their future nor; in truth, did she know what she had expected, either. But, in any case, when one stop to ponder over all the dalliance she and Luke had engaged in lately, she thought that neither should not be too surprised! Still, considering the fact that it had taken her six years to become pregnant the first time, she surely would never have guessed that she would become pregnant again upon their first love-making session, because she was certain that was what had happened! It was not that she did not want another baby, though she would admit having her first was no Sunday picnic and she had not completely forgotten it, but the point was, she had become pregnant and she and Luke both would have to make the best of it. Anyway, the only part that worried her was the possibility that their baby who was already here, would be deprived of the nourishment that she would have liked to give him through the summer. For the present though, she must do something about Luke.

She got up from her chair and walked around the table to where he sat. Speaking more severely to him than all through their entire marriage, she said, "Luke, look at me!" He raised his head. "This baby I'm carrying is ours, yours and mine. It's there because we love one another and wanted one another! Don't behave as though its within me of its own accord! That would not be right! We should be as thankful for this baby as we were the first!"

"Dear God, darling, it's not that! I'd take a dozen babies gladly, begotten of our love for each other. It's—" He stopped, asking himself, how could he possibly be blockheaded enough to think about telling her the fright he felt for her, also.

She sensed the dread he held for her, anyway, and was sorry she had spoken so forceful. She laid her hand on his shoulder.

"Luke, please dear, go on to Oak Grove and don't worry so. I know as well as I know my name, that everything will turn out all right."

He reached and drew her closer, burying his head against her body. He never said another word though. When he finally released her, rose and walked through the door, she noticed his step was heavy.

Summer. The lawn dressed in green, corn, cotton, and tobacco—crab grass and jimson weed, too. The cock's crow and the eastern sky cracking an eyelid upon a dew damp flower scented dawn. Sunrise marking spider webs hanging like grey mass around the marigolds, zinnias, phlox, and periwinkles that laced the flower beds. The glory of sunflowers and roses. Morning's warm sun closing petals of morning-glory vines that trailed around the posts on the back porch and swept from its lower beam to the ground. Noontide. An overhead sun lamp baking down unmercifully upon its victims, rendering deep tans and sweat baths. The quiet of hot, lazy afternoons when the mockingbirds chose to doze in the coal, shaded branches of live oaks and magnolias. The fragrance of new-mown hay drifting from the meadow field. The musky, perfume smell that clung around the fruit trees in the orchard. Fried chicken and fresh picked butter beans. The honey sweet smell of flue-cured tobacco. Smoke curling skyward from the big furnaces at the tobacco barns, tying gray-blue bows upon evening's faded dress—a fiery reddish—orange sun sinking at its hem. All this was summer and a lot more, too. For Eliza, another summer; that in a sense might have been the one passed, excepting for her baby and two Visits that were made to Green Sea. One was no surprise; she was expecting it. The other was a surprise and it upset her.

It was known throughout the neighborhood that Doctor Roalf had been calling on Caroline since Christmas passed. He had been escorting her to Church and to any social event that took place in the community as well as calling to Elms at least once or twice through the weekdays. The doctor made no attempt to cover his affection for Phil Carson's long waiting Caroline. He had fallen head over heels in love with her and, most people; if not all, approved the match. Though Doctor Davis' friends grieved for him and missed him, they; nevertheless, had not hesitated in taking Seth Roalf and his little boy to their bosom, also. This had not been hard for them to do, because the young doctor was an easy man to like and get to know. In fact, most his patients were already on first name basis with him. It was "Seth," or sometimes, "Doctor Seth." Hardly ever did anyone refer to him as "Doctor Roalf." Even though Doctor Davis' wealth had been on a very modest scale, he had given his services at no charge a good portion of the time, Seth Roalf was flabbergasted to learn the late doctor had named him as sole beneficiary to his holdings when the doctor's attorney probated his will after his death. Doctor Davis had stipulated only one clause in his will, "take care of his friends", and it appeared that Seth Roalf was not only determined to carry through with the late doctor's wish, but marry one as well!

Now, Caroline sat across from Eliza in the small living room at Green Sea. She was poised and lovely as ever, if one disregarded the fact that her beautiful gray-green eyes lacked the long ago sparkle and her nervous twisting of Phil Carson's glowing diamond that she still wore on her finger. The early June day was rather warm. Eliza made some lemonade though and the clinking of ice in their glasses seemed to lend a cool freshness to the room while they chatted.

After a playful hour in which he had been passed back and forth between his mother and Caroline several times, the baby had fallen asleep and Eliza had placed a quilt on the floor near the doorway and laid the sleeping baby upon it. She was a conscientious mother, always thinking more of Carr's comfort rather than following a fixed routine or formal custom, like giving him the advantage of any breeze that was likely to sift through the small house even if it did call for her to let him sleep upon the floor while she entertained company. Looking toward the baby, Caroline was saying once more, "yes, I can hardly get over how much he favors you and Phil, Eliza."

"He does look like the Carsons, doesn't he? As much as I like to think I'm seeing some feature of Luke about him at times, I'm going to have to agree, it just isn't there!"

Caroline smiled, "Well, perhaps this second baby will favor that adored husband of yours and then you'll have your wish."

Eliza laughed, "Maybe so. It would be sorta nice to have the score evened up!" Her laughter suddenly died though as she added, "But seriously. I'm thankful he favors Phil and so is Luke."

"I used to dream of the day when Phil and I could be married, and we'd have a son that looked exactly like that baby lying there. Then, one day I realized that it was never going to be. I guess one might say that I finally awakened to the actuality of my true circumstance." Caroline said, with a definite ring of resignation in her every word.

"It has been such a long time," voiced Eliza.

"Five years in July," Caroline muttered, as she continued to toy with the diamond ring on her finger.

Though she had been expecting Caroline and the doctor to get married, in the moment of silence that had fallen upon their conversation, Eliza became somewhat startled when all of a sudden Caroline swiftly pulled the ring off her finger and leaning forward said, "Eliza, I—I feel I should give this to you. Seth has asked me to marry him and I've accepted his proposal."

Certain that Caroline did not want to part with the ring and stalling for more time to decide how to handle it, Eliza hastily ignored her gesture and remark, exclaiming instead, "Why, Caroline, that's wonderful news! Seth's so nice and handsome, too, if I may add! I'm so happy for you both, though I will be honest and admit I'm not surprised, because Seth's devotion for you has been obvious from the first."

Although she still held the ring forward, Caroline seemed to want to talk about the doctor rather than the ring for the moment. She straightened up and said, "Seth is nice, and I respect him I've come to enjoy his company a great deal, and I simply adore his little boy. Of course, I've always loved children. One thing that could account for that though is the fact I was an only child."

"That could be," said Eliza. "But, I'm crazy about children, too, and I was raised up with two brothers."

"Well, anyway, it appears I'm set to become a mother on my wedding day," laughed Caroline, leaning forward again and gesturing for Eliza to take the ring.

Caroline's failing to mention that she was in love with Seth Roalf had not escaped Eliza and although she had no intention of keeping the ring, she leaned forward and held out her palm.

As Caroline dropped the ring in Eliza's hand, her laughter died away as suddenly as it had erupted. There seemed to be a strained hush dividing them until Caroline's grave voice fell upon the quiet of the small room,

"That's the first time it's been off my finger since Phil slipped it on my hand Christmas of 1860. I remember his exact words, he said, If the day should ever come that you have any doubt about my love for you, Caroline, just look down at your hand, because my love and devotion for you will forever be as strong and hard as this diamond."

"Try not to look back, dear, and think about that," said Eliza. "You hardly had any other choice except to remove it. It's only natural for Seth to want to put his own engagement ring on your finger."

"No, there won't be any engagement ring from Seth! He wanted to give me one to seal our betrothal, but I told him I much preferred he didn't. I asked him to give me only a plain wedding band when we're married, which will be in the near future. I don't want to be engaged anymore!"

She had sorta shocked and surprised Eliza again.

"Well, I think you and Seth both have a lot of wisdom and were wise to discuss your feelings openly concerning your and Phil's engagement. It's better to get things like that settled and understood before marriage rather than after marriage, I should think."

Caroline's eyes quickly moved from the ring which still held her gaze to stare at Eliza.

"Eliza, Seth and I have never discussed anything about my wearing Phil's ring or my engagement to him!"

"You haven't? But, I thought perhaps that was why you were giving the ring to me, that he—"

"No, I just thought it wouldn't be the proper thing to do, my keeping the ring. Seth has never mentioned it, one way or another."

Well, thought Eliza, it seemed Seth Roalf was ready to take Caroline any way he could get her, ring and all! "But, Caroline dear, do you truly want to part with it?" She asked. "I don't think you do."

Caroline eyes dropped toward her now unadorned left hand.

"No, to be honest, Eliza, I'd rather not part with it."

"Then, in that case, take it back. Phil meant for you to keep it when he gave it to you. To be truthful, since Seth is willing and broadminded enough to have overlooked your wearing the ring all this time and especially while your marriage plans to him are being made, I don't think he'll mind if you do keep the ring and wear it besides. Apparently, it doesn't bother him. However, may I make a suggestion?"

"What's that?"

"I don't think you should wear the ring on your left hand." Eliza leaned forward. "Here, give me your right hand." And, when she slipped the diamond back on Caroline's right hand, third finger, she saw Caroline's anxiety suddenly vanish. "There! Now you can have your ring back and your left hand is vacant for Seth!"

"Oh, Eliza, I wanted to keep it, but worried that people may think I shouldn't. I feel so foolish!"

"Caroline, my feelings have always been that we all should do what our hearts tell us to do, not what we think people may expect us to do."

Caroline brought her eyes back to Eliza's, looking at her thoughtfully.

"You're the wise and thoughtful one, Eliza. Will you come to my wedding? I'm not having a big affair. I'll be married at Elms with only family and close friends. Please, say you'll come. I do so much want you and Luke to be there."

"Well, you know I'd love being there, Caroline, but I am pregnant and don't see how I—"

"Pregnant or not, Eliza, I want you there," interrupted Caroline. "I don't see why women have to be cast aside and shut away from the public anyway, just because they're having a baby! Besides, if I didn't know you were having a baby, I'd think that it was merely a few added pounds of weight! You're much smaller with this baby than you were with Carson." Caroline jumped up from her chair. "Come on, let's go see about your dresses. We may have to add a bow or sash but you're coming to my wedding!"

And, two weeks later, Eliza did go to Elms and saw the lovely Caroline married at last, not to the man who she had remained faithful to so long and who Eliza was positive she still loved, but to a happy, proud Seth Roalf the same as Eliza had seen in a vision. There were a number of old friends present. All the Clarendon's were there, including Bill. But it seemed to Eliza those that were missing made up the greater number. In her pink muslin hoop-skirted dress that she and Caroline had added a white sash to that tied to the side in a big bow, her white straw hat that was lined with pink satin, and wearing white lacy woven gloves, she stood beside Luke, looking more like a bridesmaid which Caroline had chosen not to have, than the already one time mother and soon to be mother again that she was. She and Caroline had concealed her pregnancy so skillfully that it barely showed. Though their clever work of high fashion brought many eyes straying in Eliza's direction that probably would not have gazed upon her so long, almost and no doubt in some cases destroying their purpose, had not she looked so beautiful. As Eliza heard the sacred vows falling form Reverend Johnsons lips and saw Caroline's solemn face as she repeated them, her mind took her back to another time when she had seen Caroline's face and Phil's too, glowing and radiant—the night of their engagement party long ago.

She gripped Luke's hand and wept.

Spring turned to summer though and the days flowed on, one after another. Caroline and Seth returned from a brief honeymoon and Seth and his little boy moved from Doctor Davis house to live at Elms. Seth junior had become a steady playmate of Stuart's since he had begun classes with Stuart at Drakston Hall in the fall, and now with Seth junior closer to Drakston Hall the two little boys were together more than ever. Doctor Davis' small house became Seth's office alone. Seth ordered more modern medical equipment, and it was not many weeks afterwards til the entire dwelling shone as brightly and efficiently as though it might have been an office of some renowned doctor in New Orleans or some other big city instead of merely being the office of a country doctor, located in the midst of a farming belt. Caroline helped the doctor with his files and various paperwork, actually becoming to do all the office routine before too long. She did not help with the patients though. Seth would not allow it, telling her she was doing too much as it was. Although Caroline had never appeared to look sickish; that is, to the point of ailing, Seth was aware by this time that he had not married a robust, vigorous girl. Her whole person leaned toward fragility, which to the doctor meant something too unsteady and delicate to be exposed to what the sick room sometimes revealed. On the outside the couple seemed to be compatible, giving no reason for one to think otherwise. Still, they both were private people where their personal life was concerned. Certainly, the doctor appeared to be very happy with his marriage, and Caroline seemed no different than she had been for years to those that were close to her, namely Eliza, barring two exceptions. When she came to Green Sea, she refrained from mentioning Phil's name if she could get around it, nor did she ever ask to look at his portrait anymore. However, his ring still remained on her right hand.

Eliza's pregnancy was quite obvious now and on a hot, muggy morning in late August, she had another visitor to call upon her in the person of no other, but Frank! It had been almost three years to the day since Frank had reined Blossom through the archway at Green Sea. And, no sooner than Eliza's eyes fell upon him, she was telling herself that his visit could not have been any more ill-timed' and Frank would have agreed wholeheartedly, because he was saying to himself as his eyes ran over her in shocked disbelief, 'God Almighty! It's even worse than that day at the flowerbed!'

To be sure, there had not been any time that morning for much personal grooming; and it was doubtful indeed that had Eliza been granted the time, very little she could have done toward improving her appearance, considering her near pending confinement and the heavy load of work she was laboring under in the sticky and sultry weather. Her hair was moist and for the most part seemed to be plastered to her head except for several strands that kept falling down and sticking to her face, despite her brushing them back and resetting her comb every now and then. She was pale, bloated, and tired looking. Beads of sweat rested on her forehead and around her mouth. Her dark chambray dress which hiked up in front above her slippers was damp and hugging closely to her body, revealing huge wet circles at the armholes that extended halfway across her bosom on either side. Her ankles were swollen, puffed out over the tops of her shoes. She wore no stockings, nor did she have on but very few pieces of underclothing, which, of course, marked the ungainliness of her person that much more.

It was little wonder that her feet were swollen in view of the fact that she had been going on them since dawn. In addition to getting Luke's breakfast, doing all the usual daily household chores, and caring for her baby that morning, she had peeled and prepared two bushel of apples to make applesauce and had the fruit bubbling in a huge copper kettle over the fire in the fireplace to say nothing of a number of other pots and kettles that held food for dinner. There were green beans and ham hocks cooking together. Another pot held rice. Okra and tomatoes were steaming in another pot, and an apple cobbler and bread baking in the oven. There was still a chicken to fry, that she had dressed earlier, and gravy to make. But this would be done later when she had gotten the applesauce in the mason glass jars that she had also washed and rinsed carefully and had lined up on the kitchen table waiting. Doss had helped a lot before he had plodded off to the tobacco barn when it became necessary for every hand on the plantation to help with gathering the green tobacco if it was to be saved. It seemed all of it had ripen at once, that which was still hanging on the stalk after several cropping's had already been cropped off. Anyway, Doss had caught the chicken and wrung its neck and picked the beans and gathered up the apples that had been lying on the ground and going to waste under the heavily laden apple trees.

To say that it had not been a pleasant morning, would have been putting it mildly. Let alone all the work that was required of her hands in the extreme August heat, the baby had been fretful that morning, besides. He was sitting upon the quilt; then, that she had placed in the doorway, surrounded by spoons and clothespins which he had thrown aside, holding out his arms as he looked toward her, squalling rather loudly just when the applesauce needed to be removed from the fire or it was going to be scorched and ruined. She looked yearningly toward the baby and pleaded, "Please, darling, wait til mother removes this kettle and she'll go to you."

She turned back and grabbed up two potholders. Giving her hair another sweep with her arm, she sighed and was leaning over the steaming pots, attempting to get the kettle of applesauce, when suddenly Frank's voice cut through the baby's screams.

"For the love of God! Wait Eliza! I'll lift that tub for you!"

Startled, she jerked her head around, "Frank! I didn't hear anyone!"

Frank had already stepped over the baby's pallet and clutter and was striding toward the fireplace.

"I knocked and called out to you at the front, but when you didn't answer I came on around to the back. I heard the baby crying."

Before she could hardly straighten her back on reply, with his hands still encased in his expensive riding gloves, he reached forward and lifted the huge kettle of bubbling fruit from the fire. As he set it down upon the iron trivet that she indicated which was near the jars on the table, he said, "A tub's the right word for that, it's too big for a cook pot!" she saw the old familiar flush of anger spread over his face. "You have no business lifting loads such as that, Eliza! Where in the hell is everybody? Where's that husband of yours?"

She might have told him that he had missed Luke by a hairsbreadth. Luke had rushed from the tobacco field where he was helping crop tobacco to check on her. He did this several times a day now, and it seemed to her that each day Luke's face was wearing more strain as he continued to worry about her. In fact, Luke's leaving was what had set the baby wailing again. Knowing that Frank would never understand how it was with her and Luke though, she let his question go unanswered. And, seeing that he had charged back across the room to where the baby was, she stopped and waited in going to it, because Frank had already furiously yanked his gloves off and thrown them on the floor and was reaching down for the screaming baby. Holding the baby in one arm, she saw him quickly slid his other hand inside the pocket of his immaculate riding pants and draw forth a handsome looking pocketknife whose handles were inlaid with pearl. Now, he was saying, as he offered the knife to the baby, "Here! Here now! Sorry boy, don't you like this?

Carr suddenly cut his scream in half and looked curiously at the flashing knife for a few seconds. Then, his little hand shot forward and seized upon the novel object with force.

Pulling a nearby chair closer, Frank was saying again, as he sat down with the baby on his knee, "I thought you'd take a liking to that." But he looked back to where Eliza still stood and saw an anxious look upon her face. "Oh, don't worry he can't open it." He told her and then went on to say, "Good God! Eliza, how do you stand this place! It's like an oven in here. Why in the hell doesn't that husband of yours buy you a cookstove if you're going to be forced to do the cooking, which you have no business doing in the first place? I had a stove put in ages ago at Drakston Hall for the cooks to use. One would think Green Sea existed in the Dark ages! No doubt if Luke Heyward were forced to stand where you're standing right now, it wouldn't be long before he broke down and bought one!"

When Frank had sat down with the baby, and she had seen that he had become fascinated in his examining of the knife, she had turned back to her work. Now she was busy ladling the applesauce into the jars and thinking what a vast contrast there was between Frank's cool, fresh linens and the way Luke had looked when he rushed to check on her. It was doubtful there had been a dry stitch of clothing on Luke's body. But Frank would never understand that, either, because he had yet to crop the first tobacco leaf in the hot sun or, as far as that went, doing any other kind of work. Finally, she commented, "As long as one has to cook, I don't imagine it would make too much difference whether one cooked in a fireplace or on a cookstove, such a day as today."

"Well, at least that damn smoke and those goddamn flames would be out of your eyes and face! You should've let the damn fruit rotted, have no business canning it! Why in the hell don't you have some help? Where is everybody, anyway?" He furiously inquired a second time.

Again, she might have told him that Luke had also told her to let the apples rot, though he had said it kindly and had not used a cuss word. In truth, she was having as little to say to Frank as she could get by with. She could see his anger and frustration and did not desire or feel up to having an argument with him. Moreover, she was embarrassed over her appearance and was thankful she had an excuse to stand behind the table with the large kettle of fruit setting in front of her. It was not that she was ashamed of her pregnancy. Nor was she concerned this time over Frank's staring at her, because she had already seen his eyes falling away from her every time he did look toward her. What was bothering her though, was her soiled clothing and the fact she wore so few pieces of it. Still, with the situation being as it was with her, she had no qualms over letting him know she was entirely alone except for the baby, a feeling she had not experienced in Frank's company for a long, long time when they were alone together. Apparently, Frank had forgotten, nor did it seem he wanted to remember that this was summer, tobacco gathering time, a period when everybody at Green Sea was compelled to work long hard hours all day, every day, barring Sunday.

"Everybody's helping gather tobacco," she finally replied. "It's going to waste if it isn't taken off the stalk today. Luke's having to help crop in this hot weather. I almost feel I'm lucky to be standing where I am. I'm out of that scorching sun, anyhow."

"There you go again, always worrying about him and never thinking about your own welfare. You know it upsets me, Eliza, to see you as you are!"

Now, a longer pronounced silence fell between them. Aside from the thud of applesauce falling in the jar, there was no other sound in the room. The baby remained to be intrigued with the knife and was perfectly still. At long last, the uneasy stillness was broken when she asked him a question that in no way was relative to his remark.

"How's Elizabeth and Stuart? It's been weeks since I've seen them."

"They're alright," he replied, "gone to Charleston today. Let's not talk about them, Eliza. It's you I'm worried about and want to discuss. That's my reason for being here. I know I said and swore by it, that I'd never invite you to come to Drakston Hall again, after you refused to accept my invitation to come live there as long as you wished to when the mansion burned. But this heat wave got me to thinking about how unpleasant this house, which isn't much more than a shed, must be for you in your—well— I want you to come to Drakston Hall, Eliza, for your confinement! I heard about the rough time you had when this baby was born, and I thought that maybe if you came to Drakston Hall this time, that at least your surroundings would be more comfortable. You know you shouldn't be having another baby so soon. But—oh, hell, why talk about that fact at this stage! Will you come?"

Frank never ceased to amaze her. One second he was hard and cruel, the next his heart seemed to be filled and overflowing with compassion. She had filled the jars and was putting the lids on; Luke would tighten them later. Actually, she was not thinking about his invitation as much as she was thinking how complex Elizabeth's life must be, sharing it with this odd and complicated person, who was waiting for her answer, looking at her anxiously.

"Frank," she said at last, "I appreciate your thinking of my comfort. But really this house isn't so bad. Its home to us. Granted, it isn't the mansion, but with its high ceilings and the morning-glory vines shading the back porch, the rooms are cooler than one would think and especially the bedroom, which catches any breeze that's blowing. Carr was born in that room, and I want this baby born here at Green Sea, too."

"Then, you're refusing my invitation and my wanting to help you, again?"

"Frank, try to understand my side."

"I'm trying, but I don't think I'll ever understand the fact that you appear to enjoy living here in this shed!"

"No, you're wrong about that. Anyway, that's why Luke works so hard. He tells me I won't be living here many years."

"And, why not, if I may ask?"

"Because his plans are to build another mansion in the same spot that has always held all the manor houses of Green Sea."

"And, when is this project to be started, if I may ask again?"

"I imagine as soon as he possibly can. Of course, it depends on the crop. I hope we do as well this year as we did last. We were able to put aside some savings toward that goal, from last year's tobacco and cotton."

"Eliza, your faith and confidence in Luke Heyward never fails to astonish me! You remind me of Uncle Matthew. Sometimes, to be honest, I get a little weary of hearing Uncle Matthew singing praise to Luke Heyward when he and my mother visits at Drakston Hall! To hear him talk about this place, one would think that there was already a mansion standing at Green Sea, instead of this shed that Luke

Heyward throwed together! Luke Heyward will never build you a decent house to live in!"

It made no difference how hard she tried not to argue with Frank, she saw instantly to avoid it was inevitable, and she also saw that Frank's dislike for Luke was smoldering as deeply as in the beginning if not more so. This was obvious by his still referring to Luke by his full name. Unquestionable, this gave him a sense of keeping Luke at a distance, at bottom, still seeing Luke as an outsider and in disassociation with her, their baby, or any other family member. In spite of all, she found her temper rising and retorted back, "And, just why are you so sure he won't, if I may ask you?"

"Well, that's easy to answer. Look around you. Look at where you're sitting today, when you should have servants waiting on you hand and foot, I told you, Eliza, a long time ago that Luke Heyward would never provide for you and my words are certainly ringing true, if today is an example of how you live! Your marrying him has brought nothing but hardship upon you!"

"My marrying him has brought me happiness, a kind of happiness no other man could have given me."

"So, you make certain once again that I hear you say how much you love him. You always manage to get that in our conversations, don't you, Eliza, although you know how it infuriates me?" Instantly, he sat the baby back upon the quilt and rose from his chair. "I'll go this time before you order me to leave! I don't want to upset you. It's plain to see from your appearance that you aren't up to an argument. I'm pleading to you once more; won't you reconsider the advantages you'll have and come to Drakston Hall to have your baby?"

He stared at her anxiously.

"No, I can't, Frank. What you're asking involves a great deal more than just my having more comfort. This is my home, shabby or however you see it, it's still home. You're aware of how I feel about Green Sea, and, yes, there's Luke, too, I don't want to leave him here alone to shift for himself when he's working so hard, though I don't expect you to understand that."

"I understand that apparently he's dragged you down to his level, or you'd give this place no thought and take your baby and come with me! I loved you, Eliza, and wanted to marry you above everything else, but it seemed you wanted no part of me and look at where it's all led to. By God! I still love you! Yes, I'll admit it, and I'm telling you so, because I'll probably never tell you again. I hope that everything goes all right with you—and—oh hell, what's the use—Goodbye!"

He stepped over the baby's pallet and was through the door in a flash.

She quickly called, "Frank!" and heard the sudden stop of his steps crossing the porch.

"You forgot the baby still has your knife."

"Oh, hell!" He called back. "Let him keep it!"

She rose and crossed the kitchen to where the baby sat and stood for some minutes looking down at the knife in his hands. Then, she walked to the front door and looked out. Frank was turning Blossom through the archway toward Charleston.

Frank went to Charleston and got roaring drunk—a spree that lasted for several days, something that he very seldom did.

Chapter Eight

Had she heard that second babies come easy? No, she must have been wrong. But someone had said so. Who? Think. Concentrate on anything that might carry her mind as far away as possible from this staving giant force that had thrust her body upon a bed of spikes—anything—Carr's first little stumbling steps that he had begun to take alone a few days ago and that she now heard through the open window as he played on the back porch. Doss was keeping him well entertained with his wonder—working little games, such as their make-believe game of whittling with Frank's closed-handle knife. Luke—his strong hands clasped around hers and then as another hard pain stabbed through her, him sitting on the edge of the bed telling her to push against his body. And, it was more easing to have him beside her, doing as he had suggested, than clinging to the rods of the headboard above her head as she had done before when Carr was born. Though if it were possible Luke's face caused her even worse pain. It was nothing but a harrowed map and had been for days ever since it had been apparent that her labor was going to start before the due date. Why was it that both her babies had had a hankering to see the world before their scheduled birth and had started on their long, tiresome journey almost within the same hour? Had a hundred years passed since last night when she had told Luke he had better go for the doctor? What was today, anyway? It must be September twelfth, but she was not sure.

There that crushing giant was again—"Oh—God—Luke—help—"

"It's coming, Eliza, one more hard push. There!"

Who said that? Of course, it must have been Seth, and had she heard Seth add, "Here she is, Luke, take your daughter and, Hannah, you help me for a moment?" Yes, she was certain she bad because at long last something had lifted her body from that huge pressing grinder. Why!

That meant she and Luke had a baby girl, a little sister for Carr! She must lift her head and open her lazy eyelids, she so much wanted to see her! The weight on her eyes was so heavy though; yet, at the same time, she saw a peaceful growing darkness where everything was so calm and joyful. It was all so strange. Still she was happy. Her legs felt so good, they did not seem to be tired anymore. In fact, she wondered why she had ever thought she was tired in the first place, considering how fast her flying feet were crossing the meadow field, that was filled with yellow buttercups and twinkling fireflies—gaining ground so swiftly on Phil and Nat that she could almost reach out and touch their shoulders now. Darkness was closing too rapidly then to do so, but tomorrow in the early morning's sunrise, she would come back to the meadow field and pick a pretty bouquet of buttercups for her mother.

Upon the doctor's words, Luke felt an icy chill running the length of his body. He turned and held out his palms, barely feeling the soft blanket that Hannah let fall upon them. He was held in awe too much by the wonder that Seth held and was now handing to him. His little son was very dear and precious to him; yet, notwithstanding his deep regard and devotion for Carr, there seemed to be something special about this baby girl that suddenly caught his heart and held it firmly the second his eyes fell upon her. For the moment, he seemed to be outside of himself—elsewhere—held in the power of infinite goodness as he stared at her. It came to him that she was absolute proof in disputing the saying that all newborn babies look alike. She held no likeness whatever to her brother when he had been born. Indeed, even though she appeared to be normal in every respect, Luke thought she looked somewhat pathetic and wondered if this was why his heart had been touched so deeply. For one thing, whereas Carr's head had been full of heavy curls, hers could claim only one or two hairs that were jet black and straight as a board! Her limbs were long and gangling, with no plumpness at all about them. Her thin, fleshed scrawny little body reminded him of a pocket-sized doll, arms that looked no bigger than his fingers; and she seemed to be as weary and tired as her mother was. She lay placid and quiet in his hands, no kicking, no squalling, no nothing. But, her wide-set eyes with heavy black brows above them did move around the room a little, seeming to reveal the fact that she was wonder-stricken to be where she was as he felt at being able to finally hold her at last.

Seth, who was now gathering his medical necessities together, looked across the room at Luke and grinned, "Well, don't you think it's about time you let Hannah clean her up a bit and put some clothes on her?"

"Uh—oh—yeah, I guess so," laughed Luke.

Seth swapped his bag shut and crossed the room to where Luke still sat on the edge of the bed holding the baby. Taking a rather long gaze at her, too, he said, "Those legs remind me of a thoroughbred Colt's."

"You know, Seth, I was thinking the very same thing. A regular thoroughbred I would say, even if I do break the rule and use the word in relation to the human race instead of a horse's lineage."

"After getting a good look at her, my suspicion is that your daughter is going to take after you in looks more than she does her mother."

Looking as though Seth's remark just might tum his head Luke looked up at the doctor and broke into a wide smile, "I'll admit I've also been thinking that, too, Seth. Yes, I'm certain, she's going to be all Heyward as Carr is all Carson."

"Have you and Eliza already picked out a girl's name?"

"Yes, we settled on that a long time ago in case she had a girl. She'll be called for our mothers, Jane Anne. The Jane is for my mother, Anne for Eliza's mother."

"It's a beautiful name, I like it."

"We thought so when we settled on it," said Luke, as he turned his head toward Eliza. "I wonder if she even knows she has a daughter. I'm so thankful though to see her getting some rest at last."

"Well, I shall think she's earned all the sleep she's fallen under. Don't disturb her, she can see the baby when she wakes up. Giving birth is no easy process for your wife, Luke."

"I know," agreed Luke and although he did not disclose his thoughts to the doctor; not then, he was telling himself that come next September Eliza's torture most certainly would not be repeated for the third time—blue flowering negligees or whatever!" With concern growing deeper in his face, he went on to ask, "She will be all right this time, won't she, Seth?"

"Everything points in that direction, Luke. Her labor was long and difficult again though, more so than what it should have been taking into account this was the second baby. However, I'm happy to see that so far there has been no sign of a hemorrhage as there was the first time she gave birth; therefore, I'm sure she'll be fine. Anyway, I'll be back in the morning to check on her."

"Thanks, Seth, a hundred times over. I'll walk outside with you,"

Luke said, and finally getting to his feet he gently laid the baby in Hannah's waiting arms, saying to her, "Take care of her, Hannah."

"Sho'nough, Mister Luke," Hannah replied, peering at the baby rather keenly. Then,

looking somewhat thoughtful, she added, "Mister Luke, dis gal is qwine look just like ya!"

Luke laughed and thought, nothing escaped Hannah's eyes.

September fell to Indian Summer—a time that brought another mellow and abundant harvest—sunny, warm days that smelled of early morning hearth smoke and gleamed with the brightness of yellow golden rod that graced the numerous hedgerows and along the wayside of the river road, where the near giant forest was wrapped in a gay colored calico dress—ancient towering trees that looked as though they were touching the marching white clouds and the daily formations of geese flying through them on their way toward a winter feeding ground.

It was on a day such as this that Luke had suggested to Eliza once more to see the doctor and when she brushed his suggestion aside, assuring him that she was fine, it came out while they were eating dinner that Luke had taken the matter in his own hands. As a matter of fact, the baby was progressing along nicely, gaining weight each day and also looking more like her father as time passed. The color of her eyes, which had been difficult to determine at birth, were now an unmistakable unique shade of gray with no hint of blue about them. They were the same identical coloring of her father's. Although her brother had out shown her at birth, it was now manifested that she was coming into her own and growing into a bright and pretty baby. In truth, whereas the baby had gone forward, it was just the other way around with her mother. Eliza had become very thin and sallow looking. Moreover, even though she was quite mindful of Luke's behavior toward her again and in a sense, she was becoming nettled over it, he need not have been concerned with the possibility of his having to resist her alluring curves set off by blue flowering chiffon anymore! With two babies to care for in addition to all the other tasks she labored under, it seemed doubtful she could hardly have spared the time to think about blue negligees, much less downing the seductive outfit in order to entice him had she so desired to.

When the soft, lazy autumn days drew to a close, she was so tired and worn out by then that she barely hit the bed before she was sound asleep. Now, she was still protesting in seeing the doctor and was telling Luke again, "I'm all right, Luke, a little tired, but that's running after Carr so much. He's constantly exploring everything since he started to walk."

"No, darling, I won't hear of your putting off seeing the doctor anymore. I saw Seth this morning and I've already told him that we'd be there as soon as possible after dinner. I've also arranged for Hannah to stay with the babies while we're gone, she'll be here shortly. So, as soon as we finish dinner and dress, we'll be going. Besides, on a beautiful day such as this, you wouldn't decline an outing with your husband, would you?"

Shyly, Eliza looked down at her plate.

"I never have nor would I ever decline anything with you, Luke!"

He reached his hand across the table, tipping her chin up til their eyes met.

"Nor I with you, darling," he said, "as long as circumstances doesn't force me to do otherwise."

Viewing his remark in a rather serious light, she looked at him thoughtfully and told him,

"I'll hurry, Luke, and make ready to go."

"Thanks, dear. Maybe you'll get the chance to visit with Caroline awhile. That should compensate some for the usual bottle of brown medicine that I'm well aware you deplore bringing home with you."

"Some, Luke, but not much, though I do love Caroline and would like to see her."

After Seth had seen his patient and, to be sure, had prescribed the customary "brown tonic", she and Caroline, always eager to chatter with one another, were doing just that and upon Caroline's suggestion had strolled outside to have a look at the pretty blooming chrysanthemums in the small garden that Doctor Davis had ever taken such delight in, but never had the time to spare in it that he desired to. Thus, circumstances being such, Luke and the doctor likewise were engaged in conversation and; therefore, having a more direct and straightforward discussion than had the women been nearby.

"Seth, how is Eliza? I'm worried about her, she looks so pale, lately. I know you've told her if she followed your orders and took the medicine you've prescribed that she should be all right and feeling much better in a few weeks. I suppose though what I'm asking is for more specific details, now that we're alone"

"Certainly, Luke. Well, she is weakened and run-down somewhat, and I agree with you her cheeks aren't their usual healthy pink. But, I'm sure in time she'll gain back her normal vigor; that is, if she gets plenty of rest, stays on medication and eats the proper foods and an adequate amount I should add. You must remember she's had two babies less than twelve months apart and has lost a lot of her blood supply and especially during the first labor. This weakens the most robust of women."

"Then, there's nothing seriously wrong?" "As far as I can tell, there isn't."

"Thank God, for that. Yes, she went through two trying ordeals, but if l can help it, she won't go through another of that nature, no time in the near future, anyway!"

The doctor sent Luke a rather long and decisive look. "You sound as though you're adamant about that, Luke."

"I am! Don't get me wrong, Seth. I could kneel down right here, right now, and give humble thankfulness to God that Eliza and I have been blessed with two children, because it appeared, we would never have any. But, if I have to maintain separate sleeping quarters from my wife to prevent her going through another excruciating labor, I'll do just that, regardless of any want I may have to assuage my desire for her. I don't want to lose her, and I feel in view of past circumstances, that I'm very fortunate, I didn't."

"Well, I meant to take this up with you when we had more time and could discuss it under more favorable conditions. However, since you've brought the subject up and obviously much distressed over it, I feel obligated to tell you that in relation to that matter, it isn't necessary for you to go that far in your sleeping arrangements in order to protect your wife."

An alarm bell began to peal in Luke's head.

"What do you mean by that?" He chanced to ask.

"I'm sorry, Luke, but I'm certain Eliza will never have another baby! In truth, it's astonishing to me that she ever became pregnant the first time. I had a suspicion when I attended her during her last labor that this would be the case. I wanted to be sure though before I told you. As you've just stated, be thankful for the two children you have because I'm positive there won't be any more!"

Seeing that the news had hit Luke rather hard, the doctor quickly went on to add.

"The problem's an internal female disorder that I'd much prefer not to go into, until there's time for me to explain it in detail. It's my opinion though that this was why her confinements were so long and difficult."

"Will it hinder or endanger her health?"

"Not any more than what it's bothered her since the onset of her menstrual periods. Anyway, not that I can foresee at this time."

"Could it be corrected?"

"Yes, by surgery it could, but I wouldn't advise or recommend it, the risk is too high in any kind of surgery. Even if the surgery presented no problem, she would still have a lengthy stay in a hospital besides a long convalescent period at home. My advice is let will enough alone, or that's what I'd do if it were Caroline. I think once Eliza gains her strength back, she'll be as well as she's ever been, so that's a great consolation, though there won't be any more babies."

Although Luke was saddened to know for a certainty there would be no more children for him and Eliza, his heart lifted in gratitude in hearing the doctor say that her health should not decline.

"Of course, Seth, you're so right. Eliza's health is the most important part to me, anyhow.

"No, I thought it best not to tell her til she's had time to regain her strength back. She could fall into a deep depression if she were told now. In any event, I wanted to discuss it with you first.

"I appreciate your thoughtfulness. I agree with you that she could become upset over it. To be honest with you, I'm somewhat shaken myself."

"That's understandable. As a matter of fact, Luke, Eliza doesn't have to know, if you think it best that she doesn't. On the other hand, if you'd prefer to do so, I have no objection in you telling her yourself; that is, if you think she should be told. I'll leave the decision with you and you can let me know whichever way you choose."

"Well, maybe it wouldn't be a bad idea for me to tell her, sometime. Then, if she wants to hear the medical details, I'll let you handle that part. I think she and Caroline are coming back to join us. I'll see you, Seth, in a few days to hear the details myself. Thanks for everything and for telling me now."

"You bet, Luke."

So, in his knowledge that their union would not be fruitful anymore, Luke moved back to the warmth of his wife's bed and autumn had moved to winter and he still had not told her. True, he bad endeavored to tell her several times. Even so, in each attempt, he always allowed his heart to overrule his conscience. His overwhelming desire to keep her mind free of any burden that lay in his power to render, ever won. Moreover, at that time, it was all too easy to drift with the current harmony and order that flowed through the little house in the quiet, cozy days and nights of winter. After almost two years of anxiety, he could not bring himself to lay blight upon his happily renewed union with Eliza, whose cheeks were blooming once more—looking as fresh as an April morning. Thus wise, because of this, and the marvel he saw in their two beautiful, healthy children, he told himself that maybe someday he would tell her there would never be another child for them, but not then.

Indeed, there were few idle hours that winter for Luke's mind to be free for very many self-accusing thoughts, anyway. If he did hear a voice of conscience every now and then when he shared the fireside at night with Eliza, it was drowned in the laughter and warmth of the cozy, peaceful setting, where he did discuss other subjects with her that near had his mind absorbed at that time. He was busy adding two more bedrooms to the little house. He and Eliza had planned and worked out the details together at the kitchen table in the evenings after the supper hour, and, on warm, suitable days Luke and Doss worked on the new project. This addition did not require to be rushed and finished as the other had been. It was many months before the rooms were completed and, when they had finally been dressed in the same soft grey that the rest of the house shown with, the dwelling had shed its cottage look forever in its becoming quite a large, comfortable farmhouse. During that same winter, Luke was to make the first move toward another project that was never too far from his other crowded thoughts; that being, building back the mansion that he had promised Eliza. Though she never talked about that mansion's loss anymore, and seemed to be happy and contended in the home they now shared, he; nevertheless, could not forget how much she had loved every brick and board that had held the walls of her former home together and was certain that within her the wound of its burning was remaining to be slow in healing. Hence, the first huge trees, a few among the numerous that would eventually be cut before the project was ever finished, were felled that winter and taken to Bill's sawmill where they were sawed and planed into sills that were to be used for the foundation of the mansion that he was planning to build her. Luke was very mindful of the fact that he was taking on a full hand—a task that in no way could be compared to adding rooms to an already standing structure. He was well aware that it would probably take many years of hard work and no doubt call for a lot of sacrificing on the part of him and Eliza both to bring his ambition into the making, even if he were to be blest with luck all the way through, suffering no hindrances or drawbacks; for instance, such as having a crop failure. Still, he thought if it were possible, he yearned to see another mansion setting where the old one had stood as much as Eliza did or maybe more so. Even though the ground at the old site was now well covered with grass and evergreens; and the may chimneys clustered in heavy vines that hid their gaunt starkness as they still towered high above the hundred year old magnolias and live oaks, to Luke, they continued to quicken an uncanny feeling about him, seeming as though they were grey ghost in the night, each time he rode by the place and allowed his eyes to rest upon it. He had been unable to forget that day long ago when he had gotten his first glimpse of the stately Doric columned mansion that had shone so splendidly in the morning's sunlight and could hardly wait to have another gracing the lands of Green Sea as it had done. Accordingly, one bright, early winter morning he mounted his mare and started out for the purpose of locating the best and most convenient track of timber that Green Sea could lay claim to. He rode and looked for three full days before he finally settled upon a virgin stand of pine and hardwoods that were located less than a quarter mile from the border of Drakston Hall's acreage. The grove of timber grew upon a high, dry ridge and looked as though it had stood there for centuries. The trunks of the massive pines and oaks were enormous. But, upon taking a careful view, Luke concluded that once a wagon road was cut and cleared out, removing the timber form the high ground by mule team should present no problem. He dismounted and marked a few pines that were to be cut and sawed for the sills, beginning his first move toward replacing the burned mansion. And, not long after that, the work in clearing a road to the timbered ridge was started. Also, he and Doss began to demolish the ghostlike Chimneys, salvaging what bricks that were possible so as to use them in laying the ground foundation for the new mansion. Luke's hopes were to get the foundation to the house built that year, if he were to accomplish nothing else in the giant undertaking. Added to all this building talk though that he and Eliza engaged in during the after—purpose leisure hours, a further development that had taken place at Green Sea that winter was discussed and mused over fairly often, as it had disturbed them a great deal, particularly Eliza.

In the early hours of dawn on a cold, raw morning in the month of February, she was awakened, long before it was time for her to arise, by icy sheets of sleet beating against the windowpanes. She was contented enough though just to lie there awake in the folds of Luke's arms and think about their happiness with one another again besides a number of other things, including their children, imagining how the mansion that Luke was working on the drawings to which later on he would take to an architect for a final work—up would look once it was built, and wondering if the sleet would continue and prevent Luke form going to Charleston that day to get the additional supplies he needed in building the bedrooms. When she did arise; however, it was apparent to her and Luke both that be would not be going any place that day. The ground was nothing but a glare of ice, with the trees and shrubs bending way low from the weight of its heavy blanket. And, later on in the day, when big fluffy flakes of snow began to fall upon the glasslike grounds, it was definitely pronounced that the area had once again fallen victim to another rare snowstorm. Nevertheless, regardless of the storm that was interrupting Luke's work and delaying his plans, the Heyward's took advantage of the interruption and had an enjoyable day. Once the snow had accumulated to several inches, Luke took a large bowl and stepped outside, scooping it full of the ice-cold flakes for the purpose of making lemon or vanilla flavored sherbet—a much favored treat of every snowstorm. With Carr toddling around their knees and their baby girl lying happily in the rosewood cradle that her brother had been forced to surrender to her, Luke and Eliza sat beside their warm hearth and savored the novel sherbet. Afterwards, while applesauce pies baked in the oven and chicken jumbo simmered on the stove, a surprise that Luke bad set up in the kitchen at Christmastime even though she had never mentioned that she would like to have a stove and certainly never told him of Frank's remarks, Eliza pieced scraps of cloth together that in time would turn out to be a patchwork quilt; and Luke, forever meticulous in keeping everything around him in tiptop working order, used the idle hours to clean and oil the firing weapons once more. Strange as it was, all the firearms at Green Sea had been saved from the fire that had swept the mansion to rubble and ashes. Even the matched dueling revolvers that had belong to Joshua Heyward had escaped the fire. A few days before the tragedy, Luke had taken the entire gun collection to the kitchen for the purpose of giving them the periodically cleaning, which had ever been a must with him. Having had his attention demanded elsewhere though before finishing the job, he had left the weapons in the kitchen. Therefore, they had been saved along with the portraits that Eliza had snatched from the licking flames.

The cold, snowy but pleasant day for the Heyward's soon fell to a close though, and instead of the snowstorm subsiding with nightfall, it seemed to be growing worse—bringing Luke to reason that the fore footed occupant who had more or less taken possession of the back porch since late fall, and who went by the name of Jailor, was not barking this time just to amuse himself. He told Eliza that evidently Jailor was uncomfortable outside and as soon as she got Carr bedded down, be thought he would let the dog come inside to lay by the heart that night. Carr adored that dog and they both knew if he saw Jailor there would be no bedtime for Carr for hours Jailor was a thoroughbred foxhound puppy, a gift to Carr form Bruce. Bruce held the notion that all boys required a dog for their companion, and Jailor had been presented to Carr from a litter that was whelped at Oak Grove the previous summer. The kennels at Green Sea had gradually passed out of the picture during the war years; and due to Luke's cool indifference to ride to hounds, he had had no desire to revive the hunt, which of course, would have called for restoring the kennels. He had never gotten the pleasure from the sport that Eliza's brothers had. In fact, in years passed he had declined a number of invitations to follow the hounds from Phil and Nat both and, after his and Bruce's return from the war, he had also turned Bruce's invitation down several times. In truth, Luke could hardly bear to see any animal hunted down for the purpose of the sport only. His concern for all animals was planted too deeply in his sense to tolerate it. Thus, Jailor could not have been more lucky in corning by a master than having Luke fill that responsibility; for example as then, Luke's concern that the weather was too cold that night for Jailor to sleep on the back porch in his somewhat comfortable bed, which happened to be a wooden crate with a ragged quilt stuffed inside. True to his breed, Jailor had very keen senses, nothing escaped him even though he was just a young pup; and he was in his heaven when he was granted the privilege to lay in the warmth of the fireside.

However, rather than leaping form his box and bounding through the doorway as Luke had expected him to do once he had cracked the kitchen door open and sounded the invitation, Jailor's coal-black swift legs, looking as though someone had pulled tan stockings halfway up on each one with exact measurement, came plowing through the deep white flakes round the comer of the house and stopped dead still at the bottom of the porch step. He set his bright, sharp eyes to Luke's and gave a loud yelp. Then, retraced his steps a few feet and looking back at Luke again, be stopped and gave another loud yelp. When Luke commanded him to come back though, the dog plainly showed his disappointment in his master. His pink tongue that wallowed over the side of one jaw instantly disappeared back to its proper place, and his gleaming teeth that shone like a white picket fence from jaws down firmly together. Then, he let his head fall. Next, his tail came lagging downward between his legs farther and farther til it could scarcely be seen, as he turned back and came cowering up the steps and on into the kitchen, obeying his master's command. He cowered on to the hearth and took his usual place. His hind legs rested on the floor no longer than thirty seconds though, before he moved across the room and sat down beside the door that opened into the living room. He began to whine.

"I wonder what he wants," Luke said. "He's never behaved like this before." "Obviously, he wants back outside," replied Eliza. "But I think he's slightly confused in his direction."

Luke studied the dog for a moment.

"No, I don' t think so, dear. I'm sure something out front has gotten his attention. He came from that direction when I called him. He really didn't want to come inside; I could see his actions clearly by the light shining through the window. No, he's not confused, I'm positive he's trying to tell me something."

Eliza, piecing quilt scraps together again, stopped for a moment and studied the dog, too.

"Well, your sense of understanding an animal's behavior, Luke, is much deeper than mine, but if he's barking is any sign of he's trying to tell you something, he's been making an attempt to reach you ever since dark fell."

"That's true, and come to think of it, that was more than two hours ago. He barks so much though, I guess I've gotten so used to it, I just shut my ears to the sound. I think I'll open that door and see what he does."

Luke got up and opened the door between the two rooms. Jailor trotted direct to the front door, turned and set his dark liquid eyes to Luke's again and whined anxiously.

Eliza had laid her thimble and needle aside and had gotten up; also, watching to see what the dog did.

Luke stepped back to the mantel and reached above it to the gun rack.

"Keep away from any light, dear, that can be seen from the outside. Stay behind the door here, unless I call you. I'm going to have a look out front."

"Do be careful, Luke!" Eliza cried, suddenly, fearing for his safety. "I will, don't be frightened, dear, it's probably nothing."

With Eliza standing anxiously behind the door that had been left ajar between the two rooms, Luke crossed the living room and standing aside somewhat, he reached for the front doorknob and let the door swing open.

Jailor bounced outside.

No commotion whatever came from the dog though, as Luke had been expecting. All he heard from Jailor was the same whimpering. Quite surprised and a little put out with the dog, he stepped in the doorway and scanned the dim, shadowed white landscape for sound and sight of any disturbance. He saw nothing and heard nothing but the whining at his feet. He brought his eyes back to the dog and was gathering his breath for a rather heavy scolding when at that instant he spotted a bundle of some sort lying within inches of his boots! Puzzled, he bent down but could not make out what it was in the obscured light, reasoning at the same time that he should take caution before he put his hands upon it.

"Eliza dear," he called. "Bring the lamp."

Eliza grabbed the lamp and rushed to the doorway where she saw Luke leaning over a pile of spoiled rags, exclaiming while she lifted the lamp higher to get a clearer view, "What in heaven's name is that, Luke? What in the world has he dragged up now?"

"That's what I'm trying to find out before I expose my bare hands to it, though I don't think Jailor's had anything to do with disposing this packet here on our step this time," Luke replied, nudging the heap of rags with the tip of his revolver—causing a soiled baby blanket to slip and suddenly reveal the palm of a baby's band!

"Good Lord!" he shouted, "It's a baby! I see a baby's hand! Someone's left a baby on our doorstep!"

"What?" Eliza shrieked.

"It's a fact, dear, try not to get upset, someone's brought a baby here to Green Sea and abandoned it!" Luke exclaimed, as he thrust his revolver aside and quickly ran his hands over the mass of rags, gathering it up and diving through the doorway toward the fireplace in the kitchen, adding as he plunged on his way, "Let's get it to the fire, but I can't tell you yet if it's alive or not!"

For an instant Eliza stood in complete bewilderment and disbelief, staring at Luke as he bounded across the floor with the ragged bundle in his arms and Jailor leaping up and down beside him highly excited now that his master had finally understood. She hurriedly gathered herself together though and shut the door, making a dash for the kitchen; also, hearing Luke say, as he laid the bundle down on the floor before the hearth, "Maybe it would be better, dear, if you didn't look, til I see what we have here."

She set the lamp down upon the table and turned her back, conscious now that she was trembling.

"It's alive, dear, but barely!"

Wheeling around, Eliza's eyes fell upon a very dark-skinned negro baby, who looked to be a boy somewhere near the age of eighteen months, if the shabby damp clothes that draped the little body was any sign. The baby appeared to have fallen into a frozen state of unconsciousness.

"Oh, Luke," she cried. "Who in the world could've been so heartless and cruel?" Hastily, she dropped down beside him and started helping get the baby out of its cold and grimy clothing.

"I can't imagine, dear, who it was or their purpose for it. But, the most urgent part right now is trying to save him, if we can. We'll think about who's responsible for this act later.

Eliza sprang upon her feet.

"I'll run and get a blanket and some clothes, Luke, I'm sure Carr's will fit him."

"Is there any warm water on the stove?" He called after her.

"Yes, there's plenty in the kettle." "Good! Bring that, too."

"Of course, Luke, I'll be back in a jiffy."

Presently, she was back at the hearth with a soft blanket and several pieces of Carr's clothes, including a nightshirt. She had also gathered up towels, wash cloths, soap, warm water, and a small box of carded wool.

"Once we thaw him up a bit, we'll lay him in the box of wool, Luke," she said, falling down beside him again and going on to ask, "Why didn't we hear him cry, Luke? Surely, he must've cried."

"Probably because he was asleep and also half numb from lack of suitable clothing in this type of weather, when he was laid out there. Naturally, if he did awaken after being brought here, he was too frozen to cry out loud enough for us to hear him. If this baby recovers, which looks doubtful, he'll owe thanks to no one but Jailor. He'd still be on those steps if it hadn't been for jailor's sharp and watchful eyes."

"Yes, you're a good dog, Jailor." Eliza added, bending over the near dead baby and laboring at what appeared to be a useless endeavor.

Suddenly, Luke jumped to his feet.

"Dear, I'm going to run for Hannah and Doss. It looks as if this might be an all-night ordeal and I think we could use their help. Just keep on applying that warm cloth to him as you're doing, I'll be right back."

Frightened at the thought of the baby dying in her hands, Eliza pleaded, "Please hurry back, Luke."

"I will, darling. I'd send you and stay with him myself, but its better that you stay out of that weather out there."

She heard the door close and, all of a sudden, she felt as though she had been tossed in another world where no single person dwelled.

Sometime later, after four weary and concerned people had bent and stooped over the baby for what seemed like countless times, while Jailor sat perched like a hawk looking upon its prey and watched them, the baby began to stir a little and at last the anxious circle heard a faint murmur fall from the tiny mouth.

"He gwine come round," muttered Doss. Hannah nodded, "Y'us right dis time o'd m'n."

"I hope so," Luke replied. "It seems we've done everything that can be done. In the morning, I'll go after Seth to have a look at him. Later on, I suppose I'll have to pay a visit to Sheriff Walt Hawkins and report this, even though I much prefer to have as little to do with that man as possible."

"Luke, there was no clue whatever, footprints or anything?"

"No, dear, we saw nothing. Doss circled the back with his lantern, and I circled the front.

If there were any footprints, by the time we began our search, the snow had covered them. Whoever put this baby out there, realized the snow would conceal their steps, that's why they chose to pull this deed at this time."

"Luke, I'd rather you wouldn't report this to Walt Hawkins."

"Why, darling? The louse that did this should be tracked down and prosecuted. Besides, we could get in trouble with the law by keeping this baby here!"

"I hardly think that bunch would care one way or another what happened to this baby," Eliza replied, as she looked down at the baby pensively. "She could've requested that he be brought to me."

Luke jerked his head up and stared at her, Hannah and Doss, also.

"What are you talking about, darling? She? Who—"

"Julia! He could belong to Julia!"

"Julia?"

"Yes, Julia."

"But, dear, this baby doesn't resemble Julia in the least. Julia was very light-skinned."

"I know, but Jake was very dark-skinned."

"Then, you think he belongs to Julia and Jake?"

"I'm not certain, Luke. Still, I have a feeling that it could very well be. You know the last few years have been rough going for so many people."

"Well, times would never become so hard for me that I'd leave my children on someone's doorstep in a snowstorm. It's difficult for me to see Julia and Jake doing such."

"I agree with you to a certain extent. I don't think Julia could've forsaken her baby, but let's not rule out the possibility of her asking Jake or someone else to bring him to me, though my belief is, that it was Jake!"

"Why would she do that? You just said—"

Solemnly, Eliza said, "Because, it could've been her last request."

"Well, if that was the case, why in the world didn't Jake come to you like a man and tell you?"

"Because, Luke, Jake was a shallow and weak person with many shortcomings. I became aware of this after Julia married him. He would rather risk the life of his own child than face me. Our parting was bitter when he took Julia away that morning. In fact, I threatened his life!"

"Oh! Well, maybe Jake will show up sometime if this baby belongs to him." "Then, we may keep him here?"

"For a while, anyway, dear, if he survives."
"Thank you, Luke. I truly do have a feeling about this baby."
Luke's face softened, "All babies, dear," he said.

Chapter Nine

Pete, the baby who had fought all odds and pulled through. As he had suddenly been dropped at Green Sea, from nowhere, he had come by his name likewise. In an unguarded moment, the name bad popped from someone's lips, but no one could seem to recall having heard the name said for the first time in connection with the little castoff negro boy. He had simply become Pete.

With Eliza, Luke, Hannah, and Doss watching over him painstaking diligence Pete had occupied the box of wool for several days; and during this period, it began to be visible that Hannah's grumbling over the fact that she was not a grandmother, was going to be heard less often. It seemed as though the deserted baby had come along to fill this void in Hannah's being that provoked her so insistently. The chance that Pete just might belong to Julia, who Hannah's fondness for had been lacking a great deal of steadiness and this had carried conviction more than ever the day that Julia had rode away with Jake, did not curb her interest in the baby none at all. The fact that Pete's dark complexion though would have stirred little of Julia in the mind's eye, could have played a factor in Hannah's attitude. Anyhow, when time revealed that Pete was going to recover from his brush with death and every attempt had been made by Luke and to no effect at that to track down the party who had deposited the baby upon his doorsteps, Hannah and Doss made it known that they would like to take Pete to their cabin. Luke granted them their wish, but not before he made it clear that he and Eliza would be answerable for Pete's welfare and needs as long as he remained at Green Sea. Moreover, he also warned them about becoming too attached to the child in case his real parents should show up someday. Hannah and Doss had merely nodded in accord and taken the baby, anyway.

Luke might as well have let his warning rested, for a year had gone by and still no one had come forth to claim Pete. In this time, Eliza had learned a lot about the small, sober faced child; for example, that he was never happier than when he was allowed to sit in the wood box beside the stove and watch the preparing of the meals. He would sit quietly for hours, staring at every move that she, Hannah, or anyone else effected with the pots and pans and the many other gadgets that were required in cooking a meal. Very seldom did he appear to be interested in playing with Charlie and Sam's children, who numbered five by now—two for Sam and Bessie and three for Charlie and Ruth. Nor did he make too many moves to play with Carr and Jane Anne. He was bright but very reserved and dignified—way old beyond his years. Sometimes, Eliza was positive that he came by these traits through no other except Julia. If he ever desired to lick the cake spoon and bowl, be never made it known. What could have influenced his behavior in this though was the fact that Eliza, who he seemed to hold much affection for, always rendered him this favor. Even doing this though he was unchanged, ever licking the spoon in an orderly manner, no cake batter spilling on himself or anywhere else. While she observed Pete one day as he sat in the wood box, Eliza told Hannah that if he continued to maintain his interest in Culinary art that she would be most happy and have no objection, because she thought it would be a suitable and proper occupation for Pete, if he should eventually turn out to be a chef. Besides, she held the opinion that men were the better cooks. Did not most renowned resorts employ them as such? Thus, without her or Pete being aware of it at the time, she had proposed the role that he was to start fulfilling at Green Sea in a few short years.

In this year following the astounding arrival of Pete, Luke had seeded and planted more of the long-fallowed acreage that the war had brought, and the warm and fertile land had sprouted and grew another rich and productive crop—giving one high hopes that the rebuilding of the mansion was not too far off in the making. Indeed, another brick foundation was almost completed now on the same knoll that had caught the eye of that young attorney adventurer of long ago. Luke and Doss were laying every brick with a vigilant eye, taking care that each one was fitted to precision. But, one Sunday in late October, a day the land looked as though it may have been polished metal, so brightly in shone in fall's shimmering colors, Luke and Eliza came home from church to find hardly a whole brick standing in its normal place! What had taken place in their absence staggered them so, they just continued to sit in the buggy, held aghast in silence, unable to make any sense of what had met their eyes.

Of course, everyone on the plantation had been away. Even the watchful Jailor had been absent, due to Luke having been powerless once again to resist the dogs mournful look when he had told him to go back to the house, as they all were climbing into the buggy to start for church that morning. Jailor was more Luke's dog than anyone else's, with Carr being no exception. He followed Luke every place that was possible to be approached by his four feet and begged to be allowed to chance the places that were restricted to them. His devotion for his master was seemingly unending. He was happy most though, when Luke kept silent and allowed him to hop upon the back of the buggy and ride blissfully along wherever Luke was headed to. It was getting to be no new common sight to see him perched upon the buggy as it waddled through the rough ruts toward the Baptist Church on Sunday mornings. Upon arrival he would hop down and accompany the family as far as the church door, and there he would stay quietly planted throughout Reverend Johnson's long, stormy service. Luke had felt a little mistrust as Jailor had suddenly leaped off his perch and gone racing down the driveway, barking excitedly. He looked at the dog now sniffing around the wrecked foundation and was glad that he had given in to the plaintive face that had gazed at him so imploringly earlier in the day. Leastwise, the dog was safe, not shot down or reduced to what Bullitt was enduring. Though he felt the worst aggravation that anything like that could bring, he was aware, too, that it could never equal the distress and vexation that would have been his to borne, had he come home and found Jailor lying dead through someone's obvious endeavor to strike back at him. It had been such a long time since any disturbance of that sort had taken place at Green Sea, that seldom did he and Eliza give any thought to the past raids and the possibility that they would start all over again.

After some minutes of staring in baffled silence at the wreckage, that reminded him of places he had seen during the war that had fallen to rubble under the blast of cannon shells, Luke clucked his tongue at the mare, and she moved on down the driveway.

Eliza sighed heavily and said, "Luke, you worked so hard to lay those brick. I think I could shoot down the party responsible for that deed, without giving a second thought to what I was doing."

"Well, right this minute, I feel that perhaps shooting would be a little too quick! I can't imagine anyone's revenge being such that they would stoop to this kind of contemptible evildoing."

"Apparently, Walt Hawkins still holds his grudge against you, Luke, and sent his Yankee friends and those scalawags to do this, even though he is the sheriff and is supposed to see that law and order in the county is maintained."

"It's for sure and as clear as this day, that there's a grudge or something existing." "What will we do, Luke?"

"There's nothing much we can do, dear, since there was no eyewitness, except go on as usual. Certainly, I'll rebuild it, if it lays within my power to do so. The next time around though,

I'll hold myself in readiness for the evil day and guard against having to rebuild it for the third time," he replied rather forcefully.

"Regardless of my remark about shooting, Luke, if rebuilding the mansion is going to

cost us to live with guns and violence in addition to all the other things that its building will require of us, I would as leave we live out our days in the house, we're in now and have you never make another move toward a mansion. I don't want to live in fear of you getting hurt or perhaps have the worst to happen."

"In view of how those attacks have been carried out, it's my opinion that it won't progress to that stage, darling. No, I surely wouldn't want you to live in fear, either, and would never expose you and the children to that type of living. What I meant was, I'll just keep a more watchful eye for the guilty. Building back the mansion is very important to me. Besides my desire to do this for you and our children, it's my hope; also, to achieve this in your father's lifetime. It's not that I think Mr. Carson is getting to be feeble and could depart from us, because, actually, he doesn't seem to grow any older. It'll be my way of letting him know that I haven't been blind to his kindness and generosity over the years and the opportunity that he's made available to me here as well as expressing my own sentiments for this plantation. To me, Green Sea is set apart, sublime in every respect, and I think deserves a mansion to grace its lands."

"Oh, Luke, what could I or Green Sea have ever done without you?"

He turned his head to look at her and, for the moment, his rage and frustration eased somewhat.

"Well," he teased, "There's a supposition forming in my mind right at this minute that tells me your charms most surely would not have deteriorated and gone to waste, hidden under the cloak of spinsterhood! I also have a feeling that you'd manage somehow, to have held Green Sea together."

"Luke, I'm serious!"

"You think I'm not?" he asked, reaching to give her ear lobe a tweak!

Early on Monday morning, Luke set out in an attempt to find some clue in perhaps a few answers he might receive in connection with the smashed foundation, that Doss had already begun clearing away in preparation of starting to rebuild it all again. Luke scouted around most all that day and saw and questioned several people, Early Cole and his sons among them. Even so, in the end, all his effort and above all his conversation with Early, proved to be as ineffective as his vain endeavor in tracking down the party who had placed Pete on the cold and snowy steps of his house, many months before that.

Lying spread-eagle in his favorite spot upon his rotting, rickety porch, Early Cole let his head fall sideways toward the voice that had aroused him from his siesta. Then, with his eyes squinted so tightly that it made Luke wonder how Early Cole could possibly see who was making an effort to exchange a few words with him, he slowly began to drag his fat legs forward inch by inch. Gradually, his head began to rise along with his body and, while he grunted continuously but not too distressfully, he finally swung himself around and let his feet fall upon the ground, facing his visitor but not with his eyes. He moved them as far away from Luke Heyward's face as possible, spotting a few geese sweeping along on a southward course which he focused them upon, as he at long last muttered, "M-hum," going on to ask, "Did I hear you right? You say the whole foundation tore plumb down?"

"Yes, that's what I said. It happened yesterday while my family and I attended church.

Our tenants were all gone, too, unfortunately."

"Well, that's a down right shame! I know laying them brick was a mighty hard job."

How could there be even a bare possibility of your knowing that, thought Luke

"The bricks! Pappy?" pipped job, scrambling upon his feet all of a sudden, his thoughtless expression beginning to show a glimmer of light.

Thinking that Job was still sound asleep where he had been curled up, as snugly as though he were a baby inside a flannel blanket, in the warm and cozy sunlight that shone upon the end of the porch, Early suddenly became startled and let his flying geese go. He quickly realized that Job's sudden outburst had put the situation on slippery ground, making it necessary for him to come up with some fast thinking if it were to be saved. Blinking the brightness of the blue sky from his eyes, which, at that moment, were having difficulty of seeing his son, he swiftly replied, "Uh, yes, son. Have you watered Maybelle like I told you to do? She's plum

tuckered out from all the miles!"

"Miles? Water Maybelle?" Job asked, puzzled by his pappy's question, because Maybelle

had been in her stall all day and had had her water besides.

"Yes, son, do as I say and go on and give Maybelle a bucket of water.".

The bricks completely forgotten by now in this unexpected chore that his pappy had diverted his impaired mind upon, without another word, Job leaped to the ground and headed toward the well.

Sighing deeply with relief, Early turned his attention back to his visitor.

"Excuse me, Mister Heyward, my youngest son as you no doubt have already heeded is well—" he spread his hands helplessly.

Hastily, Luke replied, "Certainly, I understand."

"Now, let me see, where wus we? Oh, yes, it was that house foundation of yours that we wus discussing."

"Yes, I was inquiring if you or any of your sons had seen any unaccustomed riders

passing by here yesterday or perhaps had heard the sound of any unusual commotion coming from the direction of Green Sea, and, if so, about what time?"

"N—o—o—o—o, I don't believe so; that is, I didn't. But, let's say if that could've been the case, I sho—sure don't recollect it, today!" Turning his head toward Joseph and Jonah, both of whom were still stretched out full length on the porch; also, only a few feet from the spot that Job had occupied—though the sunlight has not reached them yet, his lazy drawl sang on, "Boys, I don't suspect that you've seen any riders or heard anything, either, out of the everyday run of things, have you?"

Luke noticed that neither put forth any attempt whatever to move or get up. Nevertheless, while they both gave him a long and straight eye and seeming as though they were speaking with one voice, they did give their pappy a rather prompt reply.

"No, Pappy, we ain't seed nobody," they said.

Early sighed with ease, delighted that he could at least give his gentleman visitor his undivided eye—quickly fastening his sharp and cunning gaze direct to Luke's.

"Well, there's your answer, Mister Heyward, and I'm plum sorry that it's such a poor one as fer as being of any help to you. I know you're dealing with a very perplexing matter. But, just try to rest your body and mind as best you can, and you'll see that the days will pass by with less troubles to contend with. That's what I always tell the boys and I'm giving the same advice to you, because it's plain as this very day that you work too hard. I—"

"I'm running late, I have to be going," Luke suddenly interrupted, feeling that both Early and his sons had lied and also telling himself that he must have been bereft of reason to have stopped and asked the Coles anything. "I'm sorry to have disturbed you from your rest, good afternoon." Turning on his heel and with his head and shoulders high, he made good time in reaching his mare—leaping in the saddle and heading for home.

While his mouth remained to hang open at the words that had begun to flow and that Luke had suddenly stopped, Early fingered his drooping, tobacco stained chin, which in recent years the stubby beard that clung to it had turned totally white, and looked at Luke's back for some minutes.

"Boys," he finally said, "I hope we never have to tackle that man in a direct fight. It's too gosh—dam bad that his own married kin's crazy jealousness puts such a hardship on him. I wish he'd stayed longer. I was just beginning to enjoy his visit. Now not only my siesta is ruined for the balance of this day, I have no one to talk with that's capable of conversing with me on my level! Oh, well, such is a man's lot for getting educated!" He sighed again and stood up, squinting at the westward morning sun. "Jump up, boys, and find Job. If we make haste, we just might make it to the still and back here before good dark."

"Yes—Pappy," they yawned.

Although he was to keep a watchful eye, Luke gained nothing of consequence in the recent raiding matter. All the same, he was determined not to give up this time, averse to be incredulous anymore. His rage had subsided considerably but by no means had it died. He held little doubt that in time the molesters would be back, and he had made his mind up that if it were years before they returned, his eyes would stay open and he would continue to wait in readiness. He was resolved never to leave the plantation unguarded again, til the rioters were revealed. He had told himself that someday or some night they would be back and when they did arrive, he would be all set to greet them!

Indeed, there were one or two firearms above the mantle that gave evidence of Luke's earnestness. Firmly secured in their brackets, way beyond the reach of the children, the weapons lay prepared for sudden attack. Luke had asked Eliza to pass over the guns in cleaning and dusting the house. In fact, be made it known to Eliza, Hannah, and all the others who sometimes helped in the housework, that the weapons were to be left alone and handled by no one but himself. He was so anxious to welcome these unknown adversaries of his with the speedy and warm salute that they deserved, he could not see delaying his greeting by keeping unhandy firing pieces! Meanwhile, though, there were other things besides this business with his enemies that needed his guidance and attention. Though it was winter, once again his hours were long hours. Along with Doss' help, he was engaged in rebuilding the proposed mansion's foundation back, to say nothing of his other tasks and obligations.

On one bright, sunny winter day while Luke and Eliza were discussing the building of the planned mansion, a mountainous load that Luke appeared most willing to shoulder, actually becoming more enthusiastic about it as time went along, he suggested that they ride to the ridge of timber that he had selected for felling. He wanted her to see the timber before it was cut. He had a few more trees to select and mark, anyway; did she not think that it would be quite unusual and rather interesting to help him pick out the most choice trees that would eventually become the walls that would protect and shelter them in their future years? Moreover, Bullitt needed the exercise and, as far as that went, she did, too. Eliza had laughed, telling him he need not have put up such strong defense in support of his suggestion. She would love to go!

Though she was a superb horse woman and did enjoy riding; it was true, she very seldom took to the saddle any more just for the enjoyment of the sport. Even though Bullitt remained to be maimed in his gait; nevertheless, she and horse alike still got a great deal of satisfaction out of the few horseback rides she did take. Had she been able to have squeezed in the time, she certainly, would have taken the horse out more often. But her days had become so taken up with the raising of her children and the endless household duties that seemed forever to be waiting for her hands, that she found it was almost impossible to get away, anyhow, merely for the pleasure of horseback riding, alone. Thus, she was very pleased that Luke had asked and; indeed, had insisted that she chuck her chores for that one time and go along with him. Hannah came to sit with the children. Pete was toddling along beside her, flushed with a happy grin in prospect of spending the afternoon in Eliza's kitchen. After seeing that all three children were settled down and happily preoccupied with their playthings nearby Hannah's chair, where Hannah now sit with the never-ending basket of mending that was ever waiting and that she always pulled forward to work on when she stayed with the children, Eliza turned to Luke and eagerly taking his hand, they slipped through the door. Doss had brought the horses to the end of the walkway; Bullitt was prancing somewhat wildly in anticipation. His peppy behavior though did not daunt Eliza none whatsoever. Confident and sure, she took the reins from Doss and sailed upon the horses' back with no less facility and expertness than that exhibited by skilled cavalryman. Her poise in the saddle was so natural and unaffected that for those observing her actions, it was hard to believe that she seldom rode any more. Luke also observed that she had changed into her old riding habit and that it still fitted her to perfection even though she had had two children. As a matter of fact, while looking at her, he noticed that she did not look one day older than the eighteen-year-old girl he had married, a fact that told him she was going to be as ageless as her father was. He inwardly rejoiced in discovering it' and in sensing that her heart had quickened as his had done when she had turned her head to look at him, too, he gloried in that, also.

The sun shone warn, for December, a perfect afternoon for horseback riding. The weather was mild, more like the beginning of spring than the nearing of the Christmas season. Reaching the river road, they reined their mounts toward Drakston Hall and rode for about a quarter mile. Then, cutting across the lower South field of Green Sea, they headed for the opening in the edge of the woods which was the beginning of the road that had been cut the winter before. In point of fact. one could hardly call it a road. It was scarcely more than a wide path sliced through the heavy thickets, dodging here and there around the bigger trees. It was the route though, that would lead them to the deep, righty timbered ridge. Thus far, only the timber for the sills, which were still stacked at Bill's sawmill, had been snaked over it. Therefore, it had grown over somewhat through the previous summer. But both horses were nimble-footed and both riders capable. It was not too long before they bad reached the stand of timber without having any difficulty.

"Well, what do you think, dear? Can you vision the house I want to build for you, contained here in these trees standing before us?"

Slowly, Eliza's eyes moved through the timber around her. She bent her head backwards and gaze at the massive trunks that towered above them.

"I vision more house in these giants, Luke, than we would ever want to build," she finally told him. "I wonder how many years they've been standing here."

"There's no telling," he said, "no doubt, centuries. I imagine way long before your great grandfather came here."

"In a way, Luke, I hate to see them cut."

"Now don't go getting sentimental over them, darling," he laughed. "Think of it this way. Sure, they won't be alive anymore, but once they become boards to be raised in walls and laid in floors in making up our house, they'll still creak, not form the elements I hope, but form the liveliness and laughter of our home."

She looked at him rather wistfully.

"You are truly looking forward to those days, aren't you, Luke?"

"You bet I am!"

His eyes traveled to the highest part of the ridge where the land began to slop toward a ravine that appeared to be a shallow tributary leading from the river, though water could seldom be seen running in its bottom. They could not see the gully from where they sat upon their horses, but Luke knew it was there and planned on showing it to Eliza because the slope was so pretty. For the present; however, he had bis mind on something else.

"See those big white oaks over there on the edge of the ridge?" He went on to say. "I can't wait to swing you to the tune of a waltz over their broad gleaming boards!"

She laughed, "You really do make it sound as if this timber will come pretty near living on, even though you do plan on taking an axe to it."

"As near to living as dead timber can be made alive," he quipped, breaking into a wide grin. Then, he turned more serious. "I realize it won't be an imported mahogany floor, but—

She was already saying, "I think white oak will make a lovely floor, Luke, and I'll be looking forward to having that waltz with you, upon it. Besides, I'll think our oak floor will be better than mahogany anyway, because it came from our own land."

Knowing the depth of her devotion for Green Sea, he believed her. He let his reins fall over the saddle bar and jumped to the ground. He walked around to Bullitt's side and raised his arms to her. "Well, in that case, Mrs. Heyward," he said, "won't you come and stand by while I mark them, though I fear we may have to wait for our Waltz longer than I had hoped for. I've already been delayed a year or darn near to it. I should be placing the sills this winter instead of rebuilding that foundation."

She saw that he could still be stirred to a degree of anger when he thought about the sneaky and cowering attack that had destroyed the foundation.

"You'll make it, Luke," she encouraged, as she slid off Bullitt's back into his arms. "I'm going to do my best," be replied, turning to tether Bullitt to a nearby tree branch

since he remained to become somewhat restless at times. He left his own placid mare, the Morgan mare that Matthew had given to Eliza and the one horse that Luke had mostly ridden after his return from the war, standing quietly where she was. He picked up the axe that he had thrown to the ground from the scabbard on his saddle with one hand and reached for Eliza's hand with the other. While they walked toward the nearest of the big oaks that be wanted to mark, she asked, "What's on the other side of this ridge, the same timber?"

"You'll see in a minute. That's another reason I wanted you to come along with me. I've never seen a prettier wooded area. It reminds me of the trail we rode on at Windsor.

"Windsor? Well, if it looks like the hills at Windsor, I can't wait as long as a minute!" She suddenly let go of his hand and ran to the top of the ridge, stopping and gazing into the sloping woods in amazement. "Oh, Luke! The hollies! Come and look at the holly trees!" She cried

Luke, having marked the first oak, was walking on to the next one. He looked up, surprised to hear her exclaiming over the holly trees. But, letting his eyes follow her gaze since he was on higher ground now and could see farther over the summit of the ridge, he could see why she had forgotten everything else for the moment except the hollies. In the thick of their every green, glossy leaf, clusters of bright red holly berries were shining like balls under a big glowing Christmas tree. It was a stunning sight, lovely as a pretty watercolor.

"I knew several hollies were here," he said. "But I hadn't thought about them having this whole hillside lit up like a glowing Christmas tree."

"They are so pretty, it's simply indescribable." Anxiously she looked toward him. "You won't cut the hollies down, Luke?" she inquired.

"No, dear, I won't touch them or allow anyone else to bother them."

"Thank you, Luke, I hope they stay here forever. All that's missing from this scene is seeing a red bird gracing those limbs."

He was propped against his axe, now looking at her more than he was looking at the holly trees. "Well," he laughed, "if we wait long enough, maybe we'll see one of those, too."

Making no comment to his reply, she appeared to be having other thoughts. Presently, she said, "Luke, I've just thought of something."

"What's that?"

"Next week, I'm going to come back here and gather some of this holly to decorate for the party."

"So, you and Martha did decide to have a party this year?"

"Yes, Martha seems to think we're way overdue one. It really didn't make much difference to me whether we had one or not, but I went along with her. It'll be at Oak Grove and she mentioned that she'd like to decorate the rooms with a lot of pretty holly. "

"I agree with Martha, I think we all would enjoy a party. But, darling, don't you think you should bypass gathering this holly. It's a long way between here and the house, you know. It'd take a whole afternoon to come back here, gather the holly, and return to the house."

"I'll come back, Luke. I know you want to finish laying the brick if the weather is pretty next week. Don't worry about it."

"You mean by yourself? Alone?"

"Don't look so surprised, Luke. I'm not afraid to come back by myself You're forgetting that I've ridden many times in the woods all alone and especially during those years you were away."

He knew this was true. Still, he was not completely convinced to the idea. But, desiring to keep her from seeing that he did have deep misgivings, he asked rather lightly, "What if a bear should suddenly make a lunge from behind one of those trees?"

She sensed his purpose and skepticism but retorted back in the same frivolous manner. "I'd just back off a few feet and go on about my business!" Though she did go on to add, "Luke, please don't be so concerned. I'll be fine. I'll hang a sack on Bullitt's saddle and keep him close beside me while I fill it. That way, there will be no problem of lifting or tugging it around. I'll enjoy gathering the holly. You said yourself that I should get out more, remember?"

Ever submissive to her wishes and also seeing that she was definite decided in carrying through her notion of supplying Martha's holly, he resignedly shook his head, saying, "Well, all right, but let me finish marking these trees and then we'll sit there on the base of that big trunk for a spell. I want to hear more about this holly business and what you and Martha intend to do with it." He smiled, "What's more, while you're telling me about the plans for the party, we just might spot that red bird you were wishing for."

A merry light danced in her eyes.

"We might at that, Luke," she told him.

Swinging his axe, he moved on to cut a notch in the remaining oaks that he hoped to fell in the ensuing weeks. She turned and raked up additional leaves with her hands and piled them near the big tree that was already surrounded by a thick carpet of last summer's leafage and pine needles. Sitting down upon them, she leaned against the tree's huge trunk and gazed at the flaming hollies; and every now and then, she turned her head to look at Luke, too. Presently, while she sat in the lap of nature's earthy, pungent smell and felt as though she were wallowing in all its lush of beauty, a strange sweet happiness began to flow with every intake of breath that gave life to her body. Thinking about all the loveliness in the universe that God had created, the miracle and glory of the Christ Child on the Christmas so long ago, thoughts of celebrating his birth with Luke, their children, and their family and friends, she became totally wrapped in a gentle peace that seemed to stretch in infinite dimensions of divine goodness.

The feeling was not hers to keep for very long though. Soon, all too soon, a cold hard bitterness was to occupy a portion of her heart, always there to spoil her hope of ever recapturing the joy that was hers to know on that day, no matter how hard she strived to bury it.

Chapter Ten

Frank Drakston sat motionlessly, as he had done for some minutes now, in his huge, easy chair that was upholstered in fine Morocco leather, a leather that was identical in grain and to the leather bindings of the numerous volumes of books that lined the walls of his cherry paneled library. His eyes were fixed solidly upon one of the many rich deep-colored patterns in the luxurious handmade Oriental rug that covered most of the gleaming Cherry wood floor, which matched the wood paneled walls. It was doubtful though if he could have told one what color made up the design, he had his eyes set upon. Moreover, as a trail of mild December sunshine streamed through the window, cutting a bright pathway across the rug where he had his booted foot sprawled, it was dubious once again if he really were aware the sunlight was there. His mind was too preoccupied and; in some instances, was as far removed from the room as the far East from whence the rug came.

Another chair of the same type and size that he was sitting in was placed direct opposite him, though it was empty and, in all likelihood would remain to be so since he was not expecting any callers that day. Both chairs were within handy distance of his enormous rosewood desk and swivel chair which were part of the other splendid furnishings that the overlarge room held. For the most part, Frank sat in either of these two chairs when he was forced to conduct business with someone. He found it much easier and more relaxing to him than sitting at his desk and peering across it. He still tended to be a very private person and; most the time, even in business transactions, found making conversation a great chore, not to mention having to gaze at his associate out of courtesy. Even though he and Elizabeth bad entertained the elite of Charleston's society quite frequently for a number of years and bad attended many other social gatherings that was no sign that he had come to enjoy it. There had been no change in his personality. In truth, it had come to the point of him being more or less dragged to these social activities by Elizabeth, than him attending of his own free will. Lately though, barring the Coopers, he had whittled his attendance down considerably, almost nil; and even when he allowed himself to be entertained by them, he most likely as not remained to be as remote bad he been in China. The number of people that he in all truth felt at east with could still be counted on one hand, with a finger or two left over. He very seldom went to the bank anymore. To attend to business of any kind. Brad and Brent Cooper came to him at Drakston Hall. Why not, if Frank preferred it that way? Which he did, he controlled the greater part of the bank's entire assets.

Sitting there staring at the floor; however, he was reasoning out many things and had finally made up his mind on one of these actions that concerned him, come to the brink of setting upon another, plus having many contemplative thoughts about other situations that touched upon him, too. First, he was telling himself that he would not be roped by Elizabeth's pleading anymore and dragged off to all those parties and social functions that she found so thrilling and he found so boring. His and Elizabeth's marriage had grown into a damn peculiar relationship, anyway. He had come to enjoy and take a lot more pleasure from Elizabeth's presence outside the bedroom than he did on the inside; for example, like having her sit there in that chair opposite him reading a book as she sometimes did, while he looked over business reports. In fact, he and Elizabeth had become better friends than lovers, and it had been that way for a good while now! It was from no faultiness on Elizabeth's part though, the problem lay with him, that is, if one would categorize their marriage as not measuring up to the theoretical ideate of the average marriage bed; and by the very fact that he had come to envision his wife as another woman when he made love to her, he would be the first to say that a damn big problem did exist between Elizabeth and himself In short, the physical side of their marriage had become blemished and it was all his fault. That was one hell of a note! That time in London he had held back from taking Elizabeth because he had thought of Eliza! Now, he made love to his wife, fancying her as Eliza! He must be crazy as hell or damn near to it! For Elizabeth's sake, he hoped she never became aware of this duplicity on his part. That was the one and only reason he had almost stopped making love to his wife, because the knowledge of what he was doing had begun to make the whole act of their physical union distasteful to him. Well, friends or lovers, from that day forward Elizabeth might as well get it in her head for once and all time that he was through going any place that he did not wish to go. But, where would that be? He had had his damn fill of dinner parties, Charleston's society which despite the fact nobody would affirm had become filled with Yankees, the bank and, even the Klan did not hold his interest anymore. England? Could that be the answer to his disappointments and restlessness? If he and Elizabeth were back in England where there would be no chance of his seeing Eliza, would they be able to recapture what they once had? Who knew? Maybe it would be so, then again, perhaps not. One thing was for certain though and that was final, Elizabeth could forget about his attending all those Christmas parties she had been speaking of lately, rather casual like of course; and particularly the one that Martha was gabbing about yesterday which was going to be held at Oak Grove.

Sometimes, he was inclined to think that Martha had become short on common sense! He could not understand why she had harped on that one subject so much and had insisted that he and Elizabeth attend. Could she not see that he still loved their cousin? It was bad enough to face the fact that from all appearances he had lost any chance of ever winning Eliza away from Luke Heyward, besides spending a whole evening in that overseer's presence. Yes, he had come to believe on this very day that Eliza would stick with Luke Heyward, come hell or high water and would never come to him as he had envisioned her doing. Eliza had not the remotest idea what it had cost him to go to Green Sea that day and plead with her to come to Drakston Hall to have her baby, the distress he had felt when he had seen her, the confessing of his love for her all over again. Well, that had been over a year ago she had had her baby, though from what he had heard it had damn near killed her again, and she was still with Luke Heyward in that scarecrow of a house he had slammed together! He would have to say one thing for that overseer though, a more mule stubborn, headstrong son-of-bitch, he had yet to see! It was not an easy matter to fight this man. What did Luke Heyward do when that house foundation had been smashed to crumbling rubbish last fall? The debris had hardly settled where it had fallen before it was cleared away and work began over on another foundation! Now, he was hearing that it was almost completed. It was true that he could have blown those damn Cole boys straight to hell for burning the mansion that had rightfully fallen to Eliza. All the same, it was also true that he was doing his damnedest to see that Luke Heyward did not build another mansion in its place! Why? Well, it seemed that that was the only way for him to prove to Eliza that Luke Heyward would always fail to protect and provide for her in the manner she should live in! Still, even though it cut to the quick to realize that in all probability Luke Heyward was going to win over him; nevertheless, these filthy Coles had better forget the whole sordid mess! He had been certain that Eliza would get fed up with the way she was forced to live and come to him as he had warned her, she would. Now though, it looked as though that would never happen. Well, it probably would not do any harm to let things ride as they were awhile longer. Let Luke Heyward finish his house foundation. It would be safe. After that fool mistake of theirs, those thick-skulled Coles had not dared in the past nor would they dare in the future to venture one step in the matter of that business without acting on direct orders from him! In any event, it had finally become visible to him that damn money did not buy everything after all, apparently having no worth whatever when it came to buying happiness or peace of mind!

Ultimately, Frank lifted his eyes from the floor and let them rest for some time upon the empty chair. Suddenly and somewhat shocked and puzzled, too, at discovering it, because he could not recall having ever felt that way before, for some unknown reason he had the urge for a bit of conversation, certainly not to discuss or reveal anything about his private life or anything about that storage of private thoughts that ever dwelled in his mind; but perhaps exchange a few ideas concerning the bank or the stock market with Brad Cooper, Brent, or some other member of the bank's board of directors. In fact, right at that moment, he felt as though he might have welcomed the sight of that pushy Sheriff, Walt Hawkins, who had a habit of appearing at Drakston Hall from time to time on every possible excuse or pretext that he could think up or claim to have, obviously hoping eventually to make it through the front door by a formal invitation. Well, on second thought, he reasoned, he would want to talk with someone in the worst way before he would ever become so desperate that he would settle for Walt Hawkin's company! He wished that Elizabeth had chosen another day for her Christmas shopping or, indeed, if she had to shop on this day that she had not taken Stuart along, too.

The house was entirely too quiet. All of a sudden, the pressing silence seemed to be more than what he wanted to put up with any longer. He jumped up and crossed the floor to the window. Looking out upon the sunny lawn and noticing the spring-like day, it came to him at last, why he had thought he would have welcomed most any kind of company. It was the absence of the school children! Lucy had dismissed school till after the holidays, and without realizing it he had missed the clamor of their shouts and laughter during recess, the sauntering of marching feet, the hum of voices reciting and especially during French class. This idea of organizing a school at Drakston Hall had been successful way above any expectation he might had held. Naturally, he knew the greater part of its success was because of his having the good fortune to employ Lucy Randolph as its teacher. She was capable and a strict disciplinarian. He found himself smiling as he thought about that. He may miss the clamor and shouts, but it was obvious from Stuart's actions that he was most happy to be from under Miss Lucy's thumb for a few days. A more cheerful little fellow he had yet to see than Stuart was this morning. It was not only the school vacation and Christmas that had Stuart excited, it was his knowing that Whit would be there in a few days, also. Whit. Oh, yes, that business about Whit. A damn shame! True, he had thought his uncle and mother both had gone wacky, as a loon when they had announced they were adopting a baby. However, upon seeing Whit for the first time he had immediately become a little leery and had begun to suspect that Whit was not just any child that Matthew Carson and his mother had taken upon themselves to raise. Then, during their visit home when Elizabeth had roped him in on that family gathering at oak Grove, he had observed a certain glow and heartfelt look on Lucy Randolph's face each time her eyes trailed toward Whit, a poignant, pervading look that appeared to go a lot deeper than what anyone would feel for a child by merely being attached to it through a close friendship, which was supposedly to be the case, when she had lived in Columbia. In all the rumpus and merrymaking, he began to look closer and saw that Whit had the same coloring of Lucy Randolph with the exception of his deep gold curls. He started adding all together, recalling the number of times he had heard Martha talking about Nat's visit home in the fall of sixty-three, the short while he had stopped in Columbia to see Lucy, her being the last family member to see Nat before he was killed at yellow Tarven in the spring of sixty-four; and then and there, he had concluded that Lucy Randolph was the mother of Whit Carson! Of course, it had not been necessary for him to question Whit's father. It was a known fact that Lucy Randolph had hardly looked in the direction of any other suitor, and there had been those who had endeavored to make the grade with her, other than Nat Carson. She had had eyes for Nat only. In fact, up to the present date, he had never heard of her courting another man. But there had been many times she and Nat used to pair off together at parties, church, and other gatherings. He had heard Martha state several times how sad it was that Nat and Lucy were not granted more time together in Columbia. Well, he supposed it was sad. Still, it appeared their time together had been long enough for Nat Carson to leave his seed planted in Lucy Randolph! Yes, as surely as Stuart was his child, Whit was the child of Nat Carson and Lucy Randolph! So, there had always been more to that relationship than what most people had seen. How long had that sort of dalliance been going on before Nat had gone to war, if any? Hell, what made the difference? Did not the majority of couples eventually get around to doing the same or damn close to it, though in public they strived and did give the impression that they would never go that far with their stolen hugs and kisses! A chance was all most anyone needed!

True, he had been deeply disappointed and had disapproved of his mother marrying his Uncle Mathew. However, after that Whit business he had begun to view his uncle in an altogether different way. Now, he inwardly saw Matthew Carson and Lucy Randolph both as being very courageous people to have taken the step that they had and, as far as that went, his mother, also. Furthermore, Lucy Randolph must be endowed with unusual remarkable qualities that only a few people were aware of. From what he could gather she had born her burden all alone, or as some would say, her act of folly. Anyway, she had not come whining to her family, bringing her disgrace upon them. That alone was enough to tell him that she surely had to be a strong person. Were Martha and Eliza wise to the true identity of Whit? If they were, neither had never let on or said one word touching upon that one factor of the situation. There was no question that silence, which evidently is what they had chosen to keep because surely, they must know, would certainly be better for all concerned, anyhow, and was the most rational and sensible course to take. Yet, he could not help from being a little curious as to how Lucy Randolph had managed to shepherd herself through what was sure had been a trying ordeal for her. Naturally though, he had no intention of conducting a search into the matter of the sake of satisfying his pondering, probing mind. Let it lie on that dark closet shelf where from all appearances everybody had desired it to be placed, he guessed that most important part had been taken care of anyway, and that was the fact that Matthew Carson and Lucy Randolph had seen to it that Whit would carry his true name through life, though, unfortunately, very few people would ever be aware that it was his true blood name! Nevertheless, he supposed again that they had done all that could be done. Leastwise, they had spared Whit the stigma of going through life as a bastard and being called that name more than his name would have ever been called! No question but what this had weighed on Lucy's mind and had brought her to the decision to give her child up. Well, was he going to continue to stand here for the rest of the day, gazing out the window, his mind lost in other people's troubles? Was not his own plenty to warry about? Why not take advantage of the mild, sunny day and go look for a Christmas tree? Then tomorrow when Stuart was home, they would go back and cut the tree down and haul it to the house. Locating the tree would give him something to do and at the same time should take this restlessness out of his bones. He thought he knew just the place where he might find the size pine he wanted, or perhaps a small pretty holly. Another idea Just crossed his mind. Why not take his shotgun along, too? Might see a few squirrels or some other game. It had been quite a spell since he had gone squirrel hunting.

Abruptly, he turned from the window and strode across the room to the wide hallway, calling out for a house servant. Within seconds, scurrying feet came running to the hall. Frank very seldom addressed those servants by name, nor was this time to be the rare exception. As a matter of fact, he still tended to give the house servants at Drakston Hall so little of his attention that it was indeed doubtful if he were aware to who he was in truth speaking to. In his usual clear, crisp manner, he hurriedly sang his command.

"Send word to the stables for Blossom to be saddled immediately and brought to the front steps. If Mrs. Drakston and my son should happen to return before I do, inform Mrs. Drakston that I've gone squirrel hunting and to look for a Christmas tree."

Guardedly, the servant replied, "Yessir, Mister Drakston," made a swift bow and hurried away to carry out his orders, in awe every much as profound and no different than had slavery still existed.

Shortly, Frank and Blossom were sailing down the long drive on their way. When he reached the roadway, he reined Blossom toward Green Sea. This direction was also toward Drakston Hall's North Field which he had to cross in order to reach the portion of woods that he had in mind to hunt in and look for the Christmas tree, an area of Drakston Halls wooded acreage that contained the same ravine that cut through the woodland of Green Sea and the land mark that he would come upon in due course, the slight water channel that he would choose to follow and the route that would lead him straight to the ridge of marked timber and holly trees on Green Sea's lands.

He had ridden for quite a long while, observing a few small pines here and there and marking the place in his mind, in case he did not come upon a more suitable tree, so he and Stuart could cover the same places next day and select one for cutting. He had not seen a suitable holly, but he had decided that he would let Stuart make the final choice among the trees, anyhow. Thus, he sorta dropped hunting a Christmas tree and started giving more attention to the hunting of game. He saw a few squirrels and took a shot at them, but they had not been too exposed to his aim and he had missed hitting any. Missing the squirrels though did not bother him. He found he was enjoying the mere sport of the hunt far more than he had expected to and seemed to be getting as much pleasure form it had he been bagging a sack of game. He was discovering that the ride and exercise were doing wonders for his body as well as his frame of mind and began to ask himself why had not he spent more time in the outdoors that fall? The open air was exhilarating. Forthwith, he decided that he would repeat the afternoon in the near future.

In the process of circling the tract of land, he now came upon the slight watercourse. He stopped and began to take his bearing, having soon concluded that if he followed the ravine in the direction that he was headed, it would lead him direct to the river road. Noticing, too, that the sailing western sun was spotting the leafy, moss-covered ground with less and less sunlight, he decided that by the time he reached the roadway it would be time to call it a day, anyhow. In thinking about day's end, his mind turned to Stuart and Elizabeth, wondering if they were on their way home. Then, he smiled to himself and thought, would not it be just great if he were to reach the road as they were passing by? He would ride on home inside the coach with Elizabeth and let Stuart follow alongside it, riding Blossom. Stuart would get a kick out of that.

He had covered a long stretch beside the ravine, mostly thinking about his little son, the brightest spot of his entire life, past or present, when suddenly his eyes were drawn to the flaming stand of holly trees.

Likewise, as Eliza had been, the beauty of their branches moved him so that he slowed Blossom to a standstill. As he sat and took a long look at the lush landscape before him, a spirited essence of the holiday season began to fire his imagination as it had never been roused before, a strange lively eagerness filling him with an expectant readiness to meet the days ahead. He sighed contentedly and was starting on his way again when, all of a sudden, the unmistakable nicker of a stallion cut through the woods. He jerked his head around and looked toward the top of the ravine from where the sound had come from and could hardly believe his eyes at seeing a woman whirl atop the ridge to look in his direction; and, seconds later, he became more baffled to recognize the woman to be Eliza! Another loud snort was cutting through the air again. He looked more closely and now saw that Bullitt was tied to a tree limb some few feet away from where Eliza was still standing motionlessly, looking down the slope at him. Instantly, all thoughts of reaching the roadway were dismissed from his mind and were forgotten about, though his gaze held no intent, only astonishment and gladness as he stared back at her. Somewhat in awe, too, at seeing that she was alone, he began to guide Blossom up the sloping hill between the holly trees, hoping while he climbed the ridge toward her that she was not making ready to leave. Nearing the place where she remained in her same tracks, seeming as though she were sorta stunned, he heard her say, "Frank, what on earth are you doing here? You frightened me."

"I'm sorry, Eliza, but may I ask you the same thing? It's obvious though, so you don't have to tell me. They are pretty, aren't they?"

"What?"

"The hollies, silly," he laughed. "You must think so, you're standing there with your arms full of their branches."

"Oh," she said, having completely forgotten everything except the one thought that had been pounding through her head, her awareness that Frank had found her alone in such a remote, out-of-the-way place. But then, as she continued to observe him, she sensed his seldom good cheer and somehow found herself feeling less fearful for his being there. "Yes, it's so unusually pretty, that's why I wanted to gather some. I thought it would make lovely decoration for the Christmas party at Oak Grove."

"I've been hearing a lot about that party, lately. Martha was by yesterday and was talking about it again. Why isn't she here? You should've pressed her into helping you."

"She really doesn't know I'm gathering it. I heard her say that she'd like to find some pretty holly, so I decided I'd surprise her with this. I'm positive there's no place where we could find holly any lovelier."

There was still no purpose in him for making the statement, he was merely jesting. He said, as a half-croaked grin spread across his face again, "I wish you thought as much of me as you do Martha."

She looked aside somewhat and ignoring his remark altogether, she asked, "You and Elizabeth are planning on being there, aren't you?"

Suddenly, despite his decision earlier in the day that he was through with parties and quite surprised at himself besides, he heard himself telling her, "Oh, I'm really not sure. Well- yes, I suppose we will. Might as well since its Christmas. Say! I must've really scared you; you haven't moved out of your tracks yet!"

Making an endeavor to catch and hold between them for once this rare mood of Frank's, she sorta jokingly replied, "You did. In fact, when Bullitt suddenly nickered, the first thought that popped in my mind was to wonder if a bear were going to make a lunge at me from behind one of these trees."

He throwed his head back and laughed deeply, a young and innocent kind of laugh that she had not heard coming from him for many long years. It brought a smile to her face, too. Though she felt it had been spoiled when he told her, "Well, I certainly hope you were relieved when you saw that it was me instead of that bear you were expecting, though I've often wondered if you don't look upon me as being such or maybe something worse!"

"Please, Frank, let's don't start anything like that today, what's passed is passed, let's forget it."

"I couldn't agree more. But, getting back to that bear business, I don't think you're afraid of bears or whatever, or you wouldn't be way out here gathering holly all alone."

No sooner than he had said it, she decided that this was another remark that would be best dropped where it was. Finally, she was moving out of the one spot that she had stood in, saying as she turned away, "I think it's time I unloaded my arms of it, too," adding nothing more as she started walking toward Bullitt.

Quickly sliding off Blossom's back, he called, "Wait and I'll give you a hand with it."

She turned back as he hurried along beside her. They walked on together without saying anything else until they reached the sack that was hanging from the saddle on Bullitt's back.

Then, she said, "I can manage it, Frank since I already have it in my arms," and started to reach up to lay the holly inside the sack but stopped, going on to add, "I suppose it would be helpful at that if you'd hold the top of this sack wider."

"Sure thing, I'd be glad to."

He reached and held the sack wide at the top while she laid the holly inside.

"It appears that's filled this sack, unless you have another, I guess your holly gathering is all finished for this time."

"Yes, I was just before leaving when you rode up. I've probably already gathered more than what we'll use, anyway."

He jerked off his gloves and stuffed them in his coat pocket.

"I'll tie that string tighter, wouldn't want you to lose your holly leaves before you hardly get started."

She thought the cord on the sack was fastened to the saddle firmly enough, though she did not tell him so. While he fiddle-faddled with the knot, or it appeared o her that was what he was doing, a silence had fallen between them, an uncanny stillness that to her seemed to be crowding them, but for the life of her she could not think of anything to say to him. Finally, when she saw that he had finished retying the knot, as casual like as she could attempt it, she said, "Well, I suppose that does it. Thanks, Frank, I'll get on my way home now." She made a move to mount.

He quickly laid his hand lightly on her arm.

"Eliza, it's not late, yet. Won' t you stay awhile longer? It' s been so long since I've seen you, that is, alone like we are now. Well—to be honest with you, I was hoping you weren't getting ready to leave. I wish you wouldn't go. I've been wanting to talk to someone all day!"

Puzzled, she looked at him rather closely, because this indeed was something very unusual for Frank to want. She wondered what had induced him to feel that way, if anything. Nevertheless, she had no desire to stay longer and perhaps find out, wishing now a thousand times over that she had forgotten all about the holly and never came back. Knowing Frank for his touch—and—go personality, she knew she was treading upon dangerous ground and felt uncertain about any move she might take, or, as for that matter, anything she might say, though it was manifest that she had to do something immediately—he was anxiously awaiting, his eyes fixed upon her.

"Frank, I really should go, it'll soon be time for me to start supper. I—"

"You shouldn't have to cook your supper!" he suddenly exploded. "You should have servants to do that! My God, Eliza! Why did it have to be like this? Where did I fail, when all I've ever wanted was to put the world at your feet?"

She saw him ball his hand into a tight fist and thought to herself, 'well, that sure was the wrong thing for me to say.' She tried a different approach, "I know, Frank, and I'm truly sorry for any unhappiness that you've seen because of me, but—"

"Then, you will stay awhile longer?" he interrupted again to ask. "We could sit over there at the base of that big tree trunk and talk, please, Eliza."

It seemed that every word she had spoken had gone against her; she thought that Frank was being very childish and unreasonable to ask her to stay and especially after she told him it would soon be time to start her supper. Still, she was aware, too, that if she made him angry there was no telling what he might do. If she were to go ahead and leave, anyway, he might even attempt to overtake her and detain her out of sheer deviltry, and her being late would cause Luke to worry. She knew there would be no question of Frank's overtaking her, if it came to that, because Blossom could move like lightning whereas Bullitt was maimed. Even though she knew all this to be solid fact, she; nevertheless, went against her better judgment—mentally asking herself over and over was she walking into something she would not be able to handle, as she finally told him, "Well, just for a few minutes, Frank. I've been away from the children too long as it is, and I really must get back to them and see about supper, too."

"Come on, he said, swiftly reaching for her hand and leading her over to the huge oak tree, the same tree and bed of cushioned leaves that had provided her and Luke with such a snug place to rest and have a delightful talk together less than a week earlier, though she said not one word about it to Frank. The truth was, she felt like a fool and was thinking what the scene could very well suggest in case anyone else should happen to ride by like Frank had done and see them. She pulled her hand away from his and rather shrinkingly sank down on the bed of leaves, curling her legs up under her body as her full long navy-blue skirt spread out around her. She was not wearing a riding habit on this day. She had worn the wool navy-blue skirt with matching sweater and a white cotton blouse. Having gotten quite warm while she was gathering the holly, she had taken her sweater off and draped it across the saddle where it still remained. Although Frank had said, he wanted to talk, once they were seated, he seemed to have become solemn and in want of something to say. Thus, she took the lead and got their conversation started by asking about Stuart and Elizabeth. He told her they had gone Christmas shopping, and then, he asked of her children but inquired nothing of Luke, which, of course, did not escape her notice. They said a few words concerning playing the role of Santa Clause to their children, but she still did not bring Luke's name up.

Taking the lead again in the falling silence, she said, "you never did tell me what you were doing riding out this far, today."

"Well, actually two things, looking for a Christmas tree and I thought while I was doing that, I'd do a little squirrel hunting."

"Had any luck?" she asked and smiled back at him.

"What with, the tree or the squirrels?" he asked, as the trace of a smile gave evidence of his light mood returning.

"Oh, I saw several trees that will be all right, but I'll let Stuart make the final choice tomorrow. As for the game, I saw a few squirrels and took a shot at them but missed out—" he paused suddenly and looked at her deeply, no trace of the smile now as he added, "the story of my life it seems."

Somewhat irked with him for making such a self-pitying remark, clearly explicit in its meaning, she turned her head from his gaze and looking down the slope through the holly trees, she decided, come what may, she would comment upon it.

"Frank, I would've hoped that of all people you would never have make a statement to that effect. It's my opinion that so far, you've had a very full life. You've been blessed with a devoted family, good health, vast wealth, and a lovely wife and child. What else on earth, could there possibly be?"

"Well, I'll rephrase it then. Let's say I missed out on getting the one thing I wanted most, and you know that was, but—oh, hell, what's the use in going into all that!"

She started to tell him that she was in complete accord with him, because if that subject was what he wanted to talk about, her few minutes had come to an end. But suddenly, he was turning his head in all directions, staring at the trees, Exclaiming, "Eliza's someone's been chopping hell out of this timber! Have you noticed?"

"It's nothing to worry about, Frank, it's been marked for cutting."

"Cutting? You mean that's why all those damn chunks have been cut out of their trunks?

Who—" He suddenly broke off his question.

"Yes, Luke marked them a few days ago for timber."

"Timber?"

"Yes, he plans to use Green Sea's own timber in building the mansion that he hopes to build back. We certainly won't be importing any mahogany as Father did. Our floors will be coming out of these white oaks that you see marked here."

"Oh, I see," he muttered, seeming crestfallen once more. All of a sudden though, she saw a flush covering his face as he went on, "My luck again! I may have known that I wouldn't be granted even these few minutes with you, without his name coming up!"

If she had been put out with him over his other statement of self-pity, due to his failing in having won her, now he had absolutely floored her. In spite of hoping and thinking that perhaps for once they could have a peaceable conversation, likewise with him, she felt her temper rising and could feel the hot flush that was covering her face, too.

"For heaven's sakes! Frank!" she flared. "I was merely answering your question! And, yes, I, too, may have known that we wouldn't talk five minutes before you would say something about Luke that would irritate me! Besides, why shouldn't I mention his name in our conversation? He's my husband as Elizabeth is your wife, and I want you to understand that for all time! There is no reason whatever for your despising Luke as you do! He's one of the finest men I've ever known! A more kinder or considerate human being for people or animals, I have yet to see! He'd—"

"Stop singing Luke Heyward's praiseworthiness to me, Eliza, I don't want to hear about it!" He retorted, shaking his head and raising his hand, waving her words aside.

"Well!" She flared again, her voice to the point of quivering in her anger, "I was starting to say that Luke would be your best friend if you'd only allow him to be, and in my opinion, you'd do well to have his friendship. However, since the mere sound of his name is so obnoxious to you, you have no need to be concerned that I'll say another word regarding your becoming friends, ever!"

"You'd be doing me a great favor because 1 've never been too keen on forming a friendship with, well, let's just say, the more common hands!"

Her mouth flew open in astonishment. His insults could still amaze her at times.

"So, again, Frank, you have no qualms in telling me direct that Luke 1s outside your class! That's the ultimate between you and me and I mean it this time! I warned you long ago that you'd better save those derogatory remarks in relation with him! He's my husband, the father of my children, I love him; and I shall not stand for this any longer, I'm leaving!" She started to jump up, but he was too quick for her. He made a grab for her hand, jerking her back down with such impact that the dry, dead leaves went sailing every which way around them.

"No!" he sneered, "You'll leave when I say you may leave. Furthermore, you should know by this time that I don't appreciate hearing you say you love Luke Heyward!"

Even though his grip on her hand was definitely sending a signal of his powerful muscle strength over hers, causing her to feel a sudden dark fear that sent a tension fatigue from her head to her feet, she; nevertheless, forced a bold spirit over it, lashing out, "What! You mean to say you'd force me to stay here til you're ready for me to leave out of pure devilish spite, when I need to get home to my children?"

"Your children, Eliza?" He laughed scornfully, his rare light mood, that she had hoped would endure at least until she got gone, vanishing before her eyes altogether in the rising of the same old familiar imperious personality that had ever claimed him the greater part of his life. "It's not your children as much as it's that overseer you want to get home to. You don't fool me. Sure, you love him, and you always never fail to tell me how much, do you?"

"Let go of my hand, Frank," she demanded, rather forcefully.

"No, by god! Not til I'm ready, and you might as well calm down. I'll let you leave when it's time to leave!"

The instant his last word had fallen, it seemed there was only one object in her mind now, to break his grip and run! Hoping to catch him off guard, she exploded, "Well, it's time now!" as she made a swift move to leap to her feet, pulling on her hand with all her might.

But Franks hold was firm. He jerked her down again, this time much harder than he had before, and drew her closer to his side, telling her, "I be damn if it is, not till I say so!"

Panic seized her. She started struggling in his grip, fighting at him with her free hand.

"Luke, will kill you, Frank Drakston, for this!" She cried pushing and slapping at him all the harder to free herself.

Still without purpose for his keeping her there except to show her and also prove to himself once again, too, that he reigned as master of the situation, he grabbed her other hand, barking, "Goddammit! Eliza! I told you to calm down. I don't want to slap you but you're tempting me, yes, it seems you have a way in bringing out the worst in me!"

She did not calm down though. His threat of slapping her went unheeded. She struggled harder and harder to free his grip on her, screaming again between gasps of breath, "Luke—will kill you—I know—he will!" He screamed back, in a violent rage now because she had not done what he had asked, "Goddamn Luke Heyward! I'm not afraid of him or his kind. Right now, I'd welcome the sight of him. Go ahead and scream by god if that's what you want to do, but nobody else is going to hear you but me, and I have no intention of letting you leave til I'm ready for you to go!" Though her strength was wavering the screams, the sobs, and the tussle never ceased. While he held both her arms pinned down firmly to her sides, she labored on fiercely, making a desperate effort to push against him and get upon her feet. In her twisting and struggling she began to crumble fast under his strength and fell backwards. He followed her down. Even when she was down flat upon her back in the bed of leaves, she did not give up the battle to free herself, though. It continued on for some minutes with her rolling back and forth, making a vain attempt to ward him off with her knees and feet, as he hovered closely over her, more or less rolling with her.

At this point, it finally came to Frank that both their fiery tempers, and his dogged obstinacy not to go back on his word, had carried their bickering way passed what even he had no taste for, this time. Even though, as usual, she had enraged him to no end and was still kicking at him and struggling to free herself, it had become evident to him that her strength had weakened considerably, though it was true again he did not sense and had no way of knowing that it was falling rapidly into a state of total exhaustion and that her fighting him had never come to an end, because the rigidity of her arms was misguiding his reasoning, as he held onto them. At any rate, all of a sudden, he decided that she could leave! Rather again, had his decision been motivated by the fact that in their scuffling together in the leaves, having her body so close to his, his face having brushed across her bosom a number of times, he was aware now that he was becoming sexually stimulated and had no wish to take her with her fighting him? Moreover, he had suddenly found his rage with her had gone, entirely. Anyway, whatever the case, he did have intentions of telling her she could go even though he had chosen to continue on to keep her pinned down while he did so. Immediately, he put her two wrists together and now holding them with one hand while he supported himself with his other, he drew apart from her and had actually started to tell her he was sorry that their quarrel had gone that far. However, he never got around to it, for by that time, several buttons on her blouse had become unfastened, revealing a good portion of her full, high breast; and her body was lying directly beneath him with her skirt and petticoats up around her waist—hardly factors that would have induced him to press forward with his decision without taking notice of them, even had there never been any desire for her on his part to begin with. Therefore, instead of him saying anything, he told her nothing as his eyes became set to these makings that had resulted from their fight with each other. Scarcely, before he had begun to stare at her, he felt himself being drawn into a dreamlike stimulus of motivation that was to gain a mastery over his every move and every word that he was to enact. This was something far bigger than Frank Drakston, himself, this time. Something that he was powerless to control in any degree, nor did he desire to, he suddenly found. The years began to fall away, back to Drakston Hall long ago, melting away in the lust that was claiming him. No longer was this woman who lay beneath him the wife of Luke Heyward, the man he despised. He did not even think of Luke Heyward. No longer was she the mother of two children. She was the pure and innocent sixteen-year-old Eliza, his gem, his own jewel, and he would be justified in claiming her as such. He drew back from her further still and now taking her sudden quiescence as she finally gave up and stared up at him as a sign of partial surrender to him, if not perhaps even agreeability, though he thought, he was not sure, that she had whispered, “No, Frank, please no, think of our children,” he reached forward and laid his free hand on her breast and caressed it in all tenderness before he bent his head forward and buried it in depth of rapture that seemed to have no bounds, as he murmured, "My own Eliza, My darling, I'm not going to hurt you. For all the world's riches, I wouldn't hurt you. I love you so!" And later, some minutes later, he finally released her wrists and in warm softness gathered her closer in his arms. Then, one of his hands slid down between their bodies and in a short length of time; but what to him seemed like the infiniteness of all creation, he was gently but firmly guiding his flesh into her flesh, driving deeper and deeper, taking her at last in all the hallowing of love that he was certain God had put in the power of man to meet with in satiating his desire in the flesh of woman. Even so, hardly had his sense become to being assuaged in completion when he began to realize that the glory of his prize was turning to that of regret as he perceived that Eliza was not responding to him any more than the dead leaves which had become their bed, a factor that had ever been of vital importance to him in his copulating with any woman and especially now with Eliza. Also, afterwards, when he was to discover that she had actually become ill and he had taken her in that state, his regret turned to bitter heartache, turning his world around him as dark as death!

Indeed, she had become ill. Filled with terror, she had recognized the look in his eyes for what it was and suddenly had made all effort to dissuade him from going through with his act by pleading to him to think of their children. In her pleas he thought she was still screaming, until to her utter dismay, she found that her screams were dying to mere whispered words in a throat that all of a sudden had collapsed on her. She tried harder and harder to beg to him, but she heard nothing coming through the dry, harsh soreness, that now seemed to be squeezing her breathe off, but faint whispers which appeared to have no effect at all on Frank. Also, she had known by the extreme weakness overtaking her that her strength was going rapidly, but was unprepared for the dejection that crushed her upon learning that as far as fighting Frank's moves off when he did release her hands, she might as well have been a baby in his arms! Suddenly, knowing that she had fallen prey to him at last due to her overspent body which felt as if it were waving on the brink of faintness, she began to pray silently over and over for darkness to come to her as quickly as possible so that her mind may be spared if not her body. The darkness did not come though, not then. While he was having his way with her, she was conscious of every detail; the pricking of the dead leaves and pine needles upon her cheek when she had turned her head as far to the side as possible and it had sank in their foliage, Franks head lying buried in the hollow between her neck and shoulder with him murmuring love words in her ears at the height of his glory, the final taking and insertion of his body into hers despite the times she had told him he would never have her, all these crushing details she was to feel keenly, so much so, that their mark on her was long in healing. Now, that he had at long last finished with her, she lay prostrated before him, feeling as though her very soul had been trampled upon and as she were going to throw up any second besides, she tried to gain back enough strength to rise.

Frank sat close beside her fastening his pants. The silence was permeating, almost to the point of being deathlike. Now that it was all over with, he was chagrined because he had not been slow in sizing up the situation and seeing it in its true light. Though he had endeavored to be tender with her and was certain he had been, he was also aware that had not changed his deed from being short of atrocity, since she had not submitted to him willingly. Therefore, having reflected upon it for some minutes he had summed the whole matter up in one word—rape!

Besides the horror of that word though, something else began to bother him dreadfully and that was her behavior. Had she been lashing out no less ferocious than a captive tiger; in truth, what he had been expecting her to do, he thought he could have dealt with that far easier than this distressing, unstirring calm. Once he had disengaged his body from hers, he had been unable to meet her eyes, averting his gaze here and there while he waited for her to stir. But the minutes were ticking away, and she still had not made any move to get up. Glancing at her through the comer of his eye, he saw that she was lying in the same precise position that he had left her in, something that puzzled and distressed him more, to say the least. Her eyes were fixed and staring straight above her. Her clothes were disarrayed with her body still exposed. The exposure of her body alone heaped additional mortification upon him because if there were anything he knew about Eliza, he knew her for her modest and delicate charm and especially when she was in the company of the opposite sex, even if he had abused it a number of times. Growing more miserable by the second, he knew nothing else to do but try to soften the ruthlessness of his conduct through an apology, thought he was well aware that whatever he might have to say would do but very little, if anything at all, toward modifying the element of its crudity. All the same, he would try, even if he could not bring himself to look her full in the face while attempting it!

With his eyes still averted elsewhere, he slowly and rather humbly began. "Eliza—I'm—well—I'm truly sorry about—all this. I realize now that I should've let you go on home and not—delayed you. I do want you to know though that I didn't plan—well, for it to go as far as it has. It just happened—I mean—I couldn't stop, Eliza, I just couldn't" Suddenly, he let his apologizing ride for the moment. Nothing but the heavy silence meeting his words. Eliza's failing to retort back this time was more than he could fathom, causing him to gain the courage at last to look at her. Searching her in a somewhat close-up gaze, by no means was he pleased with what he saw. The pallor of her face was too white, the eyes too set! What had happened? What had he done to her? Alarmed, he edged closer to her side. He knew his questions were going to sound stupid, because it was obvious there was something wrong with her. In fact, all of it had been wrong and ill-timed, their meeting—everything! But, he had to know why she was so silent and white looking.

"Eliza, is something wrong? Don't you feel well?"

He was quick to see that even if she had heard his apology or his questions, she was not going to trouble herself answering him. While he sat and studied her, wondering what to do or say next, his eyes came to the uncovered part of her body and fastened there. Suddenly though, the dishevelment of her clothing started getting to him. He began to feel as if he could not bear to see her lying there looking so vulnerable and unprotected any longer. He was amazed at himself for feeling that way, because when it came to a woman's body and particularly in the case of Eliza, he would never have thought that a circumstance like that would bring him to have a desire to cover her endowments. Be that as it may, though, he did have an intense desire to see her clothes straightened. Thus, he cautiously let his hand steal to her waist and gathering hold of her skirt while he anxiously watched her, he began to pull it down over her body. Instantly, he saw her eyes fall from above her and move to his hand and then they came to his face and stopped. Though he was greatly relieved to see her reacting for what little it was, he was positive that he would never forget what he read in her expression as she looked at him. So cold and hard it was, it looked as though it were set in granite and especially her eyes, which held nothing for him except vials of hate. Just the same, now that she had responded to a degree, he decided that he would apologize once more, thinking that if it did not do much good in mending what he had done to her, that maybe she would allow him to help her up, anyway. He repeated his apology all over again, humbler than ever, and finally said, as he made an effort to take hold of her hand, "Here, let me help you get up."

Quick as lightening, he saw her shrank from his as though he were a serpent, as she snatched her hand back and hugged her body tightly in a seemingly endeavor to shield it from him.

Her obvious hatred for him and her refusing to let him help her, cut at him sharply. He drew his hand back to his side and stared at her for some time, reasoning that it was plain she was not going to have one word to say to him, or, as for that matter, even acknowledge his presence anymore if she could help it. He told himself though that in a way he could not blame her. Had not she had to yield to his more powerful strength? Even though he had made up his mind that he would stay nearby until he saw her on her way home, he; nevertheless, rose and stepped off to the side a few feet and began to brush parts of leaves and pine needles from his clothing. Seeing that she remained lying as she had been when he had gotten his clothes back in fair order again and; for lack of something to do in the uncertain, awkward silence, he turned away and started walking aimlessly in the direction where Blossom was still waiting quietly in the same spot, he had left her in. He had only taken a few steps though before he felt compelled to look back, seeing to his surprise and joy, too, that Eliza was beginning to rise. His joy; however, at seeing her stir at last was short-lived. No sooner had she gotten to her feet; he saw her pitch over in the leaves again! It scared him. He felt his throat tighten as he dashed toward her. He fell on his knees beside her and saw that she had fainted dead away! He became frantic. He jerked his hat off and began to fan her, wondering as he did so what on earth had he done to her, wishing a thousand times over that he had never touched her. He saw his fanning was having no effect and were wishing that he had some water when suddenly he thought about the shallow stream. He literally leaped down the slope and soaking his handkerchief in the cool water flow, he ran back and squeezed the water upon her face. Then, he took her up in his arms and holding her on bis lap he continued to apply the wet handkerchief to her as he exclaimed over and over, "I didn't know, Eliza, I didn't know!" knowing for certain now that he had indeed taken advantage of her weakness in addition to feeling the helplessness of her body cradled in his arms, he had become so upset that he was not even aware he was weeping tears for his spent lust. The first tears that he had shed for a long long time—until he noticed that water was dropping on her unconscious face and knew then that it came from the tears washing down his cheeks.

It was sometime before he was able to revive her, a length of time that for him could not have been spent any more remorsefully—time in which he had come to think that if he had his rifle, he would blow his brains out! True to his heedless nature, he did not think about the fact that if he were to do away with himself, that she could very well be accused of the crime- heaping more trouble upon her. Anyhow, he finally told himself that maybe Luke Heyward would do the deed, saving him the trouble, though his feelings toward Luke remained unchanged. In all events, she did at last come out of her faintness that she had prayed for earlier and gained back enough strength to make an attempt to start for home. Every move that she made though was still done in silence. Frank walking beside her, as she not too steadily made her way toward Bullitt, offered her his hand but she brushed it aside. Even so, when she did reach Bullitt and started to mount, still brushing his hand off as he offered her his help aside, he ignored her and lifted her in the saddle, anyway. He observed that she behaved as if he were miles away. While he anxiously looked at her, she swept her hair back from her face a number of times, rearranging hairpins here and there. And then, looking down at her clothes, she slowly buttoned back her blouse, seeming to be surprised and pleased that there were no buttons missing. The next thing she did, she brushed at her skirt. Then, he heard her give a long sigh as she headed Bullitt in the direction of home. He saw that her pace was slow though, as he stood and watched her til her back had become lost to him; where upon, be turned and clucked for Blossom. On his way home, still geared solidly to the peculiarity of his personality, he gave very little thought or worry; if any, to the fact that Eliza could go home and tell everything and that Luke Heyward could ride to Drakston Hall that very evening and call him out, doing the same deed that he had been on the verge of doing had not Eliza stayed fainted so long in his arms. The one thing that was uppermost in his mind and the one thing that did worry him far more than anything else now, was the fact that it looked like Eliza was never going to speak to him anymore!

Luke, keeping his eye on the bedroom door, sat on the edge of his chair beside the fireplace. His shoulders were slumped from tiredness; his face was set with worry. He was holding the baby on his knee and keeping close watch on Carr and Pete; also, as they played on the floor in front of the hearth with Carr's toy soldiers, seeing that they played as noiselessly as possible. Hannah was bustling around the kitchen preparing broth for Eliza along with hurrying in her effort not to be too late in getting "Mister Luke supper on dat table," though he had told her there was no need to rush for him but he would like to get the children fed and put to bed as quickly as they could manage it. Hannah's face showed lines of fretting, too, and every few minutes she would interrupt her cooking long enough to tum and look toward the bedroom, also. Doss was likewise, as he tramped back and forth in the chore of filling both wood boxes, one beside the fireplace and another beside the cook stove.

Now, at long last, Seth was opening the door. Luke, with the baby still in his arms stood up and took a step forward, asking, as he tried to read the message in the doctor's face before the door had hardly closed, "Seth what do you think? Is she serious?"

Seth walked on and stood near the hearth before he replied. "Well, right at this stage, Luke, let's not say serious, but she's very ill, that's for certain. She has a much-aggravated throat inflammation, congested lungs, high fever and—"

"Pneumonia?" Luke questioned again, somewhat shaky.

"No, I'm not going to use that word; yet, but I fear she's near to it. The main thing is to get busy and try to ward it off before it does tum to that."

"It's all my fault."

Searchingly, the doctor inquired, "How' s that?"

"Because I should've let that work out there on that foundation rested and gone and gathered that holly myself. She mentioned this morning that her throat was a little sore, but during dinner she assured me that she felt fine then and wanted to go on and gather it so she would have it ready to take to Oak Grove tomorrow."

"Don't blame yourself, Luke, these things have a way of creeping up on people. No doubt she didn't feel ill several hours ago. The extra exertion and this balmy weather this afternoon, which caused her to become too warm and probably perspire, certainly played a big part in bringing it on quicker. In fact, this type of weather brings on colds and other illnesses far more often, than in severe weather when people will dress more snugly."

"Yes, that's true. I recall now that Eliza didn't even have her sweater on when she came home. It was lying across the saddlebow, but she should' ve been wearing it, because the air had become chilly by then."

"She didn't realize it though; due to that high fever she's carrying."

"I guess not, I was shocked when I touched her hand. All of it sorta puzzles me. I looked for her a good while before I finally saw her at the edge of the woods. I had a feeling something was wrong with her, then. I threw everything down, jumped on the mare and rushed to meet her, and this part is more baffling than all. No sooner than I asked her what was wrong, saying that I'd been looking for her back earlier, she broke down and started sobbing. Then, I took a closer look at her and saw that she was ill. Of course, when I attempted to question her further as to what the trouble was, I found she could barely whisper. I told her not to try to talk or weep, either, that it would only worsen her condition, but she cried all the harder. I got her on to the house and to bed as fast as I could and sent Charlie to fetch you."

"I started to mention that a while ago and ask you if you knew what she's upset about.

There's no question about it, she's in a highly emotional state."

"I have no idea, Seth, that's what puzzles me so. She was in a happy and cheerful mood when she left."

Looking into the lighted fireplace that was taking the night's chill away from the house, the doctor, pondering his question, went on to say, "It could be that party that she and Martha were planning. Caroline's mentioned it several times in the past few days. She's all excited about it, too. I understand Christmas Eve was the date set for it, which is only two days away and; with Mr. Carson, Miss Amy, and Whit due to arrive that day, too, it's no doubt troubling Eliza because she's fallen ill and won't be able to go through with her plans for the holidays. Eliza has a sensitive nature, disappointments or otherwise, she's more affected by them than most people. Another thing, a high fever can bring on emotion. I've seen it happen before."

"I don't know, Seth, I think it may be something more than the party or the forthcoming holiday events that's got her upset. I've never seen Eliza behave like that before. She seemed frightened to me, even to the point of being scared."

"Well, I suppose I should be getting on with further treatment in an attempt to cure my patient's symptoms, rather than stand here and continue to speculate on what caused them. I've already given her something for fever and also painted her throat with ointment. But, I want to get a very hot mustard poultice to her chest as soon as possible. I see Hannah's got supper on the table. You go ahead and eat and tend to the children, I'll get Hannah to help me with Eliza." Starting back to the bedroom, the doctor turned and quipped, "Don't eat all that savory looking ham and rice, Luke, and I might add those peaches and biscuits as well, I want a bite myself, I plan on staying awhile."

"Thanks, Seth, I'd appreciate it. As for the vittles there'll be plenty when you're ready to eat. I'll soon have the children fed and put to bed, then I'll help you with Eliza."

Luke's eyes followed Seth through the bedroom door then he, wearily, pulled a chair out from the kitchen table and sat down with the children. He saw that they ate their supper, but he hardly ate one bite.

So, the way things turned out that night and for a good while afterwards, there was no special reason for Luke to ride to Drakston Hall. In the long run, he was inclined to think as the doctor did, that Eliza's deep depression was due to her severe illness and her disappointment concerning the planned holiday festivities. The next day, Seth was forced to use the dread word, "Pneumonia," though he did add that it was confined to one lung and her chances for recovery looked bright. Thus, the holidays were tense, days filled with strain and fear. When Matthew arrived at Green Sea, he found his only child, or the only one that he thought was living, in the crisis. He took a seat beside her bed and refused to leave till it was evident that she had come through and would survive. For Luke, it was a dark time. There was only one cheerful note about the holidays for him and that came through his old friend Tom Green. A long cheerful letter and a big box of delicious apples arrived on Christmas Eve from Tom, Betsy, and Luke. Hearing from Tom in his heavy despair seemed to give Luke hope that all would turn out well, after all.

However, of all the people who Eliza's illness did affect, there was no person more concerned or baffled through the holidays than

Elizabeth Drakston. Of course, she was concerned about Eliza, but her great concernment and bafflement centered upon her husband. Upon hearing that Eliza had pneumonia and was seriously ill, he immediately withdrew from everyone. Neither his little son nor his beloved mother could penetrate the hard, silent hell that he slipped into. Dark remorse was his constant companion, though Elizabeth nor did anyone else know this. All Elizabeth did witness or know was that Frank seemed to brighten considerably when news came that Eliza had passed the crisis, which was normal, and she understood that; but what she could not perceive was the fact that her husband would allow his cousin's illness to affect him so that he still dwelled in a state of morbidity fairly often—hours when his own child could not reach him.

Chapter Eleven

Yellow forsythia and white bridal wreath filled the garden. Flower-hued warmth was bursting over the land again, breathing life into a new season. The virulent chill; however, that had taken over a portion of Eliza's heart remained unchanged as this flowering glow spread through the air and opened the winter door of nature's house around her. The deed was still too raw and vivid, her illness too recent, her fears too keen, and her feeling of guilt for not having told Luke—too heavy. Once she had left her sickbed and had begun to take over the duties of her household again, her burdens weighted on her mind so, that she went about everything she did in a somewhat blind, unthinking fashion. Her appetite was feeble and sometimes she lost what little she did eat; consequently, bringing days that seemed to have no end for her, as she wondered and feared if Frank Drakston had gotten her with child. Counting days and remembering back; thus far, she knew if she were pregnant, the baby could not belong to Luke. Hence, she decided she had to make sure it remained that way so there would be no guessing it turned out to be that she had another baby that fall. The thought of possibly conceiving a baby under such circumstances repelled her; yet, what seemed worse still was the thought of having a child and the question of who might have fathered it always hanging over her head. So, she shuddered and feared and the night that Luke had turned to her for the first time following her illness, she had been forced to tum away from him, a move that brought an apprehensive silence to their bed for the first time since their marriage. But, although it distressed her deeply, she felt she had no choice since her illness had brought her health to a state of uniformity. The day came though when she at last knew without a doubt that she could empty her mind of that one worry altogether. No more would she tum away from Luke's arms and shed silent bitter tears for doing so! Fortunately, she found, this had been another fear, that Luke's arms still held the same meaning for her. In no way did she associate what Frank had forced her to undergo with him to her sexual union with Luke. The act was simply not one and the same. For her, the giving of herself to Luke was virtually and morally a substance within itself alone, nothing else tied in with it. All the same, instead of this happiness that she was finding in her husband's arms again lessening the guilt of harboring Frank's crude deed from him, it seemed to bring it home to bare on her conscience all the more. Her dread though of what could happen once Luke found out; the thought of possibly a killing, the scandal that would result and be heaped upon innocent family members to say nothing of the grief, the horror of thinking that Luke could end up in prison because had not she herself told Frank that Luke would kill him, all those possibilities, she thought about constantly and kept putting off telling Luke although she wanted to. She prayed to gain the courage to overcome her fears, but they continued to live with her. There was hardly a doubt in her mind as to whose side the law would favor if, God forbid, her fears were ever to materialize to reality. In fact, the fear that Luke could be taken from her and their children and be sent to prison had come to be such a mania with her that she had begun to have nightmares in which she would see Walt Hawkins leading him away bound up in handcuffs and chains! It was not uncommon for her to scream out in her sleep. One night during another frightening dream, she woke up to find Luke holding her and saying over and over in a rather concerned tone as he tried to soothe and reassure her, "I'm not leaving you, dear, I'm right here beside you." He had insisted on her seeing Seth the next day. She had gone knowing full well that Seth, though competent doctor he was, would not come within a mile of discovering what her real problem was. The source to all her trouble was of such an outlandish nature that she saw no way that the doctor could come near making a valid diagnosis and treat it in point. But there were some things too private to discuss even with one's physician.

Sometimes, she saw Luke studying her and would wonder if she had blurted out something in her nightmares that had started him guessing that something else was causing the greater part of her highly nervous state rather than her recent illness. Though if this were the case, she was also soon to observe that he was not going to say anything about it. She had not seen Frank since the day that she had left him on the timber ridge and her feelings were that she never wanted to see him anymore, concluding she had earned and was still earning the right to feel that way. And so, as time began to march by in that spring of 1870, such were her days and her nights, too—a period in which her distress was becoming more foreshadowed rather than growing lighter in the brightness of springtide, a dire time for her because it made no difference how glowingly blue the sky shone, she could still see dark storm clouds gathering on the horizon. A habitual with her though, she made no effort to meditate upon it, ever hoping that the next day would bring her dread for the near future less pronounced. But each sunrise she was to see as unpromising. Curiously, even though she was now positive of pending tragedy in some form, as the days passed, she began to feel somewhat alleviated in her fears for the reason that, she felt whatever came it would not involve Luke or her children, directly.

Although in its entity, Early Cole's over anxiety could not have been any more removed from Eliza's, that hardly made it any less disturbing to him; nevertheless. When it came to the matter of setting his eye to the future, Early could see little; if anything around him that signified spring was going to be any brighter than what winter had been. Though winter's road had been rough going, Early was beginning to think that from all appearances spring was not going to present any smoother byways for him to tread. Actually, he saw nothing about his present situation that bespoke of anything but the fact that he was approaching rope's end and the hour of decision was drawing nearer and nearer. The knowledge of all this cut at Early like a bullwhip. True, he would be the first to admit that his moonshine—no, distilled spirits was a better way to define it, more classic, had dropped in its quality; even so, he had been sure that he would be able to persuade a few of his old customers to stand by him. It seemed though that in this present postwar year most people were becoming a little more well-fixed, adjusted more to the upheaval the war bad brought to their way of life, getting back on their feet again, and in this adjusting and present well-being, it appeared that the taste buds of this majority had undergone a change, too, completely forgetting that once upon a time old Early's beverage was all they had to depend on or could actually afford, tempting the appetite with it as often as their meager means would allow. Well, it was just as well be reasoned, as he headed Maybelle toward home on an evening in early March. He had not been able to secure any more credit to buy supplies, anyway. One did not brew spirits without supplies. Hence, his livelihood had finally vanished, faded away right before his eyes!

He pulled his old tattered coat closer to his body and yanked at the frayed brim of his hat, lowering it further over his eyes. Weather—

wise the day had not been too calm, either. The unruly wind had howled all day and was continuing to sing in the treetops, though it was getting to be the time of day that it should be settling some. It was almost dark before he reached the edge of his cluttered and rundown homestead. Guiding Maybelle carefully thought the tin cans broken glass jars and bottles, rotting boards and shingles with rusty nails sticking here and there that had blown or fallen from the house from time to time, besides sticks and splinters and a dozen or more varieties of other rubble, he finally made it inside the barnyard and rather wearily crawled down from Maybelle's back. Leading her inside her stall, he flinched at the emptiness of the other two stalls between Maybelle's and Joseph' s horse. At the beginning of winter, in the face of starvation, it had become necessary to sell Job's horse, not too long afterwards, Jonah's bad been the next to go. He had decided to start with Job's horse and go up the line in the family instead of the other way round. Now, it looked a though all the horses were going, one by one Depressed almost to the point of grieving over that seemingly fact, be patted Maybelle fondly on the head and then started the process of gathering her up something to eat. Looking though the bins and cribs of the old rickety barn that seemed to be deserted without all four horses standing there, he quickly found that horseflesh was not all that the shaky building was becoming scarce of. He did manage; however, to scrape up a few com nubbins and some oats. Finally placing the grain before Maybelle, be said, "Maybelle, that's plum sorry fare, but to tell you the truth, I'm not expecting to have much better myself."

Appearing as though she understood every word that Early had said and wanted him to know it, the mare nudged him affectionately with her nose before she lowered her head to her scant supper. Early gave her one or two more loving pats, sighed and turned away to close her in her stall. He stepped through the doorway and started to draw the door to a close and drop the latch in place, but before the door bad hardly moved one inch it went crashing down and actually fell into several pieces near Early's feet! Though the fate of the door had been obvious for some time, Early gaped at the rotten, worm riddled boards and told himself that the door's falling was just about the last straw for that one day. Looking at his faithful mare though and suddenly concluding that she would not stray off, anyway, a reliving thought because it was telling him it would not be necessary to start nailing boards across the doorway, he shrugged and while beating his way toward the back kitchen door, he wondered how much more he was going to encounter before the day ended.

As he opened the timeworn creaking door with a little extra care since he had no desire to be reminded any more that day of his crumbling existence, the savory smell of chicken cooking flowed his way, instantly melting his taste buds and sending his spirits soaring in delight.

Wanting to satisfy himself about this unbelievable surprise be gently closed the door and walked on over to the small stove and lifted the lid from the old smutty iron pot that his mother, Kate had cooked in, gazing down at the bubbling chicken and rice.

Busy in the one function that he had become fairly able at, Job standing beside the stove with a big spoon in his hand, grinned, "Joseph brung us chicken, Pappy."

Early smiled back and said, as he put the lid back on the pot, "It looks that way son." He walked on to the hearth where Joseph and Jonah were stretched out on the floor.

"Joseph son, it seems you were lucky today."

"Pends on how you look at it, Pappy, cause that's one hen I had to work some fer."

Started, Early said, "Work?"

"Shore did, Pappy." "Where at? Who? —"

"Mister Heyward."

"Luke Heyward! You mean Luke Heyward at Green Sea?"

"I ain't heered tell nobody else in these parts being called that."

Quite concerned, as he began to recall Frank Drakston's warning, Early inquired somewhat fretfully, what wus you doing at Green Sea? I thought I told you boys what Mister Drakston said. Have you went and got us in more trouble, Joseph? We wus not supposed to about Green Sea till—"

Joseph jumped up, frowning, "l ain't made no trouble fer us, Pappy. I wanted to see if that there house foundation was about built back, so l rode up there and asked Mister Heyward if he had seen old Red!"

"Old Red? Our hound? Why Joseph that dog's been chasing coons and possums in heaven fer weeks now, already gone to his reward!"

"I know that, Pappy," Joseph suddenly snickered, "but Mister Heyward don't know it. Don't you see Pappy that was my excuse for riding there. Fact is, he wus downright friendly, said he sym—cent—"

"Sympathized," interrupted Early, "It means his heart wus thinking about our trouble." "Yeah, that's right, cause he said if his jailor was to go off and get lost like Old Red, it would hurt him mighty."

Impatiently, Early pointed to the floor. "Sit back down, son, that's enough about old Red!

What I wants to know is how you got that chicken. You sho—sure didn't go up there to Green Sea and ste—take that hen out of Mister Heyward's chicken coop right before his eyes, I know. Now start at the beginning and tell me everything you seed, heered, and all you said!"

Obediently, Joseph flopped himself upon the floor again.

"Well, the chicken, Pappy, is where the work came in. Like I say, I wanted to see that house Mister Heyward is startin' so just when I commenced to ask Mister Heyward about had he seed old Red, a big load of sills came from Mister Clarendon's sawmill, the biggest sills, Pappy, I've ever seed in my life. Mister Heyward asked me if I would give them a hand in unloading, being there was nobody around but that old nigger an' the two drivers on the waggin, said he would pay me, that he didn't expect me to work fer nothin'. It shore was a job, but Mister Heyward kept his word, I got this," He slid his hand inside his pocket and drew forth one or two dollar bills and held them out to Early, "besides the chicken and the rice. When Mister Heyward started to pay me, I told him I just as live have a hen and some rice, but I got money, too. Didn't I do all right, Pappy, I'm tired of eating cornbread and syrup!"

Flabbergasted, that Joseph's adventure to Green Sea had resulted to him working for Luke Heyward as well as bringing home money and a Chicken, that for once had been earned instead of stolen, Early could hardly think straight. He finally managed to mutter, "Yes—son—it's all right. Mr. Heyward's a fine man."

Jonah, silent until now, suddenly turned his head and staring at his Pappy as though he might have been a stranger, said, "Then, why does we do all them mean and aggravating things at Green Sea, Pappy, if you think Mister Heyward is so fine?"

Briefly, Early was stumped again. The day was absolutely getting to be a little too much to cope with. Besides all his other problems that his mind was bogged down with, now Jonah would have to come up with a troublesome question like that! "Well—what I meant, son, is that it appears the man keeps his word. About them—well—them other things, it all boils down to us letting ourselves become in debt to Drank Drakston—"

"I ain't in debt to Mister Drakston, I don't owe him a cent, he's never handed me a penny!"

"Well, I hate to dispute your word, son, but in a way, you are in debt to him, all we Coles here on this plantation rides in the same boat, no favors. So, even though Mister Drakston didn't put the money in your hand, you live here so that does not excuse you from being in debt like the rest of us! Like I started to say when you cut me off, unless a person stays independent in life they sometimes have to bend a lot of ways that they wouldn't bend if they had not had the misfortune to get in debt in the first place."

"But, it's Mister Drakston we owe the money to, so why do we do them mean things to Mister Heyward when we don't owe him money, seems to me—"

"No, we don't owe Mister Heyward no money and thank God for that! But we owe plenty of them greenbacks to Mister Drakston, that I've been forced to borrow from him from time to time—"

Quickly, Jonall sat up, his penetrating eyes fastening upon his Pappy's.

"Pappy, how's them mean things we do to Mister Heyward ever going to pay our debt to Mister Drakston? It seems to me if we going to be mean, Mister Drakston is our man, not Mister Heyward!"

Early leaned further back in bis chair, shaking his head. He guessed he might as well got more comfortable. Explaining some things was not an easy matter. "In the first place, Jonah," he said "life don't work that way. And, in the second place, one word could answer your question correctly as to why we trouble Luke Heyward and that word is jealousness, on the part, of course, of Frank Drakston."

"I don't understand, Pappy."

"No, I don't reckon you would. It's like this, son. We owe money to Drakston and can't pay him back with money, so that leaves us under his thumb to order us to do the things to Heyward that he would like to do his own self, because he wants Heyward's wife. Like I told you boys long ago, he's always been wild over her. Now, mind you, he don't want anybody to think that, not even us, but l know different. When I asked him why he would want us to do them things to aggravate Luke Heyward, he said something about Heyward being nothing but a carpetbagger didn't belong in these parts. Then, he looked me square in the eye and told me it was none of my damn business—forgive me, Mathilde, fer using a word like that in talking with our children. Anyway, he let me know right quick like that we would do what he said do or leave this roof."

"I still don't understand the part about that woman," insisted Jonah.

"Well, I think Drakston bad it worked out like this, son. His aim all along has been to show Heyward up in the eyes of his wife. Mostly though, he thought if he made the going rough enough fer Heyward there right after the war when people wus barely keeping body and soul together, that Heyward would get disgusted and pull stakes, go somewhere else to scratch his living out like a lot of people wus forced to do, fer awhile, anyway. Once he got Heyward out of the way, his plans wus to move in fer the kill with Heyward's wife—make the grade with her, son, take Heyward's place in her bed! Now, Drakston's sharp, mind you, about a lot of things; but that was just plain foolish thinking on his part, because the way I see it, things would never get to be rough enough fer Luke Heyward to leave that beauty he's married to fer any length of time."

"I shore would not leave her if she wus my wife, cause she shore is purtty."

"Yes, she is, son, but don't you get your mind on that woman, she ain't fer you or the likes of you or Frank Drakston, either. She belongs to Luke Heyward, bound to him in the sight of the Lord God, and Frank Drakston would do well to look at it that way and quit coveting another man's wife! My mind tells me, as bad as I hate to admit it, that in all likelihood this plantation will be as near as Frank Drakston will ever come to owning anything at Green Sea!"

Seeming satisfied, Jonah said, as he stretched out again by the hearth, "Just as you say, Pappy."

Suddenly, Joseph popped up from the floor again, exclaiming, 'Pappy, I ain't seed no supplies, did you leav'em in the barn?"

"No, son, I didn't," Early replied, as he stared into the lighted fireplace with a fairly long face. "I wu not as lucky as you wu today. There ain't no supplies to leave in the barn or anywhere else. When it comes to u getting any more credit, Joseph, I fear that is all passed and done with. I hate to tell you boys this right before that fine meal that Job's beginning to take out the pot, but it looks like we're washed up fer good, finally finished in the beverage business!"

"But, what will we do, Pappy? l don't want to sell my horse!"

"Right at this minute, son, I ain't got—I mean I haven't the littlest idea." His woes were pressing him so tonight, he could not even think to talk proper! "But, try to calm yourself and not get upset. I know you don't want to let go of your horse and when I think about the fact that Maybelle could come to the same fate, it near starts me to weeping. Just give me a spell to think in boys, and I'm sho—sure that I'll come up with something though."

"Like mebby Mister Drakston giving us some more money when we tear down that new foundation that Mister Heyward has built back, aye, Pappy?" laughed Jonah.

Though his remark had actually stemmed out of admiration for his father's shrewdness and he had said it in praise to that factor and nothing more; nonetheless, it suddenly jangled Early's nerves, causing him to tum a pouting lip toward Jonah; and he most certainly would have given Jonah one of his talking—to lectures at that very minute had not Job called out that supper was ready. Though he was still irritated and thought his second son had gone too far and should be upbraided for it, he rose from his chair anyway, and padded across the floor to the table with his mouth dropped in silence. But, as he clapped his eyes upon the huge platter of mouth- watering chicken and rice that had come by way of Green Sea, he instantly recognized why Jonah's remark had rubbed him so. It was guilt. And too, all of a sudden, he felt as though his sons had looked down his throat, taken his true measure in uprightness, causing himself to start wondering if that holier—than—thou that he had forever proclaimed, though in its origin he had ever believed in his sincerity, had maybe after all been nothing but hypocritical canting all these years. Thus, the dressing—down that he was thinking he was going to give Jonah once they had eaten, got lost somewhere in the middle of his own unsaintly deeds as they flashed through his mind.

He sat down at the wobbly table, which by then had finally become bare of any covering,

and started saying his usual blessing that he reserved for those times when the fare was more pleasing to his eye than in the normal order. He was muttering along, "Thank ye, Father, fer those nice sustaining vittles that you've seen fit to grace our table with," When suddenly, he cut off his blessing, even failing to say his habitual pronounced "Amen." So much was his hurry to make an attempt at covering up what he was positive that his sons had suddenly gained knowledge of; and to prove to himself, too, that Early Cole did indeed, for all that, possess a little of that holy righteousness that he had mouthed for his entire life, he felt he could not wait another second to hear his earnestness in the matter of Green Sea verbally declared. His mind was going father than Green Sea, though. He was also telling himself if he were counting on meeting Methilda at the gates of Paradise, perhaps the time had come for him to start walking a more straight and narrow path—the years were slipping up on him! Thus, while filling his plate with Chicken and rice, he went on to announce the sudden and startling decision that he had just arrived at. "No, Jonah, in answer to your question, I think not! We ain't tearing down no more house foundations at Green Sea! Let Frank Drakston get someone else to do his dirty work!"

Having had no thought beyond the present concerning their future welfare, his announcement sounded almost as shocking to his own ears as it did to the three stunned and questioning faces that turned upon him, causing him to have a sudden quiver of alarm in spite of all. Sinking his teeth into a chicken leg; however, he immediately took heart and cheered, "Now, don't you, boys, get upset and start fretting. Go ahead and enjoy your supper. Like I told you a while ago, if you give me time, I'll think of something. It'll give me a chance to use my head fer a change, make good use of all the intelligence that the Holy Father saw fit to supply Early Cole with! Since I wus blessed like that, how could I let you down! Like I say, go ahead and enjoy your chicken!"

Later, after having gone to bed, Early was finding that the "something" he had though his mind capable of coming up with appeared to be more difficult than what he had reasoned it would be, while stuffing himself with the lavish supper that Joseph had provided. Even though his stomach was contented for a change, that not too common fact didn't seem to affect his restlessness none whatever. He tossed and turned, pulling the soiled, ragged hand-sewn quilts about him as he tried to unlock the door to the thinking part of his mind. But, the harder he trained to find the answer to his problems, it seemed his mind worked that much harder to remain blank. He began to have doubts, wondering if he had sworn off having any more to do with Frank Drakston too soon and plunged headlong into the task of attempting to take care of himself and his own without the assurance of Drakston's assistance to fall back on. Finally, out of desperation, he reached the point of having almost convinced himself that this was probably the case; and feeling utterly defeated he turned on his back and setting his eyes to the room's darkened rafters that were outlined by the shaft of moonlight streaming through the uncurtained window, he began to ask himself, had Drakston won again? Was he going to be forced to yield to Frank Drakston's wishes once more and allow his sons to continue to harass Luke Heyward and keep destroying his property? It was a true fact that he had no desire to. Still, what then, if he turned Drakston down? Well, there was no point in wrecking his brain any further. He had already worried so much that in bis anxiety he had begun to see stars before his eyes. Stars? He blinked his eyes once or twice to see if the twinkling light were really there or just merely an illusion and found that indeed he was seeing stars! Baffled and somewhat suspicious, too, of what he feared, he raised his head from the pillow and peered closer into the darkened room above him. Why, lo and behold! That was not lights from anxiety he had thought he had seen; it was truly one of Heaven's glories shining right direct through the roof upon him! Well, now that was the final straw for this one day! The March wind had finally blown part of his roof away; in fact, over the very spot where his bed set! Well, He reasoned, leastwise the elements were tranquil enough now. The wind was calm, but, most important of all, it was not raining or snowing. Thus, Providence must be smiling down on him, anyway. So, why get excited because he had Heaven for a roof tonight instead of those old rotten shingles? Might as well quit worrying and get to sleep. He would gaze at the stars a while. Maybe that would settle his mind some and tomorrow perhaps he would be able to unscramble all his perplexing problems.

Resigning, at last, to the many trying ordeals and disappointments of the day, he let his head fall back down to the pillow and pulling the covers up around his shoulders he set his eyes to the twinkling, inky sky through his rooftop and gave the working on his mind full rein. Strange though it was, rather than his thoughts dwelling and deliberating on his present worries, he found himself recalling his childhood—his and Matthew's bare feet running through the freshly plowed earth behind the several mule teams at Green Sea after they had read their lessons for the day—the awe of being invited by Matthew's pretty and smartly dressed mother Anne Carson inside to share cookies and milk was a wonder out of fairyland—his own gentle mother, Kate, and her delight that he was learning to read and write and her gratitude to the Carson's for making it so. But, whereas Matthew had stayed to his studies in the schoolroom, he, himself, was soon to lose interest and instead of his mind following the pages of the books before him, it began to stray to other things and places—places that all too soon his feet were to carry him to, which were from every fish lake in the swamp that he could find to the streets of Charleston and back to O'Henry's general store; and his separation from Matthew for all time had been imminent, though he had not been aware of it at the time. Had he not allowed his mind to be lured to other wonders other than what had been in his books would his life have taken a different direction? He mentally asked himself. Well, there was no use in thinking about that at this late date. HE had been happy in his adventures, after all. In addition to all the merry making and hilarious capers he had gotten into, there had been the excitement and joy in going back to the hill-country on their annual visits, seeing his Cousin Jim again, their going possum and rabbit hunting together, their wishing upon the evening star when they were small, and later, their confessing to one another that each had wished they could remain together and not be separated by so many miles. Jim? Cousin Jim? Why in the world had he not thought of Jim before this hour in all his trials and tribulations? Cousin Jim! He had thought of it at last! Jim was the answer he had been searching for! Jim would take him and his sons in till they could get on their feet again. He would leave the low country, go back to the hills and mountains from whence his ancestors came and where his kinsmen still dwelled. Let Frank Drakston have these scrubby rundown acres that bordered Green Sea, there was no way that he could ever raise the money to get out of debt to him. Yes, by Jove, that was it! He would pull stakes and give it all to Drakston! When he had realized a while ago that, among all his other troubles, there was actually no roof left over bis bed to shield him from the forces of nature, he had been on the brink of thinking he was forsaken. But now he knew different. Even though the good Lord had sent that fierce wind today that had blown his shingles away; nevertheless, through that very making of the Holy Creator—exposing his eyes to the stars tonight through that hole up there in his roof, He had been showing Early Cole the way!

Elated, Early suddenly threw the covers aside and lumbered out of bed. Shuffling bis feet across the floor, he headed for the comer of the room that held an old crack-mirrored dresser and the oil lamp that set on its top. Fumbling around in the darkness he found the match box and striking one the matches on the wall, be turned the wick up in the lamp and lit it. Then, with lamp in hand, he turned and waddled to another comer of the room that held the one item in the house that still clung to most of its original charm and elegance—the handsome trunk that his mother had brought with her to the low country as a bride, though its gilt-edged tapestry-like cover was now faded considerably. Squatting down beside the trunk, he set the lamp on the floor and unsnapping the center metal hook, he lifted the dusty creaking lid. Digging into the musty, crowded inside among the numerous time honored and outdated articles such as a flimsy, narrow-waisted bridal gown that had turned yellowish with age, a few timeworn dainty handkerchiefs and palm leaf fans, the likeness of several family members well-preserved in a number of daguerreotypes, letters, hair ribbons and combs, and many other old and dateless things, he finally found the document that he had gone in search of the aged, crumpled deed to the fifty acres that made up the Cole holdings. Holding it in his hands, he gazed reflectively at it for some minutes in the dim amber lamp flame. Then, shrugging his shoulders to what seemed inevitable to him, he rose leaving the lamp still setting on the floor, he hurried to the door and flung it aside, calling excitedly, "Boys, wake up and come out here! I promised you I'd see a way fer us and I have by golly!" He lumbered on into the kitchen and fell into his chair beside the fireplace.

It was not long before Joseph, looking as though he may have been walking in his sleep, appeared in the doorway, yawning, "Pappy—did you say fer us to git up? Shore ben a short night."

With a little impatience creeping into his voice at the obvious untroubled mind of his son, Early retorted, "Night' s hardly begun, son. Get your brothers up and tell them to come out here, too, I said I had something to tell you."

Joseph turned back through the door and in a very brief while all three shaggy, tousled haired and heavy-eyed Cole boys were once again sprawled on the floor around Early's feet.

Early looked down at the seemingly half-conscious group and wondering fleetingly what it would take to put some life in his son's listless nature, he decided it would be wise of him this time to get to the point quickly and refrain from the usual warming up chatter and rhetoric of wording that he was ever famous for before making what he thought was an important announcement.

"Boys, first thing in the morning, I want you to start mending the wagon."

"The weggin, Pappy?" inquired Joseph, as he raised his head to no great degree with a trifle of interest, while Jonah and Job remained merely as they were, without a fraction of movement.

"Yes, the wagon has to be repaired to tiptop condition and as soon as possible tomorrow, because by this time tomorrow night, I want us to be on it with our most important belongings and well on our way out of here!"

Surprising somewhat to Early, his news suddenly brought all three sons to a sitting position as they turned their still sleepy eyes toward him, though their faces bad taken on a bewildered look, as Joseph went on to inquire further, "On our way, Pappy, where we going to?"

"To the hill-country, boys! I'm taking you back to live among our own kind, our relations in the hills. I'm going to let Frank Drakston have this rundown plantation make him a present of it fer the debt we owe him! Give him this deed here in my hand. Should've done it a long time back. I've become too old to plow, anyway!" Early told them, his words hitting with an electrifying impact.

While Joseph searched his pappy's face in openmouthed disbelief, appearing to be beyond the power of asking any more questions for the moment; and Job became more wide-eyed, Jonah, seeming to be the least unruffled by the explosive news and also more thoughtful as he bad appeared to be all evening long, ventured to get on with the questioning where Joseph had left off.

"Where to in the hills?" be asked soberly.

"Of course, Jonah, to my Cousin Jim's place, where else? We're heading straight fer Jim's house. Should be there, too, in a few days."

"He won't be spectin' us."

"Well—that's no doubt true, son. But me and Jim, we always been just like brothers, you know that, so why fret bout that business of him spectin' us," encouraged Early.

"If you say so, Pappy." Jonah replied, his skepticism concerning their welcome vanishing.

"Well, I do say so, because that's the way it will be," promiscd Early. "Jim will welcome me and you boys, too, like long lost brothers come home!"

"If you say so, Pappy." Jonah echoed again, as he let his head descent toward the floor once more, seeming indifferent to anything now save getting back to his interrupted sleep.

"Home to hills!" Job suddenly interposed, though his now wide-awake face was turned to no one in particular.

"Yes, son," said Early, "we' re going to the hills and your job will be to get your pans and cook pots together after you fix us a few eatables, in the morning. We'll be needing them pots and pans fer you to cook in along the way." Then, as Job turned his head back toward his pappy, beaming with delight, Early went on in voicing bis plans and instructions to bis other two sons. "The bedding and clothes, Jonah, I'll leave to you to see about, and the outside, Joseph, will be your lot, such as seeing that we have tools along to mend the wagon with in case it breaks down, and buckets to serve the horses a drop of water, if the situation calls fer it. Now, as fer my own functions, after I see to storing away a few things on the wagon in a safe place, like your mother's trunk fer instance, I'll be busy paying a farewell call upon the likes of Frank Drakston!"

Joseph, whose face had taken on a look of near idol-worshiping as he had listened carefully to every word that his pappy had said, finally broke his silence and in doing so some of the secret yearning that he had held form time to time was revealed to Early. "Pappy, you is so smart," he praised "You can think of so much. I wish I wus that smart, but I don't know nothing 'cause I can't read and write like you, Pappy."

His disclosure brought guilt and regret both striking bard at Early's conscience, but sticking tight to his inveterate habit of covering up any and every deed that became unpleasant for him with excuses, this time was no different as he made an attempt to soothe his son's longing by telling him, "Listen, Joseph, don't you get to fretting over not knowing much; because, believe me, son, there ain't anybody in this whole wide world that ever bas been or ever will be so smart, that they know everything!"

But, as Early scrutinized the intent look that came to Joseph's face, he was not too dumb to see that he had not been too successful in crawling out of his negligence this time by coming up with this bit of shrewd philosophy, though the substance of his words bad been will conveyed All the same, he was not daunted and in his instant desire to see the obvious unhappiness over the like of schooling wiped form

Joseph's face, as always Early's sharp and quick mind suddenly glimpsed a way out.

"I'll tell you what, son, when we get to the hill country, I'll see what I can do about getting your Cousin Polly, Jim's wife, you remember her, to give you some book learning. Just this minute, it hit me, that Polly is most gifted in that sort of business. Would you like that?"

For a moment, Joseph gaped in awe. Then, catching his seemingly loss of breath, he exclaimed, "Oh, Pappy, you is somethin', I shore would!"

"Well, don't you worry no more about that school business. It won't be long before you'll be educated just like me. Now, I want you boys to get back to bed and like I say, come morning, I want that wagon mended. Remember, them wheels will have to roll over a lot of miles in the coming days ahead, so do the very best you can," Early cautioned as he rose from his chair an padded back to his bedroom, his ragged nightshirt flapping round his legs. He bent over and blew the lamp out, padded on over to the bed and crawled back under the covers. Tucking the deed under his soiled and smelly goose feather pillow, he told himself yes, tomorrow was the day—the beginning—in a way the working of his very salvation—his deliverance form what surely would have been purgatory for him in his afterlife, bad be kept on engaging in that shady business against Green Sea, or he should say, allow his sons to. What would be Drakston's reaction when he threw this deed in his face? Well, he would have to wait till morning to find out. But, no doubt about one thing. Frank Drakston would be surprised to see Early Cole.

A smile played in the depths of bis grey, shaggy beard as sleep began to claim him.

Chapter Twelve

By mid-morning the next day, a lovely, tranquil spring day, Early Cole, clutching his battered felt hat in his hands and dressed in his near about everyday attire, save his clothes were clean on this day—tattered, faded overalls that had crude patches splashed here and there and a gingham shirt that was almost out at the elbows, found himself planting his dusty, snagged brogans inside the magnificent mansion, Drakston Hall. He had not been inside its walls since that day long ago when he had gone there with Matthew and Matthew's parents, Cable and Anne Carson, while he had been attending school at Green Sea. Its splendor had awed him then, but nothing like the elegance that met his eyes now. As the butler ushered him down the long wide, impressive hallway, the architectural frame cut that symbolized the plantation's title, that heavenly threshold the "Pearly Gates" that Early so often referred to in his speech, flashed across his mind. He was certain that this celestial passageway that he had pictured in his imagination so many times, could not be too far different in all its holy majestic state than what his footsteps were carrying him through, at the present!

As he and the butler approached the open door to the library, the butler stopped and gestured toward the inside, made a slight but not too pretentious bow—Early observed, and then preceded to move on down the great hall, disappearing form Early's view through another doorway. Standing there nearly stuck fast in his amazement as his eyes still moved over the grandeur and luxury around him, Early finally took another step forward and peered into the library's grand interior, seeing that Frank was sitting behind a huge desk with his head bent forward in preoccupation. Noticing that Frank was rapidly sailing the pen that he held in his hand back and forth across the sheet of paper lying before him, Early guessed that he must be writing a letter, but, of course, he was not sure. The one thing that Early was certain of was that it appeared Frank Drakston was rather annoyed if the frown on his face meant anything; and that he seemed to be unaware that anyone was standing in the doorway, though the butler had trotted at least three or four times between the front door and the library carrying bits of information from himself to Frank before Frank even relented to his insistence that they talk in private, to say nothing of the loud whacks his rough shoes had made upon the glasslike floors—a sound that Early was positive had had to reach Frank Drakston's ears.

While he waited and wondered if his presence was going to be acknowledged or ignored after all, Early's eyes caught the fashionable and splendid dress of Frank Drakston, bringing something to his mind that he very seldom gave any thought to, if any at all, his own shoddy appearance. Even so, he never let it bother him, brushing it aside, as he told himself that even though his appearance was inferior to Frank Drakston, that by no means meant that his principles were any lesser. True, he would admit, the scion of Drakston Hall was a big man, so to speak, powerfully wealthy; and he, Early Cole, was a nobody in the eye of this rich, arrogant aristocrat, who continued to sit there ignoring him. But, basically, in the main, Early Cole would say they stood on the same level—the quality wanting—when it came to the weighing of character, and he was there to tell Frank Drakston this and a whole lot more! In truth, it was much easier to hide inside a pocket that was stuffed with money than one that stayed empty. Nevertheless, high-class or low-class, this rich, stuffed shirt bigot had better climb down from his high horse and be soon about it, recognizing Early Cole's presence! Never again would Early Cole hang his head and hold his breath for the likes of Frank Drakston or anyone near his mold. That day at O'Henrys when this upper-cruster came to his aid and payed the back taxes on his land, he should have known then that favors are brought, not given. Well, that had been over four years ago—a long time to bend and engage in this man's shabby revenge against Luke Heyward. One never became too old to change and try to set one's house in order; the moment had arrived for Early Cole!

In a rare flame of rising temper with Frank, for still having not bothered to show one sign that he was there and waiting, Early cleared his through and started forward but, instinctively, halted as his unkempt brogans hit the costly, handmade oriental rug. He dropped his head to stare at the unique wealth that he stood upon, though his hot blood did not keep it hanging very long. Momentarily, it was raised again to stare instead at Frank Drakston's sullen face, as Frank rather irritably threw the pen down and glared across the desk at him. Holding one another's eye, Early strode on across the elegant rug—his head high—his dander up.

The irony of the situation was that even though both men highly disliked one another; in a sense, they were allies for the reason that both had once again reached a major decision at the same time that not only tied in with one another concerning the same matter; but paralleled also in self-condemnation in connection with the same circumstances—Early's pangs of conscience in regard to Green Sea—the never-ending bitter regret that Frank lived with in the matter of Eliza. In point of fact, Early's guess had been correct. Frank was indeed writing a letter and one that touched upon the whole affair. Moreover, he had told himself a few minutes earlier that someday soon he would have to go see Early Cole' yet, that had carried no weight in Early's favor when the butler had announced he was there because of two things. First, Frank was not pleased that Early had chosen to come to Drakston Hall, disturbing him. Second, he was infuriated with Early for having insisted that they talk in person after he had sent word by the butler that he was attending to a matter that he wanted to post in the mail that day and had no time for Early Cole's prattle!

Indeed, Frank was writing a letter, another one among the many that he had exchanged with his mother after she had gone back to Columbia following her holiday visit home, though the contents of this letter were different somewhat; in that, they revealed his final plans for the near future and also expressed a few hopes that he held. True to form, as ever, in his turmoil he had at last reached out to her, but naturally he never conveyed the real reason for his misery and restlessness. To disguise his main distress to her, he filled his letters instead with chatter on various subjects and his own point of view concerning them, mainly the political situation of the day, something he blamed for the greater part of his woes.

It was true, even though the Yankee troops of occupation had been removed and the activities of the Freedmen's Bureau terminated; the South's plight still remained to be grave. Though for all Frank's moaning over it, he had yet to suffer any real hardship and it was not likely that he ever would because of his immense wealth in cash assets. But, for the majority of other southerners it was entirely a different matter. In fact, in this spring of 1870, under the rule of the triumphant Radicals, the Southern landholder found his taxes four times higher than what the tax had been on the same land in 1860, while the value of the acreage continued to decline and, this was only one of the numerous burdens that the former rebellious states were being forced to deal with. Corruption was overflowing in state legislatures. Moreover, to make matters worse, or what seemed to be the ultimate for the greater number of the South's people, the mud-spattered Union General, Ulysses S. Grant, who General Lee had surrendered his army to, five years prior, was now sitting in the White House as president of all the people in the preserved but still disunited States—the result of another Republican victory in the national election of 1868.

In the chaos of this additional Radical victory, Matthew had managed to hold his seat in the state senate, but, assuredly, he was retaining it in the Democratic minority whose power had been reduced to nothing, by this date. Matthew's close friend, President Johnson, who had pardoned Matthew shortly after the war for the "crime" he had committed by serving the South in its struggle for independence, had finished out his term as president in March 1869 and gone back home to Tennessee, despite the Radicals bringing him to stand a trail of impeachment, for which he was acquitted, before he could do so. Thus, with Ulysses S. Grant in the White House and the Radical regimes in full control of all legislative branches of government, Matthew's enthusiasm for his senate duties had long disappeared.

Having heard his uncle talk of his disappointments with the present controlling political body; in fact, he had heard Matthew say at Christmastime that he just might resign his senate seat and take a position with the South Carolina Railroad, Frank was suggesting in his letter that morning to his mother that perhaps the time had come for her, his uncle, and Whit to come back home and live at Drakston Hall. He would feel more comfortable about leaving. It depressed him when he thought about no one being there except the servants. Yes, he had definitely decided to sail for England and abroad the middle of April, and, of course, Elizabeth and Stewart would be accompanying him. They would be gone a year or longer. Now, he had no wish to disrupt her life, but owing to Uncle Mathew's bore with the present state of politics, did she not think this was a sensible solution? And too, besides there being no family member living at Drakston Hall while he and his family were abroad, if she did not come back, there was this problem of what to do about the school, also. He would like for the school to continue on in his absence since the children and their parents, too, seemed happy with the arrangement. Most important though or leastwise to him, Stewart would still have a few grade years when they did return, even with his private tutoring; and he would like to have Stewart close by, as he was now, during those few years. There was quite a bit of business to take care of in connection with the school, such as the parents' contribution in funds, books and other supplies to be ordered from time to time, and also Lucy's salary to see about; therefore, maybe Uncle Matthew would be interested in taking over those duties. Moreover, they could enroll Whit in the school. Lucy was an excellent teacher. This was another thing that was bothering him. He had been the main cause for Lucy leaving her former position in Columbia by offering double her salary, a bargain that he had kept, and he was not sorry, because she had proven her worth in her field long back. But, he sorta felt responsible for her employment now and would hate to see the school fold. So, would not she and Uncle Matthew think all this over and let him know as quickly as possible as to what their decision was going to be?

Frank had been smiling to himself while writing the part about Whit attending school under Lucy's teaching. As strange as it was, he and Lucy Randolph had begun to cultivate a warm and steady friendship with one another and particularly after his ill-fated encounter with Eliza. It was through this atrocious wretchedness that he himself had brought down upon his own head that he had begun to see and think of his distress as being in striking likeness to what Lucy without question had gone through—drawing him to her in an one and indivisible affinity that he had never sensed before with anyone else. Though it was fact, he never would have dreamed of discussing his burden with her and still remained to be aloof in his manner toward her nonetheless, he felt that out of family, friends, or any business associate—had his act be' come known which thus far it had not—that it would have been Lucy and Lucy alone who would have to an extent understood how he could have allowed his all consuming passion that he had ever held for Eliza, blind and deafen him to everything except the maddening desire of its burning flame. Save the depth of his love and desire for Eliza, mesmerized in its ecstasy, he had been insensate to principles and everything else, even the state of her physical condition through the whole act of his taking her, and that factor was the part that tortured him so. Every time he thought about it, he felt as though he were a son of the devil. For what short time it had been, it appeared that he and Lucy Randolph both had been destined to know the glory and the hell of yielding to reckless, forbidden love, because there was not a chance that Lucy's love for Nat Carson had brought her every much as untold misery as his own passionate love for Eliza had brought to him. Both of them had lived and would continue to live with the anguish of a denied love. Nat Carson lay in his eternal sleep and, as far as Eliza and himself, he knew now that she had become lost to him for all time.

As he sat behind his desk and thought about all this still continuously to hold a cold eye upon Early Cole, he wondered what had induced him to make these suggestions to his mother and why he had this earnest desire to see them carried out, before he set sail for England. Was it his subconscious trying to get through to the conscience in an effort to restore a little peace to his mind in realizing that for the first time in his life, he was making a move at last that did not pertain to money or for the benefit and well-being of Frank Drakston, alone? Or was it the sadness that he had seen cloud Lucy's face, a short while earlier, as she had stood at the window and watched the children playing during recess? Then again, could it be the knowledge of knowing that no doubt his uncle would have brought his mother and Whit back to live at Green Sea long back, had not those damn sons of this shiftless louse standing before him, burned the mansion at Green sea? Well, whatever the reason, he was glad he had been moved into taking this action if, in anyway, it would bring a degree of comfort into Lucy Randolph's life, relative to what she had endured because of her love for Nat Carson. No, there was nothing he could do about her unquestionable yearning for the love she had lost, but he could try and do his best to bring the essence of that love back into her life in the being of Whit the child begotten of that love. Finally, breaking in upon his thoughts that Early Cole had interrupted he growled surly, "Cole I thought you understood that if there were to be any more contact between us, it was to be of my choosing to say when and where, not yours. Apparently, I failed to make that aspect as clear to you as I should have."

Mentally noting there had been no greeting between them, Early quickly shot back with a leering eye, "Nope, nothing of the sort, Drakston, you made it plain all right, and I understood well enough!"

Started somewhat and puzzled, too, at the usually placid and humble Early Cole's obvious defiance, Frank averted Early's gaze for the moment, letting his eyes fall to his desk again. Picking up his pen he leaned back in his chair and while he rolled the pen slowly back and forth between his palms, his eyes went to Early once more, giving him a cold artful inspection as he said, "Then, if that's true, why did you come here? Of course, you must realize that your intrusion upon my privacy is straining my patience a great deal."

Early shifted his soft, bulky frame from one foot to the other. Standing was not one of his most common practices. Though had it been to the contrary, his position posing no irregular stress on his legs, it still would not have escaped him that Frank had not ask him to take a seat.

"Yeah, I realize it, Drakston," he scoffed, "But it sorta surprises me, cause if my bottom wus gracing that fine chair there, knowing, too, that all this elegant setting wus all mine," he emphatically gestured as he turned and waved his hand about the room, "I hardly think I'd get riled at the sight of you or anybody else!"

Along with another shot of rising blood pressure, Frank read Early's message. His cheeks coloring, he leaned forward again and laid the pen back down. Aware though that his surroundings were not the best place that he could be in to lose his temper, since the school children, Lucy, and Elizabeth were so nearby, he made an effort to curb it, managing to say rather calmly, "Perhaps not, Cole, but what you may do or may not do, if our positions were reversed, cuts no ice with me. Yes, I resent your coming here and insisting on seeing me. However, since I did permit your presence to enter my home, I will grant you the time to state your business providing you dispense with your usual discourse and keep your insulting remarks to yourself. Furthermore, if it's money that you've come to trouble me about, that's all over with, starting this very minute!"

Now, Early's purpose for being there seemed to be deflated to an extent. It appeared that Drakston had been making a few plans too. "No, it's not money, Drakston. Oh, I could use some, but I didn't come here fer that. As fer as the insult goes, I wus only trying to tell you how lucky you are to have all this finery to live in. Why, this place looks right out of Versailles. It's—"

"I warned you, Cole, Frank cut in. "That it would be far better and wiser if you didn't start your rhetoric with me today, I have no time for it. Get on with whatever you came here to see me about!"

Early's seldom flared temper over Frank's reluctance to grant a personal meeting between them had calmed considerably by now, though he still remained to be piqued with Frank for not having shown him the courtesy of allowing him to rest his legs in one of the several comfortable looking chairs that were setting empty around the room. It caused him to carry his jeering a little further than what had come in his mind to say when Frank stopped him. "All right," he replied, "I'll state my business after I finish what I started to say. I started to tell you that this is sho—sure one fine mansion you have here, the finest that graces these parts and that's for a fact, cause we both know there wus one more that did measure up to this here one, but it's gone now." The look he sent toward Frank was that of near mourning.

Frank's flushed face was far from mourning. As it turned to a deeper crimson, he rose from his chair. His hands gripping the edge of the desk in rage, he bent further over it and despite his surroundings, he barked, "Yes, by god, it's gone, and all because of those damn idiot bastards that belong to you! I deplore and despise the day that I ever became involved with you or your kind—"

"Hold it right there, Drakston," Early cried, "I'll not stand here fer another second and let you insult Methilda like that! And, speaking of my kind, what you got to say bout your own mold? When did you git to be so saintly? You may be high-class in your book and to a lot more people round here, but to Early Cole, you ain't so high!"

"Get out, Cole, or I'll throw you out!"

"No," Early defied, "I'll leave when I finish my business here and not before!"

"Well," Frank bellowed again, "that had better be quick," as his raging temper contorted his livid features, turning his flaming cheeks and bulging veins to a purplish hue.

Early braved Frank's obvious rage and snappishly barked back, "Quick or slow, I'll have my say, and bout getting mixed up with me and my kind—well—that can work both ways, Frank Drakston! Course, we both know the real reason that made you come to my aid that day, don't we Drakston?"

Frank narrowed his eyes and setting them direct to Early's, looking as though he were taking aim down a gun barrel, another warning peeled from his lips, "Cole, you'd better stop where you're at, before you tempt me to blow your brains out!"

"You won't do that, not here, anyway," Early declared, and to a much-surprised Frank Drakston, a lot more began to spill from his mouth. "I know you, Frank Drakston, inside and out. You thought I was too dumb to figure you out, think I ain't got no education and all. Well, you forget dat I went to school with your own blood uncle. I played like to you I didn't know what you was up to, but I been on to your scheme ever since you told me dat trumped-up story bout Luke Heyward. Trying make me blame dat Luke Heyward was a scalawag thing to do and siding with dem Yankees. Saying dem awful things bout dat man cause be wouldn't jive dat Klan o'yours an' ride from here to kingdom come with you, when all de time you didn't want him nowhere 'bout you, cause you can't stand de sight o' him. I knowed—knew—" Early paused for a second or two. There be was, in bis excitement, using all wrong words after he had just told Frank Drakston that he was educated! He would have to take it a bit slower and give more thought to his wording, he told himself, as an appalled Frank continued to give him a look that was black as thunder, while he made an attempt to resume having his say by using better English, "I knew all the time that this wus not the true story, Frank Drakston. You used that story fer your own protection, to cover up your real reason to get back at Luke Heyward. It's that eye-filling daughter of Matthew's, Drakston! That's been your trouble all along. You've burned fer her ever since the minute you wus on to your manhood! Even with a nice, comely wife of your own, you still bum fer Luke Heyward's wife! Don't you know what the Bible says 'bout such things as that? You ought to be ashamed of yourself, lusting fer another man's wife. Why—"

Suddenly, Early called a halt to his calling Frank to account, wondering what had impelled him to be so bold as to venture upon it in the first place, as he threw his hands high above his head in a mortal fear for his life. Unable for the moment to make a sound come from his throat, that felt as though it had become paralyzed, and thinking that he surely had not known Frank Drakston as well as he thought he had, he gaped in horrified disbelief at the gleaming pearl-handle pistol that was pointed on a straight course within inches of his mouth!

In a flash as quick as lightning, Frank had jerked the pistol forth from the inside of his waistcoat and was now holding it in a not too steady hand, as another vehement ear-splitting threat poured from his lips. "One more word of your hypocritical sermonizing, you dammed old windbag, and I'll stop that tongue of yours for all time! It's a good thing for you that you were not slow in putting your hands where they are, or your mouth would've served for my target! Now, I'll allow you to drop your hands, but if you want to stay alive, you turn around and get the hell out of here and stay out of my sight from here on!"

Heart in hand, Early ungrudgingly agreed with Franks orders. He had already decided that he would as leave tum his back on Frank Drakston's pistol, as having it hang near his face, anyhow. While letting his hands fall, one swiftly found the back pocket of his overalls that held the ancient deed to the Cole farm. He drew it forth and quickly, gaining back his voice that had been choked off with fear, he muttered, as he threw the deed down upon Frank's desk, "Sho—sure—sure thing—whatever you say, but that wus my business beer. There it is, the deed to the whole fifty acres. You can have it all fer the money I owe you. As fer as staying out o' your sight, that won't be hard fer me to do, I'm leaving for the hill country, so you can drop your pistol and keep it down!" He turned and in his lumbering gait he made for the doorway, as Frank, throwed off his guard for a moment, stared down at the yellow-colored paper.

However, it seemed that for all his cold fear for Frank's pistol, it was going to take more than that to quiet Early's tongue, entirely, when it came to the matter of Frank's open desire for his cousin, forjust before he cleared the doorway Early looked back and said, "Take heed, Drakston, she ain't fer you. You'd do well to fergit her, cause she ain't yours to have!"

I'll damn well kill you, Early Cole, for that," Frank yelled, as he jerked his head up and raised his hand that still held on to the pistol, but before he had time to aim for his target again, Early Cole had made a fast exit from Frank Drakston's viewing range.

Frank was still holding the pistol pointed toward the door, when presently Elizabeth came rushing through it, saying, "Frank, what's going on? I heard you yelling clear to the supply room where I'm sorting the linens, and I'm positive everybody else inside these walls heard you yells, too, wherever they were. What's upset you so?"

"Nothing? Do you expect me to believe such absurdity as that, and you standing there with a pistol in your hand looking as though your face may catch on fire any second?" she insisted.

Turning away from her surveillant eye, he laid the pistol down and walked over to the window where he saw Early quickly reining Maybelle down the driveway. In the smoldering of Early Cole's warning that still burned him to his shoe soles, he cynically replied, "Don't bother me, Elizabeth, with your meddling, not today. It's over with. Go on back to whatever you were doing and leave me alone, please."

"I'm sorry, Frank, I suppose that would be better for you and no doubt for me, too," she told him, turning away to allow him to stew alone in the wake of the tempest that Early Cole's last words had aroused.

Passing by the entrance to Green Sea on his way home, Early turned his head and looking down the oak-lined driveway, he suddenly become filled with nostalgia for the plantation. "Let up, girl," he muttered to the mare, bringing her to a standstill in the center of the road. "Just want to take a last look, Maybelle, cause in a way, I reckon deep down in my bones, I all'us felt that this here place wus my home 'bout as much as any place else. Fact is, when I wus a little snapper, I spent more time at Green Sea playing with Matthew den I spent anywhere. You know, girl, I wouldn't be surprised one bit that this fact wus what made me never scold the boys too much 'bout all dem chickens they brought from Green Sea over the years and, yea, that shoat, too, that we eat this past winter, cause you see, Maybelle, I must've felt that this wus food right from home!" He puckered his lips and sent a long trail of tobacco juice flying through the grizzled tassels of his beard and then swept over the spray of tobacco stain with the back of his hand as he continued with his long and final look. After several more sentimental minutes had passed, he started muttering his thoughts aloud again. "I'd stop and say goodbye to Matthew if he wus beer, but I reckon it's just as well that he ain't, might stir up more memories den ol' Early could handle." He turned his head and pulled at the mare's reins, "Git on, girl, we got to be on our way, at least, ol' Early is finally making a break to git out o' de whole dadblamed perplexing mess, should've done it long ago."

As Maybelle snapped into her usual briskness, Early's head turned back over his shoulder once again.

Day had given way to night, but the veil of its darkness seemed to add rather than diminish the impaired state of the ramshackle homestead that had been that of the Cole family for four generations, for now, its other dwellers that the Coles had shared it with had been given free range and its weather-battered walls and floors trembled and creaked from their gathering. From the scurrying of rats and mice between the empty crib bins at the barn and the broken-down safe in the kitchen that had held the crude and, most often, meager food supply, to the crickets and ants on the cold, silent clay hearth, the marking of its near doom was brought more to disclosure than what the light of day had seemed to reveal. Even the holes in its rooftop caused its shadow to take on a look of some unsightly carcass lying on a vast lonely desert—a homestead that had finally fallen prey to deprivation of care. If there were any nostalgic thoughts though for the old familiar chimney comer in Early's mind as there had been with Green Sea, they were deep within him—hidden from the observation of others; and the lonely looking silhouette of the old forsaken shack had by then been cut from his view, anyway, sparing him any deeper languish that he may have felt. True to his convictions at last, Early was well on his way toward making a new start in life—late in life. Still taking it easy though, Early, in the luminosity of the warm spring night, along with Job and Jonah, was sprawled out upon a musty, soiled feather mattress in the creaking wagon. Maybelle was tethered behind it, while Joseph sat on the wagon seat taking his tum at the reins in guiding his horse in its task of pulling the Coles and their sparse belongings to the hill country. Whether Joseph was even granted the chance to learn to read and write and Early kept his word and lived up to his sudden conversion, Early's acquaintances in the low country were never to hear, because they did not see Early any more, nor were they ever to see the likes of Early's mold or anything near to it ever again.

Chapter Thirteen

Pushed aside by Frank Drakston's angry hand from where it had landed on his desk, an area that was restricted to the hand of everyone but Frank himself, even to the maid's dust cloth to say nothing of the turkey feather duster that was held in the hand of Elizabeth from time to time as she went about the rooms scanning the surface of everything for any particle of dust that might have been overlooked, the old ancestral deed that bore true evidence of the Cole purchase in a younger time remained lying untouched a fortnight later. In these ensuing few weeks that had elapsed since his wrathful encounter with Early Cole, Frank—once Early had vanished down the driveway, had allowed little of his thoughts to center on Early Cole much less focalize on his worthless document. That is to say, the old deed was worthless in so far as serving any purpose in constituting the legality of ownership, as Frank could have already foreclosed the mortgage for nonpayment that he had been holding on the Cole acreage long back and taken full possession, depriving Early and his sons of continuing to live on in the near tumble-down shack, had he had a mind to.

Early had been no dumbbell. He had known and had knowledge of the fact that he was; in truth, occupying Frank Drakston's property, and had been for a long time, when he bad gone to Drakston Hall, knowing the old deed was worthless because Frank only had to foreclose the mortgage and record it with the county registrar to make it all legal. However, regardless of all this, Early—just for the hell of it and also in his ever desire to add a bit of drama to any situation he was involved in—had been urged to throw the deed in Frank's face, which he had more or less done. As far as that went, had fate worked in his favor, Early could have made an excellent living in the theater. Had he been given the chance to make use of all his whimsies and fancies on the stage, there is not a chance that he would have become one of the world's greatest actors!

Actually, when it came to the value of the Cole property, Early had triumphed over Frank in the deal and was well aware of this when he had finally decided to throw up the cards and take his departure for the hill country. Frank had not only paid back taxes and kept current taxes paid on the land, the sum going above the farm's worth, but had in addition handed Early ten times or above the farm's value in cash, had his handouts to Early been totaled. Moreover, Early's timing in his decision to abandon his old homestead had worked in his favor as well, because by going to Drakston Hall he had spared himself any humiliation and indignant displeasure he might have felt by being thrown out by Frank, which, of course, would have been the case before the latter set sail for England, since Frank had; also, decided to hang up his ax in his endeavor to cut Luke Heyward down. Indeed, Frank was contemplating his final meeting with Early Cole to inform him that their dealings had come to an end not to mention that Early no longer had a home, on the same day that Early had arrived at Drakston Hall with the old deed lying hid in his back pocket. Just the same, for all Early's desire to dramatize his final meeting with Frank; and, it was true, he had been fairly successful in playing the scene up a bit with his impassioned diatribe that not only had shocked Frank but had driven him into a frenzy besides, Frank had scored rather well; also, for he had been hoping that when he did foreclose the Cole mortgage that his actions would remove Early as far away from Green Sea as possible. Thus, he could not have been any more delighted when Early had informed him of his decision and, that Early and his sons had; indeed, said their farewell to the low country. Though he, himself, was leaving the low country, too, sailing within another week, his mind was much easier now than what it would have been had he left the Cole family behind to possibly air his dealings with them once he got gone. He did not want it known that his main reason for leaving was Eliza. He was certain her feelings for him had been reduced to the lowest ebb and he had no wish for more to be added.

As far as his foreclosing the mortgage on the Cole farm, be knew that would never be questioned as something uncommon. lt was almost a routine business every day and had been that way since the war ended families unable to hold out any longer in the wake of war's destruction, forced out by the capitalists, or, in some cases, their holdings abandoned for the more affluent to grab. Anyway, Frank was not concerned about the foreclosure. His lawyer would only present the unpaid mortgage that covered the farm's worth. All those other unpaid accounts that Early Cole had signed his name to over the past few years would continue to lie on in Frank's safe, hidden from any eye that might be curious. At any rate, Early Cole had departed for the hill country taking the entire Cole brood with him and Frank was more than happy to know there was nothing near him, anyway, to remind him of Early Cole, save the yellowed Cole deed that still lay upon his desk and which his eyes now had come to rest upon. [n the matter of the Cole homestead and those few scraggy acres that surrounded it, property that he had never had any aspiration for to begin with, he was thankful it was separated from Drakston Hall's acreage by a good distance. The less he saw of it, the better that would be, too.

The weeks that had followed his end-all dealing with Early Cole had been a flutter of activity for Frank. Each day had been packed with plenty to do, from getting his business arranged and the fuss of social activities which he loathed but felt it was his obligation to abide, to putting on an animated front for the benefit of his house guests. Yes, his letter to Columbia had carried a lot of weight with his mother as well as his uncle, too. Within a very few days, Amy, Matthew, and Whit had arrived at Drakston Hall and, from all accounts it appeared its walls would still vibrate with the sound of family voices after Frank, Elizabeth, and Stewart had taken their leave for England. Matthew had already more or less let it be known that he welcomed Frank's suggestion and would favor it over the current stand of politics any day. Matthew's reaction, of course, had not been too surprising to Frank. By this time, Frank was aware that had his uncle still been gripped in the exciting and affecting clutch of the politic machine as he once had been, its power; after all was said and done, would have weakened Matthew's earnest desire to please Amy. What had been obvious to everybody else at the time of his mother's marriage to his uncle, was now obvious to Frank. He could see that they adored one another, the other's happiness their ever-primary concern. Moreover, Frank was to see something else, that if their marriage lacked what perhaps younger years may have brought to it, there was Whit, who they both appeared to idolize, to make up for that one element that the middle years had denied their love.

Astonishingly, Frank was not jealous of his mother's attention to Whit. He thought the circumstances that had brought Whit into the family circle was the coaxer of that though. Yet, he would have admitted, too, that it would not have been an easy matter to resist the little boy's charms even if there were no irregular circumstances surrounding Whit. Though however much excitement and joy that his house guests had brought to Drakston Hall, Frank was finding that this still had not been enough to unburden his mind or turn aside the one thought that seemed to absorb it—Eliza. And, it was true, he did have cause for his concern in more ways than one- mainly her state of health—a factor that was bothering him more and more as the approaching date for his own departure grew nearer.

Frank had not seen Eliza since the day she had turned her back on him in antipathy and silence, heading down the ridge toward home. He yearned to see her something furiously, though. Even so, he did recognize that he had only himself to blame for the position he found himself in. He had thought about going to Green Sea several times but had kept putting it off, more because of his thinking he most Likely would be forced to endure Luke's company since Eliza was ill, than having qualms about facing her. She had been ill the greater of the winter and her health was still poor. She had just recently started going back to church; however, but Frank had quit attending church altogether, thus his chance of seeing her had so far not come about. It had been so long since he had gone to Green Sea on a social basis that no one in the family questioned his behavior concerning that factor anymore, not even Luke.

The fact was, though this was not an open subject for discussion, either, among family members, there was no deep warmth between Eliza and Elizabeth. Their relationship was barely lukewarm, actually, sometimes, more cool than warm, hardly ever going beyond a certain degree of dignified respect for the other. It was a relationship that was built on what each saw and considered as fulfilling one's duty to family, more than anything else. The friendship that both had desired in the beginning had drown and sank to the bottom before it had scarcely begun to surface, due to Frank's open desire for his cousin. Even though Elizabeth saw and fully understood that Eliza loved her own husband and did nothing to encourage Frank's infatuation that her presence always seem to fire in him, she; nevertheless, could not bring herself to smile upon the situation and ignore it; and Eliza saw Elizabeth's point, reasoning that in all likelihood she would behave no differently if she were facing the same problem. Therefore, the situation being such, it had gotten to the place, saving family gatherings, the two couples' social life was strictly set apart from the other.

Be that as it may, none of this did not hinder Frank, or, as for that matter, Elizabeth; also, from hearing about most any event that was going to take place at Green Sea, those that had taken place at Green Sea, and, all other aspects that were related to Eliza and Green Sea, though none other than Frank's sister, Martha! And, she had come to Drakston Hall several times bearing detailed news regarding Eliza's serious illness—never dreaming how much the news distressed her brother, since he felt partly guilty for Eliza having become ill in the first place. He had even been forced to hear Elizabeth's frequent reports, too, concerning Eliza's health. Yes, Elizabeth had made several calls to Green Sea through Eliza's sickness, and she had gone more out of tender compassion and sympathy many times over, than what she had felt was meeting an obligation, ever bringing more news home to Frank, ignorant, too, that Frank could hardly bear to hear about any of it. Moreover, to make matters worse, or to Frank what seemed the ultimate, since their arrival from Columbia, his mother and uncle had not held back in the least in expressing their deep concern for Eliza's health, to say nothing of another lengthy rundown that Martha had gone into a few days prior!

Now, in the spreading quietness of Drakston Hall, school had been over hours earlier and Matthew, Amy, Whit, and Stewart had accompanied Lucy and Maggie home to Oak Grove to spend the rest of that day, part of the evening, too, because they would eat supper at Oak Grove before they started back to Drakston Hall, Frank still sat at his desk in the sunless grey light of early evening staring absent—mindedly at Early Cole's deed. As he fleetingly told himself that he was going to get rid of this one reminder of the Coles for all time once he rose from his chair, he was also telling himself that it was no wonder his mind was becoming more burdened each day with the thought that was near driving him crazy—the fear that he may have gotten Eliza with child that day on the ridge! Thinking back to how everything had gone that day, he would have to conclude that his fear was well-founded. Even though Martha nor had anyone else mentioned babies so far and he most certainly had not dared ask them such a question, that was no reason that he was doing his best to think of something to see Eliza and ask her before he sailed—if he sailed at all—that would depend on Eliza's answer! He had just made up his mind about the aspect Even if he were to be so bold as to ask such a question, no one could give him the answer he was seeking, but Eliza—not even Doctor Seth, because how in hell could the doctor determine who had gotten Eliza pregnant if this happened to be the case? That factor was the most distressing part linked to this troublesome question. It could very well be that Eliza may not know herself which of the two had fathered her baby if she were with child, him or Luke Heyward!

Well, although Eliza would not speak to him that day after it was all over with, he still believed she would tell him whether she was or was not carrying a baby and if he were responsible; that is, if she knew. For all Eliza's temper, one could not say that she was not honest and straightforward. Yes, she would tell him the truth, once he got the chance to ask her. First though, if he were going to Green Sea which he was seriously thinking of doing, time for his sailing date was drawing nearer and nearer and he could not put off seeing Eliza much longer, he had to think of a valid excuse for his visit. He certainly was not in the habit of merely making a social call to Green Sea. What few times he had broken down and gone, he always went on business. But, what kind of business could he possibly come up with this time? Wait—hell—why there lay his excuse right before his eyes! Early Cole's damned old deed! Those fifty acres bordered Green Sea's land. Why not call on Eliza and that no-account cad that she married and tell them he had acquired the Cole farm through foreclosure and was putting it up for sale. Since it bordered Green Sea, he wondered if they were interested, if so, he would give them first chance. True, Green Sea's lands were vast, but as a rule with the majority of people, the more one owned, the more one desired to own. He sure as hell did not want any more land to have to pay quadruple taxes on. As far as that went, neither did Eliza need any more. Even so, who knew? Eliza could welcome the idea, she had children now.

He leaned forward and pulled the worn, yellowed paper closer to him, reading near indistinct names that were unfamiliar to him, long ago dates, and the local and dimensions of the land's boundary lines scrawled on its forefront. Yes, this old battered deed that Early Cole had thrown on his desk had served a purpose after all, he thought, as another important question raced through his head. But, how was he going to arrange it, that he would be alone with Eliza? There was that ever problem of Luke Heyward to think about. If he went to Green Sea this evening, he most likely would not get the chance to ask Eliza anything in private and privacy he must have to ask her what he so desired to. Well, he would take the risk anyway. Surely, once he got there, he would be able to think up some excuse that would give him a minute or two alone with her. If he failed, the effort would be worth the try, anyhow, because he would still have his chance to see Eliza. It had been so long since he had, over three months now since—since—Oh, God, would he ever escape that hairbrained—wanton, yes, wanton—that was the only name for it, act of his? There was no point in letting his mind start to wallow in despair again over that business though, he reasoned, and especially if he was going to make it to Green Sea and back before bedtime.

Suddenly, the old Cole deed was thrown aside once again as he sprang from his chair and made a grab for his light windbreaker that was lying on the couch where he had thrown it earlier in the day and pulling on the bell rope to summon a servant—all in the same move. While he hurriedly slipped his arms into the jacket's sleeves, he vaulted from the room to the hallway, bellowing orders to the first guarded face that came hurrying to his call for his mare to be saddled and brought to the usual spot where he always took his leave-taking—the front veranda. Then, he rapidly went on down the hall toward the rosewood hall tree to get his hat, calling loudly for Elizabeth. Feeling somewhat peevish with Elizabeth because she had not appeared instantly, he irritably snatched his hat from the hook that it hung upon and undiscerning he whirled, thinking that he no doubt would have to ramble all over the house before he found her, if indeed at all. Suddenly though, his head shot up as he heard her say calmly, "yes, Frank?"

"Elizabeth—I—" his message, that he was to attend to some urgent business, stopped short in his throat. Instead of saying anything else for the moment, holding bis hat in his hand, he walked on toward her in silence, looking at her as though it may have been their first meeting.

Dressed in an eye-catching pale—yellow gown, she stood in the dining room doorway that led directly into the hall, looking as lovely and as much like springtime as the yellow daffodil that she still held in her hand, obviously one of the cut flowers that she was arranging for the dining table. Her gown was cut on modest, yet, simple lines. The style draped her tall, lithesome figure enchantingly. Her long, silken blonde hair was parted in the center and caught in a large bun at the nape of her neck, with tiny curls falling on her forehead and framing her face on either side. As she stepped forward to meet him, he caught the sure, soft fragrance of her person finding it refreshing and invigorating to his senses, something that he had not felt for a many a day and night and; all of a sudden his annoyance with her melted away and his hurried flight seem to lose some of its importance. Finally, breaking the somewhat spellbinding inexpectation that her charm had affected, he said, "Don't tell me we're to entertain guests again tonight and I've forgotten bout it."

"No, you didn't forget," she replied, holding her eyes on his hat, as a shadow seemed to fall across her face. "There's no guests expected tonight."

"I was certain I had when I turned and saw you, isn't that a new gown?"

Her eyes lifted to his quickly but dropped back down immediately in seemingly timidness.

"Yes, it's new. I bought it the other day when Mollie and I went shopping."

"Well, it certainly is pretty. You made a good choice."

Lifting her eyes in a face that was lighting as rapidly as a child's, she asked, "Do you really like it, Frank? I was hoping so much that you would."

"Yes, I do. The color blends so well with your hair and coloring, too. In a way it's a pity we aren't expecting guests, so you could show it off."

"As long as you like it, Frank, that's all that matters to me. I wanted to wear it just for you. That's why I chose to wear it tonight. It's been so long since—well—since we've had the opportunity to be completely alone together—I mean—have the house all to ourselves—just the two of us. I thought—well—perhaps we could make an occasion of it," she finally confessed with down cast eyes again and blushing cheeks. She quickly regained her composure though and moving her eyes back to his hat she went on to add, before he could think of anything to say, "But, it looks as though you're getting ready to leave. "

She had sorta ruffled him. He was still searching for the best way not to hurt her—a fact that he had not been too concerned about, lately, feeling almost unworthy of her devotion.

"Yes," he acknowledged at last, "that's why I was calling for you, I wanted to tell you that I have some business to attend to and probably won't be back before bedtime." He saw his words were leaving no doubt about her disappointment. "I'm sorry, Elizabeth, I do feel I shouldn't put this matter off another day. Maybe there'll be some other time that we can dine alone together and have the evening to ourselves."

"Of course, Frank. But, what about your supper? I was having something special prepared, though it'll be sometime before it's ready to serve. I could send to the kitchen for something else though before you leave, if you'd like, or do you plan to dine someplace else?" she inquired with concern.

"No, I won't be eating anyplace else, but don't send for anything, I'm ready to leave. I'm really not hungry, anyway. I'll eat something when I get back. You go ahead and eat though when it's ready, don't wait on me."

Observing his casual dress, she asked, "You're not going to use one of the carriages?" "No, since the weather's so nice, I thought I'd ride Blossom. Remember, after this week, there's no telling when I'll ride her again."

His remark sounded more wistful than what she had expected him to say. She stepped closer to him and laying her arm around his waist, she said, as they began to walk slowly toward the front door, "You're not having doubts about sailing, are you, Frank? If you are, let's call it off. Although England in a sense is home, and I'll always love it, I've come to love Drakston Hall as much or maybe even more because, now I think of it as being my true home."

His steps slowed, bringing them to a stop altogether as he looked down at her. "Drakston Hall is your home, Elizabeth, and my hope is that you'll never forget it, you belong here. As for sailing, no, I've not changed my mind about that. I think its best that I get away for a while. In fact, I'm sorta looking forward to it." He told her, his unusual openness surprising her and, at the same time, causing her to feel a cozy intimacy with him again. And, when one of his rare smiles began to show and he went on further to say, "Surely, you must recall some of those delightful frolics that we used to revel in quite often, when we lived there. Who knows, maybe it'll be so again." She felt her flesh quiver in response to the thoughts he had stirred in her mind and instantly were wishing she was back in England, sharing the same with him at that very moment. She had no wish to appear aggressive though and particularly in a circumstance where she had already made her person as attractive for him as her capability allowed in such art, let alone that he was getting ready to walk out the house to boot. Accordingly, she did the only and next best thing that she knew to do to show and tell him of her yearning, without seeming too forceful and forward.

Returning his smile, she stood on her tiptoes and removing her arms form his waist, she cupped his face with the palms of her hands. "Yes, Frank, I bring those days to my mind rather frequently and feast on the goodness that we shared there," she replied and brushed his lips with a kiss, going on to add, "But, why could not Drakston Hall serve just as well as England, darling?" Then, she dropped her hands and gave him a quick hug and whispered, "Hurry home, Frank." She turned away and started to leave but to her surprise, he reached out and pulled her back to him.

"Hey, where you going?" he laughed. "I haven't told you yet, that I like that perfume you're wearing, isn't it new, too?"

It seemed all her endeavor had not been lost on him after all, she thought, and told herself that she would be a fool not to make the most of it. "Yes, it is," she giggled hiding her face against his chest, "and I'm glad you like it, but I'd much prefer to know that you pulled me back for another kiss rather than desiring another whiff of my perfume!"

She felt his arms tighten around her, instantly, as he gave another amused chuckle, "Well your perfume is nice, Elizabeth, but Frank Drakston would never put its pleasantness over that of a kiss and you should be well aware of that by now. Look at me, Elizabeth!"

Thinking of his recent behavior, she disagreed with his remark, but she let it go. Instead, she willingly raised her face to his and even though she saw his smile vanishing in his deep- troubled expression, as his mouth sought hers, the question of why the instant diversity, did not cause her to pull back from his embrace or refrain from allowing her warm lips to send their urgent message. Though she certainly would have preferred there been no question in her mind to blotch this new communion that seemed to be igniting between them, after so many months of icy cold indifference, all the same, she had lived a good many years within the circuity of her husband's labyrinthine nature; and, in a matter of speaking, had conditioned herself to it. It was true, she had not been able—until the present moment, to break through this complexity that had kept him chained in his isolation for so long a time and reach him as she had so yearned to do and had failed; yet, her affection had not become impaired because of it. He had hurt her—yes. But her emotions had not been so damaged that it had reached her heart's care. She could still open wide the door of her heart to him and this she did, as she locked her arms around his neck.

He was not insensitive to her deep devotion and her need for its fulfillment. Setting his mouth to the warmth of hers, he found himself realizing for the first time since their marriage that he had not been as deserving of this pretty English girl's generous and unselfish gifts to him and one in particular—her giving him a son, as he should have been. Though he was aware now and had been form that day on the timber ridge that he had yet to know with Elizabeth, the overwhelming exquisite ecstasy those few short minutes with Eliza had given him—never hoping to find it with her or ever again with any woman even if he had wallowed in the torturous wake of its rapture ever since, the fact remained he was finding that Elizabeth's passionate devotion could still stir him deeply and indeed was delightful overmastering, too, if he would only allow it the liberty to show itself.

In this instant awakening to his wife's faithful and unwavering love, he came to recognize something about himself that he had not been able to see until then. His suppressed continuance of late had come about not because he had ceased wanting Elizabeth altogether, but out of nothing save his guilt and regret of his treatment of Eliza; and yes, another important factor, too, that he had refused to face or had no desire to face, he did not know which—Eliza's ever complete impassive behavior toward him, sexually. Elizabeth's trusting eager responses had made it all clear to him, at last. He had been punishing her for his wrongdoing as well as Eliza's unresponsiveness toward him.

Suddenly, and astounded at himself for feeling that way, he wanted to make it up to Elizabeth, reasoning that loving Eliza and his infidelity was bad enough to say nothing of having been cruel enough to force his wife to endure a state of celibacy along with him. Just for once, he wanted to push all thoughts of Eliza aside and make love to Elizabeth for herself alone, without tarnishing the act with deceptive and fanciful visions as had been his habit for some time now.

Determined to carry through with his sudden desire, he began to strive as he had never strove before to match Elizabeth's love as generously as was in his power to do and giving a little more thought to what he was doing, he was soon to find that this was not going to be near as difficult as it had seemed—if indeed at all. Elizabeth's ecstatic welcome—her eager, moist lips, a sharp, breathless gasp, and the fall and rise of her bosom pressed so closely to his chest—had already sent a forceful responsive call through him, settling in his loins. And, he was finally beginning to see that it was one thing to reach the ultimate in rapture, for what short duration it had been, with Eliza even though she had been totally unresponsive; but it was quite another to know that the woman who he now held in his arms was fiercely seeking his every pulsing nerve with ardently devout love.

With his mouth still sealed to hers, be fervidly gathered his arms closer about her and was rather shocked when suddenly Elizabeth broke their long-impassioned kiss and whispered, "Darling, the groom's calling again, your mare's out front." He had not heard one sound save the pounding in his heart and Elizabeth's rapid breathing!

"I be damned if it isn't!" he exclaimed, as his head shot up and he looked toward the front door in anxiousness when the groom let another, "Heigh, ahoy!" sang out—a signal that never took place—to be sure—save when there had been specific orders given for it by Frank himself from time to time on the occasion he bad Blossom brought to the front steps.

In spite of her great disappointment over the interruption, Elizabeth could not help being somewhat amused at his remark and nonplus look. Had she not been so aroused and frustrated at this point, she could have burst out laughing. Instead though, she dropped her arms from his neck and, for the second time that evening pleaded, "Hurry back, dear, I'll wait up for you," wondering if he was going to tell her where he was headed to—something he thus far had failed to do and something she never ventured to ask him if his choice was not to volunteer it. However much though she was conversant with his off and on personality, he throwed her completely when without saying another word, he abruptly released her and turned away, made a fast dive for the front door.

After what they had just shared, she felt so let down by his abruptness, her heart welled inside her. She pushed the tears back; however, and noticing that the daffodil was still clutched in her hand, she sighed and turned away, too, starting back to the dining room, asking herself where had she failed and wondering what she could do, reasoning that if he could tum from her then so affected—her marriage was no doubt headed for doom. To her utter astonishment, though, she suddenly halted in her tracks as she heard his voice bellowing out, just beyond the doorway, "Take her back to the hitching post and tether

her there, I'm not ready to go yet!"

She turned back and meeting his smile with one of her own as he came striding back down the hall toward her, she thought that of all the tender moments her marriage had ever held or would ever hold again, none had ever or could ever be any more precious to her as the feeling that seemed to be transporting between them. To her, it seemed as though their hearts and very soul had truly become one and the same—a moment that was separated and far removed from any other that she had ever shared with him. Of course, she had been aware that their passionate embrace had aroused him; yet, that fact was not removing that thin thread of uncertainty that ever dwelled in her mind as to what he had his mind on or was going to do. Whatever his reason; though, for turning back, whether it would be to make love, merely tell her goodbye, perhaps tell her where he was headed to, or having decided to eat supper before he left—would make very little difference to her in the long run, she was thinking as she smilingly studied his face. The main point was, he had turned back.

He came on, his smile growing to a grin and as he reached out for her hand, saying, "Come on, dear, like you say, it's not very often anymore that we're granted the quiet of these walls all to ourselves, let's make good use of it," steering her toward their bedroom suite on the first floor beyond the dining room but on the opposite side of the hallway , there was little doubt left in her mind as to what his intentions were then.

In truth, she had not contemplated that their newborn harmony would take them to the bedroom before supper and did—raise, though she did it happily, the question of time by muttering, "Now, darling?" as he ushered her on down the long hall and through the bedroom doorway—making sure the door was firmly closed behind them—that one door inside Drakston Hall that still remained to be held in awe by one and all, if it bad not been left a jar. When Frank Drakston walked through that one particular door going either in or out, closing it behind him no servant dared knock of enter, those were his orders and last rule. When he had made certain he had not left the door ajar. With this ridged and drastic rule in regard to his privacy, there was no need for him to give one thought to the door's begin opened.

"Yes, now," he blithely told her, as he turned and took the flower from her hand and laid it on the dresser top, drawing her closely to him again, "and don't play coy with me Elizabeth' not after that flaming invitation I received from you out there in the hall, just minutes ago!"

Notwithstanding his remark, her head dropped against his chest; nonetheless. "Frank—I—" Her demure whisper sank to nothing.

He gave forth with an amused light guffaw. "Oh come, Elizabeth, surely you're not self-conscious about it. What the hell difference does it make, anyhow, we're not strangers to one another!" he cheered. "Besides, if I've never told you before this, I'll do so now even if you should know without my saying so, I'm certainly glad you're not one of those women who merely submits because she sees and thinks of it as being duty only. If I thought that were the case with you, I most assuredly wouldn't be in this bedroom with you now." He tilted her chin up and looking down into her face smiling he went on cheering, "Remember, dear, take this as though it were gospel being shouted form the pulpit by Reverend Johnson or that Marsh Reed, who convinced you that you were a sinner and needed to be converted, no man wants to make love to a block of ice!"

Well, she thought, if you believe that, Frank, and know me so thoroughly, why have you not crossed the floor between our beds and come to me more often especially since Eliza Heyward's illness? Telling herself; also, that in view of his present actions—behavior that she had been incapable of inducing in him until now that it was obvious Eliza Heyward would recover though she was still below par, that surely there was something else other than her husband's concern and infatuation for Luke Heyward's wife that had affected him so—something that tied in with his cousin's illness. Reasoning though, that it simply was not the time to dwell on that matter, not then when she had finally reached him, she tightened her arms around him and chuckling, came back with a gamesome reply, "Had it been your misfortune, Frank, to have married a block of ice, you still wouldn't have had to endure her coldness too long, because it's for certainty your kisses would've soon melted her!"

"Well, thank you, dear," he jovially returned as he lowered his amused grin closer to her upturned face, "but one could take your worthy appraisal another way, though. Do you realize according to what you just said, that had that been the case I could've put an end to her altogether, once I started kissing her—something I intend to start with you in one more second, though I truly hope you don't melt, not to a state of disappearance, anyway, I'd like to enjoy you awhile, first!"

Blissfully elated by his jolly talkative mood that was bringing forth these rare jesting quips, she cried, "Oh, Frank, I can't recall when I've been so happy, I feel so—"

As he had warned her, he instantly smothered out her words with his mouth upon hers, taking another advantage that the privacy of the bedroom allowed and that the hall had not, raising one of his bands to the rising swells of her confined bosom where he stroked and cupped and momentarily was aware once more of an enflamed throbbed response between them that was heightened even more than it had been a few minutes earlier. Directly, he lifted his head and gaping in astonishment, exclaimed, "Whew! What are we waiting for, Elizabeth, we're behaving as though we might still be in the hall instead of the bedroom." He stepped back and as his fingers began to sail rapidly down the row of buttons on his shirt, he went on exclaiming, "Let's hurry and get our damn clothes off!"

Smiling at him, she obediently raised her hands to the back of her dress but after one or two tugs that had not brought any results, she turned her back to him, saying, "You'll have to help me Frank, if I'm to get out of this dress. It required the help of my maid for me to get in it." She laughed. "I imagine she would be rather shocked if she knew I was coming out of it, so soon!"

Throwing his shirt aside, he mirthfully quipped again, as he started helping her by undoing a snap here and a clasp there, "Oh, I don' t know that she would. I imagine we would be the astounded party if we knew how many times that certain maid and a few others among this household staff have sneaked to the dark corners of Drakston Hall, at any given hour, to indulge in their dalliance!"

"Frank, you can't be serious!"

"The hell I'm not! I've always been on to their idle amusement with one another. In fact, Elizabeth, whether you're aware of it or not, I wouldn't know, I doubt it because you're so trusting; but that one particular maid is catting around with the butler and has been for some time now. I'll be a little more specific in details, dear. Just the other day when you were out someplace, I stumbled on to them, hard at it, whirling away in gasps and moans!"

Aghast, she wheeled to face him. "Frank! You can't mean—why, he's married, and I thought happily at that! And, right here in the house! What did you do?"

"Turn back around, dear, if you want me to finish with all those damned openings and closings. Whoever designed that dress, although it is pretty, sure didn't have dalliance on the brain!" She turned back and he went on to reply, "I just gently backed away and closed the pantry door and let them finish, dear. No one will ever be able to accuse Frank Drakston of breaking in on a game such as that!"

"But, Frank, the children—what if onc of the school children and think of Stuart—Whit—" Her concern was obvious.

"Never mind, dear," he assured, "I took all that into consideration and I hardly think that they'll be too anxious to fall upon one another inside these walls anymore, not after my lecture. I want Stuart to find his own way down that one road, without any possible side shows to influence his thinking."

"I agree with you, darling, and I want to thank you for handling it so wisely."

"Well, I don't give a damn how much they go in for that sort of frolicking and they know that, what I did make clear to them was the fact that next time, they had better not just fall down any place and especially in and around this house. That butler should be expelling some of his energy on something other than her, anyway, such as trimming hedges and so on, helping the gardener too. I've already told Uncle Matthew that if he and Mother should decide to come home, to give the position of head butler to Albert, if Albert wants it. This butler isn't as capable as that damn Jake was, anyhow. If he doesn't want to trim hedges, he can find the road. He won't leave though; I pay too well. This isn't 1865 when they thought their good blue—bellied friends were going to take care of them. They all realize now that the damn North doesn't care if they starve and die." He almost raged. "There! Now, I think you can manage the rest," he suddenly added and went on to tell her, as he turned back to shedding his own clothes, "Elizabeth, if we don't soon get to that bed, we' re going to forget to do what we came in here to do. Let's leave off the chatter for a while and get on with our own fondling for a change!"

She might have reminded him that the greater part of their prattling was the working of his tongue. Understandingly though, she only smiled to herself and kept silent, because—to her—this one in a thousand streak in his nature that she so seldom had the pleasure of meeting and had rarely seemed so responsive. Finally, discarding the pretty but troublesome yellow silk gown, getting it from underfoot and out the way, she hurriedly began to tackle the rest of her clothing-shoes, hose, underskirts, then, her hands began to dawdle and hesitate.

She had come to the waist length silk and lace camisole that tightly hugged her bosom and torso, and the matching bloomers beneath it.

Even though she had ever been eager to please Frank in their walking of life's road together—their sexual relationship being no exception, she still thus far tended to remain a private person when it came to the business of body exposure. In short, she never had completely abandoned her restraint relating to raw nudity in broad daylight, and surprisingly Frank had sensed her feelings and had respected this modesty in her from the early days of their marriage-never making a fuss about it, though he himself was one to hold no restraint whatsoever in his love-making. Actually, he had been far more often taken with this trait of Elizabeth's than he had been annoyed by it.

Now having become so absorbed in wanting to pleasure him—hurrying with her several pieces of clothing in addition to trying to bring herself to overcome her puritanical quirk and chunk it for all time—then and there, she was unaware to the fact that he was already undressed and standing stark naked before her, observing her hesitating hands at the top of her bloomers, till he suddenly was telling her, "Go on and take everything off, darling, I want to see all of you."

Lifting her head in sudden surprise, her eyes met his. But, appearing as though she may have been as rooted as a tree, she silently stood in the same spot and still moved nothing about her person for some seconds. Then, from the slightly crooked smile that was beginning to appear on his face, her eyes began to move slowly to other parts of his handsome, powerfully built virile body. Cutting a trail, she let them travel freely one to the broad, hairy chest and stalwart muscular shoulders and arms, the trim waistline and flat belly, the long, sturdy legs and wide-spread feet; and then, lastly she let them rest upon his maleness where the vigorous potency of his sexual adequacy was slowly but surely gathering its able power—a fact that suddenly sent her hands moving in automatic motion, causing her to forget all about her Victorian scruples, as she continued to gaze at its rising, seeing that he had reached full erection under her provocative stare by the time she had dropped the final piece of clothing at her feet. Though she was finally naked herself and stirred profoundly by his turgid maleness, she still said nothing, nor did she make any further move from where she stood.

Neither did he, for the moment, anyway, save a slight gasp that fell from his open mouth as her statuesque blonde loveliness was revealed in full. From her high-piled flaxen curls atop her head to her bare feet, the uniform satiny sleekness of her lithesome firm curves looked as flower-like as the yellow daffodil lying on the dresser near her and instantly became no less inviting to his senses than had his eyes sighted a delicious rosy ripe peach gracing a bleak, naked orchard in the cold of winter. Looking at her in hungered amazement, it was hard for him to realize that his bands had known no bounds with the same glowing flesh before this, because she looked and seemed to him at that moment to be as unblemished as a virgin as evening's saffron shadowed light filtering through the window curtains played dancing Cherubic-like forms upon her creamy supple body.

Unconsciously, he ran his tongue over his lips and suddenly if there were any fancies hovering near and about him, they were unrelated and separated entirely from Eliza and Green Sea, affinitive only to the golden, exotic woman before him—this nymphic goodness—finally nucleus of all his senses—an obvious ruttish she—cat who was now eyeing him with fierce, flaming emerald—green eyes—a sultry lioness who was dominating one and everything in this small remote world where all else had been cast out save her and him.

Finally, as he near leaped the few feet between them, he groaned, "My God, Elizabeth! You're—You're breathtaking." She swayed toward him, murmuring, "Frank—darling—" and catching hold of one another, they stumbled to the bed and fell upon it.

At last, this stalking lioness had found her mate.

She swiftly spread her pliant thighs and arched her tremulous, eager body to him and instantly he was thrusting his hardness into her fervid flesh, driving with a force of passion that was as violent as any pent-up emotion that bad tormented him in recent months and then some. And, as be thrust again and again in an increasing heated drive, her legs hugging him, her arms locked around his neck, her cries of joy abetting him on till his blood and flesh could take no more and he was overmastered by an ecstatic explosive spasm that shuttered his whole being, bringing him to sag down into an even deeper rapture as she began to writhe and shriek more fiercely under her own convulsive orgasm—her legs tightening harder around his body in the savagery of its fury, it came to him that he had been granted his wish and he felt a sudden sense of having been purged by it—not totally but partly.

Spent for the moment; yet, feeling completely assuaged, he fell down beside her, grateful that he had at last been able to draw this appeasement through Elizabeth without its occurrence being touched by an emotional insulation bearing on his feelings for Eliza. No, he had not stopped loving Eliza. By the same token, neither had be stopped loving or wanting his wife. He knew this now. However, when it did come to his intimate longings and attachment to both, be thought he had finally put his feelings in the prospective separating one from the other.

He turned his head and met her eyes as she, too, turned toward him. A long, level look passed between them. He raised his hand and laid it ever so softly upon her breast. She covered his hand with her own. Then, as near as he ever came to telling her that he was sorry for his long aloof behavior and his sharp tongue toward her, be smiled and said, “Elizabeth, England was never any better, even on our honeymoon. I’m awfully glad you found that yellow dress!”

She raised up. Propping on her elbow, she laughed, “I am, too, Frank, but I never knew that you had a preference for that color.”

“Neither did I,” he grinned, “til I saw you out there in the ball a while ago looking like a bronze goddess.” He reached up and began to twine one of her long curls that had fallen down around his finger. “I guess you know you’ve got to redress your hair, it’s all tumbled.”

“Yes, I know and can imagine how it looks now,” she laughed again, as she brushed another loose curl back from her face.

Eyeing her rather comically, he asked, “It was worth it, was it not?”

He saw her smile fade as she laid her head down on his chest and said, “I’d redress my hair a thousand times and more for you, Frank. I’ve missed you so much, darling.”

He laid his other arm across her shoulders and hugged her closer. “I know—and—I’m—” he went no further and let a long pause pass before be said any more, and she observed what he did say was in no way connected with her last remark and the one or two words that he had started to respond with. Still twining her hair around bis finger, be stopped and replacing one of her combs that was hanging loose he surprised her by suggesting, “Elizabeth, let’s take down the rest of your hair, I want to see it spread out around your shoulders.”

She rose to a sitting position, pulling her legs under her. “l guess I might as well,” she readily agreed, raising her hands to her hair, starting to remove the pins.

"Now," he told her, as he laid the last pin and the two combs in her hands, "you can raise your head, it's all finished." And, when she did, the long, thick blond tresses flowed over her shoulders and fell to her hips, a few flowing over her stomach as well.

"God, you're pretty, Elizabeth! Lean over here again, I want to kiss you. Besides, I'll let you in on another factor. I Like the feel of your hair on my stomach!"

She chuckled, holding out the handful of hair pins. "First, darling I think I should get rid of these, don't you?"

"Oh—Sure but make it snappy," he laughed, setting his eyes to her velvety nakedness and swinging breast as she jumped from the bed and scurried over to the dresser and back, where she again snuggled down close to his side and leaned over his chest, offering her lips to him.

He was quick to take possession of them and also her cheeks, her neck, her firm breast and hard nipples, too. And, with blood and pulse racing again, she began to reclining backward, readying her body once more to receive him. He followed her moves and got in desired position, satiating their fierce hunger for one another's flesh again.

Languid, but completely relaxed and now fully satiated physically, he finally said, "I'd better get up from here and get started if I'm going to get that errand seen to, it's already growing near twilight"

Sleepily, she stirred in his arms, whispering, "Must you go tonight, darling?"

"Well—I feel I must," he replied, "Though it may turn out to be unimportant after all. Whether it is or not, calls for my making the effort to find out, that's for certain. So, I guess I'd better get on a move." He brushed her lips lightly and pulled his one arm from under her and made a spring to the floor. While he was dressing with her looking on lazily, he added, "I shouldn't be too late in getting home. In fact, if I get on out of here and let Blossom stretched her legs the way she loves, I could be home before the others return from Oak Grove or soon after, anyway."

"I'll wait up for you, Frank, no matter how late it is," she murmured.

Hastily, donning his jacket and grabbing for his hat again, he turned toward her and grinning broadly he teased, "You don't have to do that Elizabeth. Besides, after all that frisky frolicking that we've just engaged in, I would think you'd be too worn and beaten to hardly crawl out of bed and dress, much less wait up for me!" She took his witticism quip in stride and while they exchanged a merry, all—knowing look, he dashed to the bed and gave her a quick loving pat on her sightly buttocks before he bounded to the door and vanished like a flash.

She lay and looked toward the closed door and smiled for a long while, basking in the afterglow of their love-making—a long awaited gift that his turning back had brought to both. One hour only it had been, but it had been a full and happy hour made up of many things that sometimes not even years could grant one. It had been a hour of fiery passion, a hour of touching tenderness, a hour of open and easy communion, a hour of giving, a hour of receiving; but she felt above all these things the one and most important of all, had been the mellow togetherness that had flowed between them. It had seemed as though the whole hour had been filled with a delicate easiness—leaving her feeling as if she were clutching a pillow of soft happiness in her arms. And, so affected, she reached and gathered the pillow on which his head had lain and held it closely to her bosom—joyfully certain at last that she had entered a portion of his heart where no one else had ever dwelled before—not even Eliza Heyward, and that he gladly welcomed her being there.

This was good, because this gift that he bad bestowed upon her was to become the force of her unwavering strength and indestructible courage for the days and nights that lay ahead of her and, yes, for him too, sustaining her for the rest of her life; in that, it was to give her a lasting happy memory to cling to—holding and hugging it to her in her loneliness without him.

Overtired, nervous, and deeply depressed, Eliza was hurrying back and forth between the stove and supper table, finally setting the dishes of food amidst the plates, silver, and water glasses that she had; also, just hurriedly set at each place around the table that the family group normally occupied. The day had been an unduly strenuous one, overloaded with so many pending chores, she had been hard put that morning in deciding which should take priority over the other. It seemed since her illness she ever felt tired and no matter how much she hurried or did, there were always household duties awaiting her. And, added to her heavy workload on this particular day and more profoundly than ever, had been that same penetrating gloom that had beset her all spring. All through the long, tiresome day, she had been totally wrapped in a cloak of dark despair and it was growing more troubling by the hour. Even though the spring sky had been a blue sea of marvelous sparkling brightness throughout the entire day, this still had not prevented those inky-black storm clouds from gathering and rolling toward her again. In fact, a number of times, they had swept so closely to her, appearing so real, she had felt as if she were caught in the midst of their rain-driven fury and bad been appalled to find herself reaching for the hem of her apron in contemplation of wiping at the wetness that seemed to be beating against her face—realizing instantly that it had indeed been nothing but a phantasmal illusion in the figment of her imagination again and not an unfigurative fact after all. Even so, she had only despaired further and bad begun to ask herself, a thousand times over it seemed, would the flow of tears be the pith of what her mind's eye had seen this time?

Having come to the point of feeling that she could not bear her despondency alone much longer, she instinctively reached out to Luke, turning from the stove to see what he was doing for the moment. But, seeing he was down on the floor beside the unlighted hearth romping with the children, both of whom she noticed had another stick of peppermint candy clutched in their hand while jailor sit happily on the edge of the lively group with a stick, too, she sighed and turned back to dishing up the rice. In addition to their own two children, Luke never failed to bring Pete and Sam's two children as well a nickel sack of candy, each time he made a trip to Charleston for the plantation supplies as he had done today. She knew now that neither child would scarcely touch their supper nor instead of letting Luke in on her fears, she heard herself admonishing him about the candy. "Luke, you shouldn't have given the children so much candy this close to supper. Besides it taking their appetite, it's also bad for their teeth, you know."

Luke raised his head and looked at her. Her tiredness and distress were obviously disclosed. He quickly rose from the floor, explaining to the children their game was finished for that time. Then, he crossed the room to the stove and standing beside her he said, "I know, but I just couldn't disappoint them. Is there anything I can help you with, dear?"

She instantly regretted her seemingly sharp tongue and in spite of her dark fears she tried to act natural and make amends both. "Well, I suppose you could pour the children's milk, but fill their glasses only halfway, Luke, and speaking of the candy, I don't reckon I should fret too much over their teeth or their appetite, because you surely don't go to the city that often."

She had expressed his own thoughts and stepping to a nearby side table along the wall where the water pail always set, he agreed verbally, as he picked up the jar of milk that Doss had brought from the springhouse when he had done the usual evening chores, "Not when the weather is as nice as it's been today, anyway. But, if I get the rest of that tobacco planted tomorrow which I hope to do, I had no choice save take the day and go get those supplies that we need."

Following him to the table with the bowl of rice in her hands, she remarked about the weather, too, and went further than she had intended to. "It has been such a pretty day. That's one reason I'm late with supper. I was ironing and time—"

"Don't tell me that you've been bending your back over a washtub today as well as ironing and tending the children and all the other work you do?" he interrupted as he stopped pouring the milk to look at her worriedly, knowing that Doss and Hannah bad been busy that day in the garden and couldn't have helped her in addition to all the other hands having been busy in the fields. Moreover, he bad asked her not to do the wash herself. "You know you haven't gained your strength back."

She had never lied to Luke and she had no intention of starting now.

"Don't get upset, Luke, the weather was too pretty not to take advantage of it. Besides, Bessie helped me."

"Well, I would as leave wear dirty clothes for the rest of my life as have you bending over that washboard ever again. Sometimes, I get to thinking if everyone on this plantation were to workday and night during planting and harvesting season, we still would never catch up with all there is to do. Maybe I shouldn't have gone to Charleston today, after all."

Although he bad not reminded her that she had gone against his wishes, she knew he was irritated that she had and thought it best to let the subject drop where it was. She set the rice on the table and turning back to the stove, she told him, "Luke, as you've no doubt already guessed, we have your favorite tonight, perch and bream. Doss had good luck last night with his nets."

He made no reply. He brought the jar of milk back and set it down. Then, he got the children and seated them in their places at the table.

She brought the platter of fried fish and placed it among the other dishes of food. They both sat down. He said the blessing. He filled the children's plates. All this in silence, til he filled his own plate and started to eat. "They're good," he finally said, lifting his head to grin at her and went on to tell her more about his day, their first near quarrel with one another forgotten. "I did more today than just make the trip to Charleston, that's why I was later than usual in getting home. I went by to see Bill Clarendon for a while."

"You came back by Clarendon Plantation," she eagerly inquired.

"Yes, I thought I should let Bill know how much lumber I'll want ready by next fall. I certainly don't have any use for it now, but I hope to get a lot done on the mansion next fall and winter, that'll give him plenty of time to prepare it. I had no idea when I'd get the opportunity to see him again."

"That's true, and especially now that he and Charlotte have moved their membership to the Methodist Church. I can't recall when I did see them last, it's been so long How is Bill and did you see Charlotte, too?"

"No, I really didn't go to the house. I met Bill coming from the sawmill so we both stopped our team and got out and visited in the middle of the road. He said Charlotte was fine. In fact, they had been to Mollies today and Mollie's little boy had come home with them for a visit. He had gone with Bill to check on things at the sawmill. Bill sure dotes on that little boy, and young Bill appears to certainly return it."

"I can imagine how devoted Bill would be to his only nephew. I think it was nice that Mollie honored her brother by naming her son after him."

"It was thoughtful of her and Brent both. Answering your question, Bill seems to be fine, too, though the war left a mark that I fear will never heal. He still limps badly on his wounded leg. He's surely done well; though, since the war. He was driving a new carriage with a pair of magnificent looking bay-colored horses pulling it."

"Yes, he has prospered greatly and I'm thankful that he bas. Still, we must remember,

Luke, that he hasn't bad the roof that covers his head and maybe a hundred thousand dollars in household property to go up in flames as you have and trying to replace, and I thank my dear God again, that he hasn't."

Her ever loyalty never ceased to amaze and move him.

He raised his head again and met her eyes across the table. "I have no hopes of replacing it all, dear. All I ask is to be able to build a mansion that will partially bring back to you the comfort those other walls granted you. l feel I have a good start, and I' m more pleased with this foundation than I was with the first one. My guess is unless it's destroyed as before, or by an act of God, it'll be there for our children's grandchildren or maybe longer."

"Well, if those hoodlums should ever happen to come back and start smashing again, I hope I'm here. I won't fire over their heads like I did before. I'll aim straight for my target. You've gone through too much and worked too hard to be forced to build that foundation for a third time!" She said defiantly.

"No, dear, if I'm forced to rebuild this one, too, I don't want you ever to expose yourself or the children to any gunfire or anything of that sort. Remember those are my wishes."

Her answer was silence and, what he thought to his dismay, was a hard look of determination in her eyes despite what he had told her.

Besides those that had been created in God's image, there had been other occupiers at Green Sea on this balmy spring day who had been rather busy, also. One in particular—an old slow-moving Eastern diamondback rattler, had exerted itself considerably and it was still busy, though it worked sluggishly, slithering along inch by inch in the chilly, damp grassy mound that lay between the driveway and the outer buildings. The aged rattler was working its way back to the warmth of its bed which was located beneath the ground a little way under a snug concealing canopy, the heavy dark-green foliage of a huge gardenia bush. The flowering keen-scented evergreen set at the far corner of the yard where the circular drive leading to the front of the small grey, white shuttered house branched off from the long driveway.

Except for visitors calling to the modest house, this one spot in the yard saw a small amount of activity. Thus, the rattler had been bedded down in the quiet of its disclosable den all through the fall, winter, and early spring with little disturbance coming its way. Occasionally, it had slithered off through the grass for short distances in search of food. But, for the most part, it had hibernated in its den til the balmy weather that morning had aroused it in coming out to go in search of a tastier meal than what the surroundings of the gardenia bush had to offer. It had gone laboring clear to the stalls and corncribs. Most all day, the sluggish, deadly reptile had crawled lazily around the stables and corn bins unobserved, preying on mice and other varieties of animal life until its full stomach and the growing twilight, too, had prompted it to start covering the trail back to its familiar sleeping place.

Now, in the near dark of night, having gained the curve of the driveway just opposite the gardenia bush, a distant vibration on the ground caused the rattler to halt and lift its head cautiously. Wanting to reach the coziness of its bed; though, it went against its intuition to stay put and lowering its head again with its beadlike eyes set straight ahead, it contacted its complex body into motion and slid on down into the first rut, across the center mound, and on into the other rut. But, as it started to crawl out of the last rut and proceed to cover the few remaining yards of its long journey, the near approaching increased pitter-patter jolted its body more severely, causing its habitual sense of over wariness to finally win out and bring it to a full stop. Stretched full length across the rut and some few feet beyond, the feared serpent, by man and beast alike, lay motionlessly on its disquieted belly and waited as the vibration grew closer at hand!

Frank, excited and somewhat qualmish also in wondering what Eliza's reaction would be when she saw him, eased up a bit on the reins and looked through the trees toward the small frame house as he cantered Blossom on down the oak-lined avenue. It still chafed him plenty to see Eliza living in the house; his eyes never fell upon it that he did not think about her turning down his invitation to live at Drakston Hall as long as she liked. The very idea, he thought, continuing to keep his eyes clapped on the house as he started to pull on Blossom's reins in taking to the circular drive of her living in those rooms that Luke Heyward bad slapped together rather than have the pleasant luxury of Drakston Hall to her disposal. Instantly though, be had no more time for that kind of thinking or anything else. He was too busy concentrating on staying in the saddle as Blossom suddenly gave a violent start and reared backwards, whinnying frightfully.

He knew immediately that the mare's behavior could mean one thing only—a deadly snake and in all probability a rattlesnake at that. Calling to her in soothing words while she kept sidling in fear, he at once gripped the reins with one band and bugged her sides tightly with his legs as he groped inside his vest to reach his revolver—looking hard in all directions on the dark-shadowed ground while doing so. He reached his gun quickly and closed his finger around the trigger and when Blossom swerved again, he finally spied the coiling reptile and within another second knew his hunch had been correct by the clattering sing of its rattles. He aimed straight for its slightly raised head and fired.

By then, his endeavor to soothe Blossom by talking to her had calmed her considerably for she had stopped whinnying, though it was apparent she remained to be badly frightened with the writhing snake so nearby. Giving the mare an affectionate pat, he peered closer in the rapidly falling darkness and was not certain that he had mortally wounded the rattler with the one shot. To make sure the snake would prove to be no menace ever again, he took aim and squeezed the trigger for the second time, seeing it flatten out full length, instantly. However, at the same time, he was to wonder fleetingly if he had been careless enough to shoot himself, too, because another shot had followed simultaneously with a hard blow hitting his middle.

The sudden impact of the bullet shocked his body with a severe jerk, throwing his head up and he saw instantly where the shot had come from. By the reflection of light inside the house, he saw Eliza standing in the front door with a raised rifle in her hands! Stunned disbelief ran through him, and he wondered again if he were becoming confused and seeing things that did not exist. But suddenly another loud crack split the air with another bullet singing by his head, and the truth of his doubt hit home with no harder force than the sudden cutting pain that seemed to be slicing him in half.

How seriously he had been wounded; Frank had no idea; but the knifing pain in his bowels and the beginning of a warm, sticky wetness trickling under his clothes told him he was losing blood and that somewhere in his insides he was carrying a slug of lead. Even though it was difficult for him to fully grasp what his going to Green Sea had resulted in, all the same he did realize be needed help and quick; yet he never hesitated once in thinking be had no choice save turning back since he was aware now that it had been Eliza who had shot him rather than having shot himself by his carelessness.

He dropped his revolver in his jacket pocket and clutching his middle with one hand, he quickly pulled on the reins with the other, turning Blossom back down the driveway, saying to the mare, take me home, Blossom," as he let the reins go and seized onto the saddlebow for support—slumping down over it in misery and shock.

There was no doubt in his mind that the mare he had rode since he was a boy would do what he had asked of her, and Blossom instantly proved out his trust in her by falling into a fairly fast but easy canter—seeming to sense the urgency of the situation as well as his agony. Blossom had only covered a short distance though, when Frank heard another crack and the humming of a bullet splitting through the treetops and then following that he heard the loud noise of a door slamming shut

Running from the center bedroom where he had dashed with the children, leaving them there for their safety, Luke had run on to the front door and grasping hold of Eliza's arm he had pulled her back from the doorway. Then, some of his terror for her safety and a great deal of his fury, too, had gone into the banging of the door as be bad given it a hard push with the toe of his boot.

In spite of what he had told her—only minutes before that, at the sound of the first shot, Eliza bad jumped up from the table, exclaiming, "Speaking of the devil!" and had made a dash for the fireplace where the loaded weapons, a shotgun and rifle, had hung above it for months, waiting for the avengers to come again. Paying no heed to Luke's shouting for her to leave the guns alone, she had snatched down the rifle and racing on to the front door and flinging the door wide open, had fired the three shots while Luke had been grabbing up the children and carrying them to the bedroom where it was not likely they would come to any harm by a bullet flying through a window.

Still shaken and aggravated, too, Luke could not help from showing it by the sternness in his voice, when after pushing the door closed, he wheeled to her and said, "Give the rifle to me, dear, and go to the children, they're in the center bedroom. I want the three of you to remain there, till this is over with." As near death as she had been just a few months earlier and knowing she had not fully recovered in addition to her highly nervous state, which he pondered over frequently, he could not bring himself to say more—right at that moment, anyhow.

She was not so overly emotional that she was unable to realize her recklessness, reasoning that she had more than tried Luke's patience as well as scared him half to death besides. She could see now that standing in an open doorway firing at the avengers had been a foolhardy thing for her to do—neither she nor Luke bad given one thought that it could be anyone else but the avengers since the sudden crack of Frank's pistol was too similar to past experiences.

Handing the rifle to him, she said somewhat meekly, "I think it's already over with, Luke, I heard a horse trotting down the driveway just before you banged the door shut. Maybe now that they've been served a taste of the same medicine that they've dished out to us more times than I've got fingers and toes, they found it was a little bitter and decided they didn't want any more for tonight, anyway."

Taking the rifle—the same rifle that Matthew had carried through four years of war—Luke had instantly positioned himself beside a front window that gave him the best and nearest view to the driveway. Lowering the window from the top, he had the rifle poked through the opening and was bracing it against the side of the window as he peered into the darkness with a rather vigilant eye, silently.

After waiting a moment and seeing that Luke was not going to comment on her remark, Eliza attempted to defend her actions, "I'm sorry, Luke, that I've upset you, but I just couldn't sit and not do anything while they tore down your work all over again that you labored on so long and so hard. I—" She paused again, giving him a chance to reply. But, when he still did not respond she turned away and started to leave the room, saying, "I'll go see about the children."

"Wait a minute," he finally said and still keeping a strained eye on the darkened outside and trying not to lash out too strongly, he now made an endeavor to point out to her how she had mocked danger and at the same time convey his feelings as well, "And, I will think neither could you began to fathom the anguish I' d suffered, had I found you lying in that doorway shot. Try to remember that, dear, and also our children, too, if you should ever have another urge to run and stand in a line of gunfire despite my pleading for you to come back."

She could see there was no point in attempting to explain any further and had she started to, she would suddenly have been drowned out by the sudden clamor of voices and footsteps on the back porch along with Jailor's scratching and barking at the back—kitchen door. Luke jerked his head around and for a split second they shared a terrified look, with Luke wondering if he were going to be forced to hand the rifle back to Eliza regardless of what he had told her so that she could defend herself. But instantly, that blasting resound pitch that Doss could belt out when he became excited was rending through the walls and over Jailor's barks, filling the room!

"It's Doss and the others!" Shouted Eliza, as profound relief and gratitude swelled through them. While she ran toward the kitchen door, Luke took a final look outside and still seeing no sign of anyone, he concluded that Eliza must have been right about the raider's hasty retreat. He drew his rifle inside and pulled the window back in place and latched it. Then, he went hurrying to the back porch where he heard Eliza, in a flurry of edgy nerves, explaining to Doss and the rest of the hands what the commotion was all about.

In spite of his being moved by these former slave' s stanch loyalty and recognizing the situation for what it was—apparently the attacks on Green Sea were starting all over again, Luke almost laughed out loud once he joined Eliza on the back porch and saw the conglomeration of weapons that the hands had grabbed up in coming to his and Eliza's aid. With the exception of Willie and Allen, both of whom were carrying shotguns, the rest had come running with everything imaginable, hoes, rakes, house brooms, axes and knives, a pitchfork which Charlie was carrying; and even the children were carrying sticks and switches!

Through all the "ah's" and "oh's" and exclaiming "Lawd sak's!" no one had seemed to notice that Jailor had made a beeline for the front yard and had been barking some few minutes rather viciously at that before he got anyone's attention.

Doss, who had taken time to light a lantern before hurrying form his cabin, along with his two sons and the shotguns and Charlie with the pitchfork, all set out across the yard toward the agitated hound who appeared to be standing guard over something near the large gardenia bush. Luke remaining to be warry of what the dark might still expose and uncertain of Eliza's reaction in case something could be amiss, in spite of his revealing his obvious displeasure to her a short while earlier, chose to stay close beside her and asked all the rest to stay back, also. In wonder, everybody waited while the others went trampling off cautiously into the darker night and disappeared from sight behind the obscurity of the bush.

Promptly, they saw the four men coming back with Doss holding up the huge lifeless rattler by the numerous horny rings on the end of its tail which were to number fifteen when counted and once the snake was measured, its length was to reach five-and-one-half feet. As Doss approached the waiting crowd, whose faces bore a look of awed fascination in seeing that some length of snake was trailing on the ground despite his holding it way high, he searched for Eliza's face and grinned, "Look heah, Miss Eliza! You gits yo'self dis heah ol'rattler wid dem shots. He sho' is a big'ne an'deaders den a doornail."

Ever terrified of rattlers, Eliza only spared Doss a slight glance. The thought that such a vile, loathsome creature who was capable of rendering death in a mere flash had been crawling around in the yard where her children might have run in their play, chilled her to the bone.

Clapping her hand over her mouth in horror, she muttered, "Dear God, what if the children—" breaking off to say no more as she whirled and made a dash for the center bedroom.

Luke wheeled and hurried after her, grabbing the lamp from the kitchen table as he passed it. Entering the bedroom though, they saw that apparently the evening's calamity had not bothered the children at all. Both had fallen fast asleep on the bed where Luke had left them. He held the lamp while Eliza, quietly and seemingly more tender than usual, removed their shoes and socks only and let them remain where they were, tucking a light cover around them before she and Luke both brushed the healthy pink cheeks with a kiss and softly closed the door.

Even though in truth he did not relish any more supper, he; nevertheless, in an effort to restore a degree of normalcy to the evening and also to divert her mind from the rattler which he knew had added to her strain, he took her hand and said, "Let's finish our supper, those fish were mighty tasty. Then I'll help you do the dishes."

Morning was to find her still wan and depressed.

Chapter Fourteen

Pain. He felt as though he had never lived without it, so constant and without variation it gnawed at his insides. Yet, odd as it was, from the moment he had slumped over the saddlebow in the force of the pain's grinding intensity, he had felt a certain degree of outer calm throbbing in company with it. It seemed that in his knowing the bullet had been fired by Eliza, that somehow by the occurrence of it, his distress and guilt over his abusive and dishonorable treatment of her had at last been mitigated—having tempered his mind to the point that he was close to feeling as if she had laid a soft, easing poultice on his head rather than having sent a bullet tearing through his stomach. In so many words, he felt that she had given him his comeuppance—balanced the account, so to speak.

Fully rational, the shock to his body having tapered off by now, he lay in the giant size mahogany four-poster in the master bedroom suite where he had been born and thought that if he were going to have to face what appeared to be the inevitable—his pending death—that in a sense Eliza's hand had softened the blow by giving him the tranquility of mind. He would know what to expect in a very short while, just as soon as Seth Roalf and those two surgeons that the doctor had summoned from Charleston had finished their consultation, which they obviously had no desire to discuss before him. Well, if it turned out that they could do nothing more for him save making him as comfortable as his condition allowed, he would do his damnedest to face it as valiantly and unfearingly as possible. Had not he told Eliza once that he would have made a brave and capable soldier? Now it looked as though he would have his chance to prove it, after all. Though in all honesty he would have preferred meeting it quickly and unknowing and on a battlefield at that, instead of under present circumstances. Furthermore, as strange as it was, he could see now that if the worst was going to be his lot, had not he partly sealed his fate by his own unwise steps? Had not he lived the greater part of his life by his own set of rules—holding his own court and passing judgement regardless of cost to others? No question that he had caused Eliza and, yes, Luke Heyward, too, untold distress and hardship and he supposed he should lay bare the facts and ask their forgiveness. Though in all sincerity again he surely could not say that he had begun all of a sudden to like the man. Moreover, there was still that other business that he wanted to see Eliza about and it sure as hell was not that damn Cole farm! However, after all was said and done, it was not likely that he would be able to do anything about it now, no matter what she should tell him. And it looked as though the same applied to everything else where he was concerned, including his ever—taking Elizabeth back to England.

If there were only someway to spare Elizabeth, his mother, and Stuart from all this. Seeing that naked anguish on their faces was in a way more painful to him than any suffering he was having to endure and especially those times when Stuart stood quietly beside his bed and looked at him with a face that only a six year old could reveal—solely exclusive in its saddened wistfulness and it had looked that way ever since he had screamed out those few times last night of course, as far as that went, was not everyone's grief uniquely solitary in being? Take Elizabeth, as much as she was trying to hold her composure and conceal her fears from him, she revealed how she truly felt in every glance she sent his way in spite of all her efforts. She could not help letting the tears well any more than she could stop breathing, while, on the other hand, he believed his dear mother would actually hold her breath till she met the final summons herself, before she would let him see her give way to one emotional tear, even though her ashen face reminded him of the departed as much as anything that was associated with this whole situation—even the length of time that Seth Roalf and those two internal specialists were taking to discuss his condition.

There really must be little hope or Seth Roalf would have already come running with the news that they had decided to operate and remove the bullet. Well, he was growing weary of suspense and wished the doctor would come on and give him the report as to what they had ascertained and settled their minds on, because he had things to attend to while there was still time—square a certain account! Yes, he guessed that would be the only and right thing to do, confess that he had been the main instigator behind all that trouble at Green Sea. Now, why had he come to think he wanted to do such a thing as that? Hell, stop kidding yourself, Frank, you know why—Eliza. You want to do this for her, bring what comfort to her mind that you can in regard to the mansion's burning at Green Sea and, in order to do that, it was going to take divulging the whole mess. But so be it! Had not he heard Martha say more than a half dozen times that Eliza attributed the misfortune of the Mansion's loss to her not having given one thought about it burning that windy March night and going on off to church? Well, it just was not right to let her continue to be saddled with the notion for the rest of her life when he could relieve her mind and place the blame where it belonged—on him. He should have told Eliza that her negligence had nothing to do with the mansion having burned a long time ago. He had had a most propitious opportunity that day she had been canning that damn applesauce—the day that he had declared his love for her all over again, begging her to come live at Drakston Hall but she would have none of it.

Whatever he had to say about all that business; though, he had no wish for it to go any farther than the walls of this room. He never wanted his mother, his wife, or his child to know that he had schemed to get back at Luke Heyward and possibly wreak his and Eliza's marriage. Why had he suddenly become so soft and concerned over the feelings of others having no desire for his family to know what he had been involved in, Hell, he didn't know unless it was for the reason that in the last few hours, he had fully come to know and appreciate the value of his family's devotion, and he supposed he wanted nothing to blemish it so that he would continue to ever be mirror bright with them as well as keeping their minds unburdened regarding his scheming deeds. But, what about Eliza? Certainly, so that she may have this easing of mind pertaining to all the great wealth that was lost at Green Sea—a good portion of it irreplaceable—he would bring her to view him in a dimmer light than she already did. Still, there was a chance that she may not—a slim hope that he would cling to for the sake of giving him the courage to go through with it. Why not have Uncle Matthew present, also? Might as well go all the way if he were going to start on the road of confession! No point in taking a short cut. He wanted to tell Uncle Matthew that he no longer resented his having married his mother—lately having become grateful they had each other.

Life was sure one puzzler. Who would ever have thought yesterday that Frank Drakston would be contemplating a deathbed confession today? To be sure, not Frank Drakston himself! Nevertheless, it was fact—it was—

Pressing the ice pack harder against his stomach, Frank set his eyes on the doorknob and waited for Seth Roalf and, while he waited, he wondered if Eliza would come when she got the word he had been shot and wanted to see her.

Indeed, Elizabeth Drakston could no more have agreed with her husband's concept in thinking that the realities of life was beyond human understanding at times. While Frank waited for the doctor's report and decision, she herself was hearing it and, at the same time, was asking herself was this actually for real or was she dreaming it in her sleep? Half in shock, she could hardly grasp what Seth Roalf was telling her in the most gentle manner he could gain—the staggering news that her virile, vital husband was in all likelihood dying from a rifle bullet lodged in his stomach and there appeared to be nothing the surgeons could do about removing it. No, he was sorry, but the two specialists were certain that Frank would never survive, even for a short while, the shock of an operation. In order to remove the bullet it would take a considerably length of time as well as the risk of working in an area that was considered extremely perilous, if indeed they would be able to work in the area at all, once they had begun to attempt it. Yes, he was bleeding internally and had already lost a great deal of his blood supply, but his shock had stabilized, and he was at present holding his own.

While Matthew Carson stood beside Elizabeth with his arm draped protectively around her shoulders, he had finally persuaded Amy to lie down for a while, Elizabeth heard more questions falling from her lips and was wondering again was it really, she who was asking them or was she hearing the quivering voice of someone else, as a chill as cold as death itself ran over her.

"You—said in all likelihood he's—" Could she ask? She would try again. "You—say his condition is grave, does that mean—there's no—chance at all of his recovering?"

"There's always a chance in hoping, Miss Elizabeth," replied Doctor Seth Roalf. "I wouldn't want to mislead you though; your husband's condition is very critical."

"And," she inquired once more, "The surgeons can't remove the bullet? There's no way they—they can help him?"

"In regard to operating for the bullet, that's what they've concluded," assured the doctor for the second time. "Judging the location of where the bullet entered the abdomen and other signs which indicate it's lying perilously close against the liver, they're positive that any attempt to remove it would put your husband in even greater danger than he's already in, if not in all probability bring on instant death. I'm terribly sorry I can't be more encouraging."

"But you do think—there is—he does have a—a chance?"

"Yes, but it's a very slim chance, Miss Elizabeth," the doctor warned again. "If the internal bleeding were to arrest itself, there would be a fair chance of his pulling through even with the bullet unremoved, less other complications, of course. However, in any case, his condition would remain to be grave due to damaged and torn tissue."

Elizabeth was not so numb that she became unmindful of Matthew Carson's comforting support. She felt his arm tighten more firmly around her. And, as he laid his other hand on hers, she grasped onto his sustaining strength, steeling herself against the growing weakness in her legs to further inquire, "Then, what—what—can be done for him—since operating is—out of the question? And—how long—how long will it be—before you can tell about the bleeding?"

"In answer to your first question, we'll continue with the ice packs and give medication for his pain along with other drugs in an endeavor to stabilize blood pressure, pulse, and other vital functions—" the doctor paused, asking himself should he be more blunt with Elizabeth Drakston? Should he give her the facts of his true opinion—that it was astonishing to him Frank Drakston was not dead already—that in all his experiences as a doctor—even his war experiences never had he seen the hardness of Frank Drakston's endurance. No, to tell her that, it would sound too cold and make him appear as if he were indifferent to the strain and pain, she was undergoing herself. Elizabeth Drakston was a sensitive and intelligent woman. He could tell her in a less harsh way, and she would still be able to see the true facts for what they were. "In the matter of the other question, Miss Elizabeth, Frank's amazing alertness is basically due to his having been in perfect health when he was shot, his age, and his remarkable constitution when it comes to bearing up to pain. It could be several hours or even a day, perhaps two days before there is any great change. It's difficult to set a time limit on something of this nature. Why don't you try to get a little rest? I promise I'll call you at the first sign of any varying turn that could arise although my own opinions is that it won't be right away."

Yes, Elizabeth was intelligent, but, right at that moment, she most likely was thinking in terms of its benefit being a curse to her instead of a blessing. She had seen the true harrowing facts clearly enough. She saw what Seth Roalf was trying to tell her in a round—about—way, that it would probably be a good while before Frank died—but die he would! Her husband was slowly bleeding to death on the inside and there was nothing they could do about it! She studied the doctor's face for a moment but ask no more questions. There was nothing else to say. While the doctor excused himself and was leaving the room, she automatically let Matthew guide her to a nearby sofa where she sat down before her trembling legs might have buckled under her. Matthew sat down beside her. For some moments, she sat totally submerged in an apth of dazed silence overcome by the unsureness of this shattering tragedy that had suddenly exploded and crushed the light form last evening's radiant world and left her groping in a chaotic darkening madness that was beyond her to take in or rationalize.

Finally, though, her whirling thoughts began to settle enough that she was asking herself, why now, at this particular time—if it had to be—when she and Frank had at last discovered and embraced a closeness that their marriage had never known before? It had been there. She had felt the glorious sublimity of its tenderness and there was no doubt in her mind that Frank had soared in its radiance, too. No, they hadn't had to wait till they reached England to recapture anything that they once may have shared, they had found all of it again as well as so much more in the shadowy quiescence of last evening's growing twilight inside those very walls of Drakston Hall, Now, all so quickly, Frank was dying! Never again would she know his strong arms about her. Never again would she feel the rapture of that divine ecstasy for any man, because only Frank could grant her that and carry her to such sublime heights of glory.

Last evening when Frank had left her, she had lain in their bedroom long after it had grown dark, but she had not been seeing the darkness. She had been seeing nothing save the light of their union, feeling as though the darkened room was still a glow in the brilliance of this beauty that God in his infinite wisdom had willed to man and woman to share. She had finally gotten up though and lit the lamp, noticing the glow that still covered her face and how her eyes shone back at her in the mirror. She picked up the yellow dress that Frank had said looked so pretty on her and slipped it back on over her head, smoothing its shimmering folds down over her hips and smiling to herself as she thought about what her personal maid no doubt was going to be thinking, when she called for her to come and fasten the dress and redress her hair all over again. But, what of it! She had told herself, taking an unusual disregardful and indifferent view to anything the maid or anyone else may have thought. Frank was her husband. He had wanted her. She had wanted him. When and what they did behind their bedroom door was their doing and should not be of any concern to nobody else!

When she had finished dressing for the second time that evening, she had asked the maid to bring her a light snack to the library, she thought she would read awhile, nothing heavy just a cup of tea and a muffin would be fine, because she had decided to dine later with Mr. Drakston when he returned home, and be sure to tell the butler and the dining room maid to forego serving supper until then. She had been certain that Frank would come home early. But, Heavenly Father! At no time would she have ever thought what his coming home earlier than what she had even expected would bring forward. Would she ever be able to, at least, see it all less distinct?

Still wrapped in the blanket of placid serenity that Frank had draped around her, when she had reached the library she had been drawn to a book of Shakespearean poetry. Buried deeply in the book's romantic verse, she had eaten the sweet muffin that the maid had hurriedly brought and was leisurely sipping her cup of tea when the sudden sound of a galloping horse coming up the driveway caught her attention. Looking at the clock on the mantel and seeing that it was only a few minutes past eight p.m., she had been surprised but swept with elation as well to know that Frank had chosen to come back home so early—at least an hour sooner than she had been expecting him. She had found herself smiling in thinking that apparently Frank's mood was something near to her own. Why she had been so positive; however, that it was Frank, she would never know unless her exalted heart had refused to think it could be anyone but him. She had put the book of poetry aside immediately and was rising from her chair to go meet him when the groom's terrified scream for help, followed at the same instant by a shrill neigh from Blossom, suddenly cut the evenings quiet as though a peel of lightning had struck—shocking her into an ice cold fear and complete standstill as it told her something had happened to Frank!

Somehow though, she had quickly gathered her shattered nerves together. Snatching up her dress high above her ankles so as to give her feet more freedom to move in, she had gone sailing from the library and on down the long hallway to the outside and almost froze in her tracks again at facing the horror of Frank's ashen, dazed face and his blood-soaked white linen shirt. Suddenly, she had felt herself growing violently ill, the muffin and tea churning round and round in her stomach. But seeing that Frank needed help and needed it desperately, she had thrown her feelings to the wind and sailed on down the steps and reached him just as he let go his hold on the saddlebow and tumbled into the arms of both her and the groom alike.

Thus, her maddening nightmare had begun to move under sail.

To add to the horrifying situation even though her gratitude would forever remain solid for the capable presence of Matthew Carson, the Drakston coach from Oak Grove came rumbling up the drive at the same time. There had been no way to prevent Stuart from taking in the alarming scene. He had had his head leaning out the coach's window—looking anxiously—and as Matthew had jumped from the coach to lend a hand with Frank, Stuart had leaped right after him and had begun screaming with every breath at getting a closer view of his father's shocking appearance. Whit tumbled from the coach, too, and after taking a rather long look, his screams began to echo Stuart's. She knew both young boy's screaming and especially Stuart's had deeply distressed Frank as much as it had her, although their wailing had soon quieted down. Frank's mother—bless her—her face as ashen grey with shock as Frank's, had not rushed to her own son but had turned immediately to Stuart and Whit and, in her gentle, calm manner, she had quickly soothed both boy's tears away.

The butler and several more servants came rushing outside. The groom raced for the stables to get a fresh mount to rid for the doctor, and by the time they had gotten Frank inside to the bedroom, she had begun to see how fortunate she was to have Frank's uncle beside her. He promptly took charge, making Frank as comfortable as his condition would allow, while they had waited for Seth Roalf. She thought that Mr. Carson had been able to do more for Frank's comfort than what he normally would have had it not been because of his experiences in the past war. Certainly she could never have handled the situation as well as he had, even if it did now appear that all their efforts to save Frank had come to no avail.

She still did not know if Frank had shot himself accidentally, been waylaid on his way home by some secret adversary, gotten in a dispute with someone and it had resulted to them pulling guns on one another, or what. Even though she had sat beside his bed for hours and hours, him appearing to want her there as he reached and gripped her hand from time to time, he still had not told her anything about his being shot. Nor did she believe he had disclosed any facts to anyone else.

When she had reached Frank at the steps, he had murmured, "Elizabeth, I'm shot, send for Seth Roalf," and once, after he had dozed off for a few minutes, upon awakening he had looked at her blood-splashed yellow dress that she had not taken the time to pull off and had murmured again, "Elizabeth dear, I'm sorry about your pretty dress," and that had been the most of what Frank had said to her except a few words about his upsetting Stuart. She had assured Frank the dress did not matter. She would buy another yellow dress just for him. She also had assured him that Stuart would be fine and to prove it she had allowed Stuart to visit his father before going to bed last night, and several times today they had visited. Whit had also visited Frank but not as often as Stuart.

Even had things not become something near to a terrorized nightmare with her having no desire to wear Frank's strength with questions, one did not question him about his personal business, anyhow. She was no exception, though she had been his wife for several years. Moreover, Frank would only say so much regardless of the circumstances. If he did not volunteer to talk in depth concerning any situation or subject matter, which he surely didn't very often, one had to accept what little he did reveal and forget about the rest of what one hoped he might go ahead and say. That was the way Frank was and she had become reconciled to this particular stamp in his nature long ago. If the worst came and the doctor might as well have said it would come, what difference did it make, anyway? Frank, the person, was all that mattered to her. She loved him. She had loved him from the first and her parents had approved of her choice for her husband, especially her father. Mother. Father. How she needed that solace that only their presence could grant her—to feel her father's protective arms about her. Never could she remember having yearned so intensely to see them. It was an impossible yearning though and she might as well accept it. There was over a three-thousand-mile ocean between them and her—an unyielding impasse that blocked any way she might try to reach them—that wide expanse of water that she had been looking forward to sailing with Frank. Now, without any warning, the whole world seemed as though it had crumbled into dust at her feet and left nothing in its wake but her—frightened and alone.

Elizabeth's lost, troubled gaze drifted back to rest upon her lap where she ultimately found herself staring at Matthew's hard, muscular hand covering the small hard ball that made up both her own, that she unknowingly was gripping and wringing tightly together. Though she and Frank's uncle had known one another for several years, up until the present, the link that had brought them in association with each other had never stretched beyond that certain degree. But now, looking at Matthew Carson's strong hand lying softly over hers, Elizabeth began to see more than merely a connective family tie and the observing of correct proprieties which had mostly made up their past relationship. She saw the hand that was there, not one beyond any bounds of contact—a hand that was waiting and willing to take hers if she would only reach for it that sheltering comfort that she so desperately craved and was unable to even vision coming near let alone touch. And, even though she was aware that the comfort it offered did not promise to still her fears or fill that void of family separation that she so poignantly felt, she; nevertheless, knew that somehow once she had let herself open to its warmth and seek its strength and encouragement, that whatever lay ahead of her would seem a little less frightening.

And so, Elizabeth slowly brought her head up and looked at the man who had been sitting there quietly but rather solidly beside her for some minutes now, studying him and seeing him in an entirely different light than previously. For a few seconds, Matthew held her stare, seeing in her the yearning and helplessness that might have been his very own, because he had been there, too, more times than he cared to recall.

Spontaneously and in the same move, they let the distance between them be cast aside as Elizabeth let her head fall against Matthew's chest while his arms closed around her shoulders. With no less compassion than had he been holding Eliza, Matthew did his utmost to soothe her fears and her pain while the tears, that had stayed surfaced in her eyes all day, finally washed as full and free as they would down her drawn face.

"I'm not going!" retorted Eliza, her cheeks coloring as she looked up from the mending in her lap to face Luke who had come from the tobacco field in mid-morning to tell her of the message that had just been delivered to him from Drakston Hall. “I can’t see us dropping everything and running to Drakston Hall today at Frank’s bidding.”

“Well, actually, dear, the message came from your father, it appears that Frank wants to talk with us and him, too, about something important, or so the message stated.”

“I don’t care what Frank wants,” she snapped again. “He’s always had a way of getting anything he wanted! Any desire that he’s ever held, even if he knew that desire was out of bounds to him, he’s still figured out some way to come by it regardless of what the cost to others might have been! What Frank wants; he takes! That’s the motto he lives by!” Her blazing face fell back to her mending.

Bowled over by her obvious hostility to say nothing of her cold indifference, Luke scowled as he gave her a closer look. Good Lord! What had happened to Eliza, lately? This was not like Eliza at all. Surely, he had failed to make himself clear to her.

“But, dear, evidently I didn’t state the message to you as clearly as I should have. Frank’s been shot and form what I gather it’s serious.”

“I heard what you said, Luke and I’m not one bit surprised. What does surprise me is the fact that it hasn’t happened long before now. Apparently, Frank’s walking over people has finally caught up with him.”

“Well, I have no desire to set in his judgement. The word is, he’s critical and wants to see us, and I think we should go. I’m certain the circumstances are as the message stated, or your father wouldn’t have gone along with Frank’s wish and bothered us. He knows I’m trying to finish transplanting the tobacco today.”

Instantly, he saw her bring her flying needle to a stop, sticking the needle through the patch that she was sewing on his work clothes. And, seeming to become more disquieted than hostile now, she said, as she appeared to be studying the patch of cloth, “What on earth would prompt Frank to want to see us? Judging from his past behavior, all the people I would think he would desire to see, you and I would be the least favored. I’m positive you’re well aware that Frank’s never had any liking for your company, and he and I have never remained on a good footing with one another for more than a few minutes at a time. In fact, I was just thinking about Frank as I started patching on those clothes. He throws away better clothes than what you wear to church.”

"I won't argue the contrary to that because it's true. It does seem up until the present that fate has cast a sunny light upon Frank in more ways than one. As well as having been the receiver of many life's blessings, he's also come by many windfall profits. I surely hope though that his past good fortune isn't the seed that's sprouted all this chilliness on your part in connection with him," ventured Luke.

Her head came up fast. "No, Luke," she shot back, her eyes meeting his direct, "his good fortune has nothing to do with how I feel toward him, even if my mind's eye did see his swanky overstuffed wardrobe as I started this mending. Though, in a sense, it might just serve me better if that were indeed the case. Yes, I shall think no doubt that would be better for me, as of late, anyhow."

Again, her baffling and somewhat heatedly remark had stumped Luke. Yet, in spite of it, he was sorry he had referred to her seemingly lack of compassion and told her, "I'm sorry, dear, I shouldn't have made that remark, because I'll have to admit that your Cousin Frank's behavior has left me plenty cold several times, also. He's a hard man to get to know or understand; for example, wanting to have a talk with us when I think I could almost recall every word he's ever said to me, so few they've been. Maybe that's why he wants to see us, though, is to say he's sorry for his ever-standoffish attitude. Anyway, whatever his reason is, we've wasted enough time in discussing him now. We can do that later in the buggy. I'll dash and change these work clothes and maybe if you'll hurry, too, by the time I fetch the buggy, you'll be ready, and we can get on our way. Hannah should be coming any minute to stay with the children. I came by her cabin first and told her we'd been called to Drakston Hall. Your father said it was urgent so I thought we should try to leave as soon as possible."

Following his every word with her concentrated gaze, Eliza felt a great disappointment in seeing that Luke had failed to grasp any significance at all in what she had tried to hint but could not gain the courage to tell. Still, she asked herself, how could she be so simple as to think he would? True, Luke had admitted he did not understand Frank. Never though, would he hold a notion that Frank would stoop to the level of raping any woman much less another man's wife and especially her. Luke's principles were too high for that kind of thinking. If she could only bring herself to tell him the reason, she had no wish to see Frank or be anywhere near him. Well, she couldn't! But she could do as he had asked and also tell him she was sorry for having snapped at him.

"Yes, I suppose we should do as Father's message suggested," she agreed, rising from her chair and laying her mending aside, "and I'm sorry, Luke, that I'm so grump today, snapping at you just now. But—Well—I've—"

"Don't bother, darling, with apologizing to me," he quickly interrupted, stepping closer to her and brushing her cheek with a kiss. "You've had too much to contend with in recent months, trying to regain your health back under all these laboring chores that you're forever busy at. Then, all the disturbance last evening with Doss capping everything off by exhibiting that hideous looking rattler, I would think it's little wonder that you're somewhat jittery today. But, try to put it out of your mind, sweetheart, if you can. We'd better run now and dress so we can get started, or they might start wondering if we're going to come."

In the same never forgotten intimate expression that he had shown toward her at Windsor Luke squeezed her hand as he turned to hasten toward the bedroom. He hoped he had convinced her that he had attached little importance to her unusual manner, and, at the same time, was also telling himself that if he saw Seth Roalf he would ask the doctor to have a look at Eliza as soon as possible.

Even though they had endeavored to hurry, it still was fast approaching the noon hour when Luke finally rounded the portion of the driveway that lead to the huge impressive stone steps at Drakston Hall. He pulled the mare to a stop and though his coming to Drakston Hall on this day was owing to a reason totally different from what the bringing of his person there on prior occasions had been, that by no means did not stop his eye as always from taking in the massive ferocious looking marble lions that flanked that Corinthian-like entrance on either side leading to the columned gallery above. Without fail, Luke was ever awed by this striking authenticity of sculptured art that one was forced to pass through to gain the stately mansion. The lion's glaring greenish-yellow glass eyes and ivory tusks gleaming between the wide jaws that the sculptor had so artfully implanted in his flamboyant statues, in Luke's opinion, could not have captured the look of the lion's real unfearing nature any nearer or, as for that matter, fall short of catching the eye of anyone that came within seeing distance of the mansion.

Each time Luke saw the sculptured pieces of art, he was ever to wonder why the Drakston who had had the sculptured beast erected there, had not settled for a more pleasing, peaceful looking animal; for instance the lamb, if an animal had to be and apparently it was, their choice of decoration for the front entrance. And, as much as he disliked in having such a thought, there had always been something about that unflinching look that the statues bore that never failed to bring thoughts of Frank's bearing to his mind, causing him now to instinctively shake his head in order to unload his conscience for having such a thought about anyone, as he handed the reins over to a stable groom who had been instantly on the spot to take them from his hands.

Luke jumped down from the buggy, observing as he hastened around it to give Eliza his hand that several more vehicles, with their horses still in harness, were parked under a stand of pecan trees a number of yards off to the side of the driveway on down below the mansion toward the stables. He recognized the Randolph coach and mentally noted that someone must have seen cause to send for Martha, bringing him to reason that Frank's conditions was evidently indeed serious and, that Matthew Carson had not summoned Eliza and himself to Drakston Hall merely because he was catering to one of Frank's whims as Eliza had seemed to give every appearance of thinking. Though she thus far had not disclosed it verbally.

It was true that Eliza had harbored a few doubts concerning the seriousness of the situation as Luke had suspected. It had occurred to her that Frank was not above going to any length in seeing that one of his desired notions was put into effect, even if it did come to him misleading her father in the matter of his state of health. Still, for all that, since she and Luke had left Green Sea, she had become so uptight in her silent thoughts over the prospect of being in Frank's presence again that the circumstances which were bringing her to Drakston Hall had hardly crossed her mind anymore; therefore, causing her to give the appearance of indifference when that was not the case at all. Actually, she was constantly fighting her feelings with bated breath, wondering what Frank was up to along with her dread of facing him. And now, her eyes having also caught the sight of the other parked carriages, she felt her pulse quicken even more as those visions of dark storm clouds that she had seen of late flashed across her mind; and her reason for being there dawned on her again. Even so, she was still reluctant to see Frank.

She did give her hand to Luke; however, and clinging tightly to his while she tried to hold onto her composure, she grudgingly moved alongside him up the palatial-like steps and on across the wide gallery till they at last had reached the massive double doors that Frank had had installed since the war. The doors with their silver fittings weighed well into the hundreds of pounds. Stained glass pancls graced the doors on either side as well as a huge silver Drakston crest that set just above the center opening. Within hands reach, a silver chain dangled from the crest. When pulled, it droned a bell on the inside. Luke reached up and gave the chain a slight tug and instantly a butler was swinging the heavy doors aside and reaching for Luke's hat and Eliza found herself standing in the hushed hallway, save a faint murmur of voices coming from the front parlor, which seemed to pronounce the stillness even more.

Appearing to having been already informed as to where he should usher them, since she nor Luke had said anything, the butler turned and indicating that they were to follow him, he started ushering them down the hall. Just at that moment though, Eliza saw her father step through the lower sitting room door, coming to meet them. It was the same doorway that she had seen him, her mother, Uncle Franklin, and Aunt Amy pass through many times in years long past to do their quiet visiting with one another, while the younger generation had taken over the front parlor. The memory swept strongly across her mind now as Matthew came on toward them with his tired, grave expression. The distance between was gained. The butler announced their presence quietly and vanished from view. Her father's arms had closed around her as warmly as ever-their devoted strength seeming to give her strength. While he still kept one arm draped around her shoulders, he turned to Luke and giving him his other hand, he said, "Thank you both for coming, but I'm sorry, Luke, for having gotten you away from your tobacco planting. I know you wanted to finish with it today."

"It's all right, Mr. Carson," Luke answered, "the hands will manage without me. How is Frank?"

Matthew held back his true opinion in front of Eliza.

"Well, he has weakened some, but right at this stage, he's holding his own. That's why he insisted I send for you two now, said he wanted to talk while he had the strength to talk with. The surgeons say the bullet can't be removed, so it's hard to say just how things will go. I certainly saw worse stomach wounds during the war though and some survived and under appalling conditions at that, as I've told Frank for the purpose of encouraging him."

Feeling the sooner, the better that she had some inkling of what to expect since it now appeared that her escaping the meeting with Frank was inevitable, Eliza inquired, though she was near holding her breath, "Father, why did Frank send for us? Do you have any idea what he wants to see us about?"

"No, I'm sorry, darling, I don't," Matthew told her, having become almost as bewildered at Frank's request as she and Luke were now that he had had awhile to ponder over it. "After the surgeons gave Frank their opinion in regard to their operating for the bullet, he asked to see me in private and requested that I send for you and Luke immediately. He said there was a matter of importance he wished to take up with the three of us, something he had no desire to let anyone else in on. Of course, since I felt he should preserve his strength as much as possible, I didn't question him. Knowing Frank's nature, it's doubtful he would've gone any further into then, anyway."

"How did the accident happen, Mr. Carson, or hasn't Frank said yet?" asked Luke.

"No, he hasn't disclosed any facts about that, either. I got the impression he didn't want to talk about it, so naturally I've been waiting for him to bring up the matter."

"Well, that could be what he wants to let us in on," suggested Luke, though he put little faith in his words.

"I've thought about that, Luke," Matthew replied, stroking his chin for a moment as he reflected farther upon the matter. "Still, my guess is that it's more than likely his family's welfare he wants to discuss. It could be that he's worried and concerned about Elizabeth since she's so far away from any blood relative except a six-year-old child. That does make a difference you know, and no doubt Frank has given this some thought in case—well, in case the outcome doesn't turn in his favor."

"But, Sir," questioned Luke, as all three continued to stand huddled together in the hallway, "if that were the case, would not Martha and Bruce or perhaps Aunt Amy or yourself, be the ones he would choose to discuss that matter with? As Eliza pointed out earlier today, Frank has yet to open up to me as long as we have known one another, and it's certainly puzzling and doesn't seem logical at all that he would suddenly feel otherwise, desiring my presence in any discussion he might choose to have."

Matthew set a somewhat slanted eye upon Luke, scrutinizing him for a few seconds. "I've also thought about that, too, Luke," he said, "not only in connection with you but myself as well. However, I suppose Frank has his reasons for choosing to talk with the three of us over other family members. Come to think of it, and I mean no disrespect to Frank in saying this, we shouldn't be too astonished at his actions, because we all know that he's never been one to reveal the why and wherefore of any move that he's ever undertaken regardless of the circumstances involved."

"You're right about that, sir," agreed Luke, while Eliza thought in her silence, yes, unfortunately, Father how well I know.

"It stands to reason though," Matthew went on to say,

That Frank doesn't want to distress his mother any more than she is already with talk of that nature. Amy is terribly upset, but I finally persuaded her to try to get some much needed rest and I'm thankful to say she's still resting And, I've said, when it comes to Elizabeth, Frank has good cause to be concerned even if it turns out that's not the basis of his desire to talk with us, for I fear she's near a collapse. Not until Martha and Bruce arrived a short while ago, could anyone, including Frank, persuade her to leave his bedside. Save the time she's spent consulting the doctors, she's been with him constantly. But Martha insisted and I might add rather forceful, that Elizabeth get some rest, too, promising that she would take Elizabeth's place beside Frank's bed. Elizabeth's wish is that Frank not be left alone without some member of the family with him, which, of course is wise on her part."

"This must be so terrible and frightening for her and Aunt Amy, too. I wish there were something I could do," murmured Eliza.

"I know, dear," said Matthew. "I feel the same way but there's not much anyone can do, not even the doctors, except wait." He sighed, adding, "Well, at any rate, I suppose we should go on and see what it is that Frank has on his mind. He asked if you two had arrived yet not less than ten minutes ago."

"I reckon so," voiced Luke, still stumped at finding himself on the threshold of Frank Drakston's bedroom as one of a selected group, while, at the same time Eliza was feeling as if she were bring lead off to the gallows as they resumed their steps on down the hall with Matthew walking between them.

"Oh, another something," said Matthew again, as they neared the bedroom door, "Frank's completely rational. So far today, he's refused any sedative that would induce one to sleep, says he wants to know what's going on. Well, here we are."

Matthew tapped lightly on the door. He opened it and they entered through and now the door had closed after them. And, if there had been moments on certain occasions from time to time throughout her life that Eliza had secretly wished Martha were a little more reticent in nature, those moments had become lost to her memory now. As Martha instantly jumped up from her chair beside Frank's bed and came rushing toward her with wide-open arms that provided a sanctuary of short retreat at this momentous time, exclaiming a warm greeting in the same breezy manner that had ever been habitual with her, Eliza could have fallen down on her knees in gratefulness.

She thought, never had Martha's somewhat boisterous voice sounded so sweet and welcome to her ears, Martha's exuberate personality been so pleasingly and loving, Martha's devotion so dear. In the warmth of Martha's affectionate greeting, she began to feel as if the ice that had gathered around her heart of late was finally beginning to melt and, that maybe through this sudden warmth that was seeping over her, she was at last gaining the strength she needed to be as near her natural self once more as possible.

Faintly, over Martha's hailing welcome expressions of delight in seeing that Eliza was well enough to engage in normal activities again, Eliza heard Luke's kind, condolent greeting to Frank and Frank's murmur of response in return. Then, she heard Frank say, quite distinctly, "Sis, would you mind leaving us alone for a while?"

"Sure, Frank," Martha replied, her arms falling back to her sides, whispering as she turned and slipped through the door, "I'll see you later Eliza," and once again Eliza had come face to face with Frank Drakston, though instead of her gaze resting upon him. It had averted to the floor.

Suddenly though, without pausing for one second longer, while an appalled Luke Heyward and Matthew Carson gaped speechlessly at him, Frank was telling Eliza, "Eliza, you're a damn good shot! You can hit your target smack in the center, and I've got a rifle bullet lodged in my belly for proof, in case you or anyone else should ever doubt your skill when it comes to your handling of firearms!" Causing her averted gaze to dart like a shot in utter disbelief to his face, with an impact no less shocking than had an earthquake started moving the room's walls and the floor under her.

Shocked wordless, Eliza stood and stared back at the pain-filled, deathly pale face set to hers, and seeing in spite of his suffering the same sardonic smile that had mocked her so many times in the past playing at the corners of Frank's mouth. Regardless of the circumstances, Frank, she thought, I shouldn't have come here today. I should have known that even if I did escape your hands, there would still be the scathing of your tongue to endure.

Luke had also been staring, taking in the mocking smile on Frank's face, too, and he had begun to see red. Even though upon first glance he had seen that Frank Drakston was not likely to ever leave his bed, that fact scarcely mattered to him now in his rage. Right at that moment, Luke felt that notwithstanding Frank Drakston's obvious torture and pallid face, that was almost the color of the half dozen immaculate pillows that he was propped among while he held his hand clutched to his middle, he could have pulled him from his bed and socked him to the floor.

Moving quickly to Eliza's side and closing his arm around her in a most shielding manner, it took some doing for Luke to keep his voice steady as he said, "Frank, I would think with your awareness that it has taken my wife months to gain back her present stage of health, which, by no means, bears the fact that she's full recovered even if she did come here today; and considering the state of your own affliction, that you would recognize it's not the most propitious time for such jesting remarks! Regardless of your affliction or that obvious pleasure that you appeared to be drawing at the expense of my wife or whatever difference that you and Eliza may have reached in the past, if we're to remain in your presence and hear you out in the matter that you desired to see us about, you'll have to refrain from throwing any more offbeat jokes of that nature and be serious. I won't stand for any more of it!"

"I'm sorry, Luke," said Matthew finally finding his voice. "I didn't know—I didn't think—" He let his voice fade in its seemingly hollow apology.

"It's all right, Mr. Carson, I think Frank understands that I look on this meeting as being one of seriousness, and not one to be highlighted with off-color comedy aimed at Eliza."

"Hell, call it comedy or whatever you like," grumbled Frank, "but I've never been any more serious in my life!"

"You what?" Luke shot back, while an amazed Matthew gaped again, and Eliza started shivering as if the room were filled with winters chill instead of April sunshine while she continued to stare in fearful silence.

"I mean I am serious. What in hell do you think I mean?" Frank asked rather brusquely. "Is it going to become necessary for me to keep repeating it to you? Contrary to what you seem to want to make out of it, I'm not playing a game, though I wish to hell I were."

His voice hard as steel, Luke coldly replied, "I don't believe you." He had become so completely enraged and torn, too, by Frank's nerve-rending accusation, that he never gave one second's thought to the event at Green Sea on the previous night as being connected with Frank at all.

"No," Frank drawled, giving Luke a somewhat oblique eye, "I can see that you don't. Well, how's this for convincing you? I'm positive by this time that somebody at Green Sea has found that damned rattler that I put a pistol slug through last evening, not once but twice. A rattler was found, was if tot, lying in the rut of the driveway near that big gardenia bush? If by any chance it hasn't been, go look and you'll find it."

God Almighty, the man was serious! Feeling as though Frank Drakston had tied him hand and foot and was laughing at him while he squirmed helplessly to free himself, Luke turned his head toward Eliza and met the same helpless look on her face as she looked up at him. He could feel her shattered nerves shaking her body while he read the message of fear written in her eyes. Trying hard to remove any rage, any fear, or any helplessness that might come through in his voice, he tightened his arm about her and said, "It's all right, darling, never fear, everything's going to be all right, I promise."

His eyes darting back and forth between Frank and the shaken couple standing before him that from all appearances gave every indication of being cornered, Matthew let his eyes stop on Luke's face to stare questioningly, while the electrifying silence became more pronounced by the second

The seconds ticked by as Luke returned Matthew's look and then turned his face back to Eliza. Should he believe Frank Drakston's claim? His love for Eliza was surely intense enough to induce him to lie for her, and he thought he could live with it. Still, after all was said and done, would not the standards that he had set for himself and measured others by, including Frank Drakston, since he met and married Eliza, be all lost in vain? Would not every example that he endeavored to set before his children and raise them by from that day forward, be altogether hollow from any sound principle? Moreover, although he knew Eliza was frightened and terribly alarmed of what Frank might do, he still was positive that she wouldn't want him to lie.

While Frank lay and waited; also, for Luke's answer, Luke raised his head from looking down at Eliza and lifting his eyes back to Matthew he affirmed, in a clear and steady voice, "It's true, Mr. Carson, what Frank has stated is correct. We did find a huge rattler late last evening that appeared to have been shot at twice near the gardenia bush." Then, Luke went on to explain how their supper was interrupted by two pistol shots that they thought had been fired by the raiders, who had attacked Green Sea in the past in this same fashion; and how Eliza had grabbed the rifle and fired from the doorway while he was trying to get the children to safety. He ended by saying, "I'm sorry that all our trouble at Green Sea has led to this."

Matthew was sorry, too. But, looking at his daughter's face, he was also feeling as though Frank had handcuffed him and led him down a blind alley. Again, he heard himself trying to beg an apology, "I'm sorry, too, Luke, and I want you and Mary Eliza to know that I was unaware about all this. Had I known that this was the matter that Frank wanted to discuss, I certainly would've handled my part involved, in an entirely different manner." Matthew stepped closer to Eliza's side and reached for her hand, noticing how icy cold it felt. "Don't get upset, dear, as Luke told you, everything will be all right."

"Well," drawled Frank once more. "I thought that would clear the fog out. I can see that I've convinced everybody—" Abruptly though he impatiently waved his hand, appearing to be suddenly irritated. "That matter can rest for a while, though, I have other things I want to talk about besides that—" He broke off again at the sudden unmistakable sound of boots scuffling outside the door and someone giving it a light tap. His eyebrows arched in deep creases as he looked toward it and went on to ask, rather irritable, "Now, what?" just as the door was pushed open by an obvious agitated Bruce Randolph with the exhilarated Sheriff Walt Hawkins almost in a bounce on his heels.

Bruce paused momentarily as he spoke to Luke and Eliza, overlooking in his vexation, the uneasy gaze that Frank had put in their eyes—eyes that were warily straying toward the animated sheriff as they returned Bruce's greeting. Matthew was also giving the sheriff a wary eye and, for good reason, because it was evident that day in the tax office was very much on Walt Hawkin's mind as he, too, paused in his anxious stride and tipping the brim of his hat, which he had forgotten to remove in his excitement, said “Well, well, if it isn’t—How nice to see you—” with a quick shift of his eye, he added, “Mr. Carson.” But, much to their relief—his presences cheering them none whatsoever—before Luke or Matthew could barely bob their heads, the sheriff had whirled on toward his prize customer lying on the bed.

Bruce had also turned to Frank and was saying, his contempt for the sheriff’s brass coming through plainly in every word, “Frank, I’m sorry for the intrusion. Martha told me that Luke and Eliza had arrived and were visiting with you and I asked Sheriff Hawkins to wait his turn, but he would have none of it. He insisted that I admit him to this room immediately.”

Suddenly, Frank seemed indifferent about the interruption. Though he was still scowling when he replied, “It’s all right, Bruce.”

“Then,” said Bruce, eyeing the sheriff direct, “If everybody will excuse me, I’ll take my leave. The room seems to be a little overcrowded, anyway.” He turned and giving Luke a wink as he passed him, he strode form the room.

Appearing to have closed his ears to Bruce’s remark, the jaunty sheriff—while Luke, Eliza, and Matthew continued to look on suspiciously—blithely shot his hand out to Frank and said, even though his obvious pleasure in having business at Drakston Hall was giving the lie to every word of his so-called sympathy, “Mr. Drakston, I truly regret this unfortunate circumstance that has brought me to your side today. I can hardly believe, sir, that a man of your standing would fall victim to such an unwarranted deed. But, I’m here now, Mr. Drakston, and I’ll see that justice is carried out to full measure in your behalf. Don’t you have a fret about that. I’m sorry that I was unable to get here any sooner, but I was way out in the county on another important missions when my deputy brought the message.”

Frank had ignored the sheriff’s extended hand, which he had finally pulled back and let fall to his side, the rebuff causing his mouth to drop one or two degrees at the corners. Just the same, to the others present, it was still plain to see that it was going to take more than snub of a handshake to flatten the sheriff’s air, entirely; and Luke—for one—began to fear with a leaping heart if perhaps there was not another reason that had brought about the sheriff’s gleeful attitude other than the obvious pleasure he derived from being in the company of Frank Drakston.

Good God! Luke was suddenly thinking, as Frank lifted his face toward the sheriff appearing to be undecided about something—was this the opportunity that Walt Hawkins had been waiting for? Had this unfortunate accident provided way at last for Walt Hawkins to seek his revenge, if he had not already by leading those attacks against Green Sea? No, it can't be! For all Frank's shortcomings and his open dislike for him, he could not—would not—allow Walt Hawkins to arrest Eliza for an innocent shooting! Still, had Frank sent for Walt Hawkins, too, in spite of the cold shoulder treatment? What was Frank stalling for? Could not he see that Eliza had already been shaken unmercifully? Well, let this go on for one minute more and he was taking Eliza out of there and if Walt Hawkins tried to stop him, he just may find himself going through that window!

Luke's hand that was free—Eliza had tightened her trembling grip on the other more firmly than ever balled, balled into a hard fist just as Frank finally growled, "What message are you talking about?"

"Why, you're having been shot last evening, sir," replied the sheriff, narrowing his eyes at Frank. What was this? Was the man out of his head?

"Oh," Frank sighed, pointing a weary finger up at the sheriff's head.

The sheriff's eyes narrowed all the more. Now what? Frank Drakston was acting mighty strange. He simply had to be not all there. It would turn out this way. The most important happening in his whole career and the key person seemed to be irrational. Well, there was nothing to do except take pains in trying to find out why Drakston was pointing his finger up at him.

"What is it, sir?" asked the sheriff, the tone of his voice filled with compassion as he bent forward somewhat. "My guess is, you want to tell me something."

"The hat, Hawkins!" growled Frank again, his annoyance rising to the surface once more. "I would think by this time that you would've noticed there's a lady present, even if you are accustomed to wearing your hat indoors, obviously!"

Hawkins brought his head up fast, his hand making a grab for his hat, "My apologies, madame," he nervously chuckled. "Sometimes, I fear the shocking aspects of my job causes my manners to become secondary with me. I hope you'll forgive me." Damn Frank Drakston! He was all there, all right. The same high-toned, haughty son of a bitch that he'd always been despite having a belly full of lead. Drakston had given it to him again, just as he had that day at O'Henry's Store and in front of Luke Heyward at that. He might have known. Well, he was not going to give up yet.

Taking the privilege of laying his hat on a nearby table, the sheriff quickly fumbled in the breast pocket of his uniform and pulled for a sheet of paper and short stubby pencil.

"Mr. Drakston, now perhaps we can get on with the business that's brought me here," the sheriff suggested. "The details are imperative, sir, if I'm to carry out this investigation in the meticulous manner that I desire. Now, sir, what time of evening would you say you were struck down and just what did the view around you look like when the tragedy occurred?" The sheriff licked the end of his stubby pencil and waited in the most businesslike manner he was capable of ejecting.

During the time that the sheriff had been busy with the muttering of his apology, getting rid of his hat, and readying himself with paper and pencil to take down what information he hoped to gain whether it was related to the accident or not made not one particle of difference to him—the chance to converse with Frank Drakston was the main point, Frank's eyes had found Eliza again; and even though he had heard the sheriff's questions, they carried no weight whatever with him and were as unrelated to what he was thinking about had Walt Hawkins asked him if it were snowing. In his private thoughts with Eliza, he could not have been any less interested in what the sheriff was saying or doing and indeed was hardly aware that he had mumbled a response until Walt Hawkins' fanatical obsession to be recognized in some manner by Frank Drakston, drew Frank's attention to his foolish approach.

"You guess, about first dark, you say," repeated the sheriff. He started to write the time down but then hesitated, seeming to be dubious about taking Frank's inattentive answer as fact. "But, sir, you said you guessed about dark. Did you by any chance take notice if there were any of our other planets—wouldn't hurt to let these people see that he was far from being an ignorant man about the planets making their evening appearance? Time is important you understand. If I could only set down a definite hour, or perhaps say the exact minute. Of course, I suppose the exact minute would be asking a little too much, but the sheriff hesitated again. Looking anxiously down at Frank, he licked the end of his pencil again and waited.

The sheriff's nonsense and preposterous question finally closed in on Frank's thoughts. Started, his head turned toward Walt Hawkins and taking a long hard look, it dawned on him what the sheriff's actions could lead to.

What in hell was going on? What did that fool sheriff think he was doing? He had not asked that any investigation be made at all, not by Walt Hawkins or anyone else. He wanted no form of law involved, whatever. HE shouldn't have let his thoughts distract his mind to the point that he had been unaware of Walt Hawkins' damn moves to say nothing of allowing him to remain in this bedroom as long as he had. Why had he not noticed before now that Eliza was scared out of her wits? No doubt he himself had frightened her although he had not meant to. But, from the looks of her face, apparently, what he himself had lacked in upsetting her, Walt Hawkins' presence was going to be the crowning touch that without questions would soon send her to the floor, if he did not stop this damn fool and set him straight once and for all time when it came to the matter of this case.

Why had it been throughout his entire life, or from the onset of puberty he should say, that where Eliza was concerned, the result of any meeting or any encounter that had ever occurred between them had always been nothing near to the purpose he had envisioned or hoped for? He supposed he would die, never knowing the answer to that.

Eliza shouldn't be that frightened though. My God, did not she know yet how he felt about her? Why would she still doubt him so, that she was now probably afraid he was going to turn her into the law? He would have hoped after—after that day on the ridge that for what small amount it would have been, that she would have come to understand him better and see him in a different light on the part of his devotion for her, because he had uncovered his every emotion that day—stripped his being to the core—exposed the raw depths of ever hunger desire he had held or any he may have held in the past—laid it all bare before her in its vulnerable nakedness. But, if her behavior now was any sign, nothing he had done had made any difference to her.

To be sure, he had taken her against her will which not only had violated decency but had trampled the act as well. Yet, the fact did remain that he had not planned the act nor had there been any violence, fighting, or anything of that sort between them once his desire for her had begun to run on its wild course. Moreover, there was not a man anywhere, counting Luke Heyward, who could have taken her with any more tenderness, nor gone any further in proving his love for her. That alone, should have told her something of the way he did truly feel about her, but, evidently, it had not. And there was no question that everything he had ever done in regard to Eliza, he had gone about it in the wrong way. Too late, he could see this now.

"Yes, Hawkins," Frank almost barked, at last, "That is asking a little too much and I appreciate your understanding the fact. It is true, I'm sorry to say, that I didn't pull my watch out to see what minute or, better still, what second, that ball of lead hit my stomach! However, your question, sheriff, has stirred up my curiosity. Tell me, will my having failed to think about checking the exact time of day, in circumstances such as this, place me in a unique category?" The damn fool.

"Well—" the sheriff gave a little abashed chuckle, "I suppose, Mr. Drakston, my question was a might to the extreme but like I say, time—"

"Put your pen and paper back inside your pocket, sheriff," Frank suddenly demanded.

"Back—inside my pocket, sir, I don't quite get—" the sheriff stopped, peering down at Frank rather doubtfully again.

"You heard me, sheriff, and you might as well understand, if you don't. There won't be any further questioning, nor any more answers."

"But, sir," the sheriff nervously protested, frowning, "I am supposed to keep law and order in this county and, one aspect among many that my job calls for in carrying my duties out, does involve asking questions. If I'm going to track down the assassin who attempted to take your life, any information that you can give me will be a great help, and I surely would be most appreciative."

"What I've just stated, sheriff, is the way it's going to be, except I would like to ask you one more question."

"Very well, sir, and I'll do my best to answer it."

"Who was your source of information, applying to that assassin remark?"

The sheriff's frown deepened. He began to feel as if Frank had him tethered at the end of a rope as he endeavored to search for a suitable answer. After some rather long hesitating, while Luke, Eliza, and Matthew still continued to listen in baffled silence, the sheriff replied, "Well—no one in particular, Mr. Drakston, that I can recall at the moment, but Charleston is simply buzzing with the news, I'm here to tell you. I haven't met up with one single person today, that your name didn't come up upon greeting, and the majority wished me Godspeed in tracking down the one responsible."

"Just as I thought," murmured Frank, his fatigue beginning to show.

"What did you say, sir?"

"Are you deaf, sheriff? Do I have to keep repeating everything I say to you? I said I'm not surprised, sheriff, that you couldn't name your source of information, because, with the exception of these three people who I just informed as to how I was shot, I haven't told anyone else, not even my wife! So, you see, sheriff, you came here assuming there was an assassin, rather than sticking to the fact. Another question, did it even occur to you that I could've accidently shot myself?"

"You accidently shot yourself?" the sheriff repeated, becoming almost undone by Frank's question.

"Yes, Sheriff Hawkins, and if I say so, that's the fact of my getting shot! So, in that case, there's no one to track down now, is there?"

The sheriff tugged at his mustache, seeming somewhat skeptical to believe Frank, pondering over his next move. Presently, he raised the only factor that appeared to be left in defense of his position, realizing how flimsy it was going to sound in its invalidity but was hoping that it would go unnoted. The turn in conversation had more than aroused his curiosity and he was becoming desperate to have it continue on as long as possible.

"But, sir, what about my records? There has been a shooting with your being severely wounded, and I would think it's our responsibility to make the facts known to the people. Now if you'll—"

"Hawkins!" Frank almost bellowed, cutting the sheriff off, stressing his every word with a marked meaning as Walt Hawkins seemed to cringe under the finality of each statement, "Now listen carefully, I won't be repeating this. Since there was no one else involved but myself, where I was at when I was shot, what time of day I was shot, or what the scenery around me was composed of at the time I was shot, is none of your damn business. No one asked you to come here. Nor has anyone asked you to make an investigation into this matter. Now, you get the hell out of my home and don't you ever come barging inside its walls again, without having a sound reason for doing so. Furthermore, as of this minute, when it comes to this case, it's closed for all time to you or any other form of law and don't you forget it. Take your damn hat now and get out of my sight. My patience with you and your investigation has reached its end!"

Weighing Frank Drakston's heated words, Walt Hawkins let his flaming expression linger on Frank for near a moment. "I see," he finally replied, coming to recognize that in addition to having lost out in gaining any information whatsoever into Frank Drakston's mysterious accident, he had also lost the cause that he had struggled for five years to gain—his being accepted someday at Drakston Hall on a social footing. What's more, it appeared that even his feigned visits had at last caught up with him. Even so, he promptly decided that he would not take his leave of Frank Drakston and his visitors resembling a whipped dog, though that was exactly the state of his feelings.

The sheriff brought his shoulders up and tucked his pencil and paper back inside his pocket and reached for his hat, slamming it down on his head defiantly in spite of Frank's sneering put down concerning it. Then, before he turned to stride for the doorway, he ran his eyes once or twice between Frank and the others and went on to conclude, "Very well, Mr. Drakston, I have no choice it seems but do as you've ordered. However, I would like to add that perhaps I would, not have taxed your patience so, had I heeded upon my arrival that you were already closing the case. Such is the strength of power though and since I never fail to be awed by it, so be it." Let that son of a bitch figure that out and die to boot, who cares? Not Walt Hawkins, not anymore, he was thinking as he whirled from the room and found his way back to the front entrance and down the steps to his horse.

Confused somewhat by the conversation they had witnessed in addition to having become almost to the point of being awe-struck at Frank Drakston's exceptional steadiness and indefatigability—despite the wringing pain he was obviously enduring—Luke, Eliza, and Matthew's scrutiny followed Walt Hawkins' back as he bowed to Frank's suggestion and removed himself from the room. Now they had turned their gaze back to Frank, continuing to study him. As they minutely examined him in their confusion—wondering about his twisting the facts around concerning his getting shot—he floored them once again, clearing away any doubts they may have begun to harbor, by telling Eliza for the second time, as he looked at her with a look of near amusement on his face, "I still maintain, Eliza, that you're a damn good shot!"

Eliza said nothing. Neither did Luke or Matthew.

Surprised that Frank had held back the true facts from the sheriff, all three puzzled people remained to study him and wonder why he had brought them there. Unlike Eliza and her father though, both of who had been exposed to Frank's personality more often, Luke had become near hypnotized at seeing Frank shift the many sides of his nature back and forth and was beginning to have a change of heart—seeing Frank in a more pleasing light. After all, Frank had saved Eliza from being subjected to the clutches of Walt Hawkins, had he not? Even so, for all Luke's gratitude and swinging thoughts, Frank immediately destroyed all and everything when he gave forth with a deep sigh and instantly plunged into disclosing his startling news—never blinking an eye even though he could see that his started listeners were staggered beyond description with Eliza beginning to weep—never hesitating or seeming to be qualmish about unfolding all of it, the riddle of the raids against Green Sea, the burning of the mansion because the nitwit Job had misunderstood the few words he had exchanged with him, the unfortunate circumstance concerning Bullitt—telling everything that had been brought about due to his being envious of Luke save his personal encounters with Eliza never appearing to be restive in any degree until he concluded his story by saying, "I realize it's a lot to ask, but what I've told you, I'd prefer that you keep it among yourselves. I'd rather that Mother, Elizabeth, and Stuart never know about it."

As he fell silent, obviously weakening, he appeared instantly to drop any unquietness he may have been feeling, looking straight into their startled faces without another wince, seeming to focus his eyes on Eliza's face more than the others. Not once had he said he was sorry. Nor did he ask to be forgiven, even if it had run across his mind earlier in the day.

Dumbfounded, Luke stared Frank back in cold silence. He volunteered no promises nor anything else. Too many thoughts of all the hardship he and Eliza had endured and was still laboring under, not to mention their seemingly never-ending mental anguish in thinking the mansion had burned because of their negligence, were spinning too rapidly in his mind. He was so shocked he could hardly think straight much less make promises and especially to the man who was responsible for bringing about so many uncalled—for burdens and distress. He kept on staring, trying to perceive some light that would bear favor on the part of Frank Drakston's position But, he was finding, he couldn't.

Neither did Eliza say anything. Shivering, she continued to cling to Luke's hand and weep.

Finally, even though he, too, was shocked almost speechless as well feeling sicken at Frank's revelation, Matthew broke the silence as he told him, "You have no need to fear that I'll ever disclose anything that you have told us to your mother, because I'm certain if she were to hear about it, it would near kill her—"He turned away, adding, as he started toward the door, "If everybody will excuse me, I think I'll get a breath of fresh air," slipping through the door in seconds.

Abruptly, Luke also turned away, saying, "That goes for us, too. Come on, dear," ushering Eliza for the door which Matthew had left ajar in making his hasty exit. As Luke reached for the doorknob though to swing the door wider, the stillness was broken again when Frank suddenly requested, "Eliza—I'd like for you to stay a few minutes longer, if you would."

Startled again and also puzzled, they both turned back, fastening a penetrating look on Frank with Luke presently inquiring, "You mean you wish to see Eliza alone, in private?"

Showing not one flinch, Frank set his eyes level to Luke's and replied firmly, "Yes, I do." Although in truth Luke felt that any request Frank may make involving himself or Eliza was not coming and certainly would remain unmerited, he; nevertheless, took another long look at Frank Drakston's ashen face and promptly decided not to stand in the way if Eliza was willing, for he was more positive than ever it could very well be the last or one among the last that Frank would ever make. "Of course, you realize, it's up to Eliza," he told Frank. He turned to Eliza. "How do you feel about it, dear? I have no objection to your granting his request."

Eliza looked form Frank to Luke and then back again, appearing to be uncertain of what to do.

"Please, Eliza," Frank pleaded.

Even though he was not sure he was doing the right thing, finding himself in a hard spot, Luke dropped Eliza's hand. "I'll be just beyond the door, darling. If you get upset or feel you need me in any way, call and I'll be here." He gave Frank another long look that was loaded with an unmistakable warning before he stepped through the door and quietly closed it after him.

Without delaying, Frank said, "You've never told him." Seeming to shrink away from him, Eliza dropped her head faintly murmuring, "N—o—o."

"Please, Eliza, raise your face so I can look at it and if you won't sit down, would you come closer to the bed—I'm becoming a little tired. I—swear I won't lay a finger on you. Even if I'd be fool enough to try, you can see my hands are pretty busy holding on to this ice bag."

With emotions that were plenty mixed, she raised her face and looked at him, her long eyelashes sticking to tear—wet cheeks. There was grief for the things that had been lost through hatred. Pain for all the needless sacrifice. Distress in knowing that it had been her hand that had held the rifle, putting him where he was. A deep hurt aching inside her for the cost to Luke and her father. Most of all; though, was the bitter bruise of his lust upon her that would not heal. Yet, despite all those weighted emotions crowding her heart, it still could make room to hold a certain degree of humanity—taking her feet forward; because she could see that indeed Frank's strength was caving in rapidly and knew he had spoken the truth.

As she came nearer and stood at the edge of the bed, he said "I—guess I've already asked too much of you, but I wish you wouldn't cry. Anyhow, getting—back to my question—I knew you hadn't told him when he came here today. I—don't care about that though, the part I do care about is you. That's—why I made it my business to go to Green Sea last evening. I—didn't give a damn whether you were interested in that run down, weedy spot that Early Cole lost. All I wanted was to see you. I—couldn't sail for England without knowing. Tell—me the truth, Eliza. Did—well—did I get you with child that day? All—those damn clothes that you women wear makes it hard to tell even if it has been months. I—know you're still ill—and I've gone through hell wondering about it." He looked up anxiously into her face.

She cut her eyes sideways somewhat as she told him, "No—you didn't—" then, seeming to suddenly gain more control over her emotions, she added, "There were several weeks when I worried an awful lot, more than I could possibly tell you, but I finally knew for certain that I wasn't."

He sighed deeply, "Well—thank God for that much. I'd never—want you to go through that ordeal again on my damned account. Eliza—I know you'd never believe me in a thousand years, but I never planned to take advantage of you that day—as I told you then—I'll tell you now, I just couldn't—"

"Please, Frank," she suddenly broke in, "I don't want to talk about that."

"But, by god, I do," he blurted back, fighting his sinking strength with a grit as hard as iron. "Because, in spite of what I did to you, I've always felt and still feel, no damn man should spill his seed in a woman, if she isn't willing to play the game with him! I'll admit I've always wanted you, and I realize now, I thought that day what I wanted to think, that you may have begun to feel something, too. Then, too late, I woke to the fact you weren't responding to me at all. Regardless of what you may think, Eliza, it wasn't all lust with me that day. I took you in love and I still love you."

Ever put to it in trying to understand him, baffled, Eliza moved her eyes back to Frank's face, studying him once again. Had she heard him correctly? Yes, no question that she had, she thought, because it would seem to be nothing out of the ordinary with Frank to reveal the things, he had done with one breath and profess to love her with the next. Apparently, Frank thought that she should be as unaffected by all of it as he appeared to be. A sudden eruption of resentment flared over her and—despite all she found herself contending his alleged devotion, "If you do love me, Frank, or have ever loved me, how could you have brought yourself to send so much trouble my way? And, there's something else, Frank, that I don't understand. What about Elizabeth? Have you forgotten you have a wife?"

She saw a sudden flash of anger color his pale cheeks as he retorted, "I told you long ago, Elizabeth has nothing to do with the way I feel about you." He drew a deep breath. "I—I love you both!"

"I don't see how that could be." She replied.

He shifted the ice bag around, pressing it tighter against his stomach, appearing to have no desire to challenge her remark. Presently though, he cocked his eye up at her and said, "That's understandable, but someday you may and come to realize that it is quite possible—" he sighed deeply again, the flush of color gone. "I failed with you, Eliza, on every score though. Maybe—if I hadn't tried so damn hard, things would've been different between us. Anyway—

another reason I asked to see you in private, was to tell you not to let any of this bother you. Whatever the outcome, I suppose I have it coming, and I've accepted it."

The senselessness of everything, the waste, the distress, and fear, her pain, his obvious pain—all of it came swarming down on her again with an agony no less stinging than had she fallen prey to an angry band of bees. Her throat tightened, causing her voice to tremble as she told him, "I—I truly didn't mean to hit anyone."

"You—don't have to tell me that," he softly said, "I—know your heart, Eliza, even if I did score out with you."

Suddenly, she wanted to escape—to where it did not matter—any place would do that would provide her welling emotion the freedom it demanded. She, instinctively, looked toward the door.

His eyes followed hers and without one trace of sarcasm in his voice, he said, tiredly, "You—want to leave, don't you?"

She turned her head back to him, letting her eyes fall upon the floor as she replied, "yes but it's the baby. She seemed fretful when I left and it worried me. I feel I shouldn't stay away too long." She told herself that in a sense she had not lied to him even if she had not revealed the main reason for wanting to leave.

"I'm sorry—I hope she'll be all right."

"She probably will be. I think it's just a cold, but you know how—" she stopped.

"It—is to worry over one's child," he finished for her. "you—bet I do. I know exactly how you feel. I've worried lots of times about Stuart when he had a cold—wondering if it was going to turn into a damn case of pneumonia—" he suddenly broke off, thinking, I hate to see you leave Eliza, for I have a feeling this may be our very last meeting even if those damn doctors did refuse to level with me. Even though I did raise hell with them to tell me the truth, I still got nowhere. I won't try to keep you any longer though—not this time. Nor will I allow any of my fears and anxiety to show, possibly burdening you. He drew another deep breath, something he seemed to be doing more and more, resuming to say, "Yes—you probably should hurry on home and see about her, I feel now that I've kept you too long as it is—" he hesitated again, searching her face as though it may have been unfamiliar to him and was trying to recall some former meeting that might have occurred between them. Then, he added resignedly, "Besides—let's not forget that he's still out there waiting on you."

Her eyes left the floor to find his and while they stared at one another in pressing silence, she thought, how ironical this is. For once in our entire lives, both our tongues have finally become tamed toward the other and under untold pressure at that, his intense pain, mine emotional—in regard to Frank the worst I have ever known.

Finally, torn a dozen different ways, she turned from him, saying, in a voice that had ebbed to nothing but a whisper, "Yes—I know—I'd better go."

As she reached the door though, he called again, "Eliza?"

She turned back, taking in the amicable smile that was gathering on his face as he told her for the third time, "I—still say you're a damn good shot!" Another long look passed between them, then, she turned her back to him and once more softly opening the door, she was gone from his sight.

No sooner had she closed the door behind her, the tears burst forth, gushing down her face. Quickly, grasping Luke by the hand, she sobbed, "Please—Luke—take me home."

Long fingers of early afternoon sunlight sifted through the green wooded curtain that towered high above the roadway on either side, splashing the ground here and there with the light softness that had come with the spring day. Clapping along at a rather spirited gait, the mare's hoofbeats seemed to be beating a lively chord to the notes of gaiety resounding around them, but nothing about the cheerfulness of the season appeared to touch Eliza. Head bent, she continued to sob on in her handkerchief which had long become soaking wet.

Filled with self-reproach and growing exasperation, Luke once again—laid his hand on Eliza's shoulder and begged, "Please, darling, try not to weep. In my opinion, since I've had time to think it over, he's hardly worth a tear let alone yours. I regret now that I left you with him one minute longer. I should've known that there was more he wanted to confess to your ears only, and did, or you wouldn't be so upset."

If anything, she wept more violent, sobbing automatically, "N—o—o, he—didn't," barely aware she had even spoken, least of all, her exact words. It was not going to be an easy burden to carry, realizing what her and Frank's past collision courses had led to and where it all was going to stop—apparently. If Frank did die, there would ever be the sting of his death even though, in all truth, she knew she had shot blindly into the air and had never given one second's thought that he could have been coming up the drive. For all that; however, the knowledge of it was giving her little comfort. It had been one thing for her and Frank to constantly be at cross-purposes with one another for years and years, but it was something else again to suddenly be laboring with an oar of realism.

Dismayed all the more by her unanticipated reply, Luke frowned, looking at her intently. His one hand gripped tighter on the reins. Holding back the mare's pace, he said, "He didn't? Well if he made no more outrageous confessions, I'm wondering what he did say to you that would cause you to become so distressed—" Luke paused, hoping she would say something. Though when he saw that she appeared to be hardly listening as well as making no effort to reply, he endeavored harder to comfort her. "Darling, if it's because Frank was shot, please try to put that out of your mind. It was an accident, an accident that Frank caused himself, indirectly, by his own guileful conduct. You nor anyone else shouldn't carry the burden of it ever, and I would've hoped that Frank would've understood that part concerning this whole mess and spared reminding you about it anymore. It's evident he didn't though."

To Luke's surprise, again she sobbed, "N—o—o—, he—didn't—not really." Then lifting her head and dabbing at her eyes with her handkerchief which of course had reached the state of uselessness by this time, she stared blankly in space and continued through sobs, "He—was—truly worried—that's why he was shot—he—came to ask me if—he'd gotten me with child that day!"

Had she made a sudden leap from the buggy; Luke would not have been any more astounded. Nor would he have jerked the reins any harder, bringing the mare and buggy to an abrupt stop with both hands. Neither would his astoundment have rang any clearer in his voice as he said, "Lord, God! What do you mean?"

The abruptness in which they had stopped, and the tone of Luke's voice startled her tormented thoughts back to the present, and—too late she realized what she had said. She turned her troubled expression and water eyes to face him, staring silently and seeing plainly enough while she stared, that the worst of her day was yet to come. Though, odd as it was, she slowly began to feel she did not care—glad that it was finally in the open—reasoning that maybe in some way she would gain a little relief, in that, her guilt in keeping it from Luke would be less burdensome.

Likewise, still held in bewilderment, Luke was also staring and being no stranger to every lineament of her face, he soon saw his answer all too glaringly cruel as recent past events began to pop off in his head with the ringing impact of pistol shots. "Dear God!" He finally said, when she still had not spoken, "Don't tell me that he's had you, too!"

The phrasing of his words rendered her a brutal blow. Yet, for all the hurt that was running through her, it suddenly seemed that she was going to gain a little benefit from it as well, in realizing that her sobs were dying a quick death as she rephrased his remark, "Took Luke, not had!"

If he were cognizant to the fact he had hurt her, she noticed that he never made no attempt to apologize; however, the reins fell from his hands and looking as though someone had knocked him senseless, he slumped his shoulders resignedly and stonily staring straight ahead at nothing, he said at last, "You—mean to tell me that he—that Frank Drakston—" the word was too bitter in his mouth to utter aloud.

"Raped me?" she said for him. "I can't see why that word would be any less hard for you to say than what you just said to me a few moments ago. Yes, he raped me! That's why I didn't want to go to Drakston Hall today. I didn't want to see Frank ever again!" Although she was aware of Luke's obvious distress, knowing that he had been dealt a terrible jolt that still did not prevent her from being resentful at his reaction. She thought he might have been more understanding and concerned on the part of her feelings at the present to say nothing of the stigma she carried.

She observed though that notwithstanding what she had reminded him of, he still appeared not to be concerned about anything she had said save the one thing that she had finally confirmed. She noticed the hard set of his jaw line as he asked, "When?"

"The day I gathered the holly."

"I might have known," he replied, "just as I thought—" he broke off, seeming to be probing for something. "yes, I was certain that's the day it had taken place," he continued, his face itched in lines of hardness. "He knew you and Martha were planning that party. No doubt he had rode that holly ridge for several days, going there to linger for hours, hoping that you'd do just what you did."

She saw that he had hardly heard a word that she had said and was instantly sorry that she had spoken to him as harshly as she had; even though she had no desire to recall it to her mind, much less discuss it with Luke, she still felt that she should stop him from harboring false thoughts.

"No, Luke," she said softly, "as much as I hold Frank's conduct in contempt and deplore that something like this has become a topic for conversation between us, I can't hold back and let you start thinking and believing things that never happened at all—" she hesitated, wondering if she should start at the beginning and disclose the entire episode to him or merely brush over it. Just at that moment though, he turned his head to stare at her searchingly. Seeing his expression ended her wavering then and there. It promptly launched her into giving him an account of the whole event form the time that she had left the house. Without any more break offs or pausing surprised to find that this was not too difficult for her to come by, she was covering it quite thoroughly with him listening patiently, till she came to the part where she pleaded to Frank to think of their children. Then, suddenly and rather bluntish at that, Luke stopped her. Brusquely, waving her aside and turning his head back to stare unseeingly down the road, he said, "Please, I don't want to hear any more, particularly that part. I only wish that you'd seen fit to have told me about it, then."

"When I reached you, Luke, I was too ill by then to tell you anything, remember?"

"I mean when you did get better," he said somberly. "I would've thought that you'd placed more confidence in me. It's always been my belief that we shared everything, the bad as well as the good. I must've been mistaken though."

Realizing now the humiliating position that she had subjected him to—his dropping everything that day to grant the wishes of a man who had raped his own wife, and sensing his hurt and disappointment because she had not confided in him, she gently laid her hand on his arm and as tenderly as she could, she told him, "No, Luke, you haven't been wrong in thinking that. My faith and trust in you remains as strong as ever and will never alter as long as I draw breath. I so dreadfully wanted to tell you, darling. You couldn't begin to imagine how much I wanted to tell you and the guilt I've born in keeping it form you—"

"Then, why didn't you!" He suddenly snapped, cutting her off again before she had a chance to explain her reasons for keeping silent. "Was it because you were afraid, I'd kill him, was that it?"

"Yes!" She instantly flared back as she jerked her hands away from his own, "if that's the way you want to put it, but not for the reason your behavior seems to be indicating!" She had become intensely aggravated with him again for not trying to understand or not wanting to. She was beginning to wonder which. "I've held my tongue for several reasons, not because I was actually concerned for him, but mainly to protect you and our children and, yes, his family, too. I know if I did disclose what he did, you'd waste no time in hunting him down and that it could end in tragedy, with either of you getting killed or maybe both. I can live with the affliction he brought down upon me, Luke, I've often wondered though if I could live without you. Concerning him, as I've just tried to explain to you, I thought about that grief that would've come to Aunt Amy, Elizabeth, Stuart, and Martha, had you gone to Drakston Hall in a rage of revenge and possibly killed him. Then, there was the scandal that certainly would have rang down on all of us and especially our children to think about, not to mention the fact that in all likelihood you would've gone to prison for the crime, or worse still, been hanged for it. Night after night in my sleep, I've dreamed seeing Walt Hawkins dragging you away by chains. So, those are the main reasons, Luke, for my silence and my silence and my hope is that you'll try harder to see that they are sound reasons."

A tense hush fell between them.

Finally, in a somewhat matter-of-fact manner, he said, "I still wish you'd been willing to have given me a chance at handling it."

"I did have the will, Luke, but I thought it best not to."

Another silent pause followed. Then, he suddenly exclaimed, the unexpectedness of it caused her to jump, "God Almighty! I've always known he burned for you, but—the thought that it would come to something like this, did I ever allow to enter my head. Even if he is half dead, it wouldn't take much more to tempt me to turn this buggy around and head right back for Drakston Hall and walk straight to that bedroom where he lies and smash his damn head in!"

The oath was something new, startling her again—the first and last one though that she was ever to hear fall from his lips. She saw his hand clench, making a fist, and if she had failed before that to fully fathom the depth of his exasperation, that in itself was enough to convince her that his taut nerves were straining near the point of causing him to do exactly what he had just threatened. In an attempt to divert his mind from possibly following through with the idea, she asked, even thought she had no desire to discuss it, "Do you think his wound may be fatal?"

"Yes, I do," he retorted, without a second's hesitation. "I think he's dying now. His case is very similar to another I've known, one that was mourned deeply by me and thousands of others likewise, and I don't suppose I have to tell you who that was. The doctors could do but very little for him, either, although they tried and tried hard."

"Yes, I know," she said sadly, "General J.E.B. Stuart. I'll never forget the impact his death made upon me when I heard about it." And, what about Frank if he should die, she thought. How will I truly feel about him?

"You and the whole South," Luke was saying, scattering her thoughts, "The north, too, General Stuart had many mourners there as well. That's the glory of honor and Jeb had plenty. It's a pity that Frank Drakston has so little to take with him when he does depart from this world." Catching a glimpse of the wistful expression that Eliza had suddenly put on, he quickly added more, "I don't want you bothering yourself about him though. Apparently, he's going to have time to do something in respect to honor and his salvation, too, if he hasn't already. Perhaps he made a decision to that effect, starting with us. I certainly hope so, even if it has left me with a brutal coldness toward him, feeling and saying things that without question I'm going have to atone for myself."

Listening to Luke, she thought he was wrong in thinking that he would be required to do penance concerning anything in the matter of Frank's deeds or confession. She thought if one were required, in order to have a pleasant afterlife, to fall on one's knees every time anger arose or a word no worse than "damn" escaped—and no doubt the oath was what Luke was more concerned over than anything else—the population as a whole would be on its knees continually expressing regret and the beauty and joys of this present world would more or less become lost in the readying for the next—making for a withering existence. To her, this would be far more baneful than giving way to temper every so often and muttering a few oaths.

She kept silent though and did not venture to voice her views on the subject. Luke had his beliefs, she had hers—both a personal matter and often times, crisscrossing it expressed verbally. Besides, there was a present matter—one that had been whirling around in her head from the moment she had begun to bear the blunt of Luke's reaction—that was very much disturbing her and seemed more important right then than concepts, beliefs, or gaining salvation to that other world. The present world was where she was and where she suffered and she thought that perhaps a more opportune moment may not arise to ask Luke this question that was alarming her—in regard to Luke a question that she had never dreamed would fall from her lips. The pain of it was searing her as though a hot iron had entered her soul.

Heart thumping and hesitant, she broke the hush that had fallen again, "Luke—well all this won't make any difference, will it? I—mean—you won't feel—you won't stop—" She paused, it seemed every word was coming out wrong.

He turned his troubled face toward her once more. He studied her for a moment and then said, "If you're wondering, have I stopped loving you, the answer is, no. I've loved you from the beginning and I'll ever love you. On the other hand, if you're talking about our physical relationship, it's my opinion that it has already been affected by all this, if I remember correctly. So, I would think you'd take your answer from that and save the need to ask!"

Another blow. Hoping, she had ventured to seek his promise that nothing had changed in the way he saw her—hoping he would still look upon her as undamaged goods as to speak. But she had been crisply reminded of something else. She thought considering the turmoil of recent mouths to say nothing of Frank's startling confession that day, that she would have become near about shock resistant by now—taking Luke's cutting statement lightly; but found quickly she was still, indeed, pregnable to pain. So, it looked as though she might as well have leveled with Luke, on all counts, from the beginning. Her endeavor to make those times she had turned away from him seem meaningless, had not deceived him at all. Though it was evident his concept of her manner was all wrong. Perhaps it might be better if she cleared up the matter. Never would she want Luke to think that she had turned away because she had no longer desired sexual relations with him.

Once again, she tenderly touched his arm. "No, Luke," she said, "you must've misunderstood my question, darling, but first let me try to explain about—well about those times that you're undoubtedly referring to. I didn't turn from you because I had come to feel different about us, I mean our relationship in any way. It was because of something else, something that was worrying me dreadfully at that time. I didn't want to risk the possibility of having a baby and be uncertain of who had fathered it, you or Frank. There was a duration of time there, longer than was normal for me, where there was nothing to do but wait. Since—well—there had been nothing of that nature between us that week, which was the same week that time for me had ended, I knew if I found I was with child that it would certainly be Frank's without question if there were no physical relations between us. Don't you see, darling, had I not turned from you, I'd really never known for sure which of you had fathered my baby, had that been the case. I don't think I could've borne that. That was the reason for my behavior, Luke, and the only reason. I love you and still want you the same as always, and I hope you feel no different toward me In fact, that was what I was trying to ask you, just now."

By the time she had finished trying to explain, he was near gritting his teeth. Hardly able to see or think beyond this one thought that her words had brought to light, he became consumed by its repugnance—lost to all else. Thinking in this pertinence—loathing Frank Drakston for having violated her body—going beyond the right of any man save a husband when he himself deserving her, too, above all things had chosen at one time to let God's law prevail rather than relent to his own weakness and demoralize her virtue the godliness of thinking in terms that their union had now been corrupted by Frank Drakston, he told her something that he did not think better of saying till he spoke impulsively, "There was no call for you, or Frank Drakston as for that matter, to have worried about your having a baby! Had you confided in me; I could've saved you both the trouble!"

The hardest slap of all. Though her sudden intake of breath was to be the only emotion that came forth. There was no wailing. There were no tears. She let nothing show. But, as he instinctively whirled his head to face her, realizing too late when he had done, he saw something that he was long in forgetting in her exquisite eyes while she stared at him from their blue-violet depths and quietly asked, "What is it, Luke, that you know, that I don't? Why could you have prevented Frank and me from worrying over the possibility of my being with child?

Feeling as though he could have cut his tongue out and not flinched once, he looked away from her, staring blindly down the road again. After some minutes while she waited calmly, he finally said, "It's—It's not that important, dear, let's forget it."

"No, Luke, since it obviously concerns me, I feel I have a right to know."

His eyes left the road and came to his hands where he had begun to finger with the reins. Although he could not bring himself to lie to her, he still tried to shun away from a straight-out answer, telling her, "I'm sorry, I don't want it to be this way between us, I shouldn't have made that remark. I only meant—I mean you"

"Can't have another baby, is that it, Luke?" she said, taking up where he left off.

Filled with self-condemnation for telling her in this manner, all he could manage was a faint, "Y—e—s."

She heard herself asking, "How long have you known?" and wondered how she could be so calm when she felt as though a cold, sharp knife was lying in her stomach, slowly cutting her insides into little pieces.

Granted, he was suffering, too. Finding each question, she asked more difficult to respond to because of knots gathering and tying in his own throat. After some time, he endeavored to answer her, "Since—since—the day I took you to see Seth—after—after the baby—was born."

"Seth told you that day, that I'd never have another baby?" Silently, he nodded his head.

"But, we've talked, Luke, you and I, several times since then about how wonderful it would be if we were to have another child. I'd so hoped to have at least one more, the same number as my own mother had."

She observed he bit down on his lower lip. The set of his jaw became firmer. Finally, he mumbled, "I—know."

She continued to stare at him, thinking that she had not been the only one keeping secrets. Seeing the strain on his face; however, she could not bring herself to remind him. Still, at the same time, she was almost to the point of feeling as if she had been put to an advantage, lately and by more than one telling him, "Luke, that's been an awful lot of months for me to hope, and apparently it wouldn't have changed, year in, year out. How on earth could you not only have let me carry this false hope all this time but discussed it with me besides, when you knew full well we'd never conceived another baby together?"

Once again, she calmly waited for his response, finally concluding that he had said all he was going to say and had started to suggest that they go on home to the children when suddenly she was to see clearly the extent the battering his nerves had fallen under. He swiftly shoved the reins aside and gathering his hands to his face, he dropped his head inside his palms, fervently sobbing, "I—didn't want to hurt you—oh, God—I have hurt you—but I didn't mean to!"

She was hurt and hurt deeply. She thought if Luke could not have gained the courage to tell her she would never have another baby that he should have seen to it that Seth did tell her.

She looked down at her hands folded calmly in her lap. Had Luke thrust her hand aside when she had tried to explain to him her silence in regard to Frank? She could not remember not did she want to, suddenly. She had told Luke the truth when she had told him she felt no different about their lovemaking. However, that had been before Luke had known that Frank had taken her body, too. How would she truly feel now? In her awareness now that Luke knew, would she ever again experience that complete abandonment that she had known in his arms? Had that been another reason for her not having told Luke? Unquestionable, that had played its part, now that she had come to think about it. What about Luke? She was still waiting for his assurance that it would not matter to him and it looked as though she would continue to wait.

From that momentous rose-filled night at Windsor she had ever felt that she and Luke had found a perfect love and had been totally convinced of it on their wedding night. She had ever looked on their marriage as being so solid and utterly full of love and devotion that nothing could shake it—unbeatable against any force. Now, she was not all that sure, because in the first place it had not been so perfect that it was invulnerable to harboring secrets and from all appearances did indeed seem shaken, for the moment, anyway. Maybe there was no such thing as perfect love. Yet, on the other hand, if she and Luke had not reached and dwelled in the ultimate of it, she most certainly had allowed herself to be tricked by an illusory concept of what the word and what marriage was all about.

Luke's sobs brought her back to the present. She had never seen him weep in anguish before. True, she had seen tears on his face and the night he had returned from the war, they had wept in one another's arms. But, those tears had come from overwhelming joy, and thankfulness to be together again. To see Luke weep; however, so profoundly as this, and the fervor of it wring her heart. Looking at his slumped shoulders, bearing under the force of his anguish, his work-marked hands baked brown as a berry from his long days in the sun—hands that she knew were filled with hard calluses and yet despite this coarse roughness that had come to them from hard work could still caress her so softly tender, her mind went trailing back to Windsor. Luke's hands then had certainly not looked work-marked in spite of his labeling himself, and many others no doubt saw him likewise, as an impoverished overseer. How ironic, she thought, there was no question in her mind that besides Frank there was also a number of others who had ever looked upon Luke as being that pauperized overseer from Windsor who had scared a bull's eye by marrying the rich girl from South Carolina, when the actual truth of the matter was, Luke had seen and endured more hardship since their marriage than all or any he may have endured in his entire life before that.

While she continued to rest her eyes upon Luke's hands that showed so many signs of the hard grueling labor they had engaged in through the years he had been married to her, Eliza thought about how Frank's hands had looked on this very day, still soft and white as a woman's even more than her own—and suddenly there came the bitterness all over again, as her mind's eye became fixed solid on all the unhappy lots that she and Luke had been forced to endure and were continuing to endure because of him. And, instantly that touch of tenderness that Frank had stirred in her heart, causing them to share those few rare moments of mellow communion, completely disappeared as though a broom had entered it and whisked away every trace of this delicate affinitive that they had finally captured together and that she had yearned to hold and keep, though fragile it was.

But, despite all, the hardness came, attaching itself more firmly than ever, even as she was gently laying her hand upon Luke's arm once more and softly saying, "Don't darling," making the same plea that he had so many times made to her, "it's all right. You did what you thought was best. Let's go on home and see to the children."

One of Luke's hands instantly fell to her arm, finding her hand, squeezing it in that special way, the first affectionate move he had made toward her since pulling the buggy to its sudden stop. His other hand fell to his coat pocket. He pulled out his handkerchief and blew his nose. Then, seeming overcome by tiredness, he wearily wiped away the tears from his sun-tanned face that only liked a fraction being baked as brown as his hands. Stuffing his handkerchief back inside his pocket, he released her hand and gathered up the reins, signaling the mare to move on. She had lived with Luke too many years to not know his way; for instance, when he felt like talking and when he preferred to stay silent, and this appeared to be one of those times for silence. Besides, she knew without doubt that he would never broach either subject again unless he felt compelled to. As they road on home in silence, she thought it might be just as well if they both chose not to discuss it anymore, because it seemed each of them had been wounded enough without taking a chance on airing it further, possibly causing the wound to grow deeper.

When they turned into the long oak-lined avenue at Green Sea, Luke reached for her hand again and held it till he stopped the buggy at the walkway leading to their front door. He jumped down and sailed around the buggy, helping her down as attentive as ever. Once she was clear of the buggy, he quickly hopped back inside and turned the mare toward the stables. Not another word had he spoken.

She stood and looked after him, near to the point of feeling as she had felt that morning at Windsor when he had turned his back upon her and walked away.

Chapter Fifteen

They came from far and near to attend his funeral. Walt Hawkins came, too. It took the sheriff only a few seconds to make up his mind when he heard the news. He disregarded Frank's upbraiding as he told himself he was merely taking Frank Drakston at his last words to him, because he could think of no better or sound reason for going back to Drakston Hall than to pay his respects at that bastard's last rites! Moreover, the occasion would provide him no better opportunity to rub shoulders with the elite of the region, would it not? So, since this had become his everyday aim in life, why pass it up? However, the sheriff's clever thinking and self-operating motive were all well and good with him until he arrived at Drakston Hall. Once he cast his eyes upon the garland of white flowers attached to the wall beside the front door, the yards and yards of black crepe draped above and around the door's facing on either side with the cloth swaying gently against spring's soft-blowing wind, his indifference suddenly became a secondary thing with him as he thought about how fast Frank Drakston's life had come to its end and that he, too, was also mortal. And later, when the sheriff caught sight of the flower decked coffin which had been placed in the center of the great hall so that the numerous mourners could file past it on either side for a last view and march on out through the back entrance, his nerves quivered and from that instant on until he took his leave at the burial ground, he made it his business not to hover too closely around Frank Drakston's grieving family.

Frank's life had slowly but steadily ebbed away despite all efforts by a number of doctors to save him. The internal bleeding continued to flow on as Seth Roalf had foreseen when he did his best to prepare Elizabeth for what surely was in the making—Frank's inevitable death. And, as the day approached that she was to see her husband laid to rest, she did appear to have adjusted fairly well to the shock of his death even if it did take her several weeks more to adjust to the reality that he was indeed gone, forever. The one factor; however, that kept Elizabeth Drakston on her feet, giving her main source of strength, was her little son who most mourners were to observe bore an astonishing likeness to his late father, a fact that was obvious Elizabeth was thankful and proud of. She never let go of Stuart's hand throughout the entire service, and Stuart appeared to want to give his mother his comfort and devotion as eagerly as she seemed to seek it. Moreover, as strange as it was and something that Frank Drakston without question would have been displeased over, was the fact that Elizabeth drew a great deal of strength and comfort also from none other than Luke Heyward, who was appalled at the number of people there in spite of Frank being a loner all his life. Luke suspected though that it was mostly the Drakston name that had done the luring rather than the deceased. Anyhow, Luke's arm was finally to be the grown-ups arm that Elizabeth held onto with her one free hand as Frank was lowered to his final resting place.

What Frank said to Elizabeth before he died or what he told her or perhaps requested she do, if anything, no one else was ever to know. After she arose from her rest and the short nap that she fell to on the first day of Frank's accident, she went straight to her husband's bedside and barely left it any more until just before death claimed him at evening's twilight of the next day at twenty-nine years of age.

It went without saying that another factor which was to help sustain Elizabeth through her trying ordeal was the way that Frank had endured his pain and faced his fate. His manner had given every evidence of being mentally at peace with himself and all—a calm acceptance of everything. Though if anyone was to notice that this had been particularly true concerning his mental state, anyhow, after his visit with Eliza, no one mentioned it.

In fact, odd though it was, the accident that felled Frank, causing his death two days later, was to bring him high repute when it came to showing bravery and was to glorify him among his acquaintances no less than any soldier of the region who had fought or met their death in the late war. It all started even before his death and it stands to reason that this appraisement reached Frank's own ears before he died. It all came about through a comment that Seth Roalf, Frank's personal physician, made. As one or two neighbors were asking of Frank's condition, the doctor obliged and added, "A man of more courage and valor in Frank Drakston's, plight, I have yet to see, including my war experiences," and the heroic acclaiming commenced immediately. And, the laudation never ceased, appearing to have immortalized Frank, by a large number, anyhow, among the greatest and the bravest, even those soldiers who had earned this statue in the conflict that had torn the nation in half, by the time he was laid to rest, though he never marched one foot in defense of his country much less having seen action on a battlefield. Nonetheless, the irony of the situation was the fact that no one could disclaim Frank's record of bravery. Too many had seen him brave his struggle of pain and trial without as much as a whimper. For all that; however, Frank was merely making good his promise to himself, mostly because of the remark he had once made to Eliza, something no one else was aware of and something that Eliza failed to recall herself for a long time.

Amy Drakston Carson was devastated over her son's untimely death. Yet, likewise with Elizabeth, she, too, had derived a great deal of comfort from Frank's behavior. Though the one person who gave her the solace she needed, making it easier to bear, was Matthew. As she had not only given him her consolation at Nat's burial but her hand as well, he was there now doing the same, showing his deep devotion for her—standing strong, erect, and proud beside her. Also, she had others who she could turn to. There was Whit, his plump little hand clasped tightly to hers, wearing a grave and curious expression as his solemn brown eyes stared in puzzlement at the dismal event, his first encounter with this gloomy aspect of life. There were Martha and Bruce and their two little girls, Maggie and Laura. Then, even though their grief was as profoundly stinging as her own if not more so, there was Stuart and Elizabeth, too. No, she still was far from being alone and should be grateful for this blessing, she was thinking, as Matthew softly laid his arm across her shoulders and tenderly suggested that they leave, finally guiding her away from the high mound of flowers under which her son now slept in the Drakston burial ground beside his father at Drakston Hall. She turned away with Matthew supporting her on one side and Whit, though small he was, supporting the other. As they headed for the Drakston coach there were many mourners observing, Lucy Randolph for one, that Whit's staunch short legs were not put to any trial at all in matching the faltering stride of the woman who he addressed as "Mama" and the attentive man supporting her who he called "Papa."

Nevertheless, while all this was going on, where was Eliza? She was alone. Even though her bitterness over the things that Frank had done lay as perpetually deep rooted inside her as ever, she still, in a certain sense, had been hit harder than anyone by his premature death.

Feeling as though she had done her share in shaping the tragedy that had ended his life, she had been unable to bring herself to attend his funeral and had retreated to the place where she always eventually ended up in times of great sorrow and distress—the Carson cemetery.

Scarcely seeing what she was doing because of her teary vision, she was squatted down between the graves of Nat and her mother, picking away the tiny weed sprouts that spring's sunlight seemed to coax so quickly through the warm, sandy soil. She might have known she thought, as the torment of her grief slowly streaked down her cheeks, that black cloud she had seen so many times in recent months would finally reach her and sweep her along to flounder in its chilling blackness, causing her to feel as though she were swimming in a current of dark despair with no shoreline in sight.

As she had very well thought, Luke had not said another word on the subject of those startling secrets that each of them had been keeping form the other and had at last been uncovered through their anxiety and exasperation, the result of their visiting Frank. Nor had Luke had much to say in regard to Frank, not to her anyway. Luke may have said something to her father when he came to Green Sea yesterday. After her father had visited with her a while he had gone on to the tobacco field where Luke and the others were still planting the tobacco crop. What was said, she had no idea. But she was positive they had discussed Frank as she and her father had, because her father had chosen to come himself and tell them of Frank's death.

She had been certain her father would come to her as quickly as he could. She had seen him from the window as he had jumped from the coach, agile as ever it seemed; but she had known from his grave expression that as well as coming to see how she was that he was also bringing bad news. She ran to the doorway and as he hurried up the steps, gathering her hands in his, he said, "Mary Eliza dear, I came as soon as I could, but I have sad news, Frank's gone, late yesterday evening. You are all right, aren't you, dear? I've worried so much about you since well, since all that business with Frank day before yesterday. I hope it hasn't upset you too much or burdened you in any way, but I'll confess all of it has more or less throwed me and no doubt you feel the same."

She regarded her father's anxious face, asking herself if she could actually tell him about all the things that did burden her. No, what purpose would it serve? She had no desire for him to know about

Frank's ever unceasing lecherous eye, too, in regard to her anyway, that had finally moved him to actual rape, causing a breach between her and Luke. It was there. She could feel it in spite of Luke's endeavor to behave as normal as possible toward her. That one sordid deed that Frank had committed, indirectly playing a big part in his own death, it appeared would ever be with her. Still, she could not burden her father with it, too.

"He was so young, Father," she heard herself saying, as an icy chill ran over her, "And, in a way, I feel I killed him." It was difficult for her to picture Frank as being gone. It seemed as though they were discussing someone other than him.

They were still standing in the doorway.,

"No, dear, come let's sit down," suggested her father, taking her by the hand and guiding her to the sofa where they sat down. "That's another reason I wanted to see you; you can't let yourself start thinking that way. It was a tragic accident, Mary Eliza, and for the sake of yourself, your children, Luke and me, too, please think of it as such and nothing more. In fact, that's my main reason for wanting to see you. When Frank saw the end coming, he asked me to tell you to never let his death bother you in the way of feeling responsible. He said had he actually known how things would've turned, that he wouldn't have said anything about seeing you in the doorway with the rifle. He said he was sorry for that, sorry that you, me, and Luke didn't think the same as Walt Hawkins thought and what he wanted everybody else to think, even his own wife, that he accidently shot, himself."

Frank's message had torn severely at her already shattered nerves and, then and there, she had known that she could not look upon his funeral. She thought her father had understood her feelings. HE had agreed with her that it might be best if she did not attend, saying he was positive no one would give a second's thought to her absence because she still had not fully recovered her former state of health. He had also promised to give her regrets and sympathy to Aunt Amy and Elizabeth—her message, too, that she would see them in a few days.

Now, however, with the last weed pulled away from the graves, she sat sifting sand through her fingers and reflected over the dinner hour, telling herself that her father may have understood her feelings in regard to Frank's funeral; but she was certain that Luke had not. In truth, she had doubts that Luke would attend, either. She had found though that she was not as wise to what went on in Luke's head as she had thought!

Few words had been exchanged between them while both had gone through the motion of trying to make a normal meal out of the dinner, she had prepared that day. Mostly, they had given their attention to the children, seeing that they ate, hardly touching the food on their own plates. Finally, giving in to this lack of appetite, Luke pushed his chair back, saying, as he looked at the clock on the mantel, "We'd better rush a bit, dear, your father said the funeral is set for two o'clock sharp."

"You're going to Frank's funeral?" she asked, seeing immediately that Luke was looking at her as if she had suddenly lost her senses even though this was the first remark, he had made concerning it.

"Yes, I am," he replied rather emphatic as he rose from his chair, "What made you think I wouldn't go?"

Now it was she who was thinking that his question was ridiculous. She let it hang though, concluding that it was no doubt best not to remind him. Silently, her eyes fell back to her plate as she began toying with her fork.

Observing that she was going to let his question pass as well as making no move to rise from the table, he questioned her again, "Aren't you?"

"I—I can't, Luke, I don't think I could bear to look on any of it."

He regarded her thoughtfully for a moment. Then, he said, "I respect your feelings, dear. Still, there are times in life when we have to lay our own aside out of regard for someone else's, which in this case, happens to be Frank's family."

"I know, Luke, and I truly mourn for them but—I—" she went no further in trying to attempt an explanation. How did one go about explaining a feeling of bitterness, despair, guilt, regret, and grief all wrapped up together when the pathway to each should be set far and wide apart, one never crossing over the other? She didn't know.

Still studying her, pondering her decision, Luke ventured to tell her, "I hope you won't place upon yourself what was positively and certainly no one's doing but Frank himself. It's my opinion that Frank Drakston's unfortunate destiny was brought about by his own frailty of character. I realize to say something of this nature just before setting out to attend the person's funeral is ill fitted, but Frank's weaknesses were plenty, if you ask me!"

She raised her head to look at him as she said, "What you say is true enough, Luke. Yet, at some time or other we all are weaker and more susceptible to wrongdoing than what we'll allow ourselves to believe, aren't we not? Some are stronger than others. That's what sums up the difference." I sound as though I'm actually defending Frank, she thought. But, what of it? Luke and I both have failed to meet what each of us took for granted in the other—complete trust.

It was plain that he had read the message between her words. He made no comment upon it; however. "I'd better dress or I'll be late," he said, turning away toward their bedroom.

And, a short while later, Luke had set out to attend Frank's funeral without her and, here she was as miserable as ever. Had the hours been any less stinging than had she gone on with Luke to Drakston Hall? She doubted it. No darker spring, she was certain she had ever lived through.

Reverently, Eliza let her head fall lower as she began to pray that the day would not be too far away when—all of it—the day she had gathered the holly, the last meeting with frank, the anguish his death welled inside her, his unwarrantable moves against Green Sea—every unpleasant memory that involved him, would become less distinct, fade until it was there no more. Then, there was something else that burdened her even more than those things that involved Frank, if it was possible. Frank was gone. There was nothing to mend with him now. But there was the harm that had been inflicted upon her marriage. It could be mended. It had to be mended. It was not too late to repair the damage it had suffered. That gap between her husband and herself had to be solidly closed, somehow, and she found herself again unhesitant in asking God to help her find the way in that, too.

Ultimately, she raised her head and pushed her bonnet back from over her eyes, observing that evening's sunlight was growing pale and thin as the ebbing sun sailed lower over the western horizon on its way to light the day in another part of the vast universe. She brought one arm up and to her face and wiped away her tears on the sleeve of her calico dress. She rose and brushed at her skirt, the sand and wilted weed sprouts falling to her feet. She must go. Her children who she had left with Hannah would be growing restless waiting. Her two babies, her only two babies because there would be no more.

Doleful, she reset her bonnet and turned her back on the two marble tombs she had retreaded to, her head bent pensively toward her dispirited feet as she moved along. She had only gone a little way though when something compelled her to lift her head higher. Luke was coming across the field toward her! She stopped noticing as she looked at him that his head was also hanging downward. Suddenly though, it seemed as if someone had whispered in his ears that he was drawing attention. He brought his head up sharp and slowed his steps, gazing at her across the space that separated them. Returning Luke's gaze, she began to feel as though God had held an open ear and was already guiding her in that direction that she had so earnestly asked He show her. Heart racing as she saw that Luke was quickening his steps, her feet began to move, too, her steps growing lighter and lighter as the distance between them was rapidly closing.

She was near enough now that she saw Luke smile at her. And not only did she see his smile, but she also saw that he had picked a small bouquet of blue violets along the way and was holding them out to her.

www.ingramcontent.com/pod-product-compliance
Lightning Source LLC
LaVergne TN
LVHW012041160826
845678LV00014B/2657

* 9 7 8 1 6 3 0 6 6 4 9 4 7 *